The NIGHTMARE EX-BOYFRIEND BEFORE CHRISTMAS

A modern day Christmas Carol

"Putting the Ex back
in Merry Xmas"

DEVON HARTFORD

COPYRIGHT NOTICE

Want to find out about my next book before everyone else and get free novellas not available anywhere else? Then sign up for my mailing list!

Sign up here:

devonhartford.com

DEDICATION

To my loyal fans who wanted a classic Devon book. This oughta do it. And to Megan Christmas, because she *really* wanted one too, and I wanted to do a Christmas book.

Here the twain shall meet.

The Nightmare Ex-Boyfriend Before Christmas

From bestselling author Devon Hartford comes a new standalone second-chance romance, told as a redemption story in the spirit of *A Christmas Carol* by Charles Dickens.

Channing Peyton.
College football legend.
Business tycoon.
National heartthrob.
And my ex-boyfriend.

Channing screwed me over in college.
Every way you can imagine, the good ways and the bad.
We had two passionate and unforgettable years together, until he blindsided me for no reason, and with no explanation, kicking me to the curb like yesterday's trash.
He ruined all other men for me, and almost ruined me.
But I'm stronger than that.
I don't need him.
My biggest regret was not kicking him to the curb first.

To this day, I still wonder: was there a reason he dumped me?
Or did he never love me?
I'll never know.
But you know what?
I don't care.
I'm done with that man.

Now it's ten years later and I'm back home for the holidays in King City, the town where I grew up and we both went to college. It's also the epicenter of our past scandal that nearly killed me and my parents when it broke.
Trust me, it made the local TV news every night for two weeks. One night, it went national.
Guess who never left King City?
Channing.
The curb turd.

As relentless as he was on the field, I would've thought he'd go on to play in the NFL. He never did. Knee injury. Oh, the cliche.

Small pond, meet big fish.

Only this fish has grown bigger than anyone ever expected, built up his own business empire. Turns out he's better at business than he ever was at football, and that's saying something. Despite his knee injury, he managed to keep his college football body, abs and all. Wherever he goes, it's raining money and marriage proposals.

When he finds out I'm home for the holidays, he just has to come knocking at my parents' house bearing meaningless gifts.

News flash, unless he's hoping for an immaculate conception, he has another thing coming, and it definitely won't be me.

* * * The Nightmare Ex-Boyfriend Before Christmas is a second-chance romance with an enemies-to-lovers twist. It's gift-wrapped for you in a steamy stand-alone holiday package, and tied up with a heart-warming bow of an HEA.

Pour yourself some hot cider and start reading.

Old Ghosts

"God bless us, every one."
—*Tiny Tim, from A Christmas Carol, by Charles Dickens*

"God bless ass, every one."
—*Me, Channing Peyton, every time I see one. You're welcome.*

Chapter 1

CAROL

I was already seated in coach and buckled in for my United Airlines flight home to visit my parents this Christmas. To my pleasant surprise, young love would soon bloom right before my eyes.

Don't get your hopes up.

It wouldn't bloom for me.

I wasn't bitter (and you shouldn't be either!) because I was still young. Less than a month ago, I had turned 29 for the third time. I heard the bitterness didn't kick in for at least another decade. At the rate I was going, I would work myself into an early grave long before then. Problem solved.

The lucky pair of young lovers were the two strangers on this plane who were settling into the row across from mine. They were college age, both of them J. Crew approved, their innocent eyes jeweling with untarnished hope from the moment they exchanged their first prophetic greeting.

Jack Crew tossed out a laid back "Hey."

Jill Crew answered with a girlish "Hi."

When she nervously tucked a lock of blonde hair behind her ear, I felt a sizzle in my chest that signaled this couple's inevitable happily ever after. The stars had aligned and were shining on them, I could feel it. Sometimes, you just knew.

I had to smile.

Then jealousy pinched my heart.

I reminded my heart I was content being alone and told jealousy I'd resigned myself to spinsterhood years ago. Being permanently single meant you never argued over toilet seat politics. Forget about there being a second Civil War over Red vs. Blue. It would be fought over Up vs. Down. Toilet seats, that is.

So what if I wasn't enjoying my dirty thirties like most women? I was still 29! I had plenty of time. And I was more than happy to spend a few hours vicariously enjoying the sight of burgeoning love between two innocent kids who clearly deserved it. Their coming together would make for more pleasant inflight-entertainment than any of the movies listed on the United app.

I settled in with a smiling sigh.

While I was relaxing, a steady stream of impatient holiday

vacationers crowded onto the plane. The seats were fairly full already, and the overhead bins were bristling with luggage.

A frustrated and rumpled grumbling man stepped between me and the two young lovers, who were sitting with an open seat between them, with young Jack on the aisle and Jill by the window.

"That's my seat," the grumbler grumbled. "Move."

Jack unbuckled and squeezed into the aisle, making room.

A forlorn Jill frowned disappointment.

I did too.

If the grumbler sat between the young couple, their love might not have a chance to take root. Worse, I sensed the grumbler had his eyes on Jack's prize. I was not letting him ruin their chance at romance with his negative energy and leering grin.

I tapped the grumbler on the back, intending to suggest he let Jack sit beside Jill, and he take the aisle, which would give him extra elbow room, a win-win for everyone.

The grumbler didn't notice my tapping because he was too busy forcing his hardshell Samsonite suitcase into the bin across from me, the one where my softshell Briggs & Riley bag was already parked. He flailed and swore under his breath, "Get in there, you stupid f—!"

You can imagine the rest.

If you can't, or you prefer a bit more candor in your commentary, I'll simply say that sailors everywhere were either cringing in awe, or applauding this man's crude use of the English language, your choice.

"Excuse me," I said to the grumbler in a stern voice. "You're smashing my bag." Jack & Jill's love story would have to take a brief backseat to my luggage story.

His back to me, the rumpled grumbler answered with more flailing, more swearing.

"I said excuse me, sir, you're going to smash my Christmas presents." I'd put the gifts for Mom and Dad in my carry-on to avoid breakage. "Sir? My bag? Do you mind?"

"What?" He whipped around to face me where I sat in the aisle seat.

"You're crushing my bag with yours. It looks like there isn't room in the bin. Sorry. Can you put yours somewhere else? Please?"

"There *isn't* somewhere else, lady!" he crabbed, his face lobster red. "Why don't you shut your hole and mind your own business?!"

"I am minding my own business," I sighed. "That's *my* bag you're crushing." My preference would've been to turn this into a teachable moment that focused on when — and when *not* — to use the term "hole" while talking to a woman. Potholes, knotholes, foxholes, fine. Not as a derogatory term for a woman's mouth.

Crabby leaned over me, his crusty red face inches away, his words flicking spit, "Shut your f—ing c— hole, you stupid f—ing b—." We all know he wasn't em-dashing his words, I was. He was dropping letter bombs with abandon. "I'll put my f—ing s— anywhere I want."

Silence whip-cracked the nearby passengers who, until a second ago, had been busily bustling themselves into their seats. Many were parents with young children. Now, their frozen and frightened eyes were on me and Crabby.

I was ready to summon Lady Vengeance and rage in his face, but I kept calm. Of late, I'd discovered a level head was one of the few perks you got from being 29 three times.

In a low voice, I said to Crabby, "You will not talk to me that way, sir, and you will not force your bag where it won't fit. Now, either you find someplace else to put it like a civilized person, or you will check it with the flight attendant. Have I made myself clear?"

Crabby's beady eyes blackened and his face fractured with rage. He hulked over me, fisting his index finger at me, and hissing razored words, "Now you listen to *me*, you stupid f—ing b—! If you don't shut your f—ing *hole*," he should *not* have said hole a second time, teachable moment or no, "I am going to OOG!"

Like lightning, I had just shot my arm out and clamped claws on his crotch. Good thing I went to a rock climbing gym three times a week. I had a strong grip.

Crabby flinched and his eyes bulged into cue balls with black dots.

"I'm sorry, sir," I said, donating a beauty pageant smile to the charity of his choice, "would you mind repeating that without the swearing?"

"Oog!"

"Is something wrong?" A female flight attendant asked, squeezing past the gawking passengers blocking the aisle.

"Ask him," I said smugly.

"Oog!"

"Sir?" said the flight attendant. "Is there a problem?"

I finally released a very flustered Crabby.

"You b—!" he hissed hoarsely and turned to the attendant. "This c— just grabbed my f—ing balls!"

"Language, sir," she warned.

He coughed, "Language?! F— my language!"

"Sir, I'll have to ask you to please tone it down. There are children."

"I don't care about any f—ing children, b—! This c— just grabbed my d—!"

A lesson in learning the alphabet it was not, but the kids sure were listening.

"Mommy, that man just said—!"

"Sir!" the flight attendant was now angering.

I was too. What was it with men who got put in their place by a woman only to then go crying their eyes out to the first person of authority they could find? If you asked me, that was daycare behavior fit for toddlers, not grown men.

"Tracy?" asked a concerned male flight attendant who'd come rushing up from the back of the plane. He was obviously addressing the female flight attendant after having heard the commotion. "Is everything okay?"

Tracy said, "It's—"

Crabby ignored her and whined at the male attendant, "F— no, it's not okay! This f—ing b— grabbed my d—!" There he went again. Appealing to authority.

He went on from there, more B-bombs, C-bombs, D-bombs, and F-bombs raining down like the proverbial can of Alphabet Soup that would surely start World War III, if you believed Crabby.

Within minutes, airport police and TSA were escorting him off the plane to a round of applause, some of it directed at me for saving the day. I brushed it off with plentiful "Thank yous" and "It was nothings."

Eventually, everyone settled in, including Jack & Jill Crew, who looked visibly relieved that Crabby would no longer be sitting between them.

Tracy the attendant was thoughtful enough to offer me a packet of Sani-Wipes for my hands. She'd seen me grab Crabby.

"You might want these," she winked mischievously.

I took them with a guilty laugh, using them to wipe away the bad memory more than anything else. By the time we took to the air, I was quickly forgetting it because I was too busy tending the garden of love where Jack & Jill were frolicking. By tending I meant eavesdropping on their conversation. They owed me for Crabby.

The two junior lovebirds told each other they were traveling to see their respective families over holiday break, and both admitted they were pathetically single, followed by mutually cute laughs.

They wouldn't be single for long.

I sat rapt the entire flight, resisting my growing urge to get jealous-drunk on mini bottles of Stolichnaya. I had no doubt Tracy would comp me one or a dozen if I asked nicely.

In case you're wondering, I didn't ask.

As much as I wanted to drown my pain in vodka, my obsession with Jack & Jill as they migrated cautiously from being complete strangers to fast friends was stronger. Their carefree laughter was constant and genuine, his-and-hers tokens of openness. I got high on that instead, popping those tokens like holiday Hershey's Kisses.

Their connection deepened when they oddly bonded over their mutual love of quirky 1980s sitcoms, a guilty pleasure for them both. They traded punch lines from Perfect Strangers (fitting), Cheers (I raised a mental toast), and Married With Children (ominous but avoidable). They were too young to have grown up on those shows, as was I (still 29!), but they had discovered them on Hulu and Netflix, the digital Cupids of the internet age.

At some point, Jack moved boldly from his aisle seat to the middle. When Jill initiated the subtle touches, he reciprocated. Their fingers, then hands, found each other and their hearts knit together somewhere over the friendly skies of destiny.

Later, Jill let down her guard and allowed Jack to raise the armrest, blending them into a single being, shining bright. Finally, they cuddled into oneness under the privacy of a United Airlines blanket for the remainder of the flight, leaving me to my thoughts.

If I'm being honest, watching their love unfold hurt.

Oh, how it hurt.

Not because I'd never known young love.

I had.

The first time in college had been a mistake, a false love that didn't last.

The second, also in college, changed my life forever, in good ways and bad. For over two years, I had surrendered to what I thought was true love, giving myself completely to Channing Peyton, only to have him tear his love viciously away with hateful resolve shortly before graduation.

His love might not have been true, but mine had.

The sad truth is, I *should* have known better.

I'd been warned beforehand by someone who knew a thing or two about young love.

\#

&

&*&

&*&*&

&*&*&*&

M

"Never give it up your first time to some dumb guy who doesn't love you," Jordyn Hoyle had said casually between cigarette puffs one lunch back when we both went to King City High School.

The two of us were hiding behind the gym on a gray November day, leaning against the back wall amongst the dusty cigarette butts, none of them Jordyn's. She always carried hers to the trash. I saw.

Jordyn smoked Marlboros religiously, a badass rocker chick with dark hair and a darkly angelic beauty who took me under her wing my freshman year, her senior. Before she graduated high school and left me to fend for myself, Jordyn taught me a little bit about the ways of the world, ways I would never learn trapped inside the stifling cocoon my conservative parents had wrapped tightly around me since birth.

"Once you give it up for a guy," Jordyn had warned, "your heart goes with it. If he leaves you, and they always do, you never get your whole heart back. Just pieces."

I had nodded, wide-eyed and naive, wishing I could be exactly like Jordyn Hoyle, who knew everything about everything.

"Wanna puff?" She had offered me her lit cigarette.

"Yes," I had giggled and reached out eagerly.

"Fuck no you don't," she laughed and elbowed me affectionately with her leather jacket before taking another sultry drag. When Jordyn smoked, she made love to the cigarette, and did it with the same luscious burgundy lips that drove the boys at school crazy. All she had to do was smile at them and they were under her spell. I'd seen that too. Like magic.

Boys were another reason we hid behind the gym at lunch. Jordyn explained she was taking a break from them. And me? They hated me, so I avoided them.

Looking thoughtfully at her cigarette, Jordyn flicked ash and said, "These things'll kill you quicker than a broken heart, Rolo." She'd dubbed me that the day we met, when she'd found me angrily shame-eating Rolo's candies by the handful while standing by myself behind this very building. I'd had a bad day.

"But you smoke."

"Girl pirates *have* to smoke. It's the rules."

"Gosh, Jord, can *Iiiiii* be a girl pirate too?" My too-cool-for-school attempt at sarcastic apathy was amateurish, and in this case completely dishonest. I would give anything to be a girl pirate, if only someone like Jordyn would show me how.

I vividly remember her aloof eyes surveying me thoughtfully for a long time, somehow knowing me better than I knew myself. She took a drag from her cigarette and gave me her favorite boilerplate wisdom:

"Don't do drugs, Rolo." Then she had laughed rakishly, her cigarette dangling precariously between plump lips as she'd given my ponytail a friendly tug like she often did.

After she graduated, I never saw her again.

Over a decade later and I still miss Jordyn like it was yesterday.

Because of her, I never once smoked, and had resolved to save myself for a man who truly loved me. That didn't mean waiting for marriage like my parents had. I hadn't placed my virginity on some impossible pedestal. I didn't expect an army of shining knights to fight over it, but I didn't want to throw it away either. Jordyn spoke truth and fourteen-year-old me had taken her words as gospel for six years.

A week before I turned twenty, my views changed drastically and immediately.

The reason?

I caught my newly ex-boyfriend Evan Urleigh in bed with my no longer best friend Whitney Vinson.

Them together came as a surprise because Evan had frequently sworn up and down until the cows came home that he wanted to save his virginity for me, to wait until we were both ready.

Catching Evan mooing in bed over Whitney, his sweaty ass rising and falling in time with her squirrelish squeals, had suggested otherwise.

Did I mention that before catching Evan cheating, he and I had been exclusive for a year and a half, ever since we'd met in Chemistry class our first week at King City University? Or that his life and mine had become increasingly intertwined in symbiotic bliss, he my honey bee and I his orchid? He had once written me a love poem expressing that exact sentiment.

And did I mention Evan's bed, the one where he was getting busy with Whitney, was the very bed where he'd professed his undying love to me on several occasions? The one with the comforter I'd given him because he didn't have his own when it turned cold last winter? The comforter he'd taken home with him to Arizona the previous summer because it reminded him of me? The one now crumpled thoughtlessly on the floor beside the bed where he was valiantly slaying our love with one fleshy stab after another?

"Is this what saving yourself for *us* looks like, Evan?" I snarled from his dorm-room doorway, crushing the doorknob in one hateful claw and biting back tears.

"I'm almost there!" Evan grunted, eyes clenched, oblivious and still pumping.

"I thought you locked the door!" Whitney snipped.

"Wait! Almost!" Pumpa, pumpa, pumpa.

I wanted to pump Evan full of holes, but I'd left my giant sewing machine at home.

"Glorg!" Evan coughed and dropped sagging on top of Whitney.

Was that the sound he made when he came?

Glorg?

Maybe I was better off without him.

"It's not what you think!" Whitney gasped toothily, making eye contact with me from beneath Evan, her fingers digging into the frail shoulder blades of the man I loved.

Or thought I did.

As for Whitney, now that we were no longer friends, I was free to speak my mind. "Eat another acorn, you chipmunk-cheeked bitch," I imagined myself telling her, but she was very insecure about her looks and her cheeks, and I would never hurt her feelings like that. One heart had already been broken in this room today. There didn't need to be two. So I kept my mouth shut and whirled to go.

"Wait, Carol!" the squirrel pleaded.

"Carol?!" Evan gasped, flipping over in bed, his amber-gold eyes turning into sunny-side eggs. "What're you doing here?!"

How could I have ever thought those runny yellow eyes loved me? They weren't golden. They were diseased. Whitney could have him.

I glowered, "This isn't the first time, is it?" Neither of them answered. "Evan, how long have you *not* been a virgin while telling me your are?"

The yolks broke and Evan's eyes fluttered surprise. "Carol, I..." He couldn't finish his sentence because the ugly truth was afraid to come out from hiding where it cowered behind Evan's secret monster of dishonesty.

I slammed the door like a cannon and stalked off, determined to lose my virginity to spite Evan. To spite Whitney, I'd find someone better looking than Evan. I'd try, anyway. On my best day, I didn't look half as good as Jordyn Hoyle on her worst.

I didn't care.

If I had to hand out my virginity like a free lunch, I would. Somebody was always hungry.

Two Fridays later, still virginal and fully flowered, my resolve started to wilt. Alcohol and goading from my new roommate Sienna Winters peer-pressured me back on track.

Sienna lived on the same floor of Hemingway Hall as I did, and we knew each other in passing. I also knew her double-dorm room just happened to have a vacancy since her previous roommate had dropped out under mysterious circumstances a week earlier (I would later learn from Sienna that she'd played a well-meaning prank on her roommate that led to the poor girl's sudden departure. It involved a beautiful boy, fruit-flavored condoms, and an aardvark. Ask me some other time).

Now that I could no longer share a dorm room with Turncoat Whitney (we had been roommates prior to her betrayal), I moved in with Sienna without official permission from the Residence Council while waiting for them to expedite the room-transfer paperwork.

Sienna was an instigator and much freer with her sexuality than I'd ever be. Some people called Sienna a slut. After getting to know her better, I called her confident, brave, self-aware, and someone to look up to, the second older sister I never had, Jordyn being the first.

Sienna was actually younger than me by three months, but she knew exactly what she wanted out of life and never hesitated to go after it. Unlike Jordyn, who was oddly reserved for a rocker chick (I suspected her own broken heart held her back), Sienna flirted with disaster like he was the perfect boyfriend.

"What're you waiting for, Carol?!" Sienna giggled in her artfully colorful dorm room where I now lived. We'd been having this discussion nightly since I'd told her about the Evan incident and my newly inconvenient virginity. "It's just sex, Carol. Pick a boy and do him already!"

To my surprise, I picked Channing Peyton, the starting quarterback for the King City Cheetahs, our university's Division I football team.

For him, I would throw away my virginity any day.

Most girls would, and many had, or so I'd heard.

One good look was all it took.

The night the Biggest Manwhore On Campus made a pass at me at a frat party (Channing's bedroom reputation was legendary), he threw it so expertly, I couldn't help but catch it. I didn't catch anything else, but I did catch him.

The biggest surprise of all, without either of us realizing it, Channing and I both followed Jordyn Hoyle's advice to the letter:

Never give it up your first time to someone who doesn't love you.

Believe it or not (I know I didn't), Channing was also a virgin when we met. Not for long. I may have hastened things. Oops. If you saw him, you would too. The other surprise was how quickly we both fell into each other, and from there into bed, where we gave each other every piece of our hearts to hold forever.

At least I did.

I wouldn't know until a decade later just how many pieces Channing had held back from the beginning.

Or why.

Chapter 2

CHANNING

"Raise your hand if you hate making money," I lifted my champagne glass and smirked at the men gathered around me on the 48th floor of my in-progress skyscraper in downtown King City. Windows held back the frigid December chill, but the rest of the floor was bare concrete and open rafters crawling with an overhead web of electrical conduits, plumbing, and HVAC ductwork.

All eyes were on me.

I was used to it.

For years, random women had been handing me their hotel room keys or tossing me their panties while screaming my name. Random men had been asking me for my autograph or buying me beers for the sole purpose of rubbing elbows with legendary greatness. And the men who played on my team had always looked to me to bring them victory.

Put a lid on your attitude because I wasn't exaggerating. The fact was, I held more records than any college quarterback in the history of NCAA D-I football. I'd quit football ten years ago at the age of 22, but people hadn't quit adoring me or looking to me for leadership.

What can I say?

I had a bad habit of winning more times than any man deserved, and people gravitated to that. Everybody loves a winner. At this point in my life, I worked it to my financial advantage.

I held my champagne glass high. "Who here hates making money?"

Not a single man standing in the chuckling crowd raised his glass completely. Some of the men in slick suits *almost* had, but they nervously sipped their champagne to cover their social slip up.

"Then we agree," I grinned. "We all love money. Am I right?"

Cheers and whistles from some men, doubtful smirks and chuckles from the others.

These men fell into three categories.

The smirkers were the marks, a slick group of power-suited high-dollar investors, all of them older, all here because they were interested in this building, the King City Spire, which I owned. I called them the Gray Whales because I was the Killer Whale aiming to take a bite out of their bloated bank accounts.

Unbeknownst to them, a second group was mixed in: suited friends of mine with enough money and business savvy to talk a good game. My

Friendly Fakers. Their job: pump up the Gray Whales with competitive enthusiasm.

The third group, the cheerers, were a hard-edged group of my best builders wearing well-worn tool belts, work clothes, and their burly attitudes on their sleeves. It was the end of their shift and I'd called them down from the higher floors where they worked to assist in my little spectacle here. Their job: intimidate the Gray Whales with their presence.

In my experience, older white-collar men with money like these Gray Whales often felt the need to impress younger blue-collar men by flashing their cash, making this the perfect atmosphere to close a sale.

You want to show these construction toughs how tough you are? Buy the big fucking building they could never afford. Didn't matter to the Gray Whales that these Burly Builders were the ones building it. In fact, it made the purchase even sweeter. It allowed the Gray Whales to gloat over the Burly Builders and wallow like pigs in the unspoken truth, "You may be building it, tough guy, but I'm the swinging dick around here paying for it. Don't you forget it."

What the Gray Whales didn't know was, I was the biggest swinging dick of all, pulling their strings without them realizing it.

"To making money!" I again raised my glass in a toast.

This time, everyone raised with me and we drank.

Alcohol always helped.

So did pretty pussy. Nothing like eye candy to close a sale.

Circulating amongst the suits and carrying trays of champagne glasses were six strippers serving drinks. My Sexy Santas. They were bursting out of their tight and skimpy red-and-white costumes. Their job was obvious. Encourage the Gray Whales to say yes to anything that might impress the breasts off the Sexy Santas.

"Drink up, gentlemen," I said, pounding the rest of my champagne.

One of the strippers, a gorgeous eye-popping blonde named Natalia (she was easily the best of the bunch), was quick to saunter over and take my empty. She handed me a fresh glass of fizzy liquid gold from her tray saying, "Here you go, Mr. Peyton."

"Thank you, Natalia," I said.

"You can call me Naughty," she whispered mintily in my ear, pressing her cleavage against my suit-jacketed arm.

"My favorite name," I chuckled, sipping champagne. "We'll talk after I finish up."

"I'll be waiting," she bit her plump lip and winked over her bare shoulder before sashaying into the crowd of suited men to tend to their drinks, the white puffball of her hat bouncing in counterpoint to her ass.

Except for the Sexy Santas, everyone here wore yellow hardhats, even me. I didn't wear mine because I was worried about the safety overlords at OSHA (Occupational and Safety Health Administration) slapping hefty fines on my construction company or shutting us down. The opposite. I had plenty of friends who worked at the local OSHA branch who got Christmas cards and gift baskets from my office every year. They liked me. I wore my hardhat so the Gray Whales would feel like they were on my team. The winning one.

"Show of hands," I raised my glass again. "Who hates doubling their money in five years or less?"

More chuckles, but this time, all hands stayed low.

I had invited the investors here to help pay for my skyscraper and earn back their money on rents. The projected final bill for construction alone was $400 million. With the rents I'd already inked, I expected to double that in five years. I was billing out space in this building at close to $1,000 per square foot. But we still had another $80 million to finance for the construction loans (don't get me started on insurance). If I could sell some of the Gray Whales on my vision, they could easily bridge the gap.

Two in particular.

Morris Pilkington and Warner Olinger.

Pilky and Old Oli for short.

They could easily scrape together $80 million between the two of them. The other Gray Whales were guppies, $1 and $2 million investors at best. They were here to up the energy. I'd take their money, but there weren't enough of them to make eighty.

For that, I needed Old Oli and Pilky to sign on.

Time for me to start gabbing.

My presentation was purely verbal. No distractingly boring Power Point charts and graphs that would lull a tax accountant into a coma. Just the sound of my awe-inspiring voice, the one that inspired my team to win game after game on the gridiron. I wanted every man here thinking about two things: profits and pussy. One would get them the other.

During the talk, the Sexy Santas continued to circulate amongst the Gray Whales and my Friendly Fakers asked solid and knowledgable questions about dollars and cents.

I answered them with reassuring ease. This deal was on the up-and-up. I knew how to turn a profit.

Old Oli and Pilky asked a few questions too.

Pilky was impressed with my answers.

Old Oli was a bit more crotchety about them.

When I finished my spiel, the small-dollar investors were lining up to sign contracts on the spot totaling $10 million.

Pilky was ready to sign on for $30 million. Naughty Natalia and another Sexy Santa hung off his arms. His eyes dancing between their cleavage, he laughed, "You're a smooth operator, Channing. I'll give you that. You really know how to work a deal. And I thought you were good back when you were quarterbacking the Cheetahs on the field."

"I try," I smiled.

"You do more than try," Pilkington laughed to himself. "I'll have my people look over your paperwork tomorrow, but you can consider it signed." He lowered his voice, "Can you throw in these two girls as a signing bonus?"

They giggled.

"And don't tell my wife," Pilky winked.

"Never," I grinned.

I wasn't exactly fond of Pilky's wavering loyalty to Lena Pilkington. I'd met the woman several times. She was hard not to like, the kind of woman who wouldn't let you in her house without baking fresh chocolate chip cookies for you. That she was still married to Pilky after forty years was a testament to *her* loyalty. But my priority was on closing this deal. "If I tell Lena anything, Morris, it will be how much money you're going to make on this deal."

"She'll be happy to hear it," Pilky grinned, his eyes dripping back into the breasts of his Sexy Santas.

I would trust for Lena's sake that neither young woman had any interest in Pilky beyond making him feel good about signing over his money to me.

My focus turned to Old Oli. For this evening to be a success, I needed him to sign on for $40 million. He was never an easy sell, notoriously twitchy with his money, a rumpled old man who made Ebenezer Scrooge look like your generous grandfather.

I led him over to the windows so we could enjoy the sparkling shine of the downtown lights.

Good Old Warner Olinger said, "I appreciate your youthful enthusiasm, young man, but real estate here in King City isn't what it used to be before the recession. The market has yet to recover, I'm afraid. I don't see how I'll earn back my investment in a timely manner."

"It's recovering now," I soothed, "and downtown is hotter than ever. Look around." I motioned at the view, then at the interior. "We're on the 48th floor. Only twelve to go. The King City Spire is nearly finished and nearly paid for. Everything is state of the art and completely green. My architects incorporated an array of my patented solar panels into the building glass design that will cut annual utilities costs in half."

"I heard about that," Old Oli allowed.

"I have dozens of businesses locked into ten and twenty year leases or longer, chomping at the bit to move in and start saving money. We have 90% occupancy already." We only had 60%, but you didn't get to 90% or 100% by telling people 60%.

"Show me the contracts." Warner Olinger was shrewd. He'd been rolling in dough for so many decades, his pale skin had a money-green tint, but he'd earned his riches through hard work, which gave him the unfortunate quirk of believing his word was gospel when it came to business in this town.

"Trust me, Mr. Olinger. My company has been leading the wave of revitalization that has transformed downtown King City since the recession. We have big tech businesses from out-of-state rushing in to take advantage of our low overhead and newly modernized urban center. Our city's mayor was wise enough to follow my lead on electrifying our public transportation fleet, and Morris Pilkington here was wise enough tonight to hop on board this deal for $30 million. Has Morris ever lost money on anything?"

Old Oli snorted, "Morris Pilkington is a philandering nincompoop lacking a single thimbleful of class. Your pretty ladies won't sway me, young man." Old Oli hadn't been swayed by my Burly Builders or Friendly Fakers either. He was too old to care and required a subtler tack.

"I didn't bring the women for you, Warner. Can I call you Warner?"

"I'd prefer it if you called me Mr. Olinger."

"My pleasure. I know how pious you are, Mr. Olinger." I also knew he was such a self-righteous asshole, rumor was he wore a Papal tiara over his crack and shat into a holy water font. "I brought the girls for everyone else. For you, my good man, I have something more suited to your tastes. Follow me."

I led Oli past the Christmas-themed bar tables and the busy bartender, and from there across open concrete. We turned a corner, stopping at a velvet-covered pedestal positioned in a quiet open area and spotlit from above so it glowed like hidden treasure. Two imposing men stood on either side, wearing mirrored sunglasses that hid their eyes. Both were ex-Special Ops who worked for a local security firm I used from time to time when I needed to impress people like Old Oli.

"Gentlemen," I nodded.

Neither guard moved or acknowledged my existence, according to their professional code. Do not act or react until a genuine threat has been identified.

Behind the pedestal stood Gerard LaPierre, my favorite rare book dealer. I had an antiquarian book habit few people knew about. It clashed with my former-college-quarterback turned real-estate-mogul front I led with. Books were only sexy to a select crowd. I knew Old Oli was part of that crowd.

He chortled, "What are you doing here, Gerard?"

"I'm representing Mr. Peyton." Of course he knew Oli. Gerard had been selling rare books in King City for thirty-six years.

"Gerard," I said, "if you would be so kind."

"My pleasure, Mr. Peyton." Gerard wore white gloves and removed the draped velvet covering with careful flair, revealing a glass-enclosed display case featuring two large pages from a 500-year-old book. The connected pages lay at an angle atop a wooden presentation platform nestled in a bed of royal velvet, all lit by hidden pin lights in the rafters overhead.

Oli gasped. "The last of the Birdsong Fragments!"

"That's right, a single leaf from the Holy Grail of collectible books, the Gutenberg Bible, the first ever book printed with movable type in 1455," I narrated. "As you know, Mr. Olinger, this loose leaf was originally purchased as part of a complete Gutenberg Bible in 1891 by Horatio Birdsong, the infamous San Francisco book dealer who started selling off individual leaves in 1906."

"A colossal error on his part," Old Oli grumbled gravely. "The value of a complete copy greatly exceeds that of individual leaves."

"I agree. After the great San Francisco earthquake and fire of 1906, poor Birdsong found himself deeply in debt, and his complete Gutenberg Bible was his only asset. He couldn't find a single buyer quickly enough but he found dozens interested in single leaves. I managed to track down this leaf with the help of Gerard. I believe you've been seeking this particular one for a long time, haven't you, Mr. Olinger?"

Old Oli grunted evasively.

I smiled, "It's the last leaf of the Birdsong Book you *don't* have, isn't it, Mr. Olinger?"

Oli's wrinkled jaw dropped, "How did you know?"

"Antiquarian book lovers are a very incestuous bunch, aren't we?"

"You're a collector?"

"Yes, Mr. Olinger. I suffer from the same addiction as you." I smiled. "If you invest in my Spire, I'll throw in this fragment as a favor."

"How much?" Oli's eyes whitened greedily, his pupils pinpoints.

"Morris already put in $30 million on the Spire. If you put in forty, you'll own more of this building than he does, and I'll throw in this Birdsong Fragment for free."

"F-f-f-free?" Oli stammered.

I nodded.

Rich people like Oli lost their shit over free, but it was more than that. Two years ago, I had paid $75,000 to the estate executor of Sachihiro Yamamoto, a recently deceased and secretive collector in Tokyo. Yamamoto's executor had no idea of the value of the fragment. On the open market, it would've fetched somewhere in the neighborhood of $140,000. Had they known about Warner Olinger, it would've fetched substantially more.

To Oli, the final Birdsong Fragment here on this pedestal would multiply the total value of his individual fragments to the tune of $100 million. To me, if I sold it as a single leaf, it would be worth a mere $140,000. Or, I could trade it with Old Oli for $40 million worth of his investment money.

I said, "Five years from now, Mr. Olinger, when your $40 million in the Spire doubles itself, I'll have effectively paid *you* to buy this leaf from me today." It was a bold claim I was willing to gamble on because rents in King City had skyrocketed. "It's win-win for you no matter how you look at it, Mr. Olinger."

Oli wrung his mottled old hands. "I'll have to think it over."

"Don't think too long," I said. "I have a hungry buyer in Germany lined up if you're not interested."

"Who?"

"Albrecht Röthschwert."

"Him?" Oli gnashed.

"Oh, you know Albrecht?" I smiled, already knowing he did.

"Do I know Albrecht," Oli chuckled bitterly. "That itinerant thief has been trying to steal Birdsong Fragments out from under me the world over since before you were born, young man."

"Has he?" I asked innocently. I knew that fact from Röthschwert too.

"He has, but he has yet to succeed."

"I would sure hate to see him succeed on this one, Mr. Olinger. Should I call Albrecht and ask him if he wants to steal this one before you can lay claim?"

Old Oli glared at me. "You wouldn't."

Albrecht Röthschwert wasn't interested in American real estate, but he was passionately interested in buying the last available Birdsong Fragment before Old Oli did. I'd already dangled news of it over his sauerkraut-loving nose and he'd sniffed it like an Oktoberfest blood sausage hot off the grill of revenge. In case you're wondering, revenge isn't a dish best served cold. One look at Old Oli's burning eyes said otherwise.

I said, "Mr. Olinger, I'll give you two hours to make up your mind." I made a show of whipping my wrist and checking the time on my

Vacheron-Constantin chronograph.

Old Oli shook his head, "I'll need more then two hours if I'm to verify its provenance."

"This is the real deal, Mr. Olinger. Gerard can verify."

Gerard nodded, "It is, Mr. Olinger."

Old Oli cringed. Antiquarians across the United States flew into King City to buy from Gerard LaPierre's downtown shop all the time and Oli knew it.

I said, "Two hours is all I can give you, Mr. Olinger. Albrecht flew in from Köln this morning to pick up this leaf himself." That was a lie. Albrecht was still in Köln, but I did have him on speed dial. "That's how badly he wants to steal it from you, sir. Albrecht is dying to get his hands on it."

Old Oli scowled, "And he will die before he ever does. I'll do it." Oli shot out his liver-spotted hand and we shook.

"For $40 million on the Spire?"

"Yes, forty, and I take the fragment with me immediately. You have got yourself a gentleman's agreement, young man. Forward your contracts to my attorneys for me to sign."

"You can have it *after* you sign, Mr. Olinger. I have contracts waiting." I motioned behind me to the crowd we'd left in the main area. "Maybe you should call your lawyers and have them come here." Again I whipped my wrist and checked the time. "One hour, fifty-seven minutes, Mr. Olinger. The clock is ticking. I'm sure you understand."

With that stew simmering, I needed to leave Old Oli to sweat. I went to rejoin the crowd and got another drink, whiskey this time. Setting up this show had been a stressful day capping a stressful several months, and an entire year if you counted the other investors already locked in.

It didn't take long for Naughty Natalia to saunter up and start flirting. She purred, "I love watching you work, Channing. It's a total turn on the way these men do whatever you want." The curving lines of her cleavage were smiling at me with purpose, also a total turn on that clearly made every man do what Natalia wanted. "You can make people do anything you want, can't you?"

"Given the proper motivation," I smiled and swallowed whiskey.

"What kind of naughty things can I motivate you to do?"

"Ahhhhh, Natalia," I smiled. "You drive a hard bargain."

"How hard?" She pressed her body close.

If we'd met a few years ago, I would've given Natalia a tour of the building. When she gave the go signal, I would've backed her into the nearest naughty corner so my naughty hands could take a naughty tour under her naughty Santa costume, and we would've rewritten the meaning of the word naughty with my dick.

But times changed.

As hot as Natalia was, I just wasn't interested. A tight fucking body and willing fucking pussy weren't enough for me anymore. I was longing for something I'd once had but tragically lost.

Or should I say, someone.

Lately, one willing woman from my past had been haunting my thoughts like the Ghost of Christmas Pussy.

Chapter 3

CAROL

"Carol!" Mom gushed, her arms out for a hug.

"There she is," Dad grinned, eyes twinkling and hands pocketed in his slacks. He'd always been less touchy-feely than Mom, but he made up for it with an infinite supply of heart-warming smiles.

My parents stood waiting for me just outside the secure doors at King City International Airport near baggage. Glitzy Christmas decorations hung from the walls and ceilings or sprouted up from crafty faux-snowdrift displays on the floor. Twinkling trees, gift-wrapped packages, gem ornaments, Santas, sleighs, reindeer, elves, candles, stockings, and mistletoe. Holiday cheer was in full effect.

Mom and Dad wore matching his-and-hers knit Christmas sweaters, his green, hers red. I felt a twinge of fear when I realized both of them suddenly looked much the worse for wear than I remembered.

It had been ten years since I'd moved out of King City after college, but only a year since my last visit. I guess dimly lit video calls with my parents sitting in front of their lone home computer and a desk lamp (they were very old school) had disguised the quiet ravages of Father Time, but here they were. My parents were growing old, and there was nothing I could do to stop it.

"Hey guys," I sighed while Mom squeezed a hug out of me.

"Did you meet any nice men on your flight?" Mom asked, now holding me at arms length. "Looking this good, I don't see how you couldn't."

"Moooom," I groused, instantly regressing twenty years in a matter of seconds. Mom was always trying to matchmake, and always exaggerating about my looks. I hated her for the former, loved her for the latter.

"Doesn't she look good, Jack?" Mom asked Dad.

"Never better," Dad beamed. He withdrew one hand from his slacks and gave me a vigorous side hug. "So good to see you, kid."

"When do we get grandkids, Carol?" Mom demanded with a laugh that was more desperate than jubilant.

That question always set the mood, didn't it? In years past, it always grated like sand paper, especially when it was the third thing she'd said in the thirty seconds since she'd set eyes on me. Considering that she and Dad had waited so late in their lives to have me (they were in their late thirties when they had me), it rankled. But now, with my parents looking frighteningly frail, her asking made me feel... guilty. My biological clock hadn't quite kicked in, but theirs were spinning wildly out of control like the springs and gears might go sproinging out any minute.

"Working on it," I said with a fretful laugh.

"No rush," Dad said meaning it but not looking it as he watched the conveyor belt clatter into action and spit luggage out the hole in the wall.

"I'll get my bag when it comes out, Dad," I said. "It's heavy."

"I can manage," Dad grinned stubbornly.

Mom said, "Maybe you'll meet a nice man while you're here in town." That was code for: move back home, Carol. It wouldn't be code a week from now when she said it outright over Christmas Eve dinner, her smiling eyes shimmering with hope that I'd give her the greatest gift a daughter could give her mother.

Both the dinner and the question were an annual tradition at the Duffey house. Whenever Mom asked, I always made elaborate excuses that left her sniffing and apologizing in a watery voice for even asking, and me feeling like a horrible daughter.

The sad fact was, she and Dad both knew the truth, a truth we never discussed because we had jointly cut off its head and thrown it in the icy Tabor River (some people called it Taboo River, always without explanation, but fittingly due to the secret we'd thrown in it) that ran through downtown, hoping the frigid water would wash away our heartbreak.

It hadn't.

Old ghosts never died.

The one truth my family did admit?

I had left town permanently because of what Channing Peyton had done ten years ago. No one in King City who'd been here then could ever forget that scandal. Not only had it almost killed me and my family (literally), it had almost killed King City along with us.

\#

&

&*&

&*&*&

&*&*&*&

M

"You have got to be kidding me," I groaned when my parents' sedan passed the sprawling car dealership lit up with bright fluorescent lights, a vivid beacon of twinkling Christmas colors surrounded by a vast, cold white snowfield. I saw glowing signs for every automaker you can think of: Ford, General Motors, Chrysler, Honda, Toyota, Nissan, Hyundai, Volkswagen, BMW, Mercedes, Porsche, even Tesla. "It's bigger than a city."

One sign stood taller than all.

Peyton Auto Circle.

Dad narrated. "They finished construction this summer. We got a flier in the mail and the grand opening was on the local news. Some people drove in two and three hours for the free food."

"What about free cars?" I quipped.

"There weren't any of those," Dad chuckled.

Of course there weren't.

Mom commented, "They have really good prices, I hear."

Nobody was saying the obvious, so I did.

"Which Peyton owns it?"

Mom sat silent.

Dad grit his teeth and grumbled.

That was answer enough.

Confirmation came by way of two freeway billboards we passed on the interstate as we neared the heart of King City, both of them cold haloes lighting up the darkness.

Peyton Construction, Inc. — "We Build Your Dream Home"

and

Peyton Solar — "Go green! It's the new thing!"

Both featured Channing's devilishly handsome face.

"What," I sighed quietly, "does he own half of King City now? Or just all of it?"

Silence from my parents.

#
&
&*&
&*&*&
&*&*&*&
M

My childhood home was the same as I remembered.

Modest, cozy, and seasonally appropriate.

It sparkled with the same colorful Christmas cheer I saw every year I visited. Everything was covered in snow, except the driveway, which I knew Dad snow-blowed with surgical precision, and the streets, which had been plowed and salted recently. Having grown up in snow country, and left it for warmer climes, I didn't miss it. I would begrudgingly admit that fluffy snowbanks did enhance the holiday ambiance, amplifying the sparkling rainbow of lights strewn about the house and yard.

"I see your light collection is growing," I smiled as Dad parked in the driveway. "The light-up snowman is a nice touch."

"It runs on a fan," Dad offered. "We turn it off during the day to save electricity." Same old Dad. "I have to inflate it every night."

"Your father bought it at Walmart," Mom added. "It was on sale last January." Same old Mom.

They were always pinching pennies.

Inside, the house remained unchanged since my nineties childhood, a time capsule of a bygone pre-internet era. We took off our winter coats, hung them up, and I went straight to my old bedroom, which was identical to how I'd left it, a shrine to my high school years.

Mom and Dad hovered by my bedroom door as I set my luggage down and sat on my old bed. My annual visits didn't change the fact that my familiar cocoon was becoming increasingly unfamiliar with each passing year.

You know which comforter Mom had put on the bed?

The one I'd loaned to Evan Urleigh. The one he defiled with the help of Whitney Vinson. I would've been happy to forget it had ever existed, but Mom had inevitably asked for it back a year after I'd ended things with Evan.

Mom then, "Whatever happened to the quilt you borrowed last year for that Evan boy you used to date?" My mother called them quilts. If quilts could kill, this one already had…

Me then, "Ummmmm, yeah. About that." Insert long, rambling, cringey explanation filled with hand-waving excuses and half-truths, and me somehow trying to pull a conversational rabbit out of a hat to obscure the truth.

Mom then, hands folded resolutely, "Do me a favor and see if he doesn't still have it, would you?" She was a very determined woman.

I went and got it. Evan still had it. He said, "Oh, this old thing? Go ahead and take it. It's yours anyway." Because he had *cared* oh so much about it when I'd given it to him to keep him warm on his cold nights alone. I'd had more than enough of those to know how important a good comforter was.

And here it lay, the comforter that at age 20, I would've rather burned, though I did wash, bleach, and Febreeze it. The smell of Evan was long gone. Only the stench of bad memories still lingered.

Things changed at age 21.

One weekend, Channing Peyton and I had dirty, desperate, doggie sex on this comforter, on *this* bed. Yes, he had *taken* me from behind on my high school bed. *Taken*. Hair pulling was involved, as was me screaming when I came harder than I ever had, screaming in the most unladylike fashion you can imagine. Channing left bruises on my hips from that encounter. He'd had to hold on tight with hard fingers because I wouldn't stop bucking. Don't worry. I made it up to him with the scratches on his back. Like whip welts, I'd clawed so hard. These things happened when you came hard enough to start a lawn mower.

Our memorable encounter happened that year because an old friend of Dad's living in Ohio had died of a heart attack. Mom and Dad had flown out on a Friday for the Saturday funeral and asked me to house sit for them until they came home Sunday night. Channing had insisted on coming with me.

Oh, how we came.

We fucked all over my parents' house like it was ours.

Most of all, we fucked in my high school bed.

Again and again and again.

That weekend, Channing and I effectively revised my sexual history, and we did it together, turning dreary high school innocence into a sordid thing, a wet and lusty collection of orgasms, the sort of which a young college woman like myself could be quietly and demurely proud. Had you been there, you would've seen the lax, spent, and satisfied gleam in my eyes for over a week afterward. I hadn't walked around the KCU campus that following week, I had floated, a ballerina of sexual bliss whose toes never quite touched the ground.

Now, all those memories meant so little.

Slowly but surely, I was starting to feel like a visitor in an old life that was no longer mine. I hadn't had sex with anyone since Channing, not in ten years. Sex wasn't something I did. How could I? Without Channing, sex would be...

It wouldn't be sex.

It would be movement devoid of meaning.

This bedroom, this house, were evolving into a foreign thing, the abode of an adventurous acquaintance I once knew, both the wide-eyed and innocent teenaged Carol Duffey, and after her, the college-aged Carol Duffey, a sex rockstar I once knew who did the wildest things in this bedroom and elsewhere with the wildest man I'd ever loved, and if I'm being honest, the only. Both those distant young Carols I'd once known so well were slowly dying due to neglect, victims of circumstance, fading memories, and the passage of time.

"Carol," Mom nagged primly. "Your father is asking you a question."

"Oh, sorry. What?"

"Can I get you anything?" Dad asked.

"I'm fine, thanks," I smiled and pulled my phone out to distract myself, studying it to help cool the heat of my wet recollection.

"I'll make some tea," Mom said and walked off.

"Did your mother mention I bought a drone?" Dad was always tinkering with new technology.

"One of those annoying flying ones?"

Dad nodded.

"Are you spying on the neighbors?" I teased.

"No," Dad chuckled guiltily, straight-laced as ever. "I belong to a flying club. We race them at the park on Sunday mornings when no one's there." Now that Dad was nearing retirement age, his hobby activities had been steadily increasing.

"That's great, Dad," I beamed. "Have you met some new friends in the club?"

Dad slid his hands into his slacks, "Great bunch of people."

My phone chimed in my hand.

"I'll go help your mother with the tea."

"Can you cut me a slice of fruitcake?" Mom made it every year like clockwork. Hers was quite good. Fluffy, moist, not too sweet, and bursting with flavorful fruit chunks.

"If I do that, she'll want to make you dinner. You know how she is."

"No dessert before dinner," I sighed, reciting the rule. "Skip the fruitcake. I had a sandwich on the plane."

"We ate too." Dad winked, "I'll go sneak you a slice. We'll eat them after she goes to bed."

"Perfect."

I read the new message on my phone. A company-wide announcement from work I could ignore until my long vacation was over. Every year, I spent most of my vacation days visiting Mom and Dad over the holidays. I didn't have anyone else to visit the rest of the year, so I spent an extended Christmas with them. It was the only time I saw them in person.

I checked Facebook.

A new message from Sienna Winters. I hadn't seen her in ten years. I'd told her I was coming for Christmas. She had recently moved back to King City for reasons she had yet to explain. I knew exactly why she had left. The same reason I had. The scandal. When it had spread its endless tentacles over King City like an ancient plague, it had ensnared Sienna along with me and so many others. Soon after, Sienna and I both retreated to the farthest shores we could. I had gone west to the coast and she had gone east to New York City.

Sierra's message read, *Hit me up when you land. I'm dying of boredom over here.*

I had landed over an hour ago. Not expecting an immediate answer, I replied, *At my parents house. We're having tea.*

The message dots immediately danced, then it said, *Skip old lady tea! Meet me at TT's, bitch! Imma buy the first round!*

Tipple Town, AKA TT's, was a college bar near the KCU campus, which meant it too was haunted by old ghosts I didn't want to see.

I replied, *Anywhere but there, bitch. How about Applebee's?*

Sienna messaged, *I'm unfriending you if you're not at TT's in an hour.* She added an emoji of the middle finger, one of a martini glass, one of a vomiting smiley, followed by a slutty winking smiley with its tongue hanging out.

Me, *See you then.* Emoji of a nun.

Sienna, emoji of a padlock.

I'd already told her I'd been celibate since college. Normally it was an embarrassing secret I kept buried, but I had to tell someone. Sienna seemed like the perfect person to safeguard my shame while helping me shine the light of self-acceptance on it. She was very sympathetic. I trusted her.

Sienna, *I'll bring a cutting torch for your chastity belt. We'll power it with this.* Twenty emojis of frothy beer glasses, wine bottles, and XXX moonshine jugs.

Clearly, the gasoline for the cutting torch was drinkable, and would require we drink it for safe operation of said tool.

Snickering to myself, I set my phone on my bed. Seeing Sienna after all these years was exactly what I needed. I dearly missed my sister from another mister, or whatever we were. After what we'd gone through in college, we were as good as blood relatives.

Sighing, I looked around my high school room and the older memories slowly seeped in. Whenever I thought of high school, I thought nostalgically and lovingly of one person.

Jordyn Hoyle, the first girl pirate I'd ever befriended.

Sienna was definitely the second. Because of Sienna, I had finally paid my pirate dues in college and earned my Lady Rrrr! She had vetted me herself.

But Jordyn Hoyle would always be the first. Too bad she had sailed off the edge of the ocean in her black pirate ship when she graduated high school. Knowing her, the Jordyn Roger was crewed entirely by hot shirtless men with gold loop earrings in both ears, perfect hair and perfect tans, each one ready to swashbuckle for the honor of being her cabin boy for the remainder of the voyage.

I could imagine Jordyn laughing at that lusty fantasy. If only I knew what had happened to her. It had been fifteen years since I'd last seen her. She could be dead for all I knew. Painfully morbid to say, but it was possible. Women *did* disappear, never to be heard from again.

Oh, Jordyn.

I wanted desperately to believe she was out there somewhere, living a quiet life that made her happy. Living on a fishing trawler in Alaska (with the most handsome *real* cabin boy you can imagine), or some remote Caribbean island with no internet and her boys Friday, Saturday, and the other five bad boys of the week. Anything other than dead forever.

At times like this, I missed her so bad I wanted to cry. I blinked away tears and sniffed back sorrow.

Every so often, I scoured social media looking for her, hoping she'd returned to King City. Never had any luck. I knew she'd grown up here, but little else. Sadly, she hadn't returned.

Mom's kettle whistled merrily from the kitchen.

On a whim, I did a quick search for Jordyn on Instagram. I'd checked it six months ago to no avail. Then, there'd been only two Jordyn Hoyles. It wasn't exactly a common name, but neither of the profile pictures had been hers.

Suddenly, there was a third profile.

I tapped the new one.

A private account with a single tiny photo.

I zoomed in with two fingers.

It was *my* Jordyn.

My heart tightened with hope and flapped little wings, wanting desperately to soar.

I quickly messaged Jordyn from my account. If she replied, I would die.

"Tea's ready!" Mom called from the kitchen.

"Coming!" I called, eyes on my Instagram inbox as I headed toward the kitchen.

My phone dinged the second I sat down at the kitchen table across from Dad.

Jordyn's reply, *Rolo? Is that you girl?*

I tried not to cry in my tea between making small talk with Mom and Dad, and messaging Jordyn. Turned out she was back in King City to see her mom, who still lived here, and yes, she could meet me and Sienna for drinks at Tipple Town in an hour.

I never imagined my mini-reunion with my two friends would lead to Channing "He Who Must Not Be Named" Peyton knocking drunkenly on my parents' front door and waking them, me, and the rest of our neighborhood with his arrogant shenanigans later tonight, but he did.

Chapter 4

CHANNING

These days, when I wasn't hip deep fishing in a multi-million dollar money river and hooking Gray Whales like Morris Pilkington and Warner Olinger on my line, I drank.

And I always drank alone.

Standing beneath my vaulted coffered ceilings, and next to my gratuitously tall leaded and beveled-glass living room windows (the stained glass in Sainte-Chapelle's cathedral in Paris didn't have shit on my windows), I sipped my whiskey and winced.

Outside my mansion, the carolers were—

Excuse my language.

I never used *that* word.

Hated it with a passion.

Tried to have it removed from the dictionary. Didn't work. You can't buy everything. I know. I've tried.

As I was saying, the *singers* were going at it with gusto, belting out the twelve days of Christmas. I would've loved to hang them by their belts and balls from the nearest tree. For all I cared, Christmas could suck a bag of twelve dicks-a-dicking, and a partridge in a dick-shaped pear tree. The tree *and* pears are shaped like dicks. So's the bird. Figure it out.

Anyway, I fucking hated Christmas.

Jingle Hell is more like it.

Every year, I had to drink my way through the Season to be Sorry.

Again wincing, I gulped down a $6,500 dollar swallow of whiskey and walked over to my marble bar to pour myself another. You heard right. Six-and-a-half grand a shot. Dalmore 64 Trinitas. The hand-crafted crystal bottle alone costs more than your car. The entire bottle, more than your house. The whiskey itself was a rare blend of four vintages dating back to 1939, 1926, 1878, and 1868. I know, you're impressed. I was too. First time I tasted it, I thought I came in my own mouth, it's that good.

I wasn't drinking for flavor tonight.

I couldn't. As good as the Dalmore was, from tonight's first sip to the last, it had tasted more like the stock market crash of 1929.

Abject failure.

Didn't matter. Whenever the Christmas season slid into town on the coattails of December snow, I drank only the best. I needed the distraction. At the moment, I was so far in, it could've been a nine-dollar bottle of Old Crow and I wouldn't have noticed the difference. To be fair, with my sour mood, Old Crow probably would've tasted just as good, but I didn't have any on hand. Whatever got you drunk.

When the *singers* outside started in on The First Noel, I decided it would be their last. I couldn't give five golden fucks what the angels had to say.

"Somebody set the hounds on them," I snickered to the empty cavern of my living room. I didn't have hounds. Who had time for pets? Unless you were the CEO of Petco, pets were worthless, nothing but muddy carpet pissers and roving shit machines.

"Shall I ask them to leave, sir?" Terrance asked quietly from the arched doorway and nearly scared me out of my leather Cucinelli's.

"Jesus Christ, Terrance?! Can't you announce yourself instead of this ghost whisperer shit you're always doing?"

"Sorry, sir. Shall I use a megaphone next time?"

Terrance and I had an understanding.

Last year, as a joke, I'd put out a call for a British butler. Thought I might class up King City with a little old school charm. Terrance answered. He was between jobs. His last boss at the country manor where he worked had recently keeled over and the heirs thought Terrance was an antiquated waste of money. They all lived in London and had no respect for the country or tradition. Terrance didn't talk much but I had a way of charming the secrets out of anybody. He told me over the phone he was living temporarily in a friend's cottage somewhere in the English countryside near the old manor. Yorkshire or Oxfordshire or some other shitey shire.

I could read between the lines.

Terrance was hard up for cash. Guy was in his sixties, had no kids and no wife. Lonely as fuck and too old to retrain. That meant he was desperate. Never hire someone who isn't.

When I told him King City was in the armpit of America (technically, it was closer to the scrotum), Terrance balked.

I asked if he liked money.

He said how much.

My kind of man.

I had to grease some palms and pull strings to get USCIS (US Citizenship and Immigration Services) to rush his six-year H1-B work visa. They got it done in seven days, a record they told me. My business partner Jake had told me Terrance was a waste of money. I told Jake that good old T-Dog was damn good at his job. Best part, I had no desire to fuck him like I had my last eight teenaged maids-a-milking (18 and 19 are teenaged, so get your mind out the gutter and shut the fuck up) before I would inevitably inspire each "girl" (over 18, remember?) to quit of their own accord. I can be nasty, and I'm a slow learner. Ninth time is the charm. Word of advice: if you want something done right, hire an old guy. Or an old lady like Rosa Ramirez, who ran accounting for my many companies, and was older than dirt. Nothing beats 40 years of experience in her case or his.

"Well, sir?"

Watching the singers outside, I smirked, "Can you ask them to sing *Grandma Got Run Over By A Reindeer?* Lighten up the mood, maybe?"

"I'm not familiar with that one, sir. Might I suggest *Frosty the Snowman?*" He meant me.

"Very funny, Terrance."

"I'll call the police, if you like. Have them escorted away."

"Nah. Let them sing," I chuckled morosely. "If I drink enough, they'll sound like Alvin and the Chipmunks."

"Very good, sir."

"I take it you haven't heard the Chipmunks sing their Christmas song?"

"No, sir."

"It's a kid's song. The voices are sped up to sound like chipmunks. Hits your ears like shrill drills."

"I can imagine, sir."

From over on the marble bar, my phone suddenly sang a song that stabbed my heart. I visibly winced. The tune was a goofy 1960s kid's TV show theme everybody hated, the kind of ear-bleeder that made you want to go postal on purple dinosaurs and those chubby Teletubbies.

This song was worse, for personal reasons.

The TV theme song in question: H.R. Pufnstuf.

The first line: "Who's your friend when things get rough?"

Nobody, kids. Be your own fucking friend. Life will kick your teeth in if you trust the wrong people. I had, and had the tooth caps to prove it.

I hid my bitterness behind a grim grin.

That song on my phone meant only one thing.

"Is that them on the phone, sir?"

"Huh?" I asked, distracted.

"Your Alvin and the Chipmunks, sir."

"No."

Pufnstuf continued to play while I stared at my phone like I would need to cut either its red wire or its green wire, but if I cut the wrong one, my entire mansion and all of King City would be cratered out of existence.

The song droned on with jaunty cruelty that made shrill drills and chipmunks everywhere plug their ears and wince.

"Shall I check that for you, sir?"

"No," I choked out. "I'll get it."

I already knew who it was.

It was the singer.

She was back.

Chapter 5

CAROL

After tea, Dad put me in his Ford with the studded snow tires, and sent me on my way. I drove the snow-banked and slushy streets of King City by memory. I'd grown up here. I'd never need a map.

Red neon letters flickered on a sign that looked retro, but had in fact been shining above Tipple Town since long before I'd gone to KCU, and long before I'd first seen it from the backseat of my parents' car when we'd drive past on our way to church Sunday mornings.

The full name was Tim's Tipple Town, but the letters for "Tim's" were flickering weakly in the winter night. The bar was a King City institution. A series of historic black-and-white framed photos inside showed Tipple Town back in its glory days when it was built in the 1940s by Tim Farkas senior. The last time I'd been here was back in college.

Then, Tim Farkas junior had been running the place, his dad either too old or no longer with us, I didn't know which. Tim Sr. was before my time. But I knew Tim Jr. (and he knew every regular's name) was in his late forties back in college, putting him in his late fifties now. Assuming he still worked here.

I hoped he did.

It wouldn't be TT's without Tim.

I parked in the snowy lot and headed for the front doors, stepping with confidence because Dad had ordered me to wear elastic shoe cleats over my snow boots in case there was ice. According to him, boots weren't enough. I had humored him, inspired by visions of him and Mom hovering over me in the emergency room while my medical bills rolled out of control and they fretted over whether or not their meager savings would cover the cost of rehabbing their overly-confident daughter's broken back.

Sounds of approaching calamity caught my attention. A rattletrap sedan limp into the parking lot, its muffler farting and engine clanking as it struggled through the slush. It stopped in an empty space and the engine sputtered a complaint before going quiet. The door squeaked open. In sultry contrast to the rotten automobile, out stepped the sexiest pirate you've ever seen.

Black leather jacket (the same exact one!), black knit scarf bunched up in several wraps yet still dangling to her knees (it clearly doubled as sail rigging or a hangman's noose in a pinch), big mittens, tight leggings, a floppy pom-pom beanie, black biker boots, and that mane of black hair that was as much a man-magnet as the rest of her.

Jordyn Hoyle, the pirate queen.

"Rolo," she grinned, her lips plump, now painted black. "Bring it in, sister." She held out her arms and we hugged. I tried not to cry. I told myself she tried too, but I already knew Jordyn was too cool for crying. When I pulled away, her eyes shimmered.

She sniffed, "You're taller."

I giggled, "You haven't seen me since I was fourteen."

"Right?" Her breath puffed. "You're gorgeous, girl! Growing up did you right," she laughed. "I can't believe how good you look."

"You too," I gushed, ecstatic to see her finally. We had so much catching up to do.

"I knew it!" someone shrieked behind us.

I spun around.

Sienna Winters.

The front upholstered leather door of the bar was closing on its own behind her.

"Knew what?" I giggled nervously.

"Look at you two lipstick lesbians!" Sienna laughed, eyes all over Jordyn. "Is it serious? Please tell me you're married, Care, because if you're not, I'm hitting on your date." Sienna had started calling me Care a week into our tenure as Hemingway Hall's resident pranksters back in college. She was a bad influence. Piratically bad. I wouldn't have had it any other way.

She walked right up to Jordyn and I.

"Now I know why Care here gave up on men." Sienna's eyes roamed over Jordyn. "I'd give up dick for a slice of you, sexy."

I rolled my eyes, "Jordyn, this is Sienna, my college roommate."

Sienna looked like a Pinterest post for what to wear down the winter catwalk. Everything was brand-new sheepskin, faux suede, and cable-knit, plus the mandatory winter riding boots for when she needed to gallop through the snow on her clydesdale. With her flowing auburn hair, Sienna was equal parts action princess and sinful elvish pixie.

I winked, "I can't decide which of you is hotter."

"See?" Sienna gestured. "You don't skip ten years of dick unless you're a lesbian deep down."

Jordyn said, "What is she talking about, Rolo? Are you gay?"

"For you she is," Sienna flicked. "I'm thinking about it."

Jordyn waved a casual queenly hand, "If you know how to go down, I won't stop you."

"Rawr," Sienna giggled, either blushing or her cheeks were pinking from the cold air, I couldn't decide which.

Jordyn gave me a questioning look.

I was a tad worried these two wouldn't get along. I felt they were my sisters, but they'd never met, and were very much fire and ice, Sienna the fire, Jordyn the ice. Not wanting things to get catty, I cut the tension with a slice of lightness. "Should I get you two a room, or do you need a dildo, Sienna?"

"I've got four already," Sienna flitted. "But I could use new batteries. Mine are dead."

"I like her," Jordyn hmphed a laugh and reached into her leather jacket with her sensual fingers, pulling out a pack of Marlboro reds, same as high school, and a disposable Bic lighter. She shook out a cigarette and lit it before I could stop her. "Tell me about your dickless decade, Rolo." She punctuated her words with a smoky exhale.

I said, "It's a long story. Maybe I should tell it inside."

"Good idea," Sienna shivered, rubbing her arms. "I forgot how cold this place is. I'm already getting witch nips."

"That's just me," Jordyn winked at her while coaxing her cigarette into an orange ember, seemingly unaffected by the frigid winter air. "I have that effect on most women."

I laughed.

Sienna nodded knowingly and hiked her excited eyebrows at me while pointing between herself and Jordyn, implying they were already an item.

Jordyn V-ed two fingers around the cigarette perched on her plump lips and dragged while rolling her sultry eyes with her usual Cleopatra cool. "We'll do a dick check later, Sienna. If you're packing, we can work something out. Otherwise... no dick, no dice. Sorry. That's how I roll. Right, Rolo?"

I hid a snicker.

Sienna winked, "My tongue knows things no dick ever will."

"The night is still young." Jordyn nonchalantly flicked the orange coal of her cigarette into the snow, still holding the filter. "Let's go inside. I think Sienna's witch's nips are contagious." She sauntered toward the teardrop metal ashtray stand and poked her butt in it. The cigarette, that is.

"Did you see that ass?" Sienna hissed. "Your friend Jordyn is gorge!"

I knew Sienna had dabbled with women in college, but she generally preferred men. Her sudden obsession with Jordyn was unexpected. I'd never seen her so head-over for most men, let alone a woman. I knew Jordyn could hold her own with the witty repartee, she was the Queen of Pirates after all, but I really wanted them to like each other, not have

Sienna burn the bridge of friendship before either of them crossed over it for a hug.

I warned, "You heard Jordyn. I'm pretty sure she's straight."

"Now I finally have a good reason for sexual reassignment surgery!" Sienna winked.

"You two coming?" Jordyn called out, holding open the bar door.

"I am!" Sienna grinned as she pranced inside.

\#

&

&*&

&*&*&

&*&*&*&

M

"Get out! You three can't come in here!" The familiar face smiling from behind his Coke-bottle eyeglasses and swinging toward us on crutches was Tim junior. He had Spina Bifida and had spent his entire life on crutches. His body appeared shriveled and broken under his TT's T-shirt, but his spirit was unbreakable and shone with good humor. "I never gave permission to the cast of Disney's Frozen on Ice to come into my bar!" Tim was always cracking wise.

Sienna whispered in my ear, "I told him you were coming when I got here."

"Go drink down the street at Applebee's!" he added.

Sienna said, "I may have also mentioned your Applebee's threat."

"Thanks," I laughed.

While Tim approached, I couldn't help but notice that, despite TT's timeless retro hipster charm, the interior of the bar was starting to show its age.

So was Tim.

Ten years will do that.

At least the bar was busy and buzzing with cheerful Christmas customers. Looking at the cozy atmosphere slowly turned back the calendar, taking me straight to the old days.

I remembered seeing Tim sling drinks with the best of bartenders back in the day, but he preferred to play host, circulating constantly throughout the bar, entertaining patrons with gymnastic panache. Having grown up literally walking on his hands, Tim was strong enough he could walk handstands on his crutches, hop on and off chairs with them, and go up and down stairs, which he often did to animated applause.

Seeing him move now gave me a bittersweet pinch. His spark wasn't gone, but it was quickly fading, and faster than my parents'.

"Carol Duffey," Tim grinned. "I'd hug you, but I'm still learning how to levitate." Tim's legs weren't strong enough or straight enough for comfortable standing.

"So good to see you, Tim!" I leaned forward to give him a side hug and he returned it with his shoulder.

Tim glanced askance at Sienna. "Never mind you. You still owe me a thousand bucks for the business I lost the night you Rickrolled my jukebox."

"Oh that's right!" I laughed. I'd been there that night. Sienna had done something to Tim's jukebox so it could only play Rick Astley's *Never Gonna Give You Up* over and over and over. Tim had thought it was so funny, he wouldn't let anyone unplug it. It didn't take long before people were fleeing from the bar, laughing *and* groaning as they went.

"Some pranks are expensive," Sienna giggled bashfully.

"I love ya, kid," Tim grinned. "Don't do it again."

"I won't," she said like she was daddy's little princess. "Until Rick Astley writes a new #1 hit." She laughed a wink.

"I'll call him up right now and tell him to start writing," Tim chuckled. He gestured at Jordyn. "Who's this? You look familiar."

She said, "I've never been here, but you probably know my mom."

Tim's eyes gleamed recognition. "Jennifer Hoyle! You're her daughter?"

"That's me," Jordyn cringed.

"You could be her twin, kid! How's your mom? She was in here all the time when she was younger. Waitressed for me until she got pregnant. That was you, I'm guessing."

"It was."

"She doing good?"

Jordyn shrugged.

Tim deflated. "Is she okay?"

"For now. Breast cancer."

"I'm sorry, kid."

"She's in chemo. Doctors say she'll pull through." Jordyn shrugged again, looking decidedly unpiratical for the first time ever.

I wanted to cry. Everybody I loved was dying faster than they should've been.

"We need drinks," Sienna said.

"Tonight it's on the house," Tim said nobly. "For you," his Coke-bottle eyes glared at Sienna, "it goes on your tab."

"What?! I paid my tab last time I was here!"

"Never gonna give you up!" Tim's singing voice had its own boozy beauty, and did fair justice to Rick Astley.

"You said it was funny!"

"Never gonna let you down!"

"Okay! I'll pay!"

"Fucking with ya, kid," Tim grinned. "The cheap stuff is on me. No ten dollar shots. And no Rickrolling! Go find yourselves a table and I'll send Wanda over to take your order." He crutched away chuckling.

After we sat and Wanda took our drink orders, which included me getting a non-alcoholic hot spicy cider, Sienna snorted, "It's Christmas, Carol! Live a little! Put some rum in it!"

"Did you plan on driving me home?" I asked.

"I thought you were Desi tonight."

"How am I supposed to be designated driver if I'm drinking?"

"Details," Sienna sighed.

"I should be asking how *you* plan on driving if *you're* drinking."

"I Ubered."

"I hope they have snow tires."

"You sound *exactly* like your dad." Sienna had been over to my parents' house many times during our last two years in college.

"No, my dad would say he hopes they have *studded* snow tires." It wasn't supposed to be funny. It was the truth.

Sienna snickered to Jordyn, "Was she always like this?"

Jordyn had been sitting there quietly, assessing. "You want an honest answer?"

"Um, suuuuuure," Sienna said.

"The crazier you get, the saner Rolo gets."

Sienna was about to rebut, then aborted mid-but.

"Give her some breathing room," Jordyn said sagely. "She may surprise you."

For a tense moment, I waited for Sienna to take offense while her eyes danced around. Then she muttered a thoughtful. "Huh." Nodded. "You know, you're right? Care, remember that time I was sick, so I made you prank that boy Justin for me? The one I liked from Sosh class?"

"You mean the time Channing almost killed me because he thought I was cheating on…" I trailed off.

There.

I'd said it.

Named he who must not be.

"Shhhhh!" Sienna hissed. "Don't say it! He might hear!"

"Who might hear?" Jordyn asked quizzically.

"He Who Must Not Be Named!"

"Voldemort?" Jordyn giggled. "From Harry Potter?"

"No! C! H! A! N! N! I! N! G!" Sienna hissed.

"Channing who? What's she talking about, Rolo?"

"My ex-boyfriend," I scowled.

"Oh."

"Her *only* boyfriend," Sienna said. "Real one, anyway."

"Only?" Jordyn arched an eyebrow at me.

"Remember my long story?" I smirked.

"Uh huh."

"Would you like to hear it now?"

"May as well."

"Wait, before you tell it," Sienna said, "we need a selfie of us." She whipped out her phone and we leaned in for pictures, then she busied herself thumbing the phone. "This is going on Insta. #TheThreeMuskettes, #KCreunion. I'll tag you both. Jordyn, are you on Instagram?"

She nodded.

"What was your last name again?"

"Hoyle." She spelled her last name and her first.

Sienna nodded.

Jordyn said, "Now tell me about your ex, Rolo. Channing whoever."

"Stop saying it!" Sienna hissed, focused on her phone. "He's totally going to hear!" She finished with her phone and set it on the table next to mine. Sipped her drink.

My phone pinged a moment later with the tagging notification from Instagram. If Jordyn had a phone, it wasn't important enough to her to put on the table. That was *so* her. Too casual for the chaos of constantly being connected. I muted my phone and turned it over. Took a sip of my hot cider. Steeled myself.

Said, "Jordyn, have you ever heard of Channing Peyton, the first quarterback to take the KCU Cheetahs to the Rose Bowl four years in a row?"

Jordyn shrugged, "I left King City right after high school. I haven't been back since. Kinda lost touch with everyone and everything here, you know?"

"Oh," Sienna rolled a dramatic gasp, "you better buckle your ass to your barstool, bitch. This shit puts the evil back in medieval. Me and Care here?" She hooked a thumb at me proudly. "We were smack dab in the middle of that Category 5 shit-storm when it hit."

That was an understatement.

I gulped more cider, wishing briefly it was spiked with an entire fifth of rum, then told my story.

Chapter 6

CHANNING

How did I know it was her?

The singer?

I had paid Adam Kaufman, one of the whiz kids (Kid? Shit, he was only five years younger than I was) who worked over in IT at Peyton Solar, to hack together some custom code in his spare time. Why do something yourself when you can pay an expert to do it for you? This particular code kept tabs on little Miss Duffey, who had an ass that footstools the world over would pay to have sit on their faces.

Parenthetical: another name for footstool is "tuffet," which we all know is what the infamous Miss Muffet of nursery rhyme fame preferred when sitting on *her* muffet. Little known fact, she was the namesake of muff diving. Google it.

Dirty digressions aside, I had dubbed Adam's custom code the "Duff Tracker," not to be confused with "Muff Tracker," another piece of code he'd bolted together. Muff Tracker kept tabs on any and all new Tinder listings within a hundred miles of King City. Whenever a hot piece of ass went on the market, this hot piece of ass wanted to know. Every man had his vices, and ass was mine. Problem was, the more you went through, the more they blended together into hazy anonymity.

But there was one ass I'd never forget no matter how hard I tried.

Enter the Duff Tracker.

It scoured social media continuously for any mention of the Duff. If she went online, it would ping me by jingling the H.R. Pufnstuf theme song on my phone, like it was now. If you're wondering about the song, her dad used to call her Dufnstuf when she was little.

I swiped my phone off the marble bar.

Adam had rigged the software so it gave me a notification with a link to the social post in question. I tapped the link. Waited while an Instagram page loaded, followed by a unique post.

When the photo finally filled the screen, I had to sit down, stumbling onto the nearest leather barstool.

"Is everything alright, sir?" Terrance asked.

"Fine, fine." I stared at the photo. Two tens flanked an incognito eleven.

I didn't care what anyone said, Duff had a quirky beauty that got me every time. It wasn't obvious to the untrained eye, but mine was well trained.

Dufnstuf also had the hottest friends.

One of them I recognized. The photo's poster. Sienna Winters. Shit, I hadn't seen Sin-Win since I'd last seen Duff. She'd aged well. I didn't recognize the raven-haired babe. Looked like she did porn, or could have. I didn't care about that shit.

What I cared about was my dick jumping in my $2,000 Italian slacks at the sight of Dufnstuf like it wanted to split the zipper.

I didn't care because of the slacks.

I cared because Dick didn't jump for anybody these days.

Line up a dozen supermodels for the taking, with tits out to here, asses out to there, shiny high fuck-me heels, and no clothes. Point of fact: I had once done exactly that, talking twelve grown women out of their bikinis at my own private pool party. I was the kind of man who made that shit happen. And what did Dick do? Dick yawned. He fucking *yawned*. Then curled up for a cat nap in my pants. Meanwhile, I'm shouting in my own head, "These pussies want to play, Dick! Wake the fuck up!" Nothing. Snored right through it. Only thing I could do was have those twelve girls play naked volleyball in my indoor pool. Bouncing is always amusing.

Back on point, you show me Duff from the neck up in a winter parka and scarf, and Dick here pulls a muscle trying to jump through my phone?

What was up with that?

I was over her!

I didn't need Carol Duffey in my life!

The fuck I didn't, Dick said.

Horse shit! I had money coming out my ass! Women up to my ears! My life was swimming in pussy! Beautiful women with bodies built for sin! And you, my dick-feathered friend, pulled more tail than a hungry monkey at a cat show. But, whenever you reeled them in, you refused to work. That's what I call your basic bait-and-switch. Nobody likes that shit.

The solution to this situation was obvious.

I needed to track down Carol and talk to her.

Tonight, Dick said. *Not tomorrow. Tonight.*

I studied the photo. Immediately recognized the Tipple Town decor behind Duffey and her Muffey friends.

"Terrance, start the car," I growled.

"I don't have a license, sir."

"I thought you said you drove an old Rolls Royce Wraith for your boss back in the day, one of those classic thirties gangster cars."

"I did, sir. That was in Britain, sir. I don't have an American license."

"But you can drive. I'm too drunk."

"I don't think it's a good idea, sir, what with driving on the wrong side of the road and all. I'm sorry, sir. It would be a very bad idea."

I bit back a hiss. "You're right. Wake up Lashawn. He can drive."

"Yes, sir. I'll go rouse him."

Lashawn Washington was my right hand man, the best wide receiver in football history, far as I was concerned. Statistically, he *was* the best wide receiver in *college* football history. Back when we were the top dogs on the King City gridiron, I threw more completed passes to Lashawn, and he racked up more receiving yards and touchdowns, than any quarterback-receiver duo in King City Cheetahs' history.

After college, Lashawn went onto the NFL for a mere year before he injured out. I never even went, injuring myself my last game in college. Don't ask unless you like tear-jerkers. What a fucking sad disaster that was. Still couldn't think about it without taking a drink or ten.

Football was a dangerous game.

Silver lining, after a very dark year for me, while Lashawn was still living large in the NFL, I clawed my way out of the deepest pit of misery you can imagine. After Lashawn got injured, he climbed out of his own misery pit like a man on fire. Used his meager nest egg from the NFL to cover costs on his MBA from MIT's Sloan School of Management. Would've graduated *magna cum laude* for being top of his class, but MIT didn't give out honors at graduation. Graduating from MIT was the honor.

Lashawn could've gone on to work Wall Street, Silicon Valley, start his own damn company and make billions, you name it. But I made him an offer he couldn't refuse: work side by side with the best boss in the world: me. If I'd learned one thing in life, it was that money came easy, but real friends you could trust with your money did not. So I offered him the job of CFO where he could keep his trustworthy eyes on all the money going in and out of my many businesses. When he saw what I'd built up in such a short time, and how he could help build things bigger, he couldn't resist.

And here we were. He lived in the south wing of the mansion because this place was huge, 72 rooms or whatever it was. Like me, Lashawn was too busy with business responsibilities to bother with maintaining his own place. He didn't have time to worry about cleaning or decorating, and this place was a damn bachelor's castle that impressed the hell out of the ladies who came and went from both our bedrooms. It also had an army of staff keeping the place diamond bright so neither I nor Lashawn had to waste a second of thought on upkeep.

"This better be good," Lashawn yawned. His rich ebony skin contrasted against his white T-shirt and sweats. He scratched the back of his head with a muscled arm, bicep bouncing. "I'm supposed to be up balls-early tomorrow morning for that thing we talked about."

"Fuck the thing," I spat. "It can wait. This can't."

Lashawn sniffed sleepily, "Is there a dumpster full of cash waiting for us to pick up?"

"No."

"Then I'm going back to bed." He turned to go.

"It's Carol. She's back."

That stopped him. "Duff's here? In King City?"

I nodded, somewhat surprised he remembered her because I hadn't mentioned her once in ten years, and had tried to blot out her memory with a pageant of dubious women ever since. I said, "She's having drinks at TT's right now. I'm too drunk to drive over and Trey here," I smirked at Terrance who was smirking at me, his one show of disobedience because he hated when I called him Trey, "doesn't know the right side of the road from the wrong."

"The left, sir," Terrance corrected, still smirking. "I believe you have it the wrong way 'round."

I ignored him and said to Lashawn, "Can you drive me or not?" I wasn't worried about getting pulled over for a sobriety check. Half the cops in King City were in my back pocket, where they happily kissed my ass for the privilege of being there. The other half could go fuck themselves (no Christmas bonus from Channing Claus for the stockings of those miserable pricks). I was worried about driving in snow when I was half-drunk on whiskey and fully plastered on thoughts of Carol Duffey. I could barely think straight knowing she was so close. Dick, on the other hand, was straight as a ramrod. That probably explained my lack of a clear head. You better believe his was clear and focused on one fucking goal: the only hole he truly wanted. Ha. Dick, you have a one track mind.

Lashawn glowed a smile, "I'll throw some shoes on and warm up the Mercedes."

"I'll meet you in the garage in five."

"You got it, dog." Lashawn walked out.

"Will you be needing anything else, sir?" Terrance asked.

"I'm good. Catch some winks. Who knows what tomorrow will bring."

"Yes, sir. Good night, sir."

I grunted in reply and studied myself in the big mirror over the bar, making sure I looked good enough for the Duff. Who was I kidding? I always looked good enough. But I did need a coat. Outside it was colder than blue balls on a block of ice. Not that I'd know. Blue balls were for amateurs. I also needed to get something very important from the upstairs safe.

On the long walk to my walk-in (this place needed a subway or golf carts, it was that damn big), my phone rang.

Breaking the Law by Judas Priest.

This ringtone iced my veins and froze the drunk right out of my body in a single heartbeat, though I'd never let it show.

It was my business partner, Jake Martinelli, The Nutcracker himself. Together, we had become very rich men. Ask any rich person, does success come at a high price? They will never answer honestly. They can't. Honesty isn't in their blood. I should know.

"Jaaaaaake," I answered jovially. "How they hanging?"

"Like brass bowling balls. You ready for that thing tomorrow morning?" Jake was laser focused at all times and kept shit talk to a minimum.

"Yes I'm ready for that thing," I grunted.

"Good. What happened with Pilky and Olinger tonight?"

"I signed them both. Pilky for $30 million, Olinger for forty."

"Forty? How'd you get that old fuck to pay forty?"

"I hooked him with the last Birdsong Fragment."

"The what?" Jake didn't know shit about collectible books.

"Pages from the Gutenberg Bible. He wanted them. I had them."

"Pages? Can't you get those free from any hotel?"

"You're thinking of the Gideon Bible."

"Same thing," he said with total confidence.

Like I said.

"Here's the bad news." Jake always had bad news.

"Lay it on me."

"Pilky wants to back out of the deal."

"Since when?"

"Since his people called me an hour ago."

"Why didn't you open with that?" I groaned.

"Thought maybe you had new news. You need to call Pilky to-*night* and square that shit away."

My face sank. I wanted to deal with this like I wanted to deal with an unexpected lump in my balls I found while showering. Especially now with Carol so close I could almost feel her pussy throbbing around my pulsing dick. At the moment, I was literally still hard and twitching thinking about her.

"You still there, Channing?"

"Yeah, yeah. What?"

"You know how jumpy Pilky gets. He's scared his investment won't earn out."

"It will. Unless someone nukes King City in the next five years, he'll double his fucking money if he buys in. We've turned the real estate market in this town into a fucking money machine. All Pilky has to do is hand us his bags of cash while we turn the money crank for him."

"That's what he needs to hear, kid. Talk him off the ledge with that magical mouth of yours."

Fucking *hated* it when he said that. I groused, "Now?"

"Yes, now. Unless you want to throw away $30 million and six months' worth of kissing his fat pimply ass for the sake of the Spire. I don't know about you, but my lips are raw and I'm getting tired of smelling Pilky's shit while holding his dick."

Talking to Pilky would definitely ruin my Christmas Carol cheer. I repressed an irritated grumble. Jake was not a fan of insubordination. We were partners yes, but Jake was *more* of a partner, if you catch my drift. If you can't, don't get in this business.

"Call him, Channing." Jake's words were sharpened to a surgical edge that cut away flesh and bullshit with equal ease. "Now."

"Fine! I'll call him! And happy fucking holidays to you too, Jake!" I stabbed my phone with a finger, ending the call.

Like I said, The Nutcracker.

Before you ask, King City had an opera house that hosted ballet, I went to both, shut the fuck up. You get a gold star if you guessed The Nutcracker was the current seasonal production. And there's no law that says former quarterbacks can't enjoy ballet. People change. I had, for the worse, which included my new love of ballet. There was nothing noble about it. What was not to enjoy about prancing athletic female bodies in tights made up to look like sugar plum fairies, dewdrops, waltzing flowers, and marzipan dancers, many of them barely over 18?

Opera, on the other hand, was an acquired taste. Call it the Limburger cheese of the performing arts. Musically, I preferred the symphony. Also shut the fuck up. In this town, courting other people's money required that you be cultured. You seduced them and screwed them with your cultured dick. I'd done it more than once. Cultured pussy was my favorite. Cultured dick sucking, well that was metaphorical, thank goodness, but it had to be done. Success always required that you sell your soul.

I went and found Lashawn in the garage, told him to tuck his ass into bed until further notice, then called Pilky. Spent two hours on the phone with him, drinking to quell my annoyance while trying to talk him off the money ledge when I would've rather kicked him off it in the wrong direction. Eventually, Pilky saw sense and agreed to sign the contracts tomorrow. I immediately woke a groggy Lashawn, and we sped off in the Mercedes through freshly falling snow.

I had no doubt I was too drunk to drive at this point. Even if I hadn't been, I wouldn't be able to see the road through the haze of red Jake had left rotting in my head.

One of these days, one of us was going to kill the other one.

That was not a metaphor or exaggeration.

That was literal fact.

As long as it didn't happen before I saw Carol one last time, I wasn't going to worry about it. I knew what I'd gotten into when I'd signed up for this whirlpool of shit I called my partnership with Jake.

Chapter 7

CAROL

"You weren't kidding," Jordyn chortled nearly two hours later. "The shit you went through ten years ago *was* insane. I'm surprised you both aren't dead or in jail."

"Right?" Sienna nodded.

"It's ancient history," I said. "Let's talk about you, Jordyn. You haven't said a thing for the last two hours."

Sighing, Jordyn dropped her eyes. "It's my mom, you know? She's pretty much my world right now while we ride this out." This being breast cancer.

I reached over and squeezed her wrist. "Anything you need, Jordyn, you let me know. I'm here for you."

She looked at me, her eyes wet.

I had never seen Jordyn cry.

I didn't think she *could* cry. She was a pirate queen.

"Thanks," she sniffed, scraping a tear from the corner of her eye with a pinky nail.

"I mean it, Jay." I had never nicknamed her before now. In high school, she had been a goddess, me a mere mortal. I'd always called her Jordyn. Things changed. "Whatever you need, tell me, Jay. I'm here. My parents are here."

"We're here," Sienna nodded, finally serious.

"Thanks, you guys." Jordyn's voice had a fragility that frightened me. She was supposed to be the invincible badass rocker chick, the Pirate Queen, not a frightened woman like the rest of us.

As promised, when the bill came, Tim hooked us up with free drinks, and saw us out when it got late, demanding we come back soon. We assured him we would. At least while I was in town for the next two weeks, I'd make sure we went at least one more time.

Outside, it was snowing. Sienna went home in her Uber, a stout 4x4 SUV with studded tires. Driving Dad's car, I drove Jordyn home to her mom's apartment where they both lived.

"Call me in the morning and I'll bring chains over from my dad," I offered.

"I've got chains," Jordyn said, still sitting in the passenger seat. Her being here was so weird. She seemed so small in the big car. She hadn't seemed small in high school. She'd seemed like an Amazon to little me.

She said, "I didn't feel like dealing tonight. I hope you don't mind."

"Not at all."

She smiled.

I suddenly welled up. "I missed you, sister. You have no idea."

"Me too."

We melted into a mutual hug.

I wanted to tell her how often I thought about her, how important she was to me when I was a kid who needed a friend, no, a big sister, the best one I'd ever had. There were no words.

"I should go." She slid out of the hug and reached for the door.

"Hey, what're you doing Christmas Eve?"

"Spending it with my mom."

"How about you and her have Christmas Eve dinner with me and my parents? I mean, if your mom is up to it. Is she? I should've asked before offering."

"She is for now," Jordyn hitched a sigh, nodding. "I'll ask. I'm sure she'll say yes. Then neither of us has to cook." She snickered.

I laughed. "My mom's a great cook."

"So's mine. When she's up for it. Can we bring anything? I can figure something out between now and then. Just tell me what and I'll make it happen."

"No, we'll take care of everything. You just show up with your mom."

"I can do that."

I watched Jordyn make her way carefully up snowy steps before letting herself into what was obviously a small and shabby apartment. She waved and I did too, then I drove slowly home.

For a last minute reunion with the two most important friends I'd ever had, things could not have gone better.

Chapter 8

CHANNING

"You fucking asshole!" said the angry vixen who ambushed me in the snow between my Mercedes and the front doors of Tipple Town as she walked out of the retro building.

"I take it we know each other," I chuckled.

Her eyes lightbulbed. "*Know* each other? You *fucked* me, you piece of shit! Or did you forget already?!"

"You certainly look like my type," I smirked.

"What type is that, asshole?!" She slammed her little gloved hands against the chest of my wool coat without moving me an inch. Mountains never moved unless they wanted to.

"Gorgeous, passionate, well-dressed, foul-mouthed. Love the coat, by the way. Is that real mink? I didn't buy that for you, did I?"

"No, it's faux. And fuck you," she half-laughed, folding her fur-covered arms across what I would assume was an ample chest based on her allegation of our fornication. "Why haven't you called me, Channing?"

"You'll have to remind me *what* I'm supposed to call you before I do."

"It's Destiny!" She whacked me with a little fist. "Don't you remember?!"

No, and you weren't mine. I didn't say that because I knew it would only extend this already laborious conversation. "Oh! Destiny! Right! How you doing, babe?!" I had no idea who she was. Enough drunk fucking will do that.

"You are such a prick, Channing."

"In every way that counts," I teased. To my adoring fans, you'll forgive me for my full-throated flirtation. That coupled with ample empty promises seemed like the quickest exit strategy from this bad situation, though not a bad looking one. Destiny had a certain visual... charm.

"You're bad, babe," Destiny purred, clearly meaning good, and now swaying side-to-side like a horny schoolgirl, one who was over 18, of course, but only slightly. To be fair, Destiny looked at least 30 up close, a very well-maintained 30, but from a distance, and with the proper prescription of whiskey lenses, which I was currently wearing thanks to my long and joyous talk with Pilky, Destiny here easily looked 18, and a very easy 18 at that.

In case you're wondering, I had long suspected I harbored an unconscious fixation for college-age women who reminded me of a time in my life when it wasn't shit, a time when the *singer* and I were on top of the world and she seemed like she was *my* destiny, unlike this one here.

"Destiny, I hate to cut this short, but—" you will never be the one woman I love. Did my mind say that consciously? Traitor. I don't love anybody, not even my own Dick. He's a traitor too. Ask the twelve naked and frustrated volleyball girls leaping at my pool party.

"There's nothing short about you, Channing," Destiny whispered lustily.

"True, but I'm in the middle of some very important business at the moment, and—"

"How would you like to be in the middle of my very important business?"

I would be remiss if I didn't point out that Destiny was truly beautiful and smelled twice as divine. With her white fur coat, white fur hat, luxurious red hair, and black boots, she evoked visions of a sinful winter princess whose fur most men would kill for.

She leaned into me and slid her gloved hand under my coat, stroking an invitation.

"Someone's happy to see me," she giggled.

"That's not for you," I said stiffly. It truly wasn't. It was for Carol. I mean, the *singer*.

"Liar," Destiny said. "Come back to my place. It's just over there." She pointed at the two identical high-rise condo towers that had newly gone up. It and several other cutting-edge eye-sores like it had been popping up near the historical campus of King City University (founded in 1878) for several years now, and ruining the surrounding skyline, thanks in part to yours truly, the other part no thanks to Jake Martinelli.

Destiny smiled, "You should see my condo. It's the cutest loft ev-eeeeer." She popped her lip when she said it.

Most men would sell their souls for a single nibble of that lip. According to Destiny, I'd already had a king's feast for free.

"*Come* with me, Channing." No mystery what she meant by that. "You can have the grand tour," she winked. You can guess the final destination she had in mind.

Thing was, I'd been inside it more times than I cared to count, and I wasn't talking about her… *loft*. No way of knowing how many times I'd been in that wet destination. I was talking about her *actual* loft. Not only had I been there, I'd practically designed the damned place. Spent nearly a year going back and forth with Aperture + Light, the Manhattan interior design firm Jake had insisted we bring in to do Destiny's building (which was not the way she wanted me to do her).

Technically, her building was called Tabor Tower 1 (there were two, as a whole, they were Tabor Towers). The name was Jake's genius idea because the towers overlooked the river. He wasn't from King City originally and wouldn't have objected to the locals calling it Taboo Towers even if he'd known that was exactly what they did.

Aperture + Light's task was to give the interiors the proper uptown hipster feel. That had been a war and a half with Jake. I didn't want King City to be New York City. One was enough. In the end, my vision for the interior layout and design of the building won out, but not the exterior appearance. Like two dicks screaming at the city, "Look how big I am! I'm taller than all y'all put together, fuckaaaaahs!" That was alllll Jake. And you thought *I* was obsessed with dicks?

"What do you say, Channing?" Destiny ventured. "You, me, and Bubbles makes three?" The phrase was bubbly, but I wasn't here to lecture her on grammar or train her for a spelling bee.

"Destiny, my dear, as much as I would love to have the gold-ticket tour of your... *loft*, I don't have time right now. Can I write you a rain check? You know I'm good for it," I lied.

"Channing Peyton!" said the sexy blonde coming up behind Destiny at a dead run through the snow. Was she going to kill me, or... jump into what she assumed would be my waiting arms?

She jumped.

Arms weren't waiting. Blame Dick. He had no interest in this blonde.

Had she not wrapped her thighs around my waist, she would've fallen ass-first into the snow. Instead, she fell onto my hard on and gasped, "Is that... *little* Channing?"

"You may be the first woman to ever call him that," I chuckled.

"I never did," Destiny snipped.

I spared a glance at her, expecting the worst. Getting caught in a cat fight was always entertaining, but I didn't have time.

"Let's take him home with us, D!" said the blonde.

"Us?" I pondered.

Destiny spread a wide smile. "Don't you remember Bubbles? Or did you forget her too?" With names like that, these two had to be strippers. Are you surprised?

Bubbles the blonde had her arms wrapped around my neck, her nose touching mine, and she was grinding me for all she was worth, which in this case was more than the GDP of a prosperous Scandinavian nation, Sweden from the looks of her.

"Oh, he remembers," Bubbles said with cunning conviction and pelvic purpose.

I can't say that I remembered, but it was clear Bubbles took the art of Swedish massage to new… depths.

"You need any help, player?" Lashawn called out, chuckling his ass off from where he now stood outside the Mercedes. "Huh, huh, huh, huh." His breath billowed puffs of cottony laughter in the cold air.

"Any time you want to step in would be great, LD." That was short for L-Dog, for those of you who are canine inclined. "Ladies, how would you like to have my dearest friend and business associate Lashawn Washington, former star wide receiver of the King City Cheetahs, entertain you while I take care of business inside?"

"Awww," they both cooed.

Bubbles added, "We want you to take care of *our* business, Channing. Mine first."

With the help of a very generous and willing Lashawn, I managed to pry off Bubbles the Human Suction Cup. "Don't do anything I wouldn't do, LD."

"I haven't done half the shit you have, Chan Man."

"Perhaps you can make up for lost time while I'm inside."

"You got it," he chuckled.

I went to go.

"Don't leave," Destiny pleaded, dragging me by my wrist.

Grabbing my other wrist, Bubbles whined, "Show us the other half, Channing! The dirty half!"

Something told me I already had, or they wouldn't be holding on so hard.

"Sorry ladies." I pulled away and went inside Tipple Town.

\#

&

&*&

&*&*&

&*&*&*&

M

"You must be the ghost of Christmas past," Tim Farkas Jr. quipped, big eyes blinking behind his magnifiers while he shifted his weight on creaking crutches inside TT's.

"More like the ghost of Christmas piss-ass drunk." I belched unapologetically.

Seeing Tim after my ten year hiatus from drinking here was a donkey kick to the balls. He looked frail. But he wasn't dead or in imminent danger of dying, and I had a very pressing issue trapped in my Italian slacks. I also hated being in here because it brought back painful memories.

"Where's Carol?" I demanded.

"Is that how you say hello to an old friend, Mr. Peyton? After all these years?"

"Sorry. Good to see you, Tim. And don't call me Mr. Peyton. You of all people. It's Channing. Where is she?"

"Carol left half an hour ago."

I groaned. "Do you know where she went?"

"Home, I suppose."

I had only been standing inside TT's for two minutes, and already the regulars were casting side glances and mumbling about me being here. It had been years. Not since college had I set foot in this place. Moreover, I had been a certified celebrity in this town for over a decade and still hadn't gotten used to people recognizing me everywhere I went. Brad Pitt could streak naked through town with his dick swinging and his hair on fire, and he'd get less attention than I did, as evidenced by the red-carpet welcome (and blonde) I'd been given outside by Destiny and Bubbles.

"Happy Kwanzaa, everybody," I said awkwardly. "Or merry Hanukkah, or whatever the fuck it is today," I mumbled.

Scattered chuckles.

"Drinks are on me!" I said loudly and pulled out my wallet. Money didn't solve all problems, but it solved most. I handed $2,000 in cash to Tim. "If you need more, call my office."

Tim's eyes ballooned behind his specs, "I don't think I'll even need this much. There aren't that many people here, Mr. Peyton."

"Channing," I grumbled. "And keep it. Hire a topless waitress or a bottomless Elvis impersonator for the night, or shit, pay Mr. and Mrs. Claus to fuck on stage with elves popping out their asses, I don't care."

"If you know the number for the North Pole, I'll call them right now," Tim grinned.

"Sorry, don't have it on me." I snorted a morose laugh. Tim was a good guy. "Catch you later, Tim. I need to go find Carol."

"When you find her, bring her back here for drinks some time, on me. It'll be like old times."

"Yeah. I'll try." I wasn't holding my breath. Carol considered me dead and buried after what I did to her. I turned to go.

"And give my best to your friend Mr. Martinelli, next time you see him."

"Why him?" I frowned.

"He came by here a while back." It wasn't the first time Jake did things without telling me.

"Why?"

Tim offered a cryptic grin.

"Whatever. See you around, Tim."

"Don't be a stranger!" he called out.

Bundling my coat around me and snapping my collar up, I hunkered my head against a fresh flurry and trudged out into the lonely snow.

Chapter 9

CAROL

One thing about snow I *did* like, it quieted the world under a peaceful white blanket that slowed everything down, especially traffic, what little of it there was this late.

The silence gave me time to think while I drove home.

My mind inevitably drifted back to Channing.

At that exact moment, I passed a brand new auto parts supply store that hadn't been here last Christmas. What had been here was Ella's BBQ, est. 1969, according to the old sign, and Flat Tire Bicycles, where Dad and I had picked out my first grownup bike years ago, a Diamondback Axis mountain bike, no pink girlie bikes for me, thank you very much, and Chocolate Towne. Their fresh-made fudge was to die for, the store smelled like chocolate heaven, and it had been here at least since I was born. Not anymore! So sad. Gone now.

I loved those places!

I wished they hadn't been torn down.

That was progress for you.

To add insult to injury, the name on the bright sign of the auto parts store?

Peyton Auto Parts.

How many business was this man in?

I didn't want to think about *him*, or his invasive businesses. I swear, they were worse than kudzu, ruining King City one acre at a time.

I tried to never think about Channing on purpose, but talking about him for two hours with Jordyn and Sienna, and being surrounded by his name like I was trapped in a crazy hall of mirrors, only it was his business signs instead, made it impossible not to.

Like it or not, there was no King City without Channing Peyton. Based on his ever-expanding business presence, he'd soon own every business in town. Then they'd change King City to Peyton City. My condolences.

It wasn't long before I turned onto my parents' street.

A black Mercedes idling in front of Mom and Dad's house caught my immediate attention. Slow smoke drifted from the tailpipe, hanging on the frigid, still air. This car didn't belong on my street. Nobody in our neighborhood could afford a Mercedes, not one this nice and new, anyway.

First thought?

Drug dealer car.

I didn't remember our neighborhood having a gang problem. Then again, progress. Sensing something was wrong, I slowed two houses away from our driveway and stopped. Pulled out my phone and considered calling Dad to come out and meet me. It was almost midnight. My parents were already in bed. Did I wake them? Or call 911?

No, I was being ridiculous.

It was probably someone visiting a neighbor, or someone who pulled over to send a text. It wasn't a creepy drug dealer.

I pulled slowly into the driveway and parked Dad's car. Watched the Mercedes in my mirrors while I found the house key on Dad's keyring and readied it, then fished my mace out of my coat pocket, made sure it was armed, and put my finger on the button. I climbed out, eyes intent on the black car for any signs of movement.

None.

I strode through the fresh snow, thankful I was wearing Dad's cleats. You never knew when there might be ice hiding underneath.

The black back door popped open on the Mercedes and I jolted into motion, hurrying carefully up the driveway toward the front walk, the front door still an impossibly distant safe zone I was determined to reach before the rapists kidnapped me in their big black car.

"Carol! Wait!"

That voice.

It took the wind out of my sails. I stumbled to a stop, my boots kicking up snow puffs. I didn't bother turning to look.

I knew who it was.

"Carol! It's me, Channing! Channing Peyton!"

Like I could ever forget.

Chapter 10

CAROL

"What do you want?" I groaned where I stood, my back to him.

"I brought you something," he said with quiet hope.

"Go away, Channing. Please. It's cold outside and I don't want to do this." I almost added "right now" to be polite, but the truth was I didn't ever want to do this. "Please, just leave."

"Five minutes, Carol. That's all I ask." His voice had changed. It had always been rugged, masculine, somewhat raspy. Now it was all gravel, broken rocks, the kind that broke hearts and left a trail of broken women writhing and dying in his dust on the roadside.

If Channing had been born eighty years earlier, that voice would've made him a radio star. The looks I remembered would've made him a teen idol, when he got older, an A-list movie star. But he didn't need to be any of those things because he had once been the biggest college football star in America, known not only for his nearly perfect record on the field, but for his perfect looks everywhere else. Once photos of him without his helmet started getting out, Channing Peyton became a sensation, for the women of this country, an obsession. He had always been too big to remain a small town boy. One look told you that.

Ladies, listen to me closely.

Looks aren't worth it.

Looks take more than they give.

I know because Channing had taken everything from me when he left my life. The worst part? Channing the person — not the football star, the boyfriend I knew intimately — always gave more than he took. He was generous to a fault, which made our breakup that much more devastating. For a time, he had been the exception to the rule. Then he had proven it. Let me tell you, mourning the loss of what had been a perfect love for two wonderful years was like going through hell and back.

Shoes crunched the snow behind me.

"Care," he said softly, using his voice to cast a spell over me.

That's what he used to call me. Care. Because I did. Usually too much.

"Let me see you," he whispered.

I didn't move, but my hips were telling me to turn around and head straight for that voice. My heart was telling me to run for the front door, and my head was telling me to walk cautiously because of the snow. I whispered, "I'm not doing this, Channing."

"You don't have to do anything, Care—BLORCH!" He ripped a disgusting snow-melting belch. "Sorry. Too much whiskey. Does funny things on an empty stomach."

That was enough to turn me around. I could already picture a grizzled, prematurely balding and graying, jowly, pot-bellied and washed-up wreck of a man, the kind of wino I would take pity on, one who couldn't possibly hurt my heart a second time.

I should've remembered those billboards I'd seen outside of town on the drive in from the airport.

Channing Peyton had gotten *better* looking.

They say men age better than women. They are correct.

Somehow, Channing had become more manly, more captivating, if that was possible. His thick dark hair showed only slight flecks of gray at the temples. This only intensified the authority he had always projected. Now it hinted at hard-won wisdom, a man not to be trifled with. The lines of his chiseled face were cut ever-so-slightly deeper (he was too young to look old), but those lines added to his aura of resolve. Channing had never been one to back down from any challenge, for good or ill. Overall, he was stunning, a Titan of a man in a mortal's body. Tall, broad-shouldered, imposing, indomitable. Even with him half-hidden under a long black wool coat, Channing still had *it*, and then some.

"Carol," he sighed. "You're... gorgeous." His mysterious eyes were dark and foreboding, almost scary.

I wasn't accustomed to men calling me gorgeous. At best, they called me cute. With Channing, gorgeous was all he ever called me. And I wasn't genuinely *scared* of him. I was scared of what those eyes might make me *do*.

Dirty Carol wanted him to throw me against the nearest wall, tear my panties off, and start thrusting. We could kiss after.

Hurt Carol wanted to throw him *through* the nearest wall. Any hate sex to follow would be at my discretion. I still hadn't decided how I truly felt about seeing him again. That decision would likely take decades to resolve itself, and likely for the worse.

Heart Carol desperately wanted Channing to beg my forgiveness so he could offer me his eternal devotion, at which point, I would open my heart, my life, and my body to the man I still loved.

Jordyn Hoyle had been right way back in high school. Channing still had a piece of my heart, and always would. That much I'd always known. What I'd never realized was how many pieces he still had. If I had to guess, it was most of them, possibly all.

"I brought you this," he said, holding up a ring box.

I laughed, "You have got to be kidding, Channing. That better not be a ring."

"It is."

"If you get down on one knee, I will knee you in the nose. I'm serious, Channing. We haven't talked in ten years. I don't know you anymore."

"Fair enough." He opened the box, held it in one hand like a peace offering.

I snorted sourly, "Your grandmother's wedding ring?"

"Yup." The ring was a modest thing, but it sparkled rainbows, glinting back Dad's Christmas lights that twinkled around us like rainbow stars.

"Is this your idea of a sick joke?"

"Not one bit."

"You made me give that ring back when you broke up with me, Channing. Remember?"

He nodded. "I shouldn't have done that. I wanted you to have it again. Not in any engagement sort of way. Not in a promise ring way, or even boyfriend-won-it-for-his-girlfriend-at-the-state-fair sort of way. I don't know. I just... just take it."

"No, Channing! Are you insane?! I never want to see that ring again. Put it away!"

He clamped the clamshell case closed and pocketed it. "I understand. Too many bad memories. I'll buy you a knew one. Something with more karats than Bugs Bunny."

"Don't buy me any ring."

"How about I buy you a building? I have a few of those."

"What?! No. That's nonsense."

"Two buildings. Been meaning to rename it anyway. Do you know Tabor Towers near the river?"

"Yes, what about it?"

"People are starting to call it Taboo Towers, which does not help property value. How about I rename the place Carol Duffey Plaza and give it to you?"

"Don't tell me you own those buildings."

"For the most part, yes. I'll name them anything you like. Just say the word, and they're yours. You'll have a major stake in the buildings, and full stake in the name."

That was bizarre of him to say. He knew that money, flash and status weren't important to me. They never had been. As long as everyone in my family was fed, clothed, and had a warm roof over our heads, that had always been enough. Did Channing not remember that? Or any of our time together?

"What do you think, Care? Do you like the sound of plaza, or would you prefer Carol Duffey Towers? Now that I think about it, not my favorite. Too phallic. You're more of a plaza kind of girl. That's a better fit. I'll have them start work on the new signage in the morning. Something big and granite with brass inlays that will last forever." From him, forever was wishful thinking. Nothing associated with him ever lasted.

"No, Channing. I don't want anything from you."

"How about just me?"

"Least of all you."

He flashed his winning grin. It was more lopsided than I remembered, like a teeter that had lost its totter, but that only made it more genuine, more real. When he'd been younger, his smile had almost been *too* perfect. This was... relatable, inviting. I knew better.

"You know what I want more than anything, Channing?"

"Name it and I'll buy it."

"Don't worry, it's free." What was with him and the money obsession? He'd never been like this ten years ago.

"My dick is free."

"Ew, Channing. No, I want to be left alone. That won't cost you a penny."

"Are you sure?"

Oh, that voice. It was now weighty with hidden sadness. It was also much more refined than the young Channing I remembered. It had a poetry to it, a new and seductive rhythm that was difficult to resist.

He stepped toward me. Loomed was more like it. In his dark coat, Channing was a foreboding presence, a ghostly shadow that had once stolen my soul and might do it again if I let him.

"Back up, Channing."

"I'm drawn to you, Care. I always have been. You know that. I can't help it." Channing was still magically handsome, his eyes smoldering coals that were attempting to cast the same spell over me they had years ago, and likely on every woman since.

This time, it wasn't going to work.

"Channing, I—"

"Let me pitch you a cliché, Duffin my little muffin." His tone was suddenly light, amused, confident, winning for want of a better word, and it stopped me short. Channing always got what he wanted when he applied himself, didn't he?

"This should be good," I snarked. "And don't call me that anymore. You lost your nickname privileges when you rescinded them yourself."

He ignored my comment. "Broken-hearted small town girl goes to big city, throws herself into her career in a vain attempt to fill the hole that no amount of work can ever possibly fill. Sound familiar?"

I smirked.

He smirked in return, "It doesn't work, Duffin. I've tried. Work won't fill your hole. But I can." He underscored his point with a lascivious wink.

"Not mine, you can't," I snorted a laugh. "Find yourself another one."

"I've tried. Filled so many holes I forgot my own name." That answered that. What did I tell you about him and other women? He said, "It never works, Duffin. Your hole is the only one I want to fill." It didn't matter which hole he meant. He'd filled them all, time and time again with a fullness and desperate heat my body had not forgotten.

"Is that supposed to make me *want* to sleep with you?" It did, but I wasn't willing to admit it to this train wreck of a perfect memory.

"Yes. No. I don't know. Blorch! Sorry."

"How drunk are you?" I marveled, trying to ignore the sexual storm stirring my body as the memories took hold. "And how did we go from your grandmother's wedding ring to you begging for sex?"

"Who said I was begging?"

"That's what it sounds like to me. And the answer is no."

"Why are you being such a Nutcracker about this, Carol? It's just sex, and we're good at it, in case it slipped your mind."

"Not for me, it isn't."

"Bullshit. I made you come so hard you saw stars. You said so."

"I meant, it's not *just* sex for me. It never has been and it never will. You of all people should know. I can't believe we're even talking about this. It's pathetic, Channing. Go get laid somewhere else. I'm sure you have plenty of offers."

"More than you can imagine," he snickered. "Blorch!"

I laughed. "Do you hear yourself? You're gross, do you know that?" He didn't look gross, but his behavior set the benchmark.

"Please, Duff. Do you want to hear me beg?"

"No."

"Okay, I'll beg."

I shook my head in disgust.

"Here goes," he barreled on. "I haven't had sex with anyone in over a year. Do you have any idea what that does to a man? I can't get it up for anyone but you. I was starting to think my dick was broken. Found out tonight it's not. Since the minute you came into town, I—"

"Stop right there. Now that you mention it, how the hell did you know I'd be here tonight?"

"Wild guess. Like I was saying, you're the only woman who makes me hard anymore. The mere thought of seeing you gave me a rager that won't quit."

"TMI, Channing." Truth be told, I wanted to know more. It wasn't every day the most handsome man I'd ever seen, let alone loved and fucked, was telling me how hard he was for me. In fact, I hadn't heard those words in ten impossibly long years. And how long *it* had been. I'd never forgotten how thick and—

"I'll prove it." He reached down to unbutton his coat.

"No!" I held up a halting hand. "I don't want to see it." Lies! Audacious lies!

"You don't need to because you already have, right? Do you remember the contours of my cock as clearly as I remember your taste? Your scent? Your needy screams when you begged me not to stop? When I was inside you so deep you—"

"Stop, Channing." He was tormenting me with the truth, and the sweaty memories of everything he said were making me uncomfortably wet and hot despite the cold snow. If I wasn't careful, I'd start melting the snow at my feet like the rest of me already was.

"Would you like to feel it? The cock we both know you feel in your dreams? It's pulsing for you now, Duffin."

Pulse.

That word held special meaning for us both.

Very special.

Pulse, pulse, pulse.

He inched closer.

"No, Channing! You *just* said you've filled more holes than a gopher-ridden golf course."

"Not in the last year, I haven't," Channing chuckled. "A golf course. Smart and clever as ever, Duffin. I missed your sense of humor. It's half of what I love about you. The other half is a sticky mess ready to drip down your thighs right now, isn't it?" Another inch closer.

"No," I moaned and struggled to keep my eyes from hooding in sensual memory, swallowing the hot truth like so much of Channing's sumptuous cum.

"I mean it, Duffin." Yet another inch closer to me. A few more inches and his most pertinent feature would be able to bridge the distance with ease. "There's an emptiness inside you begging me to fill it. Don't deny it. I know, because I need to be inside you so bad it hurts. Your emptiness needs my excess. Admit it."

"Find yourself a gopher hole." I forced a snicker to cover my raining desire.

"I gave them up a year ago."

"Try a rat hole."

"I'm telling the truth. I haven't had sex in over a year, Duffin." He was right on top of me now, closer than his cock would be if he pulled it out.

I was on the verge of giving in, unbuttoning his coat in a flurry of desire, unbuckling his belt, and pulling him out myself. My only defense was to go on the attack. I mocked, "Oooooh, a whole year without sex. Boo hoo."

"That's a long fucking time," he smiled proudly. "A loooong fucking time." That was innuendo, which I ignored.

"Is it?" I said, suddenly irritated.

"Interesting. Tell me something, Duffin. Have you *not* gotten laid in the last year?"

I hiked hateful eyebrows and shook a smirk.

He frowned, "How long *has* it been?"

"Don't ask."

"Two years?"

I huffed.

"Three?"

"Would you stop asking?"

"Five years, Duffin?" He was now so close to touching me, the slightest winter breeze would blow me into him and his hardness, which I had no doubt was laying in wait beneath his coat.

"Back up, Channing," I warned.

"Jesus Christ, Duffin," he said, sympathetic. "How long has it been?"

"None of your business."

"Have you had *any* sex since us, Duffin?"

"Of course I have," I lied pathetically.

"Oh? Who with?"

"He was— I met him at a…" I was too frazzled to think.

"At a what, Duffin?"

I looked around hastily at the yard, "At a Christmas party."

"Uh huh. What was his name?"

"Gary, uh, Smur-erve," I mumbled under my breath. "That's who."

"Gary Smurf?"

"Yes, Gary Smurf from work."

"Was he three apples tall with blue skin?"

"Noooo," I sneered. "He was six-foot-two and had a beautiful body."

"Oooooh. You mean Gargamel. Bald can be sexy," he snorted. "Gargamel *is* a wizard, and he does have that moody cat and his own magical cauldron. Did he show you the cauldron? That would've been fun to see. It'd make for a great jacuzzi. Remember jacuzzi sex, Duffin? Remember how hard you came when you were floating on top of the water and I ate you for an hour that time?"

"It wasn't an hour," I chuckled guiltily.

"I remember it was summer, it was night, we were alone, and you said the noise of the jets was distracting with your ears under water, so I turned them off. Then I went back to eating you, and you started quivering so hard, you were making waves. I had to hold your ass out of the water the whole time so I wasn't swallowing chlorine. After you came for, I swear it was ten minutes straight, you said you couldn't *stop* coming, like you were trapped in an orgasm that would never end. You said it was like floating to heaven, only better."

"No I didn't," I lied, waves of that exact orgasm echoing through my body in ghostly remembrance of what had been tantamount to a spiritual journey, except sexual, or both, I never could figure it out, but I'd never forgotten it. And I will tell you, masturbating in a saltwater float tank, one of those sensory deprivations ones you paid for by the hour so you could hallucinate without drugs, and in my case, hope to recapture that elusive orgasmic experience Channing had once given me, was not the same thing.

I'll tell you why.

Float tanks were too public while ironically being too lonely and secluded. You were all alone in it. There was also the issue of control. You needed to be out of control to have mind shattering orgasms, not in control. Channing taught me that. You needed someone *else* to be in control of *you*. That was the key. You couldn't do that to yourself. There was just something magical about two people together that created a spiritual conduit that was impossible to find on your own.

I sighed, "Can we drop it, Channing? I really don't want to talk about sex with you ever again." Another lie. He and I could talk about sex for a week straight and I wouldn't get bored.

"Fine by me," he smiled smugly. "We'll skip the dirty talk. Go straight to the fucking."

"No, Channing!" I laughed against my will. My body remembered things about this man that my mind had forgotten but my heart would never forgive, and that was why I needed to put a stop to this, for the sake of my soon-to-be-ruined panties. Ruined because there was no way I could ask Mom to wash them.

That brought bad memories rushing back in a raging hurricane.

"No," I repeated more firmly. "Channing, you made it very clear ten years ago that you were done with me when you tore my heart out and tossed it in the toilet. Remember that? Huh? You don't, do you? Because you disappeared after dumping me like I was a bag of garbage."

"Don't say that," he grimaced.

"Why not? It's true. You never saw what your leaving did to me. You didn't see me wanting to die because I couldn't find the strength to get out of bed for three months. Literally three months, Channing. I missed an entire quarter of school because of you. The worst part was, missing that quarter threw off my entire schedule. I had to redo senior year of college because of you."

"I'm sorry. I didn't know."

"You didn't, did you? Those first three months, the only place I went was crawling to the bathroom. I had no idea heartbreak could kill you, but it almost did me. Ask my parents if you don't believe me. They were there. At one point, I stopped eating for two weeks. Two weeks, Channing. I lost twenty pounds I didn't have to lose. If my parents hadn't forced chicken soup down my throat, I probably would've died of starvation."

His face went Fukushima. Total meltdown. Not with explosive anger, not with a dramatic display of atomic energy. Everything was internal, a profound malfunction, system shutdown. It was hard to explain, but I wasn't the one who needed to do any explaining. He was, but none was forthcoming.

I folded my arms. "No snappy answer for that one, Chan?"

"It," he growled, "was," he heaved a sigh, "a very difficult," he grit his teeth, "time," he hissed, "in my life," he choked, "back then."

"Oh," I snorted. "Right. I forgot. It was tough for *you*. Me and my parents?" I waved a sarcastic hand. "We were fine. We had all those caring and concerned TV news reporters shoving microphones in our faces and helicopters flying over whenever we walked out our front door because *you* blamed *me* for something *you* did! Because of *you*, the entire town hated me! Some of them probably still do! People literally wanted to kill me back then because of what *you* did! Or did you forget that because you were skunk drunk then like you are now?"

"I remember," he muttered. "Blorch."

"Oh, good." I sneered. "Tell me something, *Channing*. Did the people of King City try and run *you* out of town on a rail too?"

He shook his head.

"Ooooooooh, well, let me tell you. There's nothing like having your neighbors throw things at you or your house or threaten to burn it down and call you names for something you didn't do! I literally moved out of

King City because of you! No, I don't know *anything* about how hard things were back then, *Channing*."

He glared at me, speechless.

"Why are you even here?" I huffed, now completely over him.

"I don't fucking know."

"Hmph. That's the first honest thing you've said all night."

"I just, I, I wanted to talk. Is that too much to ask?"

"Oh, please. If you wanted to talk to me, you could've called me at least ten thousand times in the last ten years. But you never did, did you? Not a message, not a text, not a card, not anything. I assumed you'd moved on and never looked back. Tell me I'm wrong."

"Carol, I—"

"Go away, Channing. Your being here is opening old wounds that should've healed. I deserve to be healed, Channing. You're making things worse. It's late. I need to sleep. You need to go home and sober up and never come back." I put my hands on his chest and pushed. "Go, Channing."

"Carol, please, I can explain."

"Can you explain dumping *me* after everything *you* did?" I pushed again.

"Carol! Stop! You don't understand!"

"Go!" I pushed.

Channing backed up a step and suddenly slipped on the slick snow, arms and legs flying frantically in every direction.

I gasped. I didn't want him breaking his neck or cracking his skull on the icy walk.

Somehow, he managed a sideways stumble onto the foot-deep blanket of powder on the front lawn. Poomph! He sunk right into it.

"Fucking black ice," he grumbled at the night sky, still molded into the snow. He was fine.

"Get out of here, Channing."

"No." He lay there.

"Fine. Stay out here and freeze. I don't care."

"I'll make snow angels all night. That'll keep me warm and Frosty here will keep me company." He meant Dad's life-size inflatable light-up snowman, which was quietly keeping itself inflated with its fan a few feet away. Whir!

I crossed my arms and rolled my eyes, hoping Channing here would be the one to die. "Go home, Channing. If Mom and Dad see you here come morning, they'll call the cops. They don't deserve that kind of aggravation."

"Let them call. Half of King City PD are on my payroll."

"Is that true?"

"How do you think I get things done around this city? It's who you know, Duffin. It's *always* who you know."

"You mean who you pay."

"That too."

I cringed. Why did hearing him admit that disgust me so much? I had a few ideas. But it didn't matter. "You're missing the point, Channing. I don't care about you or your money or your connections. I care about my parents. They're getting old and I don't want you disturbing what little peace they've gotten back since you made a mess of our lives." I let that sink in.

After almost an entire minute of silence, Channing started vigorously making a snow angel. "This sure is fun," he chuckled like he'd simply missed, or coldly ignored, everything I'd just said. "Care to join me? It's more fun than I remember. Haven't done this in forever. You should try it. Lie down, Duffin. Make an angel next to mine, like they're holding hands."

"No, Channing. Will you please just get up and go?"

It took a moment before he sighed. "If you insist." He sat up, extended his hand. "Help me up?"

I shook my head. "You have legs."

"Fine." He stood up and dusted off the snow half-heartedly, leaving his back completely powdered. He offered his hand to shake. "Friends?"

"No," I scowled. "Go."

"I tried," he sighed.

I watched him climb into the back of his Mercedes and it drove off.

Did he have a chauffeur? Apparently. That was odd because the Channing I remembered *always* did the driving. He hated being driven anywhere. He said it made him feel like an asshole to have anyone drive for him other than a bus driver or an airline pilot. I tended to agree.

What else was new about him that I didn't know?

I hated to think.

One thing was clear. We had both changed in fundamentally different ways. I was not the carefree and trusting kid I'd once been, the one who'd so freely given her heart to a man who, in the end, didn't deserve it.

Now he was... I wasn't sure what he was now. He didn't quite seem real. Like he'd become a caricature of his former self, an over-simplification. Tonight, I recognized bits and pieces of the old Channing, but so much of him had become... a cliché, if that made any sense. Like the real person had died ten years ago, leaving behind only ghostly tendrils of his humanity, nothing more.

Or perhaps I was being overdramatic.

Perhaps I had simply changed and he hadn't?

Young Channing *had* been obsessed with success, and it seemed he still was. The only difference, from the sound of it, his focus had shifted from winning football games to making money and scoring social status points. Not the kind of man I wanted in my life. Based on what I read and heard from others about relationships, obsession of any kind didn't work well over the long term. It certainly hadn't worked out for me and Channing. Our two years together *had* been obsessive, especially when it came to sex. My college-age self had thought that was the secret to a lasting relationship. Obsessive, passionate sex, and everything that went with it.

The ignorance of youth, I guess.

Everyone said you needed balance to make a relationship last.

We hadn't had that, had we?

Not a bit.

The only thing I couldn't figure out now was how I had ever come to love Channing Peyton in the first place. Lust, yes. But love? I was having trouble seeing it. Had it ever been love?

Or merely a potent cocktail of my hormones and my youthful naïveté?

When I crawled into my old bed that night and snuggled under the covers, a galloping herd of old memories came storming through my dreams, answering my question in vivid detail.

Christmas Past

"The Scrooge I knew was young and hot and loved to screw."
—*a blushing Carol Duffey, later in life*

Chapter 11

CAROL

You can probably guess my college relationship with Channing Peyton started out with a bang.

Literally.

It would be my first.

The first time we actually met was at the Sigma Epsilon Chi house, during a rowdy frat party. My new roommate Sienna Winters dragged me along, only to immediately disappear with the first suitable boy she found.

"I'll be right back, Care! Promise!" She giggled as he dragged her into the swallowing crowd.

Famous last words.

The boy was cute. She'd be a while.

An hour into it, I was seriously considering forgiving Evan Urleigh, my recently ex-boyfriend who I'd caught screwing my newly ex-best friend Whitney Vinson. She I'd never forgive. If Evan did a citywide apology tour complete with begging, crawling, and scraping, I was open to the possibility of taking him back. On the condition that he hired a Thanksgiving Day Parade float to drive him around for the tour. No, the Oscar Meyer Wienermobile. No, both.

You're thinking I'm an idiot.

Not because of the Wienermobile, which Evan obviously was in his own right, sans wheels, and with a much smaller hot dog.

No, you're thinking I'm an idiot for considering Evan's apology tour.

Once a cheating ass, always a cheating ass.

I know, I know. Blame my moment of mental weakness on the frat brat meatheads here at the party. I could only take so much of their drunken keg standing, beer can shotgunning, bottle-shotting, and beer bonging behavior. If you don't know what those things are, they're all a race to the bottom of a beer container.

I would've liked to join in some of the more traditional drinking games going on around the frat house, in the garage, and the crowded backyard. Beer Pong, Flip Cups (I was a cup-stacking champion, which may or may not have been a transferrable skill), Quarters, Drunk Jenga, a drinking game involving playing cards, and one involving movie trivia. Who didn't like movie trivia or Jenga? The only problem, I couldn't play with the other college-age reindeers if I didn't drink with them too.

Sadly, this wasn't my scene at all, but here I was "enjoying" myself.

Sorry if I sounded dreary. I had good reason. I'll refresh your memory.

Evan: Pumpa, pumpa, pumpa.

Whitney: "It's not what you think, Carol!"

Evan: "Glorg!"

Noooowww you're remembering.

And don't worry, I was mere minutes away from meeting Channing Peyton for the first time. He would clear away the dreary faster than you can say, "Hot college quarterback with abs flirting with you in a private bedroom!"

The one thing I couldn't stand about the party were the incessant frat brat shouts of "Show us your tits!" aimed at every passing woman, a few of whom were happy to lift their tops (and sometimes their bras) to show off their assets for a momentary token of social acceptance. To them I say, you be you.

Why wasn't anyone shouting, "Show us your dicks!"

Probably because every girl here knew that every guy here was biting their nails in rabid anticipation of the historic day when we women did just that. Can you see the newspaper headline?

MEN EVERYWHERE SHOW THEIR DICKS, WORLD ENDS.

Not gonna happen.

Right, ladies?

Right?

As for me, I'd never figure out why so many young men chose to demonstrate their sexual prowess by drinking beer and not having any. Sex, that is. Did these boys get laid because of their caveman ways? Doubted it. I was thinking few, if any, had solved the age-old alchemical quest to turn gold (beer) into head (blowjobs). Maybe I had that backwards? Was it head into gold? Or something else?

Either way, these boys drank to no effect.

I guess the majority were drowning their sexual sorrows?

I sort of understood because I was swimming in mine.

It had been two whole weeks since I'd caught my two favorite cheaters going at it. Pumpa, pumpa, pumpa. You'd think the awful memories would've faded by now, and yet, every time I closed my eyes, I saw Evan's thrusting ass and heard Whitney's sordid squeals, and saddest of all, I saw my loving comforter lying forgotten on the floor beside Evan's bed, a casualty of his infidelity.

Last week at Sienna's behest, we had printed out photos of Evan and Whitney from their Facebook pages. Both of us giggling like witches, we had thrown darts (borrowed from Keegan and Ramiro across the hall) at the photos, cut them with scissors, and burned them (the photos, not Keegan and Ramiro, they were too nerdy and nice).

When that didn't kill my bad memories, Sienna and I made paper voodoo dolls (using doll patterns we'd found online and more Facebook photos), gleefully stuck those with pins, burned them with abandon, and cast a Wiccan curse we took from the internet onto the ashes, both of us chanting the words in creepy voices while some scary movie soundtrack music played in the background on Sienna's iPod speakers, but nothing worked.

It seemed my mind would be forever haunted by their pumpa, pumpa, pumpa.

As much as I hated Evan now, I had once loved him for his quiet style and thoughtful presence. *That* was my wavelength, not the humongous stumbling infants here at the frat party. "Show us your tits!" These guys were just as fussy as babies, and needed twice as much supervision. I wanted a man, not a super-sized pubescent boy.

Sienna had insisted this party would get my mind off Evan.

"Show us your tits!"

To that extent, it had.

At least Sienna's heart was in the right place.

After losing her earlier, I'd spent the last half hour nursing a plastic cup of warm keg beer while standing defensively in a dimly lit corner next to a group of catty sorority girls I didn't know. They were pretending to ignore me while I pretended I was with them. Safety in numbers. I didn't want to be alone while surrounded by hooting drunkards fighting like apes over a watering hole, in this case the keg. Eventually, the sorority girls smelled a rat (me), and migrated to more popular pastures.

Time to find Sienna.

Sigh.

She had to be somewhere in the house.

During my search, I interrupted several random sexual encounters in hallways, bathrooms, and bedrooms. In one case, the entangled couple literally had a 5-foot boa constrictor slithering loosely around their necks and shoulders while they kissed. As for the snake, it was just doin' its thang. Very symbolically, of course. I expected an apple offering at some point, but I didn't wait around to see the apocalyptic aftermath and garden ejection.

Still looking for Sienna, I barged in on a rendezvous that was screaming #MeToo (ten years before it became a thing) at the tops of its unconscious lungs. Did you guess this was where I'd meet everybody's heartthrob darling, Channing Peyton?

I didn't.

When I opened the door, light from the hallway beamed into a dark laundry room.

A big guy wearing a gold KCU Cheetahs jersey, jeans, and the guiltiest look I'd ever seen, stood with a limp girl's arms draped over his shoulders. Her sagging body curved against his, her feet wedged against a washing machine while he was in the process of pushing down her unbuttoned jeans and panties. They were already halfway down her hips when the jock stopped.

"What're you doing?!" I demanded loudly over the party music.

"She's my girlfriend," he explained.

"I don't care if she's your wife!" I shouted. "You can't have sex with her! She's unconscious!"

"So?"

"She can't give consent! It's rape if you try anything!"

"Get the fuck outta here." He kicked the laundry room door closed in my face.

I wiggled the knob.

Locked.

"Open up!" I pounded on the door. "You can't do this, asshole! I'm calling 911!" I fished my phone out of my jeans and dialed. A large hand took my phone and ended the call. I looked up into the eyes of heaven.

Channing Peyton.

Everyone who went to KCU knew who he was. His face was literally everywhere. Online, on mammoth banners hanging outside the stadium, on roadside billboards outside campus proclaiming him the savior of KCU's failing football program, which was true. He had singlehandedly resurrected it his freshman year (and mine), ending the season by taking the Cheetahs to the Rose Bowl for a seemingly guaranteed victory, only to lose in a bitter upset. Nobody was complaining.

Most of all, Channing's youthful face was on every woman's mind. It bespoke of battlefields and victory, ancient and current. Winning was in his DNA, in his brooding eyes, in his ruthless, sword-sharp features, his savage shoulders, his granite hands. The Cheetahs had just won last week's game against the Nebraska Cornhuskers 24 to 13, and every other game this year. A perfect record for the perfect specimen of male superiority, alpha incarnate.

Drum roll...

Channing Peyton.

Me having seen reproductions of his mythic visage had not done justice to the real thing. My recently harpooned heart restarted itself, thudding out a stuttering euphoric warning in Morse code. I didn't know the code, but the sentiment was universal: the course of my life was about to be permanently altered. Meanwhile, my sane brain was ordering me to protect limp girl in the laundry room from imminent violation.

"Give me my phone!" I demanded. "I need to call 911! That guy in there is—"

"I'll handle it," Channing said. "Hold this." He gave me my phone. "Stand back." I moved. "Farther." I took another step and saw the PEYTON name block-lettered in black on the back of his gold number 12 jersey. He wound up his body and his leg exploded into the door near the handle. It shattered opened, banging against the wall and flicking splinters.

The pantsing meathead now had the limp girl's jeans down to her knees. He nearly jumped out of his own pants when he saw Channing rush him.

"Are you fucking kidding me, Blankenship?!" Channing demanded. "What the fuck are you doing?! You've been to sensitivity training six times! Hasn't anything stuck?!"

"Fuck you, Peyton!" Blankenship growled, forgetting the girl who he let slide to the ground on her naked ass, leaving her leaning against the washing machine. He bellowed, "You goody two shoes fucking rook! You think because you're a starter, your rook ass can tell me the fuck to do?!"

"You think because you're an all-star, they won't put you in jail for rape?"

Blankenship started to huff and puff. "I can do anything the fuck I want! I am fucking Rudy Blankenship! Nobody tells me the fuck what to do! Least of all you!" The big buffoon fired a bullet finger at Channing's chest that sent him stumbling back.

Channing Peyton was tall, at least 6'4" and solid muscle, but this Blankenship character was taller and much heavier, a walking wall of raging fury ready to detonate.

"This your play, Rudy?" Channing asked, standing his ground, hands at the ready.

"Calling plays is your job, rook."

"Fine. Make a move and I call it."

"The fuck you will!" Rudy roared, advancing.

"Stop it!" I shouted.

"Shut up, bitch," Rudy sneered, flicking his eyes at me momentarily.

That distraction was all it took.

Channing launched a fist that laid Rudy out with one thunderous punch. The bigger man crashed into an electric dryer. Its metallic walls boomed and its feet squeaked across concrete when Rudy avalanched to the ground like a broken mountain.

"Did you kill him?" I asked carefully.

"Not even close," Channing grinned at me before doing a double-take, eyes afire as he looked me over closely. "Who're you again?"

"Carol Duffey." I was already smitten, twirling my finger in my long ponytail.

The limp girl groaned where she sat.

"Do you know if this is his girlfriend?" I asked.

Channing shook his head. "I don't think so."

"Figures," I smirked. "We should help her." I knelt down beside her.

"No, we need to move her before Rudy wakes." Channing scooped her up, her pants and panties still down to her knees.

"At least let me pull her clothes up."

"Good idea." He held her up in a hug (she literally couldn't stand up on her own), while I got her quickly situated.

Then it was through the crowded house.

"Show us her tits!"

"No," Channing hissed, holding limp girl in his arms like he was a bodice-ripping savior running away with his prize. Dozens of rowdy people congratulated him on his upcoming conquest. "She's not a conquest," he insisted, irritated as he pushed past everyone.

I wanted to mutter she was a victim, but I didn't want any rumors coming back to bite her on her recently exposed ass.

We ended up in a random empty bedroom with the door closed behind us, and limp girl lying on a narrow bed between Channing and I. Poor thing looked very much like a corpse at the morgue. I wasn't a nurse, but I knew how to check a pulse. Hers was steady but slow.

"Put her on her side," Channing said. "In case she pukes."

Nodding, I positioned her so I could see her sleepy and frowning face.

"What should we do now?" Channing asked.

"Stand guard." I folded my arms across my zippered KCU hoodie, making it clear I was guarding limp girl *and* myself.

"I can do that. Long as you keep me company." He winked lashes that looked extended, they were so thick. "Have a seat." He pulled out a cheap office chair from under a cramped desk, the only one in the tiny room. The chair had wrinkled clothes draped over it randomly.

"I'm not sitting on that." It would require me going around the bed next to him. I didn't want to get any closer than we already were.

"I offered." He painstakingly folded the clothes from the chair and set them on top of an exploded dresser, the drawers half open with wadded clothes bursting out at the seams.

"Why are you bothering to fold anything? Nothing else is."

"No need to make the mess worse."

"Is this your room?"

"Nope."

"Hers?"

"At a frat house?" he smirked.

"I don't know," I groaned. "Does this look like my scene?"

"You're wearing a KCU hoodie, so yes."

"Just because I am doesn't make me a football groupie."

"Your words," he said.

"What?"

"I never called you a groupie. Don't put words in my mouth."

"Someone has to. You barely speak."

"Since when?" He tossed me a million dollar smile like a party favor.

"I don't know. Since now."

"You jump to a lot of conclusions, Carol Duffey."

I hid my pleasant surprise that he remembered my name and fired back, "You jump into bed with a lot of women, Channing Peyton."

"Ouch," he chuckled and turned the office chair around backward, sitting down with his muscled forearms folded over the back like some ancient Roman wrestling statue. Even with him sitting, we were still eye to eye, he was so tall. "Is that what you heard?"

"That's what the inscription says at the bottom of your statue."

"Statue? What statue?"

"The twice-life-size bronze one outside the football stadium," I giggled.

"You have a very vivid imagination, Duffey."

I knew the only statue there was a four-times life-size bronze cheetah, the team mascot. I snickered, "The inscription on yours says, one woman for every passing yard he threw."

"That many? Over two thousand this year?"

"So I've heard," I giggled.

"I'm lucky my dick hasn't fallen off," he chuckled.

"I'm sure it has, you just don't want anyone knowing."

"Care to check?"

"No! We're not alone!" I tipped my head at limp girl, whose ribs were rising and falling evenly.

"I'll write you a rain check." He pretended to write out a check, tear it from an invisible checkbook, and offer it over the bed. "For whenever you want to check."

"Check what?"

"You know," he winked his amazing lashes and proffered the phantom check.

"Would you stop! I'm not taking your rain check!"

"She isn't either." He meant limp girl. "You take it."

"No, Channing!"

"Someone has to see it."

Were we still talking about me seeing his penis? We were. "Half the women on campus already have."

"No they haven't," he insisted.

"Okay, a third," I smirked, thoroughly enjoying tormenting the hottest, most popular man on campus. To call Channing anything less was a disservice to his rugged beauty. I was also enjoying the easiest conversation I'd ever had with any male other than my own dad. Because seriously, Evan who?

"Last chance." Channing mimed like he was about to tear up the phantom penis check. I mean, rain check.

"Burn it. I don't care."

"I don't have a lighter."

"I do." I pretended to pull one out and flick it.

"Go ahead and light it," he grinned.

I giggled, leaned over limp girl, and pretended to light his check.

Our hands were inches apart, which was strangely romantic, despite limp girl's sleeping presence, and the burning of the dick check that would've been mine if I'd only had the lady balls to cash it.

"Poof," he chuckled. "Guess you'll never know now."

"I don't *want* to know," I grinned, lying.

Smirking, Channing eased onto his backward chair. It creaked under his weight. His forearms flexed, thick veins coiling and sculpted muscles dancing under smooth skin. "Come here," he whispered. "I want to tell you something."

"Tell it from there."

He shook his head.

"Fine," I sighed and leaned over limp girl, hands on my knees. He and I were still a few feet apart, but his chocolate-caramel eyes were magnetic, pulling me toward him. I resisted, not wanting to tip over onto limp girl.

"Zero."

"Zero what?"

"Women. That's how many I've been with. Don't tell anybody. Not even her."

"You just did," I grinned.

"She won't remember."

"Remember what? The lie you've been with zero women?"

"It's true." He nodded an amused smirk.

I almost burst out laughing. "You are such a liar."

He shook his head.

I frowned, "You've *never* had sex?"

"Not once. I've been eating and breathing football since I was a baby. There hasn't been time."

"Didn't your girlfriends ever—"

"Never had time for them either."

"Oh, I get it. This is what you tell women so they'll feel special, instead of like they're number two-thousand four hundred and eighty-one on your bedpost."

"Believe what you want, Duff."

Was it okay to secretly swoon now that he'd given me a nickname?

He said, "Just don't tell anyone I told you." Sitting up straight, he planted his palms on his muscled thighs and flexed his arms with godlike authority.

"You're serious?" I asked.

"About both parts."

"I am too."

"Good," he shrugged. "I don't know why I told you. I guess it felt right. Keep it to yourself."

"No, I mean, I'm a virgin too."

Like a casual lion suddenly sniffing an approaching doe-eyed gazelle (me), his chocolate-caramel eyes glinted and he said with salty sarcasm, "What's your excuse, Duff? Too much football?"

"No," I snorted. "I haven't met the right guy."

"You have now."

"Who says I'm the right girl?"

"Me." This time, he offered his smile like the Hope Diamond.

I'll get to the banging part in a minute.

Chapter 12

CAROL

By minute, I meant a New York minute, which is either one second or at least a week, depending on who you ask.

In my case, it was a week.

Did you really expect me to give up my virginity in the same shabby frat bedroom where limp girl was snoring on the only available bed?

Of course you didn't.

We can agree I needed some time to make sure Channing's virginity claims weren't just him blowing smoke up my ass before I let him do other things with it and other orifices. He would need to jump through a few hoops before he earned that privilege.

At first glance, Channing Peyton and I would be an unlikely pair, were I to allow it. He was the star quarterback stud of the KCU Cheetahs. I was a bookish nerd girl who hid myself under hoodies. The only thing feminine about me was my long ponytail.

The begging question plaguing me was:

Why would *he* want me?

I was determined to find out the truth.

There had to be an ulterior motive.

Show of hands if you guessed there was.

Everyone?

Okay, but who can guess what that motive is?

\#

&

&*&

&*&*&

&*&*&*&

M

CHANNING

"That shorty was all over my dick like an ice cream cone, yo," said my teammate, 20-year-old Lashawn Washington, savoring the memory of his most recent (alleged) conquest with the rest of the KCU Cheetahs football team.

The fellas were gathered in the locker room before practice on a

Monday afternoon.

A big veteran linebacker named Rance Pridemore piped up, "How short was he?"

Approving hoots and fist bumps from the other vets.

Lashawn ignored the jabs at his masculinity and whacked my shoulder pads, saying, "You know what I'm talking about right, player?"

"Yeah," I forced a bitter chuckle for Lashawn's sake. "Blowjobs. Can't get enough."

He gave an odd smile.

What was I going to say? That I'd never had a blowjob? Been kissed a few times, grabbed a boob or two (with permission, of course), had my dick grabbed through my pants a few times, but that was about it. The sad truth was, no part of any female body had ever directly touched Dick. He was not happy about that fact, felt he was being unnecessarily oppressed. I had to agree, but I had too many other responsibilities demanding every available second of my attention. Single-handedly carrying the team to the NCAA D-I championships a second year running was not going to be easy. At least Lashawn and I were dialed in tight with our passing game. Hopefully it would carry us through another perfect season.

"Yo, Lashawn!" Rance Pridemore called. "When that dude was eating your ice cream dick, he eat your scoops too?"

"Both," Lashawn smirked distractedly, then frowned when the fellas started jeering and he finally realized Pridemore was insinuating he was gay.

Pridemore ran with it. "Did he chop your nuts while he was down there eating your scoops?"

Lashawn frowned, "How come you want to know so much about my nuts, Pridemore?" Lashawn's eyes lit up. "Oh! I know why! Pridemore, that was *you* sucking me off the other night, wasn't it? Chocolate is your favorite flavor, isn't it?" He said it with so much confidence and dramatic flair, the entire room laughed at Pridemore. When the taunts died down, Lashawn rode the momentum and said, "You want to know the real story, that shorty swallowed my dick whole before I split her down the middle. She was crying for more, more, more of my Lashawn Johnson!"

Approving chuckles from the entire locker room.

Parenthetical, from adult Channing: as was customary, like most college ballers, young Lashawn was prone to flights of fantastical exaggeration about his youthful exploits off the field. There's a good chance his banana blowjob never happened. In a place like this, it didn't matter what *actually* happened. What mattered was what you *said* happened, and how well you sold it to your baller brothers.

Regarding the overall topics of approved conversation, you have to remember, this was ten years ago, when being openly gay on a college football team amounted to treason. A football locker room in particular was a place where men were expected to be a very narrowly defined version of male. And it was assumed they'd trade "war and whore" stories brimming with bravado and reeking machismo. Politically Correct language never entered the room. It was tied up, duct taped, and stuffed in the nearest locker where it kept its fucking mouth shut. This was Man's Land, not Bitch Town. If you weren't a Man with a capital-M, get the fuck out and go be a bitch somewhere else.

Young me wasn't exactly comfortable with the status quo, so I faked it as needed, which was constantly.

"Who'd you hook up with over the weekend, C-Man?" Lashawn asked casually, like he was asking if I'd gone camping in the mountains or canoeing at the lake. "Some hottie, right? Big tits, tight ass, right? I know what you like. Only the best for the MVP. Tell us about the last hottie you nailed, player."

"*Two* hotties," I smirked (adult Channing is laughing here because in a few years, that would be my new normal after Carol was gone. My, how things change.).

"At the same time?" Lashawn's eyes lit up. "Why am I even asking? Of course it was the same time. Tell it."

The entire locker room leaned forward on their cleats.

At this point, they knew what to expect from me.

I may not have had any idea what a blowjob actually felt like, but this wasn't my first time lying about the women I'd never been with. I'd been spinning fictional locker room sex stories since high school, and this was my sophomore year in college. I'd had plenty of practice fabricating fantasies about the women I *wished* I'd had sex with. Here at KCU, which was known for its hotties, I saw a new babe daily that made it onto my wish list. The astute observers in the audience will ask for details about the handicraft of my private fabrication process, to which I'll answer: use your imagination.

"Tell that shit, Channing!" someone shouted. "We wanna know what it's like to fuck like an all-star!"

Hoots and hollers.

Cocky and confident, I said, "It's like having your tongue up in the pussy of the perfect ten sitting on your face, while the perfect ten sitting on your dick is screaming your name like she's trying to get into heaven."

"You need to grow a second dick!" someone heckled.

Laughter.

"That's not what they said," I smirked.

"Yeah, what'd they say?"

"They said mine's twice two big already." I switched to a reedy female voice. "Oh, God. Oh, God! Oh, GOD! OH, GOOOOOOD! Oh! Oh! Oh! Chaaan-IIIINNG!"

Uproarious laughter followed, targeting the heckler.

I'd won another round of Fool Your Friends, but I was getting damn tired of pretending I'd had sex when I'd never ever touched a naked nipple. I needed to sack the fuck up and fuck someone already.

The only question was who.

I had so many women throwing themselves at me, I had unlimited options. The trick would be finding a woman who would make me proud of fucking her, one who'd make the boys on the team as jealous of my true-life sexual exploits as I was of their supposed ones.

And I knew just the cheerleader to do it.

Sexy as hell Victoria Bissette, captain of the KCU Cheetahs cheerleaders. The internet porn version of Charlotte McKinney, who was the hottest of the Burger King burger girls, the one who knocked Kate Upton off her Double-D pedestal. Too bad for those two, Victoria Bissette was hotter and dirtier than both those babes put together.

Every guy on the team wanted Victoria, but none had ever had her. Many lied that they had, but the truth always came out. No one could get Victoria Bissette. Rumors said she was a lesbian.

I was going to bag her either way.

Like the girls on the cheerleading squad and the fans in the stands always chanted when the Cheetahs were down by 6, it was the 4th quarter with a minute to go, 4th and long, and we had the ball, "Who can do it? The Chandy Man can! Goooooo Channing!"

Damn straight.

Can you envision Victoria bouncing her pom-poms and the rest of her for me and the entire stadium?

I could.

I'd seen her do it at dozens of Saturday games already.

Now it was time for me to get down to business and do her. Before I did, I needed practice first, otherwise I'd screw it up. I wasn't an idiot. Victoria wasn't just the captain of The Bod Squad (the unofficial nickname of the Cheetahs cheerleaders), she was also the queen of campus.

Everybody knew you never scored the winning touchdown at the Rose Bowl if you never practiced your passing game. Good thing I knew just the girl to practice my pass on.

That Duffey kid from the frat party.

She'd be easy.
One and done, then I'd move on to the true trophy.
Victoria fucking Bissette's rose bowl.

Chapter 13

CAROL

Boom, boom, boom!

"Open up!" someone shouted outside my dorm room, pounding on the door.

My heart exploded from my chest like a trapped bat and went flapping around the room in a frenzied attempt at escape. I'd been lying on my bed studying with the door closed so I could concentrate on the material I needed to know for my calculus quiz this afternoon.

More door booms.

Based on the sounds of pounding, I was picturing a squad of jackbooted riot police waiting outside, hunkered behind riot shields and menacingly waving their truncheons.

"Who is it?!" I shouted, scared out of my panties, which were cowering under the bed like a whimpering purse dog.

"Panty raid! Open up!" A man's deep voice.

"Ummmmm, no? I don't know who you are." I slipped off the bed and nabbed Sienna's baseball bat from under her bed. She'd once joked she used it on boys who didn't behave. Now seemed like as good a time as any to put it to the test.

"Open up, Duff!"

"Channing?"

"Who else?" he chuckled.

I was thrilled and annoyed in equal measure. "Go away!"

"Is that any way to treat an old friend?"

"Old friend," I snorted, clutching the bat laxly in two hands. "We spent a few hours together at a frat party *one* time. That was weeks ago."

"Best few hours you ever had." You could hear the cocky grin in his voice.

"Worst few hours," I smirked to myself. "I've had dental surgery that went by quicker." It was true. I'd grown up in braces, and had several teeth pulled along the way.

"Open up, Duff. I came to see you."

"How do you even know where I live?"

"Connections. I know people. Open up."

I wanted to say no, but the white doves of lust whirling in my stomach hurled me toward the door. I opened it a crack with one hand, holding the bat in the other.

"What's that for?" Channing asked.

"You," I smirked, letting the door open a few inches more and lowering the bat.

"If you wanna beat something, beat *my* bat, not that one."

"That's disgusting," I scowled. It wasn't. For years now, I'd had a certain fascination with the idea of holding a man's swollen, erect cock in my hands for the first time. Would it pulse like they said in the books? My mom was an ardent romance fan long before Fifty Shades and ebooks became a thing, and I was always sneaking her tattered paperbacks and reading them under my covers with a flashlight. Would his tip glimmer with a pearl of pre-cum like they said? That's how they spelled it in Mom's books: c-u-m.

Channing's presence pushed those dusty old memories away. In daylight, he was better looking than the night of the frat party. His skin was flawless. Smooth, tan, no pores that I could see. The only exception was his five o'clock shadow, and it wasn't even two o'clock. His chocolate-caramel eyes caught the light, drizzling with good humor. Was it safe to assume his man-bat was as flawless as the rest of him? Yes. It was also safe to assume he'd be more than happy to let me hold his while it was swollen and beading with pre-cum.

"Let me in, Duff." Like a polite vampire asking entry, he stood at the open threshold of my door, which seemed to have opened all the way without me noticing.

It took a moment to process which "in" he meant. When I decided he meant in my dorm room, even though it sounded like he meant in me, I said, "Why?" With Sienna in class for the next two hours, I was all alone, and I didn't trust myself with swollen Channing and his possible pulsing.

"Why not?" he offered.

"That's your answer?"

"Do I need a better one?"

"Yes," I smirked.

His eyes danced. "I missed you."

"Only took you three weeks."

"I was busy. I practice six days a week. We had two away games. One in Michigan, the other in Ohio."

"So I heard." My disinterest was casually misleading.

"You didn't watch them?"

"I don't have time. I have classes I have to study for."

"I study."

"With the help of private tutors. I know. I've read all about how the school bends over backwards to give you the best paid tutors they have, and easy classes to keep your grades up. I don't have that luxury, so no, I didn't watch your stupid games."

Lies!

Outright lies!

Thank goodness I hadn't sworn an oath to tell the truth on a stack of Bibles, otherwise those Bibles would be bursting into flames and they'd be hauling me kicking and screaming off the witness stand and throwing me in jail for perjury. And arson. The burning Bibles set the courtroom on fire, they were so offended by my outright lies.

After meeting Channing at the frat party, I'd told Sienna everything except the part about him being a virgin. That was his secret he'd given me to hold and I was determined to protect it. Ever since, I'd been quietly obsessing about him while trying to convince myself I wasn't interested. During the away games he mentioned, Michigan and Ohio, Sienna and I had gone to watch both at Cheetahs Cavern, an all-ages sports bar in the student center, which showed team games on their big screen TVs while we ate hot nachos and pounded bottomless mocktail margaritas.

I'd always known Channing was a celebrity here at KCU, and everyone was always talking about him, except now I *knew* him. I knew *personally* the topic of *everyone's* obsession.

Seeing closeups of him in the huddle on the big TVs, telling his teammates what to do with easy authority, or on the sidelines with his helmet off and he was talking with the old coaches, his face serious and focused, was just... enthralling. I *knew* that guy, the bigger than life superstar onscreen, the focus of everyone's attention. The leader of the team.

Whenever Channing was on the field and he completed a pass, or ran the ball into the end zone for a touchdown (he did that *twice* in one game), I'd jump to my feet cheering. The few times he got sacked, I would physically fold into myself with nauseous fear. The moment he got up and shook it off like it was nothing, relief would river over me in warm waves. It was like we were psychically connected. Could he feel it too? That was my fervent hope. One of the times he got sacked and I cringed, Sienna had teased, "Someone's crushing on Channing Peyton."

Obviously.

At the close of both winning games, the players and coaches and every other staffer on the Cheetahs' sidelines carried Channing victoriously across the field on their shoulders. I felt as elated as they looked. I *knew* their hero, the man they held above them all, their champion. And I kept safe a deep secret he hadn't shared with anybody else, not even the beautiful Cheetahs cheerleaders who mobbed him in their skimpy outfits and hogged the cameras behind him, smiling at him while the starstruck sportscaster interviewed him about his latest triumph.

Not only had I watched the games, I'd spun crazy hand-written fantasies about me and Channing in my journal.

Sportscaster, "You just won the Rose Bowl, Channing Peyton! What are you gonna do now?"

Smiling Channing, "I'm taking Carol Duffey to Disneyland!"

Or, "Yo, yo, yo! On this episode of MTV Cribs, the sprawling mansion of NFL superstar Channing Peyton and his wife Carol! Look at that backyard waterslide, yo!"

Or, my bungling version of The Hunger Games (those books were a brand new thing back then). I had no dreams of being a writer, I just wrote it for fun, as an escape. I'm sure my version was terrible. It was called The Football Games, starring Carol Everdeen and Channing Hawthorne, who fights by her side in the arena instead of sniveling Evan Urlark, who plays a very villainous role in my version and looks exactly like my ex Evan Urleigh. Only by working together intimately can Carol and Channing survive their grueling ordeal and best Evan, and the desperate tributes from the other districts helping him.

Back on planet Earth, Channing Peyton smirked in my doorway, "Admit it. You watch my games like everyone else."

"Hardly," I lied. "I just hear about them because everyone else won't shut up about it every time you win another game. Kinda hard to miss the giant hand-painted banners they hang up around campus every time."

"Oh yeah? If you don't care, what's with the sweats?"

Now that the weather was deep into fall, I always had on a KCU hoodie to stay warm. Today's was gold with a black embroidered KCU logo on the chest. At the moment, I also wore black sweats that said CHEETAHS in gold embroidered lettering on the leg, my usual study clothes.

I glanced absently at them. "School spirit. In case you forgot, *every* team at KCU are the Cheetahs. I'm trying to support all of them. Not just yours. Please tell me you know it's women's volleyball season too."

He shrugged. "The football team is the only one that counts."

"Do you hear yourself?"

"Loud and clear. You bought those because of me, didn't you?"

"What, the sweats?"

"Yeah. Next best thing to having me inside you is having me all over your outside."

"Okay, one, that's disgusting," I was lying because I was having the opposite reaction as I struggled *not* to imagine him all over my outside while filling my inside with his swollen and pulsing… champion. "And two, you aren't the only person on the football team, Mr. Giant Ego."

A mousy voice behind Channing said, "We aren't supposed to have boys on our floor, Carol." It was Genevieve Shankle. The only time she ever came out of her room was to use the floor bathroom or go to class. Otherwise, she remained locked inside her room like a jail cell. I think she was afraid of literally everything.

Channing winked at her, "I'm not a boy."

"Yes you are." Genevieve blinked her beady eyes.

"Naw, I'm all man, babe. Channing Peyton. That name ring a bell?"

"I know who you are," Genevieve sniveled. "You're not supposed to be in here."

"Mmm." He didn't care. "What's your name, gorgeous?" Genevieve was gorgeous in the same way a prize hamster might be considered gorgeous.

"I'm telling Mia," Genevieve blurted. Mia was the resident advisor on our floor.

"Why?" I demanded. As annoying as Channing's arrogance was, I wanted to be the one to kick him out if I chose, not her.

"No boys, Carol," Genevieve whispered to me, as if magically Channing wouldn't hear from where he was standing next to me.

I wasn't going to let her cat-block me. Or was it bat-block? Didn't matter. I shook my head, "That's *your* rule, Genny. You made it up."

"No I didn't. He can't be here."

"He can be in my room if I let him. That *is* the rule, and I'm letting him." Why had I said that?

"What she said," Channing crooked a smile at Genny and sauntered past me into my dorm room.

Genny sniveled, "You better not do anything. I'll tell if you do."

"Do what?" I snorted.

"*Anything…*" she whispered cryptically, flashing evil hamster eyes.

"And tell who?" I groaned.

"*Everyone…*" she glowered beadily.

"Bye, Genny," I sneered and closed the door slowly in her face.

"Nice bed," Channing grinned, already stretched out on mine with his muscled arms folded behind his head. Despite the chill fall air outside, he wore only a T-shirt.

"Get your shoes off my comforter."

"They're not on it." He was so tall, his boots were propped up on the bottom end of the metal bed frame. He wiggled them. "See?"

"Can you just move them?"

"Can't."

"Why not?"

"Temporary paralysis. Old football injury. Happens whenever I don't get my way."

"Move. Them. Now."

"I told you. Paralyzed. You'll have to do it for me."

"You're such a scammer."

"That what you tell the guy in the wheelchair when he asks for a dollar?

"Ass." I picked up one leg. "This thing weighs a ton!"

"So do the other two," he deadpanned.

"Other *two*?"

He smirked.

I rolled my eyes when I figured out his penile exaggeration and dropped his boot back onto the bed frame. "Move them yourself." I sat down on Sienna's bed. "Why are you here?"

"Just wanted to see you."

"You're seeing me. If you don't mind, I have a calculus quiz in two hours. I need to study. If you want to read a book or something, be my guest. Otherwise, you should probably go."

"I need to study too."

"Oh? For what class?"

"Carol Duffey 101."

"That's an honors class, and you sir, do not have the honor."

"Funny," he grinned.

"Thanks. I really need to study. You're on my books."

"What, this?" He pulled my open calculus textbook out from under him and scanned the page. "What is it?"

"Calculus."

"How do you understand this stuff?"

"Studying."

"I study plenty. You try reading a 4-3 defense in the clutch when those gorillas stunt their formation at the snap and they're dying to pass-rush over your O-line and sack your ass into the ground. I study constantly, believe me."

"Is football your major?" I joked half-heartedly because I literally had no idea what he'd just said, and was secretly impressed.

"Should be. If I didn't do the homework Coach gives me every damn day, I'd be injured or dead. Then I might have to do math for a living," he smirked. "You can be my tutor."

"What math are you taking?"

"Math for Meatheads," he chuckled.

"No, seriously."

"Business math? I think?"

I laughed, "You don't even know what math you're taking? Do you even go to class?"

"Yes. Took it last year. Not like I'll need it ever again."

"But you don't remember what you took?" I was having a hard time believing someone didn't remember a class they took a year ago, especially if it was hard. My hardest classes still gave me nightmares.

He shrugged, "Whatever it was, it was nothing like this." Examining the textbook, he turned it side to side like a steering wheel. "This could be Japanese for all I can tell."

"Is that your major? Business? Not Sports Psychology or Phys Ed?" I was teasing.

"I get enough PE on the team," he snickered. "No, Media Communications. Once I finish up in the NFL, I'll be a talking head on ESPN SportsCenter. My life's on a glide path, Duff. Haven't you heard? It pays to be Channing Peyton," he grinned.

"Ew," I cringed.

"What? It's true."

"Is that your personal slogan?"

"Is now," he winked.

Ew, ew, ew. I would've ego-checked him, except for the fact that all signs pointed to Channing ending up in the NFL Hall of Fame some day, which would basically guarantee him getting a TV job anywhere he wanted. Short of a career-ending injury, he was destined for greatness and fame, which again begged the question: why me? What could I possibly offer him that much more qualified coeds here at KCU couldn't? As much as I wanted to call him on what had to be his ulterior motives, I didn't want to run him off at the end of a pitchfork without proof. At the moment, I didn't have time to look for any.

"What's your major, Duff?"

"Pre-law. Technically, I'm majoring in Legal Studies with minors in Investigative Journalism and Ethics."

"*Two* minors?"

"Yup." I popped my P proudly.

"Damn, Duff," Channing chuckled. "No wonder you never leave your room."

"Which is why I need to study. On my bed. With my books and stuff."

"What's ethics again?"

"Are you stalling or do you really want to know?"

"I asked, didn't I?" His eyes glimmered mischievously.

"Ethics is knowing the difference between right and wrong, which you obviously don't." I motioned at my bed. "Do you mind?"

"Go for it," he grinned from where he lay. His massive arm muscles flexed invitingly. *Lick us, Carol. You know you want to.*

I would do no such thing.

Channing winked, "Join me. There's plenty of room."

"No there isn't, and you need to move."

"If you insist." Sighing, he stood up and the bed springs creaked the disappointment that I felt. He said, "What should I read?"

"I don't know. Pick a book and start reading."

He scanned the small bookcase on top of my desk while I sat down on my bed and tried to focus on calculus. It was nearly impossible with the hottest man anybody had ever seen loitering over my desk. If you don't believe me, just ask George Clooney, Brad Pitt, and David Beckham pouting jealously in the corner. Channing was better looking than all three put together.

When Channing's scent hit me, it caught me by surprise. It was probably Axe Body Spray, but on him it smelled like Clive Christian (young me had once smelled a bottle at the mall, remember those?), a citrus muskiness that would not leave me alone. It tickled my fancy and... other places. My body was literally oozing with desire for this man, and my brain was swimming in a bubble bath of naughty possibilities.

When I looked at my textbook, I swear, the variables in the differential equations swirled into dancing X and Y chromosomes that tangoed across the page. The next thing I knew, dozens of X's and Y's had paired off, matching each other move for move.

If you've ever watched tango, you know they love those poses where the woman's legs are basically spread, one of them dragging behind her while her other knee is climbing up the man, and one of *his* legs is right between hers, and she's basically riding his thigh with her crotch while he drags her across the dance floor. It's basically sex without penetration. For her, anyway. I certainly wouldn't be complaining if it was me getting dragged by my crotch on Channing's thigh.

Was it suddenly hot in here?

Phew!

Someone open a window!

I looked up, expecting to see Channing beaming at me with a hungry sexual glare. Instead, he was lounging on Sienna's bed, studiously reading some book or another, one muscled arm flexed behind his head. I flicked my eyes back to my textbook before he noticed me staring at his muscles.

When I did, surprise!

The X's and Y's were doing that Tango sex move I mentioned, all of them in unison, only now, when they did it (did... *it*), I kid you not, the tails of the Y's curved up between the legs of the X's, hit the X-spot in the crotch, and started a slow fuck. Dozens of Y's fucking dozens of X's. Then, the arms of the X's wrapped around the backs of the Y's and started to spasm orgasmically.

At that point, I slapped my textbook shut with a gasp.

"Something wrong?" Channing asked, only his eyes visible over the book.

"No!" I cleared my throat. "No. Just, uh, nothing. Go back to your reading."

"Sure," he smirked.

I carefully peeked inside my textbook, on guard for any sexual X's and Y's. Nothing but boring equations. Thank goodness. I had a quiz to study for, and it wasn't for Sex Ed class.

Somehow, I managed to focus on calculus until it was time for me to head to class.

"I have to go, Channing." I closed my book and notebook, gathering up my things.

"Hold up. I'm right in the middle of something."

Only then did I finally compute what he was reading.

My journal.

Normally I buried it at the bottom of my desk drawer, but I must've left it out after writing a new scene for The Football Games after getting back from my morning class. Sienna had been gone, and that was the only time I wrote in it, especially when I wrote something particularly intimate, like the scene I wrote today where Carol Everdeen and Channing Hawthorne finally had sex in a very inappropriate, non-YA way. They did it in the confines of the arena forest, even though they knew they were being televised by hidden cameras. The two of them had dirty animal sex for all the world to see, in blatant defiance of the games' rules, where sex in the arena was forbidden and punishable by death. That's how much they loved each other in my version. They were willing to die to have each other just once. Die.

In the real world, I was ready to die.

Channing had read *that*.

I gasped and my face burned. "How much of that did you read?!"

"Only the good parts," he chuckled, eyes still scanning the page.

Horrified, I rushed over and ripped it from his hands. "Who said you could read this?!"

"You said pick a book."

"Not this one! You can't read this!"

"Already did," he smirked. "It's really good, Carol. I'm hard."

"Shut up!" I swatted him with my journal, but he ignored it like it was nothing.

"How about we act out the arena sex scene? I really liked the part when she, and I quote, 'Rode him like a wolf.' That's a metaphor, right?"

"No!" It was, but I said no because I was shocked by how much he'd read.

"Thing is, the way it's written, it's not clear if he's the wolf or she's the wolf. Or both of them?"

"No!" Still shocked.

He sat up slowly on the bed. He was so damn *big* sitting there. Big and swollen and dripping and possibly pulsing. "Me," he chuckled, "I like to think they're *both* fucking like wolves. *That* is fucking hot. Don't you think, Carol? Two people fucking for their lives?"

"No!" I backed up a step and hunched over, holding my journal closed over my crotch. My thighs were quivering and I was dripping into my panties, literally soaking them through gluing to my folds. This had *never* happened to me before, not this wet, not this fast, and never with Evan. With Channing, it had taken seconds.

Channing stood up, unfurling 6-foot-4 worth of manly, muscled perfection. He stalked toward me.

I tried to back up, but I was frozen where I stood.

His heat hit me when he was inches away.

Our eyes were locked, like wolves in a death dance.

He lifted a big paw and brushed a thumb across my jaw line.

A low growl escaped his lush lips, "What do you say, Carol Everdeen? Do we have dirty animal sex here on the floor of your dorm room, or do we find a forest and show the world how much we love each other?"

My eyes awed.

Did Channing *love* me?

How could he? We barely knew each other! We hadn't even kissed! It was just a figure of speech. Or was it?

Confused, sweating, and scared, I blurted, "I'm late for my quiz!"

I raked up my stuff in a flurry of fluttering papers and ran out the door without looking back, leaving Channing where he stood.

Chapter 14

CAROL

"D-plus?" I groaned after reading the grade on my calculus quiz several days after taking it. I trudged up the steps from where the TA was handing out graded quizzes to the students lined up at the bottom of the lecture hall after class.

I was barely scraping by with a B-minus already. If I wanted to keep my scholarship, I had to maintain a B grade in *every* class. KCU was a prestigious school (the Harvard of middle America) and crazy expensive. My parents couldn't pay for it, no single work-study job could pay for it (unless you considered selling study drugs to students a viable job, which I didn't, I worked at the campus bookstore), and I hadn't been lucky enough to score a full-ride scholarship with my high school grades. My scholarship was minor, only paying a fraction of my total school bills. To top everything off, the grants available to me were minimal.

Combining everything, including some student loans, and I was just able to pay for everything each term. My educational finances were balanced on a rickety house of cards. If my calculus grade dropped below a B at the end of the semester, the whole house would come crashing down.

This was a very sexual, I mean very *serious* problem.

Stupid Channing.

Moving back in with my parents wasn't an option. Their house wasn't *that* close to campus, and I didn't own a car. Worse, there was a ton of traffic between their house and here. If I took the bus, it would take forever for me to commute every day. If I had to do that, it would cut into my work-study job. Bottom line, the house of cards where I lived, AKA the dorms, was my cheapest option. If I kept my grades up.

End result?

For the rest of the semester, if I wanted a new hot boyfriend, it was going to be my calculus textbook, not Channing Peyton.

I *could* blame him for distracting me the day of the quiz. When I'd tried to work the quiz problems in the lecture hall, the variables kept tango-fucking each other, same as when I'd studied. But we all know that was *my* fault. *I* had allowed Channing to remain in my dorm room. I *could* have kicked him out and actually focused on studying math before my quiz instead of alphabet sex.

At least Channing and I hadn't had any actual sex.

What a mistake that would've been.

Why?

I hadn't seen Channing since that day.

The worst part? He stole my journal!

I kid you not.

After taking the quiz, I'd rushed back to my dorm room only to find Channing gone, the door shut and locked, and my journal missing. Suspicious, I went knocking on Genevieve's door and grilled her for five minutes, on the off chance she saw him or *she* took it. You never knew with that hamster. Always hoarding paper scraps for her cage. Anyway, she didn't know anything and I let it drop.

Later, I told Sienna how I'd left in a hurry with Channing still in the room, and we confirmed nothing else was gone. But my journal definitely was.

Total. Ass.

I tried to track him down at football practice at the stadium, a gigantic billion-dollar indoor thing with a capacity of over 100,000 people. KCU was a huge school, and they never had trouble filling those seats for home games with rabid students and equally rabid local King Citians. Cheetahs games were the blood pumping through the plumbing of this city, and Cheetahs Stadium was its beating heart.

Because the stadium was so big, it was on the outskirts of campus, making it a 1.5 mile walk from Hemingway Hall where my dorm was. Even taking the university shuttle bus, it took me forever to get there whenever I went. So annoying. I just wanted my journal back.

Even more annoying, the coaching staff and security team wouldn't let me anywhere near the field, or the dozen other drooling groupies who wanted a few minutes with the superstar on any given day. You'd think they were protecting the President of the United States from random assassins, not college football players.

"Are you here for Channing?" one of the regular groupies asked me in the middle of the week.

"No," I lied.

"That's what they all say," she smirked. "Did you fuck him?"

"Ew. No," I scowled, also lying. "Have you?"

"Trying to," she giggled. We were standing outside one of the stadium's service entrances with a bunch of other girls, trying to see the field at the end of a long access tunnel. A gate covered in black vinyl sheets obscured our view, allowing only tiny peephole views of the field.

Bangs startled both of us.

"Step away from the gate, ladies!" An annoyed security man on the other side had whacked the gate with his metal flashlight.

"Asshole," the groupie whispered for my benefit.

Realizing this was my opportunity to gather some much needed insider info about Channing, I asked her, "Do you know anyone who *has* hooked up with him?"

"Taylor Swift."

"What?!" I snorted. "That can't be true."

"That's what I heard. Like, they saw him getting off her tour bus when she played here at the stadium for her Fearless tour."

"That was before my time. Wait, who saw him getting off her bus?"

"I dunno. There he is!" the groupie screamed, her face glued to the crack in the black vinyl. "I can see him on the field! Oh my God! That's him! That's Channing! Over here! Channing! Hey! Channing! Woo hoo! Chaaaaaaniiiiiing!" She was practically crying.

Bangs as the security guy whacked the gate again. "Away from the gate, girls! How many times do I have to tell you?"

The groupie snarled, "You'd be doing the same thing if it was Megan Fox, jerk!"

"If you were Megan Fox, I would." Whack! "Get away from the gate before I call campus police." Whack!

"Asshole!"

I had to agree.

It took several more days of trying before I found Channing. All it took was patience and some clever observation. Eventually I realized he never came and went from the stadium with the other players who usually strolled in on foot to the north side entrance.

Not Channing. He always entered through a concession entrance on the east side where the delivery trucks came and went to stock the stadium for game days, and he was always driven up in a golf cart. He never walked anywhere I saw. The first time I figured it out, his golf cart was already inside before I could do anything.

The second time, I was there waiting near the concession gate as the golf cart drove up, a two-seater like a mini pickup truck with a smallish truck bed in back. A guy wearing a gold-on-black coaching jacket (on closer inspection, it was an *assistant* coach jacket) and baseball-style KCU cap was driving. In the passenger seat was a young, muscular African-American guy who looked like a player based on his brand-new tight-fitting gold-on-black KCU warm-up suit and superior smirk.

In the back, with his legs hanging over the sides of the bed, lay Channing wearing a Slayer concert T-shirt, jeans, mirror sunglasses, and no shoes, his hair a sexy mess. He looked like a stoner, stoned out of his mind.

The concession gate was already open, so I had to jump out from behind the bushes and hurl myself in front of the golf cart as it barreled toward the open gate. Tires screeching, it skidded quickly to a stop.

"What'd you think you're doing?" The jacketed Ass-Coach demanded. "I almost ran you over!"

"Channing stole my journal!" I rushed forward and slapped my hands on the front of the golf cart, blocking the way.

"What?!" Ass-Coach was utterly confused.

"He stole my journal!"

The African-American player chuckled, "Yo, C-Dog. One of your former exploits is here."

"Lashawn!" Ass-Coach barked. "Watch your mouth! That's no way to talk to a fellow student."

I wore my gold KCU hoodie and jeans, per usual, and looked the part.

"Apologize to her!"

"Sorry," Lashawn muttered, barely making eye contact with me.

"What's the problem, miss? I need to get these boys to practice, if you don't mind."

"I want my journal back. I'm not going anywhere until I get it."

"Journal? What kind of journal?"

I wasn't going to tell him it was the one with The Football Games in it. I might get arrested for being a pornographer. "Ask him." I tipped my chin.

Ass-Coach turned in his seat, "Channing. Wake your ass up." He reached over the seat and shook something.

"I'm sleeping," Channing groaned. "Why'd you have to wake me up? I was having this killer sex dream about fucking Taylor—"

"Channing!" Ass-Coach Jacket snapped. "There's a young lady here to see you. She claims your stole her, uh, journal."

"Carol?" Channing blurted and sat up in the back of the golf cart. He tipped up his shades and grinned. "Carol Everdeen. Good to see you, babe."

"That's not my name!" I barked.

Lashawn snickered to himself in the front seat. "You're in trouble now, C-Dog. Huh, huh, huh, huh."

"Quiet," Ass-Coach said.

"Give my journal back, Channing."

"I don't have it," he said.

"You better have it!" I snarled. "That's *my* journal *you* stole!"

"Now miss," Ass-Coach started.

"Don't miss me! He stole my private journal from my dorm room! I want it back!"

"Is that true, Channing?" Ass-Coach asked.

"I borrowed it. She said I could read it."

"Not my journal, I didn't!" I was fuming.

"You said pick a book," he smirked.

Ass-Coach's head volleyed between Channing and me. "Is that true, miss? Did you give him permission to borrow it?"

"Yes, no, yes," I huffed.

"Which is it?" He smirked.

I didn't want to explain the fine details of my almost-sexual escapade with Channing to this guy. "Do you have it or not, Channing?"

"Yeah. I'm still reading it."

"I never said you could read any of it!"

Ass-Coach sighed, "Channing, do you have her journal?"

Lashawn said, "A journal? You mean like a diary?"

Channing said, "It's got stories in it."

"What kind of stories?" Lashawn asked. "Let me guess. Boring-ass stories about kissing boys, sewing, and baking cookies, right?"

"Quiet, Lashawn," Ass-Coach hissed.

I glared a dare at Channing. If he told them about The Football Games, I would never talk to him again.

He said, "It's like, I don't know, action stories."

"Action stories?" Lashawn chuckled, doubtful. "Like Bruce Willis? No, Bruce Lee. That'd be badass."

Channing glanced at me, said, "Something like that."

"Do you have it, Channing?" Ass-Coach asked.

"Not on me. I'll give it back if you want, Carol. I'll bring it by your room next week."

Lashawn chuckled and mocked, "Special delivery from the Chan Man! What else are you gonna deliver besides her diary?"

"It isn't a diary!" I grumbled.

"Shut the fuck up, L-shawn," Channing scowled.

"Are we done here?" Ass-Coach asked me directly.

"If he gives my journal back," I soured.

"Channing?"

"I said I'd do it," he moaned.

"Good. Now if you'll pardon us, miss, I have to drive these boys to practice."

"Fine." I rolled my eyes and stepped out of the way. "You better give it back!"

"Oh, he'll give it!" Lashawn laughed over his shoulder.

Channing didn't look back once while the golf cart drove into the

stadium. He was too busy lounging in the little back bed.
I'd give it fifty-fifty he was good for his word.
I was an idiot for ever letting him in my dorm room.
Never should've opened the door.

Chapter 15

CAROL

A week later, Channing picked the exact same day and time of his first visit to make his second, in the middle of the afternoon when he knew I'd be in my room alone. Of course.

This time, his knock was normal. "Carol?"

"Hold on," I said, saving the file on the English Lit 110 paper I was writing on my laptop at my desk. I got up to open the door.

"Hey," Channing said. "Brought your journal." He held it up.

"Can I have it?"

"Sorry." He handed it over.

I took it. "Thanks. Anything else?"

"What're you up to?"

"Working on my English paper. Kinda busy." I smirked. "That's a hint."

"Mind if I hang?"

"So you can read more of my journal?"

"Already read it," he grinned.

"The whole thing?"

He shrugged. Whether that was a guilty yes or a ambivalent no was impossible to tell.

For whatever reason, I flipped it open and thumbed through pages until— "What the hell?! Why are two pages torn in half?! What'd you do to my journal, Channing?" I was very annoyed.

At that exact moment, Genevieve walked by in the hallway with a bug-eyed bitch face and said, "Can't be here!"

"Yes he can!" I snarled. I did it a-*gain!*

"Telling everyone!" Genny taunted, continuing toward the bathroom.

"I hate her," I hissed.

"She needs to get laid."

"How would you know? And why the hell did you tear up my journal?"

"It was an accident." He looked incredibly embarrassed.

I shook my head, "I don't know how you can possibly accidentally tear pages out of a book. I've literally read a million books in my life, and not once—not *once*—have I ever torn out a page by accident."

"It was, I was, do you really want to know?"

"Know why you stole my journal and ripped it up? Yes, Channing.

I'm dying to know."

Red faced, he looked around warily. "I can't tell you out here."

"Why not?"

"Because, I, can I just tell you in your room?"

"Fine! Fuck, Channing! Do you realize how annoying you are?"

He pushed past me into the room.

I turned in the doorway. "Well?"

"I—"

"Can't be here!" Genny singsonged as she passed by outside on her way back to her room.

"Can you close the door?" Channing begged.

I did. "There. Now tell me already. No. You know what? All I want to know is, where are my pages, Channing? I want them back."

He ran his hand through his hair, muscles flexing. "No you don't."

"Yes I do. Jesus, Channing! You make it sound like you did something obscene."

"I did."

"Huh?"

"I, uh, I may have, hmm. How to explain."

"Words always work."

He nodded, "I may have, you know, *jerked off* on it." He winced like he'd just admitted to inventing AIDS and injecting me with it.

"You what?!" I laughed.

"You heard me."

I shook my head, trying to make sense of what he said. "Did you," I lowered my voice to a whisper, "did you *fuck* my journal?"

"No!" he blurted. Sighed, exasperated. "Okay, I was re-reading it, you know, The Football Games, from start to finish, and when I got to the part where they fuck in the woods I, well, I sort of started jerking off."

"You what?" I gasped and felt a stirring tingle.

He nodded. "I kept reading it and re-reading it, and the next thing I know, when they came in the story, *I* came."

"Okay, and?" I shook my head. "I don't see what the big deal is."

He heaved a sigh, "I came *on* your journal."

You have to remember, I had never seen a live, loaded penis in person. Yes, I'd seen porn, but that wasn't my personal experience. I knew about wet panties, which you tossed in the wash after tossing your salad, as they say. Then it suddenly clicked.

"Oh!" I gasped.

He nodded. "*On* it."

"You," I squeaked, "you *came* on my story?"

"A lot."

"How much?"

"Enough to soak through two pages before I wiped it off."

I was trying to picture it, and it was turning me on big time because I was imagining him sitting on his bed naked, my journal propped on his naked, muscled thighs, his abs rippling and his hard-on in his hand while he pumped it furiously, then him spewing sperm onto my journal, all while I knelt between his knees watching from up close.

"I only tore out the parts I ruined," he said guiltily.

I nodded, still picturing him coming. "Let me get this straight. You were reading *my* story and you were… masturbating?"

"Yeah," he cringed. "Is that weird?"

"Um, yes, no, maybe, I don't know," I giggled.

"It's weird," he said, his voice strangled.

"Not any weirder than writing The Football Games," I grinned.

"She rode him like a wolf," he quoted.

"She did," I tittered.

"What's that like?" he asked innocently.

"How should I know! I'm a virgin! How can you even ask that, Channing?"

"You wrote the story."

"For my private enjoyment," I chortled. "*Not* yours. From the sound of it, you did anyway."

"Have you?"

"Have I what?"

"Enjoyed yourself to your stories?"

"Channing! You can't ask me that!"

"I told you what I did. Have you ever?"

"That's none of your business!" I pipped, getting increasingly turned on.

"Have you?" he demanded.

"Would you stop asking?"

"I want to know. Have you ever—"

"Yes! Okay?"

His nostrils flared and his eyes burned. "Did you do it when you wrote it? It's all written by hand. If your journal was on your desk you could write one-handed and—"

"Would you stop?" I was laughing to hide my rising arousal.

"Did you masturbate when you wrote The Football Games about me and you?"

I was quavering with desire, my mouth watering with need. I swallowed nervously. My voice a weak whisper, I admitted the truth, "Yes. I masturbate when I write stories about you and me, okay?"

"Really," he grunted. "Are you naked when you—"

"No I was not naked!"

He nodded. "Have you always done that?"

"I've never done that," I tittered. "I guess you brought out the wolf in me."

He looked stunned. "That is so fucking hot, Carol."

"Yeah," I said on general principles because I was burning up under my hoodie.

Channing reached up and tugged on the zipper.

"What are you doing?" I asked.

The zipper ticked down.

"Channing? What?"

Tick, tick, tick.

I was wearing a T-shirt and bra underneath, but I may as well have been naked.

Tick, tick, tick.

"Channing," I muttered.

"Do you want me to stop?"

"I?"

Tick, tick, tick.

"Yes or no, Carol?"

I shook my head.

"I'll stop," he sighed.

"No, don't."

"Okay," he nodded.

Tick, tick, tick.

The zipper was already past my boobs.

Tick, tick, tick.

Then it was done.

My hoodie was open.

He reached into it.

"What are you—?"

His hands clasped my back and he pulled my hips into his.

"Channing," I sighed, my forehead touching his chest. His muscles were hot slabs of seduction.

He lifted my chin. "Carol, I—" His chocolate-caramel eyes melted.

I tiptoed up, leading with my lips.

His found mine and started a slow grind.

Heat.

Wet heat.

Tongues fucking.

I'd had many kisses in my life. Kissing was great. I loved kissing. This was not that.

This was tongues fucking.

Fucking, and fucking, and fucking.

Still thrusting, Channing backed me into a wall, forcing me against it with his hips, pinning mine with his grinding. I opened my legs and hunkered down. His knee was waiting for me.

We were tango fucking like X's and Y's.

I ground myself against him, soaking through my panties and sweats. Somewhere in the back of my mind I wondered if I was going to leave a stain on his jeans. Yes, please.

When Channing's hands found my breasts, a firestorm of pleasure tingled outward and downward, launching me to sexual heaven while my womanhood squeezed and shivered waves of heat melting throughout my pelvis, a hot bloom of pent up lust now freed.

Channing attacked my neck with a series of savage kisses, licked me from collar bones to chin in one long slide, grunted in my ear, and bit my neck hard but not too hard.

I moaned, "Fuck me, Channing."

We both locked up at the exact same time.

Did I say something wrong?

"I didn't mean that," I blurted.

"Sorry, I shouldn't have—"

"Yes I did."

"I should go."

"Fuck me, Channing."

Our eyes met.

"For real?" he asked.

"Yes. Fuck me. Do it."

"Are you sure?"

"Yes I'm sure! Wait. Are you?"

He nodded dumbly.

Clearly, he didn't know how to navigate this moment any better than I did. "Um, do we... I don't know what to do."

"I don't have a condom."

"You don't?"

"I wasn't expecting to get laid."

"You weren't?"

He shook his head. "I was... hoping. Not expecting."

I was partially relieved. "What do we do?"

"Are you on the pill?"

"No."

"I guess we wait," he sighed, intensely disappointed. "My bad."

"No, it's—wait! Sienna should have some condoms!"

"Who?"

"My roommate! She has a drawer full in her desk. I saw them the day you stole my journal when I was looking for it."

"Sorry about that."

"No, it's fine." I slipped under one of his muscled arms and dashed over to Sienna's desk. Ripped the drawer open. "Here they are."

"Do you think we'll need that many?" Channing asked from over my shoulder, referring to Sienna's supply of at least a dozen condoms.

Before I could answer, his heat enveloped me. My first thought was to push my ass into his hips, but I was too shy. Instead, I pressed my shoulders up into his chest and gave a little moan.

He responded by wrapping an arm around my waist and pulling me into him. That gave me the courage to grind my ass into his crotch.

"Fuck," he groaned, eyes rolling up into his head.

"Do you like that?"

"Fuck yeah."

I redoubled my efforts.

"Fuck, Carol, fuck." His weight sagged onto my back.

I had to throw my arms forward to keep from crashing my chin into Sienna's desk.

Channing threw his arms forward too, caging me hunched over the desk. Then he ground against me, thrusting hard. "Fuck, Carol Fuck!" He hissed almost painfully.

"Wait, stop," I insisted.

"Sorry." He let go and pulled away. "Is something wrong?"

"We don't need pants."

"What?"

"We don't need to dry hump."

"Oh, right."

"You haven't had sex before, have you?"

"I told you I hadn't. You haven't, have you?"

"No! This is, this is going to be my first time."

He stared at me for a long time. "Yeah."

"Should we? On the bed maybe?"

"Take your hoodie off."

"What?"

He swallowed hard. "Take it off." His voice had a darkness to it that frightened me a little. We'd just gone from the shallow end of the pool to the deep end and there were no floating life-preservers or lifeguards I could see.

"Take it off," he grunted.

"Okay." I shrugged out of my hoodie and hung it on the back of my desk chair. "Now what?"

"Strip."

"No, Channing. I'm not a stripper."

"Not like that. Just take your clothes off. Like you do when you're alone."

"Why?"

"Because it's fucking hot, like I'm seeing something I'm not supposed to."

"Oh, okay," I giggled. Awkwardly, I pushed my sweats down to the floor and stepped out of them. Peeled my socks off with my toes out of habit. I reached for my T-shirt with both hands.

"No. Take your panties off."

"But I take my shirt off first. Panties last."

"Panties first."

"Okay," I snickered. Hooked my thumbs in the waistband.

"Do it."

I pushed them down as quick as I could. I was getting so turned on, I wouldn't be able to move soon. When I stood up, his shirt was off. I laughed, "Ohmygod, you have an amazing body."

"Touch yourself."

"What?"

"Touch your pussy." He grabbed his crotch through his jeans and squeezed. His face twisted in passionate knots.

That was so fucking hot. "Channing, I—"

"Touch. Your. Pussy. Like when you're writing about us."

"Oh, okay," I sighed. I slid my hand down the stomach of my T-shirt then bunched it up, revealing myself to him. My other hand slid down and my fingers found my hot center. I was so wet, I was practically raining. When my fingers touched my clit, it exploded with raw voltage that burned a whirlwind of pleasure I'd never felt before, spinning in sinful circles that made my legs shake. Eyes closed, I bit my lower lip and moaned.

I opened my eyes to see him ripping his jeans open and frantically pulling his cock out of his boxers. When he started pumping his straining shaft, I almost melted all over the floor.

"Wait," I said. "Stop for a second."

"Why?"

"I want to see it pulse."

"What?"

"I want to see your cock pulse."

"What are you talking about?"

"Don't they pulse?"

"You mean like this?" He let go of his cock.

Sure enough, his cock ticked in time with what I assumed was his heartbeat.

Pulse.

Pulse.

Pulse.

It was so effing hot.

"Is that what you meant?" he asked.

"Yeah. Stroke it. I want to see your pre-cum."

"How does a virgin know about that?"

"I read. Stroke it."

He stroked.

Oh my, did he stroke.

Slow, sultry, gently twisting motions.

"Take your shirt off," he demanded.

I ripped it off and tossed it aside.

"Look at you," he grinned. "You are so fucking gorgeous."

"Liar." I smiled. "What about my bra?"

"Leave it for now. Touch yourself," he said, this time more casually, his eyes locked on mine.

I simply nodded and slid my other hand down between my legs. When I slid my index finger inside myself, he grunted.

"Fuck. There it is."

"What?" I asked, worried.

"Pre cum."

We were several feet away from each other but I wanted to get closer. Hands still between my legs, I stepped closer. "Ohmygod, there it is!" If I wasn't so incredibly turned on, I probably would've knelt over his cock with a magnifying glass to examine the pearlescent drop in detail. But I *was* turned on. Seeing him leaking for me was possibly the most erotic thing I could imagine. To top it off, his cock was swollen, the head purpling and pulsing, and he was still pumping.

"Oh, fuck, Carol, I, fuck!" Channing suddenly grimaced. "Fuck!"

What surprised me the most was that I could *hear* it.

This tiny little audible tick-pop of him squirting a thick white line of cum plopping onto my stomach where it stuck.

I wasn't sure if I should be shocked or offended or what, but you better believe I was turned on and didn't stop tickling my clit. Another thick line of hot white painted my stomach and stuck. The next thing I knew, gasp, "Channing! I'm coming, Channing! Ohmygod!" I flicked faster and faster and the hottest orgasm I'd ever had washed over me, quivering down to my toes where I stood.

We both stood there panting for several moments.

When I was ready, I said, "I've never come for anyone before."

"Me neither," he said, holding his cock. "Sorry about the…"

"It's okay." I looked down at his cum on my stomach. "I'll clean it." I grabbed my sweats off the chair to wipe it away.

"I'll do it," Channing said, took my sweats away, and started licking my stomach clean instead.

His hot tongue on my skin sent me shivering. I don't know why it was so hot, but it was, especially when he licked my navel. That sent spasming vibrations spinning up from my crotch. When his tongue slid down toward my center, I gasped and jumped back.

"What?" he asked innocently.

"You have cum on your tongue! You can't lick me *there* with cum on your tongue. They swim. I'm wet."

"Oh, right. Shit. I wanted to eat you out. Fuck. What should I do? Brush my teeth? Mouthwash? Fuck! That was so stupid!"

Not once had my ex Evan ever asked to go down on me. Not once. He'd begged me for blowjobs, which I'd never given. Had he offered *me* oral, I would have gladly reciprocated. But he hadn't. He had slightly less than zero interest in giving it. I suddenly wondered if it had something to do with him being a finicky eater and stingy with money? Probably both. Anyway, here Channing was, kicking himself for missing the opportunity to give. My, how things changed.

"Rain check?" I winked.

He deflated.

"In five days," I giggled. "after every last sperm in your mouth dies, you can give me oral."

"Five days? I don't think I can make it five days."

"I didn't mean you have to wait for sex." I bit my lower lip.

His eyes blazed. "You mean…"

"Yes, I mean… I should probably clean you up first." I glanced at the curve of his half-hard dick.

"You don't have to do that."

"Don't you want me to?"

"Of course," he snorted. "But fair is fair. I can wait five days for you to blow me."

"What if I don't want to wait? Would you think I was bad?"

"Not at all. Can I, can I take your bra off first?"

"Don't you want to make me take it off? Like before? Order me?"

"Is that what you want?"

"You are so sweet, Channing."

"Thanks? I guess?"

"Yes," I nodded. "What should I do?"

He looked me over. Wrapped his big arms around me. Fumbled with the hooks for a surprisingly long time. Chuckling, he finally unhooked it. "Sorry that took so long."

"No worries." With the straps still on my shoulders, the bra just hung.

He reached up and peeled down the straps and my bra fell away.

"Fuck," he groaned, staring at my erect nipples. "They're perfect." He knelt down on one knee and started sucking on one while kneading the other. He was so tall, he had no trouble reaching them with his ravenous mouth.

His every lick to my nipples went straight to my clit.

Before I could intensify the sensation with my fingers on my clit, his big hand cupped my crotch and started rubbing.

No man had ever touched me down there directly. With Evan, it had always been through clothes.

I didn't think about him for long because Channing's thick finger was zinging back and forth across my clit.

It was far and away the greatest sensation I'd ever felt.

Until he slid a single finger up inside me, which was infinitely greater.

He entered me.

Channing Peyton was inside me.

Finger fucking me.

I felt myself squeezing on his finger, resisting each retreat of this welcome invasion.

Between his hands and his mouth all over my nipples and breasts and the rest, it didn't take long for me to come hard.

I mean, *really* hard.

Panting turned to tight squeals. I would've screamed if it wasn't for being in the dorms. People would hear. My voice box clicked and coughed a whispery orgasm that was the best I'd ever had. I came hard all over Channing's hand, then collapsed onto him, gasping for breath, both hands propping myself up on his muscled shoulders, my stomach clenching and unclenching as I came down from coming.

"I want to taste you so bad right now," Channing said, both his hands now resting on my hips.

Still leaning over him, I reached between my legs, dipped two fingers inside myself, wiggled my ass in the air, then pulled them out slow. I squatted down on my haunches, my knees spread wide open, offered my hand to Channing, who was still on his knees.

He inhaled deeply, nostrils flaring. "You smell so fucking good." He closed his eyes and opened his mouth and suckled my fingers.

Oddly, though it was vaguely blowjob-ish, it was incredibly hot, his tongue licking and swallowing my wetness so lovingly. I reached down unconsciously and continued rubbing myself.

At some point, he pulled his fingers out of my mouth and we started kissing deeply, slowly, passionately.

He shocked me when his strong hands grabbed my ass and lifted me up like I was weightless. I wrapped my legs around his waist and he stood, carrying me two paces to my bed, turned me around and gently laid me down.

I lay there naked.

He stared.

"What?"

"You are so fucking hot, Carol Everdeen." He was fully hard and pulsing again.

Pulse.

Pulse.

Pulse.

I twinkled a sleepy grin and extended my arms. "Come here, Channing Hawthorne."

"Why?"

"Why do you think?"

He smirked, "I want to hear you say it."

"I want you to fuck me, Channing Peyton."

A broad smile widened across his full and luscious mouth. "I'll get a condom." He fished one out of Sienna's desk. Held it. Stared at it.

"What?"

"I just remembered something," he said, worried.

"Did you forget to turn off the stove?"

"Huh?"

I rolled my eyes, "Something my dad always asked my mom growing up whenever we went to a movie after dinner on a Saturday night."

"Oh," he grinned. "No, not that."

"Obviously. What is it?"

"This may sound weird."

"How weird?"

"Well..."

"Just tell me."

"Okay, one of the guys on the team once said, never fuck a ho, I mean have sex with a woman, without her sucking your dick first, I mean giving you a blowjob, I mean head, er, what am I supposed to call it?"

"I get the idea," I snickered. He was so cute, I wanted to give him a ball of string and watch him get tangled up playing with it for a few hours. Instead, I said, "Is this some kind of power trip thing? I mean, I offered to give you oral. All you had to do was ask. It's not a big deal."

"No," he shook his head. "He said, if you have sex with a rubber without getting a blowjob first, your dick thinks you're fucking a rubber. If you get head first, you'll trick your dick into thinking you're fucking without a condom. I guess rubbers suck? I don't know either way."

"How about I suck you and we'll find out?"

"That'll work," he grinned. "What should I do?"

"Enjoy it," I grinned and rolled onto my knees in front of his throbbing cock. "Give me a moment." I closed my eyes. Thought about all the sex scenes I'd read in Mom's books. I also pictured what little porn I'd seen, waiting there while the memories blossomed into specific actions.

"Is everything okay?"

"Fine," I nodded, opening my eyes. First, I cupped his balls and gently grabbed his shaft. I was looking right at his dick. Inches from my face. The pre-cum this time was smaller, a clear glistening dribbling out his tip. I licked it, tasting tangy skin, running my tongue up the crease from underneath. Paused to give him a pull.

He moaned, his eyes closed. His cock seemed gigantic in my little hand. I hoped he'd fit later. I'd worry about it then.

I licked his head several more times while pumping him.

"Oh, fuck, Carol." His eyes were clamped shut and his head lolled on his neck.

I ran a hand down his rippled abs. They were quivering under my fingers. I wasn't even giving him a blowjob yet, just kissing his cock, but already I felt a distinct sense of empowerment.

When his head was good and wet, I opened my mouth and took him in, easing him all the way to the back of my throat until I was kissing my fingers were they were wrapped around his cock and pumping. He hissed and grunted and I felt his balls tighten in my hand. Hugging the bottom of him with my tongue, I tried tightening my lips around his shaft. Immediately noticed they were a bit too dry. I pulled away, still pumping slowly, and licked my lips, wetting them before resuming.

It wasn't long before I felt him jolt hard in my mouth and groan. I thought he was going to come, but he only jolted once. Shortly after, I tasted something salty and pungent on my tongue.

His cum.

Not a lot.

Just a drop.

It was like nothing I'd ever tasted before. Not bad, exactly, just different. I went with it.

Up to this point, I'd been so focused on my own technique, deathly afraid I was doing something wrong, I wasn't feeling turned on. Once I fell into a rhythm that he seemed to enjoy, encouraging me with his moans and groans, I got *incredibly* turned on. I reached down between my legs with one hand to find my bliss.

It was soaked.

My entire body drenched itself in pleasure.

The next thing I knew, after I don't know how long, he started to tighten and swell in my mouth, getting even larger, even more engorged.

"Stop!" he hissed.

I slowed slowly, letting my timing subside. I pulled away and looked him in the eyes. His were hooded and dark, drunk on sex the same way I wanted to get drunk on his cum.

"Are you sure?" I whispered and kissed his tip. "I can finish if you want."

"I want to fuck you, Carol. Please let me fuck you."

I smiled a yes.

"I'll put the condom on."

"Wait."

"For what?"

"Let me..." I plunged my fingers deep inside my vagina, wetting them thoroughly. Held them up glistening for a moment before massaging them around the head of his dick. "So you'll be fucking my actual juices, not my spit."

"So fucking hot," he moaned and shivered in my grip.

Finished, I said, "Get the condom."

He snatched up the packet.

"Tear it open with your teeth," I purred.

"Why?"

"That's what they do in the books. It's supposed to be hot."

"What books?"

"Never mind. Can you just do it?"

"Sure." He bit it and ripped it. Pulled the condom out and looked around the room. "Where's your trash?"

"Such a gentlemen. Just put it on my desk."

He did, setting it there with care. He examined the condom for a moment, flipping it over.

"You're ruining the moment," I teased.

"Sorry. Just making sure I've got the right side." Pinching the tip, he rolled it on. "Now what?"

I lay back on the bed. "Oh, wait."

"What?"

"My hair." I sat up, reached behind my pony tail and pulled off the hair tie, putting it around my wrist out of habit. I fanned out my hair, running my fingers through it.

"You're beautiful," he said wistfully. "Like an angel or, I don't know. Like I pictured Carol Everdeen."

"What," I giggled, "you didn't imagine her with a ponytail or a sexy French braid or something?"

"No, she had big hair."

"Mine's too straight to be big."

"It looks big to me," he grinned innocently. "You're gorgeous, Carol."

"You are too." I smiled and lay back on the bed again and extended my arms to him, wiggling my fingers.

Smiling, he climbed onto the softly creaking mattress between my legs.

I opened my thighs. "Go easy. I've never had anything as big as you inside me before."

"Should I, is it, I'm not *too* big, am I?"

"I don't think so. Just go slow." I had masturbated so many times in my life, I wasn't worried about any bleeding or pain, but my fingers definitely weren't as big as him.

He hovered over me, his big body a hot temple roofing out the rest of the world. His weight on one arm, the muscles flexed and bulged. I caressed it with my fingers as he positioned his condom-covered cock at my wet entrance. The first thing I felt was exquisite pressure as he pushed himself inside a tiny bit.

"Go slow," I whispered, trying to relax.

He eased in.

I swear, it took an hour, the shortest hour of my life. I wanted it to go on forever, it felt so good, my emptiness now full, the hole in my heart swollen with joy, a deep hunger now sated, an eternal need I never knew I had now met. Him inside me was everything I'd always wanted.

"Fuuuuuuuuck," he groaned slow until his entire body weighed me down, filling me with every inch.

A perfect fit.

Pulse.

Pulse.

Pulse.

"So fucking warm," he whispered.

"Channing, I—" The orgasm stole over me so fast it surprised me. I tightened around him. Wrapped my legs around his waist as tight as I could and squeezed. "Channing! I'm coming! Ohmygod! Channing!" I shook so hard, my chest locked up and I stopped breathing. The pleasure was too intense.

Channing thrust into me, not pumping, just a continuous push of pressure. "Fuck!" he grunted.

Pulse!

Pulse!

Pulse!

Eventually, I caught my breath in throaty gasps.

"Did you come?" I asked.

"Almost," he grunted. "Not quite."

Pulse.

Pulse.

Pulse.

"Carol, that was so fucking hot. You have no idea."

"Oh, I think I do," I giggled, relaxing my head onto my pillow.

"Should we, should I, uh, pull out?"

"Did you come?"

"No."

"Then fuck me, Channing. Fuck me like it's your first time."

"It is," he chuckled.

"I meant, *our* first time. I'm still a virgin until you come inside me, right?"

"Right," he grinned.

Now he did start pumping, filling me with steady thrusts.

I wrapped every part of myself around him again, and he found a sinful rhythm that turned me inside out and outside in. I became squeezing need as he thrust relentlessly. We tightened together and he filled me to bursting.

When the pleasure couldn't get any better, it did.

Powerful orgasms wracked us both.

Channing issued a crackling roar as he let it all out.

I whimpered, trying to hold it in for some reason I couldn't remember.

"FUCK!" Channing grunted.

Pulse!

I shook with need, shivering with him, milking him as I came so hard my entire body knotted.

Pulse!

"AHHHHH!" Channing groaned.

Pulse!

Suddenly, everything in my body relaxed into a flood of warmth and wetness and I sagged into the bed.

Channing weighed into me, his big body protecting me from everything. Our world became this.

Pulse.

Pulse.

Pulse.

For the first time in my life, I was complete.

His big hands muscled under me and he pulled me into a hug. Were we cheek to cheek. He nuzzled me.

A whisper so soft a mouse might miss it.

"I love you, Carol."

My eyes popped in surprise.

"I love you," he whispered again.

Okay, now. *Now* I was complete.

Chapter 16

CAROL

"He said what?" Sienna gasped.

"He loves me," I said. We were in our room after dinner. Channing had gone to practice hours ago. I'd been dying to tell Sienna since he'd left, but she'd been studying at some boy's dorm until this evening.

"Are you sure you weren't hallucinating?"

"No," I scoffed. "I mean yes. I wasn't hallucinating." I desperately wanted to believe Channing had in fact said it because that's *exactly* how I felt. It was powerful, primal. After giving my virginity to him, I couldn't imagine loving anyone else, not ever. It was as if something had taken root deep inside me and started to grow. No, I didn't think I was pregnant. The condom hadn't broken and Channing had been careful to hold it on when he pulled out of me after not too long. I wasn't pregnant.

"Were you drunk?" Sienna asked.

"No," I snorted.

"High?"

"No, Sin! I was completely sober. He said he loves me."

"Maybe he is a virgin."

"You mean was."

She waved a hand, "It's not the same with a condom."

"I don't see how it's any different."

She chortled, "You *are* a virgin."

"What are you talking about, Sin?" I laughed. "We had *actual* sex with his *actual* dick inside my *actual* vagina. He came. I did too. We're not virgins anymore." I almost told her about me blowing him and rubbing myself all over his cock before he put the condom on, but that was too intimate. That was a secret for me and Channing.

Sienna shook her head, "It's not the same, Care. Trust me," she chortled. "When you have sex without a condom, and he comes inside you?" She shook her head seriously. "It's different. Waaaaay different."

"I don't see how."

"You'll just have to try it. Until you do, you're still a virgin."

#
&
&*&
&*&*&

&*&*&*&
M

"Next?" the nurse said. Some guy got up from his seat in the waiting room and walked through the door where she was standing.

I was flipping through a National Geographic magazine where I sat inside the Student Health Clinic. I was on my period, so I was here to get birth control pills.

It was weird.

Did the other students sitting here know I'd had sex? Did I look different now that I had? I couldn't tell in the mirror. Could other people tell? Or was Sienna right? Was I *still* a virgin? That was ridiculous. It was the same thing. Sex was sex. Wasn't it?

Either way, I felt so oddly guilty being here.

I knew I shouldn't, but I did.

Thankfully, when I saw the doctor, thank God she was a woman and not a man. She reminded me of Pam Beesly from The Office. Soft spoken and very kind. She smiled and told me over and over it was good I was getting the pills, that I was doing the responsible thing.

"You know about STDs, right?" she asked, sitting on a rolling stool at her little desk. She'd already written out the prescription on a paper pad.

I nodded. "Yup. Learned all about them in middle school *and* high school biology class."

"Good. You do know that the pill won't protect you from any STDs, right?"

"Oh, totally," I nodded. "He's a virgin. I mean, *was* a virgin until we had sex." I giggled. I wanted to whisper, you know Channing Peyton? The football stud? The one on all the banners around campus who wins all the games? The one *every* girl at KCU wants for her boyfriend? Him. I had sex with *him*. It was *both* our first times.

I didn't say it. But I did blush.

"What?" Dr. Pam smiled. She didn't look *exactly* like Pam Beesly, and her name tag said Dr. Sara Kendall, but they could be sisters.

"Nothing."

"You can tell me," she encouraged. "It's just us girls."

"He's a, um, he's kind of on the football team?" A girlish giggle was inevitable.

"Good for you," Dr. Kendall said thoughtfully. "Are you two exclusive?"

"Um, we haven't had that talk yet." Per usual, Channing was a busy man. We hadn't seen each other once since we'd had afternoon sex, and he'd had to rush off to practice when I rushed off to calculus. Yes, I'd considered waiting for him outside the stadium several times, but that would look desperate. Sienna had insisted I wait until he found me again.

Dr. Kendall nodded. "I don't know anything about this boy, I'm sure he's a good person, but it's important that you ask him about his sexual activity. If he's with anyone else, and you don't use condoms when he's with you, and he hasn't used condoms with them, he could transmit something to you from another person without knowing it."

I frowned, suddenly sick to my stomach. The dozen hard-boiled chicken eggs that had apparently been slowly rotting in my stomach and poisoning me with doubt since the day *after* I'd had sex with Channing, and he hadn't talked to me since, decided now was a good time to crack open their shells and announce their smell. Betrayal. Or was that just the donkey of disgust kicking me with both hooves? No, it was both.

Dr. Kendall placed a warm hand on my jeans-covered knee. "I'm not saying he *is* sexually active with other people, Carol. I'm just saying you need to talk to him. Communicate with him. You can save yourself a lot of heartache if you just talk."

My eyes heated. Why did I want to cry all of a sudden? Was it because I knew from Evan that men lied and you never saw it coming until it was coming inside your best friend? Pumpa, pumpa, pumpa. Glorg. Was there any good reason to believe Channing was a better man than Evan? Or was he, the jock-stud of KCU, a thousand times worse?

"Talk to him, Carol. I'm sure he'll be faithful to you if you just ask."

"Yeah," I sniffed miserably, suddenly unsure and wondering if Channing had even really said he loved me, or if I'd imagined it like Sienna said.

"You said he was a virgin before you, right?"

"That's what he said." Now I was doubting it altogether. Had Channing been lying like Evan?

"I'm sure he was being honest. Just be careful, that's all. And talk. Ask him if he wants to be exclusive. If he doesn't, and you still choose to have sex with him, which is 100% okay, use condoms, during penetration and oral."

"Oral?!" I gasped.

"STDs can be transmitted from genital areas to mouth, and vice-versa."

"No, I know," I grimaced. "We learned all about it in health class." Now I wanted to vomit. Why even bother having sex with cheating Channing? He was probably sleeping with half of campus, and by half, I meant the female half, which was all of them.

"Oh, Carol," Dr. Kendall said with motherly concern. "Just talk to him. Everything will work itself out if you do."

Chapter 17

CHANNING

"Mmm, MMM!" Lashawn grunted. "Look at that pussy! What I wouldn't do to cut me a slice of that!" He was looking right at Victoria Bissette. "That's some good pussy right there, dog!" He slapped the back of my pads with a gloved hand. "Tell me I'm wrong, player!"

"That is a fine piece of pussy," I agreed. "Just begging to be served *à la mode*."

"You said it," he chuckled while we both stared.

How could we not?

Victoria Bissette was stacked and jacked.

A walking fucking orgasm of a woman who knew how to move.

Watching her dance always made me hard enough in my jock to punch a hole in my cup. Today was no exception.

Around us, the team was busy practicing under the stadium's roof. Blocking drills, tackle drills, rushing drills, passing drills, kicking drills. Lashawn and I had been perfecting our out-routes and slant-routes, but had taken a brief break when The Bod Squad started practicing dance moves. They were rarely out on the field with us during practice. They had their own dedicated dressing rooms, dance rooms, and a few others alongside the countless rooms underneath the indoor bleachers. It was like an entire city inside this place.

Best part about Cheetahs Stadium being covered?

Summer cheerleading outfits year-round.

The Cheetahs cheerleaders' costumes basically consisted of gold bras with black strapping, the shortest shorts known to man (black with a thick gold belt) that left nothing about the girls' asses to the imagination, and gold boots with black tassels.

"Every time Victoria bends over with her legs spread like that?" Lashawn said conspiratorially, "I want to run over there and just fuck her doggie-style, you know?"

"I go first," I grinned, staring at Victoria in full agreement.

"No doubt."

"Yeah? Why me first?"

"If I went first, and you after, you'd be throwing your tiny hot dog down a damn hallway."

"A hallway?" I snorted at the ridiculous image, shaking my head. "Is your dick *shaped* like a hallway too?"

"Yup," he grinned proudly, trying not to laugh.

"Does it have square corners?"

"Sure does," he shrugged. "Crown moulding, baseboards, a runner rug on the bottom, you name it."

"Baseboards?" I grinned.

"With corniced edges."

"I don't even know what that means."

"Me neither," he chuckled.

Snickering, I said, "What kind of women have you been fucking that have hallway pussies, LD? That means their pussies are bigger than they are."

"Only *after* I fuck them." He was struggling not to laugh.

"Right," I nodded skeptically, also struggling, but wanting to laugh just as bad.

"Hallways for days, dog. *Days.*" He spread his hands wide, like he was overlooking acres of open prairie.

"That's a big fucking hallway," I chuckled, following his gaze.

"Yeah, dog." Smiling big, he planted both hands on his hips and thrust them forward once in slow suggestion.

"How long is it?" I asked, looking deep into the distance with him, shading my eyes with one hand for no reason. "This hallway dick of yours?"

"Don't know."

"You don't know?"

He shook his head, "Don't know."

"Because it's so long," I said flatly.

"Mmm-hmm," he nodded seriously and thrust slowly a second time.

"How do you even move that thing?"

"Don't know."

On the verge of busting up, I said, "You do realize, your dick is bigger than any woman alive. Female whales could not accommodate your dick."

"Guess I'm just lucky like that," he quipped.

I laughed, "What the fuck do you use for condoms, LD? Nothing will fit!"

"The Goodyear Blimp," he chortled. "Take the air out. Slip it on. Done."

"You can't!"

"Why not?"

"It's too small!!!!" I squealed, no longer able to hold back the laughs.

At that, we both fell over guffawing and crying, rolling on the grass and holding our bellies.

"Washington! Peyton!" Q-Coach Latham (my quarterback coach) was shouting at us from across the field, where he'd gone with WR-Coach Tolbert (Lashawn's wide receiver coach) so they could talk to Coach Rucker, the offensive coordinator, about the routes we'd been running, and how they would integrate with the overall offensive game plan for this weekend. "The fuck you two looking at?" Latham barked. "That shit don't look like no football! Get your asses back to running your routes!"

Still staring at Victoria, Lashawn muttered to me, "Before I do that, I'm gonna practice my button hook on that bubble butt of hers."

"Good luck with that, Blimp Dick," I chuckled.

"Huh! Huh! Huh! Huh!" He slapped my pads and wheezed another jubilant laugh, the kind that put everyone in a good mood. When Lashawn wasn't in the locker room defending his manhood against a hundred other rabid football players, he was easy-going and good natured, the kind of guy you wanted for a best friend. "Seriously, when are you gonna hit that, player?" He meant Victoria.

I shrugged. "Nobody can hit that."

"*You* can, dog! You're our only hope, bro! You're like the Luke Skywalker of pussy! Use the force on *Victoria's* pussy, yo!"

"Quit dreaming, L-shawn," I smiled. "Victoria Bissette isn't interested in me, you, or anybody else. I'm starting to think she doesn't have a pussy."

"What, like an action figure? Like a Barbie doll? No nipples even? Huh, huh, huh."

"Who knows," I chuckled, wishing I could check for myself.

"Goooooooooo Channing!" the cheerleaders chorused, finishing a routine, shaking their pom-poms and flashing high-kicks.

Victoria dropped her poms, spun into a pirouette, lifted one leg into a standing split, held it with both hands, and came to a stop, balancing on one foot. Her wide-open crotch was pointing at me.

Then.

She.

Winked.

At me, making direct eye contact and smiling the hottest, sultriest, most sinful grin since Eve gave the apple to Adam.

"Me?!" Lashawn laughed, pointed at himself dramatically with both gloved hands. "She winked at me, dog!"

Still smiling, Victoria shook her head and her mane of hair waved.

"Him?!" Lashawn pointed at me with both arms.

Victoria nodded.

"Aw, hell naw!" Lashawn laughed, throwing his hands in the air and stumbling back several steps like he'd been hit in the heart with a cannonball. "You're killing me, shorty! Kill! Ing! Me!"

Victoria shook her head again and slowly lowered her leg. She curled a finger invitingly at me, her hypnotizing eyes summoning me.

I was stunned, my chest peeling open like she was prying my heart out with that finger and it went floating over to her. Meanwhile, I couldn't move.

"Don't just stand there, dog!" Lashawn said in disbelief. "Go get her already!" He gave me a shove.

I stumbled forward. Considered it. What would it hurt to say something to Victoria?

"Peyton!" Coach Rucker shouted. "Eyes on the ball, son! Eyes on the goddamn ball! Don't make me come over there!"

"His eyes are on *getting* balled, huh, huh, huh," Lashawn chuckled. "You better hit that later, player, or I will cut your dick off and feed it to you my damn self."

I winked at him, "You know how much I love hot dogs."

"Huh, huh, huh, huh."

\#

&

&*&

&*&*&

&*&*&*&

M

"You gonna be ready for Saturday?" Coach Rucker asked, his feet on his desk, readjusting his Cheetahs baseball-style cap for no reason, chewing his gum like he always did, gnashing away at it with his big white teeth like a pulp machine.

"Always," I grinned. It was two hours after practice ended. After showering, I'd just spent an hour with Rucker going over offensive plays for this weekend's game.

"You know Indiana's defensive line is gonna try and tear your head off, son."

"If they catch me," I smirked.

"Lean and mean, son, lean and mean," Rucker chuckled his favorite saying and folded his hands behind his head. "Even so, I want you to spend some quality time on game tapes this go around. Really get inside the head of their D-line. They got some new bruisers ready to kill you, and they're quick. Quickest I've seen in a long time. Last thing I need is my star quarterback getting injured out the rest of the season, know what I mean?" Chew, chew, chew. He was murdering that gum of his.

"I'll be fine."

"You will if you study the films." Chew, chew, chew. "Don't over think it. Don't over analyze. Just… watch them. As much as you can. It'll seep in. We'll go over everything with Latham on Thursday."

I ran my hand through my hair, said apologetically, "I've got midterms coming up Thursday, and two papers I still haven't started on Friday. My grades are deep in the shitter already. Classes were bad enough last year, but this year? Fucking forget it. I don't know how I'm going to pull my grades out of the can now." We both knew if I didn't keep my GPA above 2.0, where it was currently balanced on a high-wire over the Grand Canyon of ineligibility, the NCAA wouldn't let me play next year.

Chew, chew, chew, "Want me to take care of it?" Rucker offered a Cheshire grin. Chew, chew, chew. "Same as last year?"

"Yeah." I hung my head in shame. "It's just, with math behind me, I thought the tutors would be enough this year."

Rucker kicked his feet off the desk and stood up. "Don't beat yourself up over it, son. You aren't the only one who needs a little help every now and then, right?" He slapped my shoulder firmly.

"Right," I sighed.

"Forget about it." Rucker shook his head. Chew, chew, chew. "Water under the bridge." He opened a desk drawer. "Got something for ya." He handed me this flat black thing with a metal back that was the size of a smallish piece of paper.

"What's this?"

"New iPad."

"You mean iPod. It's damn big for an iPod."

"No, it's a computer. Brand new. Not even out yet." He waved a hand. "Lemme see it."

I handed it back.

He put reading glasses on his nose and pushed a button. The screen turned on. "Prototype from Apple. First ones hit the market later this year."

"How'd you get it?"

Chew, chew, chew, "I know a guy in the NFL who knows a guy at Apple." It was like that around here. People handing me free stuff no one else could get, and me taking it without a second thought. Rucker was tapping the screen with hesitant touches of his middle finger.

"What am I supposed to do with it?"

He tapped the screen several more times until a still image of Indiana's last game opened on some application with a Q. Quicktime or something. He tapped the play triangle and the video started. "If you slide this thing back and forth," he dragged his finger left and right, "You can back up and go forward. Otherwise, they tell me it's like a DVD player. You'll figure it out." He offered it to me.

"This is for me?"

"All yours, son. Oh, here's the power cord. Gotta keep it charged, they tell me. Got a battery." Chew, chew, chew.

A knock at his office door.

Head Coach Slaughter. "You got a minute, Ned?"

Coach Rucker nodded, "Yeah. Come on in, Bill."

"Peyton," Slaughter acknowledged briefly when he stepped inside. He was older, looked like Moses without a beard or the stone tablets, and commanded total respect from every member of his staff and every player on the team. Nobody talked back to Slaughter because they were too busy fighting for his approval. "How ya doing, kid? You ready for Indiana Saturday?"

"Ready to feed them their dicks for dinner," I grinned.

"I'll bring the ketchup," Slaughter winked and patted my shoulder.

Rucker smiled at me, chew, chew, chew, "Watch those tapes, son. I'll take care of the rest."

"Thanks." I was dismissed.

I walked out the half-glass door and closed it behind me, already watching the Indiana video on this new iPad. Thing was amazing. While I did, I faintly heard Coach Slaughter talking to Rucker through the glass as I strolled slowly away.

"We all set for the urine tests?" Slaughter asked.

"All squared away," Chew, chew, chew.

"Everyone passes this year, no exceptions. Make it happen. Whatever it takes. I don't want another fiasco like last year."

"I'll take care of it." Chew, chew, chew.

#
&
&*&
&*&*&
&*&*&*&
M

Three hours later, I got a text on my phone from Lashawn to call him. I did.

"Where you at?" he answered, loud noises in the background.

"Studying game films in my room. Where you at?"

"TT's drinking with the fellas," Tipple Town, everyone's favorite bar.

Half the team was too young to drink legally, but we all had fake ID's and drank at TT's frequently during the off-season. Tonight was the middle of the season and I had no time to waste on a drunken sausage fest.

"Drink for me, Lashawn. I've got real homework after my football homework." No matter what Coach Rucker might do, I was still going to study for class. At least for tonight.

"Fuck that noise, dog. Get your ass over here."

"Can't." My eyes were glued to the defensive line in the video, familiarizing myself with their entire list of formations while looking for defensive tells that might give me an edge when we hit the gridiron.

"Victoria Bissette says you can."

I perked up. "She there?"

"Not exactly."

"Bye, Lashawn. I need to study."

"Wait, wait! Listen! I got Iesha right here!"

"Heeeeeey, Channing!" Iesha sang over the phone.

I knew Iesha. She was a Cheetah cheerleader, one of the best dancers on the squad, and Lashawn's dream girl if he'd only get his head out of his ass and realize it. She looked like fucking Halle Berry's sexier sister, which sounds impossible but you'd agree if you saw her. I don't know what Lashawn's problem was. It was so obvious she was pining for him. If he didn't put a move on her, one of these days, I would, and I'd told him as much, but he always made excuses. I think deep down, he was scared she was too good for him.

"Hey, girl," I said with a grin. "Lashawn giving you a hard time?"

"Working on it," she giggled.

"You'll wear him down," I laughed.

"Not if you do first," she giggled.

Lashawn said faintly, "He what first?"

"Nothing," she said to him. "I'm talking to Chandy." Iesha was always calling me that, short for Chandy Man. Quite a few of The Bod Squad girls called me that too.

Another fun fact about my life: endless beautiful women offering themselves up like a sacrifice on my dick's altar. Never ceased to amuse and amaze me. If they only knew how little experience Dick had.

There was only Carol Duffey.

That *one* fucking time.

What a fuck that was. Damn. I never would've thought sex could be so fucking good. Would've done her twenty more times that same day and every day since if I wasn't so busy with football every waking minute.

I'd told her I loved her.

Biiiiiig mistake.

I don't know why I said it.

I didn't say it because I was supposed to. I knew better, knew that dudes were *never* supposed to say that shit until the girl withheld sex or threatened to leave. It was just something you said to string them along until you were done fucking them. Every dude knew that.

I don't know what made me say it to her.

Just said it.

It seemed right at the time.

Felt right.

Now I felt bad.

I didn't have time to love anybody, not even myself. I was a tool, an appendage of a large beast of a machine called the King City Cheetahs. Some days it seemed like 99% of my thoughts weren't my own. They were Coach Slaughter's or Coach Rucker's or Coach Latham's, or my dad's. More and more, I was living Dad's dream, not mine.

I was barely my own person.

It had been this way since I started high school football, when Dad really started in with the head trips.

"What is wrong with you? He was wide open! All you had to do was throw the goddamn ball like a man! Your wrist getting limp?"

"No, Dad."

"They blitzed the shit out of you and you never saw it coming! You're not reading the formations like I taught you! You need your eyes checked?"

"No, Dad."

"Are you pussing out? That it? You don't want to play high school football because you aren't man enough? Someone cut your balls off when I wasn't looking?"

"No, Dad."

"You a she-male with a dick and no balls? You aren't growing titties, are you?"

"No, Dad."

"Damn right you aren't. Now you get your ass out on that field and kill those fuckers! You fucking *kill* them!"

And on and on and on.

Don't let it get to you.

I didn't.

That was football for you.

You know that old saying, Power corrupts, absolute power corrupts absolutely?

Same was true for success.

Dad didn't used to be such an asshole. When I was little, he was a great guy. Best dad a kid could want. Only thing Dad loved more than football was me and Mom.

Too bad, the more successful I got, the more obvious it became I had potential, the more dickish he got. When KCU scouted me in high school, he took it to another level of dickishness, the penthouse level in a skyscraper of dicks.

I think the stress of success was getting to him. Good thing he and Mom didn't live here in King City. If they did, me or Dad would end up killing each other. Or Mom might divorce his ass. One time, she'd threatened to leave him for the way he talked to me. She didn't understand. You didn't get tough treating people like babies. Save the Pampers for people who couldn't hold their shit together. I didn't need them.

I hoped Dad would mellow once I signed a contract with the NFL. First thing I'd do is pay off his and Mom's mortgage. Maybe that would take the stress off him, and get him off my back.

Don't get me wrong. As tiresome as Dad's shit was getting, I still loved him and the game. Especially the game. What else was there to life, really?

Besides women, I mean.

Women like Carol Duffey.

You might not know it from looking at her, but that chick was 100% racer back, built for fucking.

I knew that from the night we met at the frat party.

She had a sly, secret beauty, like I was the only one who knew. Not even she did. She didn't flaunt it like most of The Bod Squad. Let me tell you, that shit got old.

Carol was different.

The only thing Carol flaunted was her courage. She had guts the way she stood up to Rudy Blankenship at the frat party, little thing like her. And me in her dorm room with her not backing down? She wasn't a pushover. Don't ask me why, because I don't know, but her strength turned me on hard core.

As much as I wanted to fuck her every chance I had, I didn't have any time. What was I going to do? Keep her tied up in my suite here on the top floor of Faulkner Hall, and fuck her in the ten minutes I had in the morning before running out the door, and the ten minutes before bed each night when I crashed from physical exhaustion?

No.

No girl wanted that.

Even I knew that.

Women wanted all that romance shit.

I didn't even have time for the sex shit.

"Chandy? You still there?" Iesha asked.

"Sorry. What's new with you, girl?"

Iesha said, "Victoria said to get your ass over here."

"Is she there?"

"No, but she said call her if you show up."

That made my dick stir. "No bullshit?"

"Would I lie to you, Chandy?"

"No," I grinned. I didn't know if Victoria Bissette wanted romance or sex or what. If she wanted romance, she and Carol could take a number. But if she just wanted to fuck…

How could I say no to that offer?

#
&
&*&
&*&*&
&*&*&*&
M

"Channing! You came!" cheered several hotties from The Bod Squad partying inside TT's. They were gathered around several tall tables.

"Now it's my turn," Iesha winked, leaning into me with a laugh.

Iesha was definitely come-worthy.

"What do you want him for?" Lashawn laughed, "He doesn't know his dick from a dill pickle. Huh, huh, huh, huh."

"Maybe if *you* did," Iesha teased him.

"You hear her?" Lashawn gaped at me.

I smirked, "The question is, do you?"

Iesha hiked an eyebrow at Lashawn.

"You two are crazy," Lashawn laughed and swallowed whatever sudsy amber ale he was drinking from a pint glass.

Iesha rolled her eyes for my benefit.

"Channing Peyton!" Tim the owner called out as he crutched quickly over, blinking behind his glasses. "The man, the myth, the legend! What're you doing here, kid?"

"Taking a study break," I grinned. Tim was a great guy, an institution at TT's and KCU. Everybody knew he turned a blurry eye to fake ID's. Rarely did he card anybody. Rumor was he had an in with the cops.

"Take a break on me, kid. What'll it be?"

"A pitcher of gold."

"You got it. House refills for your friends?" Tim meant free. He eyed the half-empty pitchers on the bar tables surrounded by The Bod Squad and some of the fellas from the team.

"Can you manage?"

"Can I *manage?*" Tim laughed. "For the undefeated Cheetahs? Do you even have to ask? You pay for it with your wins, kid. You have any idea how packed this place is game nights? Before you came along, it was a ghost town. For *years*, a ghost town. I was starting to worry I'd have to shutter up my old man's pride and joy."

"I thought that was you," I grinned.

"Nah," he laughed, "I was his pain in the neck. Anyway, it's on me, kid."

"Thanks, bro."

Tim crutched off, swinging his body in high-flying arcs as he went. The way he threw himself around, he could've won gold on the pommel horse in Beijing.

I turned to Iesha.

She was texting on the keypad of her slide-out phone.

"Who you texting?" I asked.

"Victoria. Telling her you're here." She finished and gave me a cute smile. "On her way."

Lashawn said, "You are lucky as fuck, dog."

"And you aren't?" I flicked my eyes at Iesha.

"Just saying." Lashawn shrugged and drank more beer.

"Say it to her while I freshen up." I grabbed the nearest half-full pitcher off the table and pounded it to cheers from our crew. Three beers worth would barely get me started. I slammed the empty on the table and ripped a belch. "Somebody get me another one of these!"

Cheers from the fellas, snorts from the ladies.

By the time Victoria arrived, I was well buzzed and had no less than three girls from The Bod Squad hanging off me, kissing me, and grabbing my dick through my jeans with promises of a four-way later. I wasn't even sure which three and me it would be, nor did I care. Beer was driving my dick at this point.

"Hey, Channing." Victoria blotted out those thoughts with a sunray smile. She shone with beauty, brighter than every babe here.

Comparison was the only way to fully appreciate Victoria's stunning looks. The Bod Squad babes were gorgeous, no doubt. Any man would die for one night with any of them. When you lined them up like they were now, Victoria stood out, drew your eyes undeniably. She was taller, prettier, had a better body, better hair, better everything. There was no mistaking it. At the time, I thought if they ever made a Wonder Woman movie some day (this was long before they eventually did), they would be idiots if they didn't cast Victoria Bissette to play the part.

"Looking good, Vic." I offered a beer-smeared smile.

"Looks like you're already taken. Hey, girls," she said to The Bod Squadders hanging off me.

"Look who we caught," one said.

Looking perfectly content, Victoria glanced around until she saw Iesha strutting toward her.

"Hey, girl," Iesha said.

"Can we talk? For a sec?" Victoria asked, a hint of 'tude in her voice.

"Talk away."

"In the ladies room," Victoria said, more 'tude.

"Oh, right."

I was just sober enough to figure out what was going on. "Wait!" I pried myself away from the sexual death grip of three very disappointed Bod Squadders and caught up to Victoria before she got more than three steps. "Let me buy you a drink at the bar."

Victoria smiled at me, "Are you sure? Or would you rather buy drinks for them? It's cheaper by the pitcher."

"Forget them," I said. "I'm buying you a drink."

"Okay then." The sharp edges on her face softened. "Lead the way."

I glanced down into her cleavage, which was bursting out of some classy V-neck thing and a brown tailored leather jacket. Below that, tight flat jeans form-fitting to her hips. Took everything I had not to grab those hips and yank them into my raging dick. Instead, I grabbed her hand and pulled her along through the crowd.

Lashawn hollered somewhere behind us, "That's my boy right there!"

"Lashaaaaawn!" Iesha chastened.

"Huh! Huh! Huh! Huh!"

I found two empty barstools at the bar and reached up under Victoria's arms to lift her onto hers.

"Oh!" she giggled.

I straddled legs over mine and sat down, leaning over the wood bar to hail the least busy bartender. I ordered a beer for me and a whiskey sour for her.

"I didn't think you were coming," I said.

"I had to get ready."

"For what?"

"For you, silly." She bit her lower lip with a flash of perfect teeth.

"Me? You're always ready. Every time I see you, you look like a fashion model."

She shrugged, smiled, and sipped her straw.

"I can't believe we're finally hanging out," I said.

"Why?"

"Because, you're the hottest babe at KCU."

"You're the hottest stud."

"See? Already we're a perfect couple," I chuckled.

"Right?" She bit her straw, flashing hungry eyes. "What took you so long to figure it out?"

"I may be fast on the field, but I'm slow everywhere else."

"Funny," she said without laughing and sipped her drink. "You want to play some pool?"

"Sure."

We took our drinks to the room with the pool tables and found an empty one. I racked up the balls and broke. I was decent at pool, but too drunk to play well. Victoria was terrible and asked for lessons on everything from how to hold the stick to which ball to pick, to which pocket to sink. Every single thing she said was sexual innuendo. If there was any doubt, she ground her ass into my crotch whenever I leaned over her to help her line up a shot.

I won the first game, as you can guess.

"You win," she grinned.

"What's my prize?"

"Do you have to ask?" She stood there posing, one hand on the curve of her cocked hip, the other holding her pool cue straight up on the ground and stroking it slowly.

"Fuck me," I chuckled and sauntered toward her.

"That's your job," she giggled.

I took her stick and set it on the table with mine. Grabbed those hips and pulled her against my raging dick.

"Oh!" she gasped and her blazing blues burned.

"I need you to understand one thing, Vic."

"What's that?" she smiled invitingly.

"I'm a busy man."

"I'm a busy girl."

"You are," I nodded. "The way you lead The Bod Squad? Total respect."

"Same to you. You know the girls call you The Bod God?"

"They do?"

"Don't tell them I told you," she grinned.

"I won't."

"And forget I told you. You've already got enough of an ego."

"No worries. I'll call you The Bod Goddess."

"Will you now?" It was a tease, a suggestion, an invitation to temptation.

I couldn't take her up on it without letting her know where I stood. I sighed, "Here's the thing. I don't have time for love right now. I only have time for sex."

"The best sex you'll ever have." She bit her lip again, this time with coy confidence.

"I like the sound of that." I chuckled, ready to come in my boxers thinking about the splits this woman could do all over my dick.

She leaned for a kiss.

When she was a centimeter away, I quipped, "How do you like the sound of dirty animal wolf sex?"

She pulled back and frowned a giggle, "Um, as long as it's not too dirty. Or with animals."

Why had I said that?

I knew exactly why.

The Football Games.

I sighed, "I can't, Vic."

"This says you can," Victoria purred, grinding her hips into my raging length.

"No, I'm serious. I need love in my life. I know it's stupid, but I do."

"You just said you don't do love. I don't either. We're perfect for each other."

"No, I'm thinking about someone else right now and it isn't you."

"What's his name?" Victoria frowned and took a defensive step back.

"It's not a guy," I snorted.

"Oh yeah?" She scowled like I'd pissed in her drink. "What girl could you *possibly* be thinking of who's hotter than I am?"

Her answer told me everything I needed to know.

Chapter 18

CAROL

"He's not into you, Carol," Sienna sighed. "Channing got what he wanted and now he's gone. I know it sucks, but it'll suck less if you let him go."

It was late at night in our dimly lit dorm room. I was sitting on my bed, hugging my pillow and weeping when I should've been studying. But I couldn't concentrate when my heart was falling apart. It had been a week since I'd gone on the pill in hopes of having real sex with Channing, two weeks since I'd seen him. I'd diligently taken the pill every day at the exact same time. I don't know why I bothered.

Jordyn Hoyle from high school had been right all along.

Men *always* left you.

And they took your heart with them.

At the moment, Channing had every piece.

I would get them back from that asshole somehow.

When I was ready. I had a few more tears to cry first.

"He said he loved me, Sin," I sniffed.

"He lied," Sienna sighed. "They always do. It's how they get what they want from us."

"But he told me *after* we had sex."

She shrugged. "I don't know what to say, Care. Have sex with someone else? I don't know. But if you—"

A soft knock at the door stopped her.

"Go away, Genevieve!" Sienna groaned. "We're not talking that loud!" This late at night, we were supposed to keep our conversations quiet. Another knock. Sienna slid off her bed. "Ugh! Will you get a life, Genny? Just because you have no one to talk to doesn't mean—" Sienna opened the door and stopped mid-sentence. "Channing? Get the fuck out of here, asshole! Do you have any idea what you did to Carol?!"

"Move." He pushed past her into the room.

"You can't be in here!" Genevieve suddenly shouted from the hallway. "I'm calling campus security!"

Channing stalked toward my bed.

"What're you doing here?" I gasped.

"Taking you with me."

"What?!"

He leaned down and scooped me up, pungent beer breath blowing over my face.

"Are you drunk?!" I demanded.

"Slightly."

"Put me down," I laughed nervously.

"No." He turned toward the door with me in his arms.

"Where in fuck do you think you're going with her?" Sienna demanded, standing in the doorway with her baseball bat at the ready.

"To fuck the living shit out of the woman I love."

"Rape!" Genevieve shouted hysterically. "Kidnapping, rape!"

"Quiet, Genny," Sienna ordered. "Nobody is raping anybody unless it's over my dead body."

I wasn't sure what to do. The only thing I was afraid of was having the pieces of my already broken heart pounded into dust by Channing before I could take them all back.

Sienna frowned shrewdly at Channing, "How many times?"

"How many times what?"

"How many times are you going to have sex with Carol?" It was a serious question.

"As many as she'll let me."

"I need a number, Channing," Sienna said.

"A million? I suck at math. How many times can two people have sex with each other in one lifetime?"

"Right answer." A huge smile eased onto Sienna's face and she lowered the bat, stepping out of Channing's way.

He carried me toward the doorway.

"Are you kidnapping her?" Genny asked seriously.

"If she'll let me," Channing said to me. "Can I?"

"Yes," I grinned. "I give you permission."

"Good." He carried me down the hallway.

"I don't have any shoes!" I laughed.

"You don't need any. Unless you want to wear them during sex?"

"No, but how am I supposed to get home later without shoes?"

"Who says you're going back?"

"This is where I live, Channing!"

"Not anymore you don't." He kicked open the door at the end of the corridor and started down the stairwell. "From now on, you're living with me."

"Are you serious?" I laughed, hugging his muscled neck and shoulders as I bounced slightly against his chest with each downward step.

"Yes. Completely."

"But my stuff. My clothes, my books. I can't study without my books."

"We'll get everything tomorrow. Tonight, we fuck until we can't come any more."

"Okay," I giggled.

\#

&

&*&

&*&*&

&*&*&*&

M

"Everything okay, miss?" asked the campus bicycle cop as Channing carried me down the long walkway outside the main library where the fountain was lit up for the night.

"I'm fine," I giggled in Channing's arms.

"She's fine," Channing chuckled. "Finest girl at KCU."

"Be safe," the cop grinned.

"How far is it?" I asked Channing.

"Halfway across campus."

"You can't carry me that far! It's half a mile!"

"I can and I will. Only problem is, I don't have any condoms in my dorm room. Where can we get some this late? Student health is probably closed. Isn't there some pharmacy near campus? A 24-hour CVS or something?"

"Don't bother."

"Why not? Don't you want to have sex tonight?"

"I do. I went on the pill."

"When?"

"After we had sex."

"Why?"

"Because I wanted to. For us."

"So that means…"

"We can have sex without a condom," I giggled shyly.

"Are you serious?"

"Yes. You can come inside me all night long."

Channing's eyes lit up and he started running.

\#

&

&*&

&*&*&

&*&*&*&
M

CHANNING

Once we were inside an elevator at Faulkner Hall, I used my room key to activate the button for Penthouse. Then I repositioned Carol so she was straddling me, her legs wrapped around my waist. I was sweating through my T-shirt from the run, but I barely noticed because Carol was grinding my dick while we kissed.

The elevator went straight up to the top floor without stopping. The doors dinged open and I walked out, carrying Carol while we continued kissing.

I had never been more fucking turned on in my life.

Victoria Bissette couldn't hold a candle, not even a wet match, to cute little Carol Duffey.

Call it chemistry, I don't know.

But it was real.

"I love you so fucking much," I grunted as our tongues lashed together.

"Oh, Channing," Carol gasped in my mouth.

I wasn't going to ruin the moment by asking her to say it back. When I got to my room, I opened it without a key because I never locked it. You couldn't get to the top floor without an elevator key like mine.

"We're home," I said as I carried Carol over the threshold.

She turned her head, "What the hell?! This is your dorm room?"

"You like it?"

"How many rooms do you have?"

"Living room, kitchen, bedroom, bathroom. That's it."

"That's *it*?" Carol laughed. "It's like having your own apartment. I share a room with Sienna and I share the bathroom with every girl on our floor."

"Not anymore," I grinned. It wasn't luxurious, but compared to a standard plain dorm room, I guess it was.

"Do I get a tour?"

"Sure." I carried her into the kitchen, flipped on the over-bright fluorescent light and set her on the counter. "Welcome to the kitchen. You need any water? I'm dying after that run."

"And all the beer you drank. Where were you?"

"TT's. Never mind that." I filled a glass and pounded it. I'd already pissed back at TT's before leaving. I would've sprung a leak if I hadn't. I filled a second glass from the faucet. "Want some?"

"I'm good."

I pounded the glass and slammed it on the counter. Planted both arms around Carol where she sat and stared at her hungrily.

"What?" Her eyes danced.

"These are coming off," I growled and practically tore her sweats and panties down to her ankles, leaving them there. I squatted underneath and pushed my head up between her bound legs.

"What're you doing?" she gasped.

"What I've waited two weeks to do." I picked her ass up off the counter with both hands.

"Wait, Channing!" She was holding her body off the counter on trembling arms.

"Don't worry, I've got you." I dove for her dripping pussy.

"Ohmygod," she moaned.

Her pussy was a hot feast of sweet honey. And no, she didn't taste like honey. She tasted better. I ate her until she came all over my face. While she recovered on the counter and caught her breath, I ripped my jeans and boxers down, leaving my boots on.

"You're on the pill, right?"

"Yes," she nodded, propped up on her elbows. "Go crazy."

I peeled off her shoes, sweats, panties. "Look at that fucking pussy."

"You can do more than look," Carol grinned.

"Yeah." My entire awareness tunneled down to her wet pussy. "So beautiful." I grabbed my dick and slid it up and down her slippery slit, which shocked the tip of my dick. I groaned.

"Oh, Channing," Carol moaned, eyelids fluttering.

When I started a slow slide inside, my head exploded.

I didn't come.

Not even close.

Before heading over to TT's, I'd jerked off twice in preparation for Victoria. If I hadn't, one look from Victoria would've made me come, or so I'd thought. Now I knew the real reason I was hard.

Speaking of Carol's perfect pussy, it was killing me with pleasure.

I couldn't explain it better than that.

Like an electric chair.

My dick was sizzling with every thrust.

I couldn't think about anything other than thrusting.

No wonder men hated condoms.

I hated everything in the universe that wasn't me fucking Carol without one.

The longer we fucked, the louder we got.

I grunted with every thrust and she squealed.

My orgasm built to bursting. My dick would have if Carol's tight pussy hadn't been squeezing so hard.

When we came together, I roared and she screamed.

"Come inside me, Channing! Come as hard as you can!"

Every muscle in my body and hers tensed together, wrapping us in an insane knot of erotic heat and release.

I felt myself firing into her, straining to get even deeper, felt her pussy pulsating like it was trying to pull me farther inside and suck the cum out of my cock. Later I would realize it had been doing exactly that, yearning for my sperm, drinking every lost drop of cum I had and gladly gave.

After, we reveled in a sex fest of historic proportions, christening every surface and piece of furniture in our apartment with dirty fucking animal sex.

Biggest surprise of all?

When Carol finally rode me like a wolf on my queen-sized bed, I came ten times harder than I had every time leading up to it put together. Something about relaxing and giving over control to Carol while she grunted and ground herself all over my cock made everything more intense. For both of us. She was screaming when she came.

Fucking.

Screaming.

Like she might rip my dick off.

Never felt anything like it.

Did I not tell you she was built for fucking?

And now she was all mine.

I was never letting go.

Chapter 19

CAROL

Two weeks later, my private paradise was shaken to its foundations by my former best friend while I was innocently wandering the stacks at the Steinbeck Library on campus, looking for a book by John Stuart Mill and one by Jeremy Bentham I needed to reference for an ethics paper I was writing about civil liberties within the framework of a free society.

I had my nose in the Bentham book when a familiar voice called my name.

"Carol?" Whitney Vinson, my former best friend.

I can only suggest an approximation of the sound of her saying my name: it was akin to someone dropping a box of glassware shattering at your feet.

"Whitney," I said with enough saccharin sweetness the FDA would never approve my smile because the preponderance of evidence suggested it caused cancer in whoever saw it, namely Whitney. That was my hope, anyway. I wasn't sure why I was still bitter. She and Evan Urleigh were two cheating peas in a pod, and I now had Channing.

"How have you been? It's been a long time."

Since you stole my boyfriend, I did not say. "It has been a long time." Have you seen my new boyfriend? He's like a marble Greek stature who makes yours look like a child's stick figure drawing.

For the next five minutes, I made painful smalltalk with Whitney, not once mentioning Channing. I wasn't a gloater.

"I hear you're dating Channing Peyton," she said finally.

"Oh? Where'd you hear that?" I asked innocently.

"Ask anyone. It's all over campus."

Genevieve. That bitch. She had in fact told everyone.

"Great," I grinned cancerously.

"I thought long and hard about telling you this," Whitney said ominously.

"Telling me what?" Would you like to know how long and hard Channing Peyton is, I did not ask. Do you think Evan can fuck as long and hard as he can? I already knew the answer to that. It took Evan less than a minute to come in his underwear while dry-humping my leg.

Whitney whispered, "I think Channing's cheating on you."

Did I not say, former friend? I scowled, "What are you talking about?"

Whitney whipped out her phone and showed me a picture. "This is Channing at some bar in Indiana when the Cheetahs played there. That's Victoria Bissette about to kiss him. She's the head of the cheerleaders."

"No it's not."

"See for yourself." She handed me her phone.

"How do you zoom in?"

Whitney did it for me. Back then, phone photos weren't the best. "See? That's him and her."

Ropes pulled my guts out of my body spilling onto the library floor between the stacks of books. Channing and Victoria, who looked like she should be Wonder Woman except better dressed, were less than an inch from kissing each other and looked incredibly happy about it. In the background were people drinking beer.

Whitney's phone slipped from my fingers and clattered against the vinyl tiles.

"My phone!" she snipped.

I didn't even hear her. War drums pounded in my ears. Ba-BOOM! Ba-BOOM! Ba-BOOM! It was my heart hammering with rage and pain at my betrayal.

"You almost broke it," Whitney vexed.

"Can you send me that photo to my phone?"

She sneered, "You almost broke my phone, Carol! I can't afford to buy a new one, you know."

"You *did* break my heart, Whitney. Twice. And nobody in the world can afford to buy me a new one of those. Send me the fucking photo already," I hissed.

"Okay," she whined.

#
&
&*&
&*&*&
&*&*&*&
M

"Hey, babe," Channing grinned. "Why is it so dark in here?"

I was waiting for him on the living room couch in his penthouse apartment. My arms were folded, and I was an ice block of frozen rage, my face cut and chiseled with cold hate. I'd been sitting here immobile for three hours, seemingly floating outside of my body while the sun sank over the horizon, chasing my heart into darkness. I was waiting for him to come home from football practice because I literally couldn't think about anything else. Every X-rated scenario you can imagine between Channing and Victoria had played through my imagination, each more vivid and painful than the last. On top of Victoria, I pictured Channing with every groupie on campus, like those girls outside the stadium the day I'd gone looking for Channing back when.

Now, light from the hallway outside poured into the waking nightmare I'd been living since Whitney had shown me the photo.

Channing flipped on the lights. "What's wrong?"

"Tell me about Victoria Bissette." My voice was chill fury, a cold wind slapping him in the face.

"The captain of the cheerleaders?"

"Did you kiss her in Indiana?"

"What?!" he chuckled.

"Tell the truth."

"No. Why would I kiss Victoria? I love you."

"I don't know what you do on your road trips, but I know you go to bars with Victoria and kiss her."

"Kiss her? I never kissed her." He sounded absolutely genuine.

"You are a fucking liar, Channing Peyton."

He closed the door gently. "What's going on? I never kissed Victoria. This isn't making any sense."

"Liar!" I jumped up from the couch and thrust my phone in his face, showing the bar photo. "Look at the truth, Channing! Don't deny it."

"Let me see that." He walked closer. "May I?"

I hmphed and handed him the phone.

He frowned. "Is this supposed to be Indiana?"

"You tell me."

"That's not Indiana."

"Where is it then? Iowa? Where you played last week?"

"No. It's TT's."

"What?"

"Tipple Town. Haven't you been there?"

"I have no idea what you're talking about."

"The bar near campus? Tim's Tipple Town? You've never been?"

"I'm not twenty-one."

"Neither am I. I get in with a fake ID. Everyone does. That's where this photo was taken."

"Oh, so you did it right under my nose? That's great, Channing. *Just* great!"

"Carol. Listen to me. This photo is from the night I brought you here, the night we had sex."

"You kissed this bitch the same night *we* had sex?!" I was shaking with blood red rage and ready to grab kitchen knives and start slicing.

"I never kissed her. I almost did. I told myself I didn't have time in my life for love. Only sex. I thought Victoria could give me that."

"I gave you sex *before* that! Then you disappeared while I went on the pill for you! Did *she* do that for you?!"

"I have no idea what she did. I needed to get my head on straight, after you and I had sex the first time. When I got it together, I came back for you and gave you love in return. How many times have I told you I loved you since you moved in two weeks ago?"

"Every time you come you tell me! Like some sick joke! It's disgusting, Channing!" I was frightened, angry, and hormonal, a blue-ribbon recipe for insanity if there ever was one.

"How many times have you told me you loved me, Carol?"

"I don't know!"

"Zero."

"So what?! You were at that bar with Victoria! You were! You! That's not love!"

"You're right. Because it never happened. I love *you*, Carol. You don't have to say it back. You could never say it *ever*, and I'll still say it every minute of every day. Anything to convince you of the truth. The last girl I kissed before you was freshman year. That was long before you. I never kissed Victoria and never will. I've only had sex with you and only love you." He grabbed both my hands in his big ones. "Please believe me. I wouldn't ever do anything to hurt you." He really did sound completely genuine.

I sniffed back tears, smeared them off my cheeks.

"Do you believe me?" he asked hopefully.

"I want to," I sniffed.

"I'd never lie to you, Care. I'm telling the truth. Who told you this anyway?"

"My ex best friend." I hadn't told him about Whitney or Evan because there hadn't been time and they weren't my favorite topic. Since Channing and I had been living together, there had been a tremendous amount of sex and not enough talking. I was as much to blame for that as Channing. He may as well know. "Evan, my ex, cheated on me with my ex best friend Whitney. I dumped him when I found out."

"Who would cheat on you?" Channing laughed.

"It's not funny," I blurted.

"Yeah it is. Any guy who cheats on you is fucking stupid. What a fucking idiot. You're gorgeous. Was the guy fucking blind?"

"I wouldn't have sex with him," I huffed. "So he had sex with my best friend. She was the one who told me about you and Victoria."

"What does that tell you? Other than, you can't trust what she says?"

I sighed. "You're right."

The surprise was how jealous I felt. I'd never been jealous of Evan. Not once. And look how that turned out. Maybe deep down I knew that nobody except Whitney and me had wanted Evan. He was no one to be jealous of. But millions of women wanted Channing. I still struggled with the question of why he'd possibly want *me*, when not even Evan Urleigh wanted me, which made zero sense when you took half a glance at Channing naked. Channing wanted me. What was Evan's problem? Not that I cared anymore.

"I'm so sorry," I whispered. "I'm being really insecure and jealous about this. You, you're *amazing* Channing. I don't want to lose you. I don't think I could handle it if I did." Saying that out loud was akin to peeling back my skin to show my vulnerable beating heart to the entire world, a world with its claws at the ready to shred it.

"You'll never lose me, Care. I will always be here for you."

Later, after he soothed me for another hour and I finally calmed, we made quiet love that night, snuggling into each other like warm blankets in winter beside an open fire. When we came together it was different. A relaxing sweet release of orgasmic passion, a warm sauna of two bodies in slow sexual motion. It was also an emotional orgasm, something I'd never experienced before, feelings that swept over me in tingling waves as powerful as the physical one, amplifying both into a mysterious other that was more addictive than fucking.

It truly was making love.

Honestly, it was nearly overwhelming and brought me to tears. While he was still pulsing inside me, I cried quietly and whispered a secret in his ear. "I love you, Channing Peyton. I love you so much it hurts."

He kissed my tears away and told me a dozen times he loved me too.

This time, I believed him completely.

At that moment, I vowed to myself I'd never doubt his love ever again.

Chapter 20

CAROL

The rest of our sophomore year was an unrelenting festival of sex, drugs, and rock & roll.

Okay, only the sex part.

But my oh my, did we have a lot of sex.

The only reason I managed to pass my classes was Channing's insane schedule. During football season, he really was incredibly busy. Some nights, we only saw each other while sleeping.

Those nights, I woke more than once to find Channing inside me or beneath the sheets eating me alive. Either worked. Surprise orgasms were the best. Waking while having one was even better. It would start with an incredible sex dream that became real. The dreams didn't always involve Channing (don't tell him that!), but they always ended with him inside me. Always.

On the off season, his schedule was almost as busy, and he trained five days a week with the Cheetahs. Somehow he found time in his crazy schedule to do the sweetest thing for our first Valentine's Day together.

Going out, neither of us knew that dinner at a restaurant on Valentine's Day would be like being herded in and out of a pig trough with hundreds of other heart-eyed couples, all of us squeezed shoulder-to-shoulder in tiny two-person tables with slow service and limited menu options.

We didn't care.

We were in love.

Just for fun, I'd gone shopping with Mom the weekend before to pick out a Valentine's dress because I didn't have anything suitable. Never went to a single prom in high school. Ironically, Mom and I ended up renting me a short prom dress from a bridal store for forty bucks. Mom also helped me do my hair. She had decades of practice doing her own before she started wearing hers shorter like she did now. Mom did my makeup too. It was the first time Mom and I had truly bonded over girl time.

"You are gorgeous, Carol," Mom had gushed after finishing my face. "Isn't she gorgeous, Jack?"

Dad was peeking in and got all weepy. "You look just like your mother. My two angels."

"Daaaaad," I had laughed, embarrassed.

Then Channing came over to pick me up. He sat in the living room chatting with Dad while Mom put on the finishing touches and I walked out, giving a grand entrance in our little house, like the prom I never had.

Channing took one look at me and groaned, "Every time I see you Carol, you get more and more gorgeous."

"I like him," Mom laughed. "Jack, have I told you how much I like this boy?" It wasn't their first time meeting him. I'd already brought Channing home twice prior to Valentine's Day to have dinner with Mom & Dad. They liked him from word one.

"He's a good kid," Dad agreed, hands in his pockets.

Channing walked me out to a brand new Ford Mustang. Not one of the plain ones. One of the expensive ones. Even if you didn't know cars, you could totally tell it had all the extras and then some.

"Nice car," I grinned. "Is this yours?"

"Is now," Channing said proudly.

"Did you rent it for tonight?"

"Nope. It's all mine."

"How long have you had it?" I didn't remember him having a car before now.

"Just got it."

"Wow, Channing. It looks super expensive. How did you pay for something this nice?"

He shrugged, not answering.

"Did your parents pay for it? It's totally okay if they did. I won't judge. I'm sure mine would buy me a new car if they could afford it. Is that it? Did they buy it for you?"

Channing was smirking. "Can we not talk about the car?"

"So they *did* pay for it?"

"Let me get your door for you." Channing rushed over to the passenger side, dodging past me and my question before opening the door.

"It's no big deal, Channing. Just tell me. Channing?"

He bit a hiss.

"Why are you acting so weird?"

"It's Valentine's Day. I'm nervous." His lips were tight over clenched teeth.

Was he hiding something?

"Can we just go, Care? Please? We'll be late for our reservations."

"Sure," I nodded quizzically and got in the car.

When Channing got in, grabbed my hand, and leaned over to kiss me, I forgot all about the car.

Now at the restaurant, silverware and plates clinked around us, the constant hum of everyone's conversation the only thing offering any sense of privacy.

"You look so good in a jacket and tie," I said to Channing. He had a substantial formal wardrobe because of various football non-game events he attended.

"Thanks. Your dress is fucking hot. I've been hard since you walked into the living room back at your parents' house," he grinned across the table. "This is the first time I've ever seen your hair up."

"Do you like it?"

"Love it." He smiled. "And I love you."

"I love you too."

He reached into his jacket. "I got something for you."

"You did? I didn't get you anything! We didn't say anything about gifts! Channing!"

"It's totally cool. It's for both of us, really."

"What is it?"

"Open it." He handed me a small package wrapped in red.

"Is it a book? It looks like a book."

"Just open it."

I peeled the paper back carefully, not wanting to make a mess in the restaurant. "This is nice. Is it a journal? Did you get me a new journal?" I grinned, appreciating the beautifully bound book.

"Sort of. Look inside."

I opened to the first page.

"Read the inscription."

I did.

Channing's clumsy handwriting said:

To Carol, the love of my life. I will always hold your heart safe because I've given you mine. Your love story is now our love story.
Love forever, Channing

My eyes were tearing when I looked at the title topping the first hand-written page.

The Football Games

I scanned the familiar first lines.

"This is my story," I said.

"*Our* story," Channing grinned.

"You re-wrote it."

"The one in your journal was marked up and scratched out."

I nodded, "Because I made so many changes."

"I wrote it out nice."

"This is your handwriting?"

"Yeah."

"It's beautiful." It really was.

"I also added back the two pages I ruined."

"What? How? I thought you threw them out."

"They were still in my trash can at home after I gave your journal back. I fished them out and saved them."

"Weren't they… gross?"

He shrugged, "I copied down what was on them into my laptop before throwing them away."

"You did that?"

"Yup," he nodded. "Then I wrote it all out in that journal. But I got a long one so we could add to it. Your story didn't have an ending. Now we can write it together."

I hugged the journal to my chest, my eyes watering. "Ohmygod, Channing. This is," I sniffed. "I don't know what to say."

"Say we'll finish the story together." He offered a warm grin.

"What are you saying?" I was shaking.

"I'm saying we have a lot of story left to write and I want you to write it with me."

I suddenly hated the crowded restaurant. I wanted to throw myself into Channing's arms, hugging him and kissing him all over. I had to settle for reaching across the table and holding his hand.

"I love you, Carol Duffey."

"I love you too, Channing Peyton."

"Always and forever."

"Same."

\#

&

&*&

&*&*&

&*&*&*&

M

It was a huge relief that Channing didn't fly back home to his parents for the summer. I couldn't have gone three months not seeing him.

The reason?

He stayed in King City to keep training for the fall season. Normally, I would've gone home for the summer to live with my parents, but Channing had his penthouse apartment year-round, so I stayed with him and visited Mom and Dad on weekends.

I finally got over my fear of TT's, the place where "the other woman" had never kissed him. I also got over my fear of having a fake ID. Turned out Tim Jr., the disabled owner, really didn't care. He never carded anybody. Channing and I spent quite a bit of his minimal free time there, drinking and socializing with his friends and mine.

Sienna took a platonic liking to Channing, and he to her. He always called her Sin like I sometimes did. They bonded over the pleasure of pussy. Sienna knew a thing or two about how to give oral to women, having done it herself, and gave Channing plenty of tips for *my* enjoyment. Let me just say, Sienna was a good coach. They also made a competition out of telling each other the raunchiest sexual jokes you can imagine (some quite funny), always trying to top each other.

I made friends with Lashawn Washington. He was a very nice guy who I decided harbored a secret crush on Iesha Taylor, one of the Cheetahs cheerleaders. Whenever she wasn't looking, his eyes were always on her. When she was, they had more chemistry than a mad scientist's laboratory, but he couldn't take the essential next step for whatever reason. Give them time.

For me and Channing, things couldn't be better.

The arrival of our junior year brought with it our one year anniversary. Our relationship was going strong, sailing on the seas of love in the USS Sex & Romance. Channing and I were shipping heavily long before that became a trendy term.

Our biggest challenge?

Women never stopped throwing themselves at Channing and I saw it constantly. It was always worse during football season. Whether it was groupies mobbing him at games, or randomly on campus, or everywhere we went, even off campus.

There was a shopping district within walking distance of Faulkner Hall. Channing and I would often go down to window shop and sip hot macchiatos. There, I would see grown women flirt shamelessly with Channing in the shops and boutiques, especially when I wasn't glued to his side.

The minute I walked away to look at a handbag or try on a dress I couldn't afford, there would always be a random sales girl or customer talking to him with their boobs. Like shit flies hovering around my sweet honey.

It took some getting used to.

Surprise, my jealous side could be a bit bitchier than I expected. Some days, I was the Queen Hyena. I did my best to keep the hooting barks to myself. On the plus side, it wasn't constant. It cycled. Guess why.

Sienna did a lot to help me deal with my on-again off-again monthly jealousy. We didn't talk as much as we had living in the same dorm room, but I made sure to eat lunch with her twice a week without fail, and I'd study with her in her dorm room or in the Steinbeck Library on the weekends when Channing was out of town for an away game.

"How much sex are you guys having?" Sienna asked with a laugh one lunch. We'd met up between classes at the student center.

"Not so loud," I muttered, feigning embarrassment.

"How much," she demanded.

"Twice a day? Three times? More if we have time."

"I've done that. How many times a week? Every day?"

I nodded. "Is that normal?"

"Do you ever miss a day?"

"Only when he's at an away game. Otherwise, yeah, pretty much every day."

"For an entire year?" Sienna was aghast.

I nodded. "Is that bad?"

"That's like a thousand times so far."

"Probably more," I shrugged, sipping Pepsi through my straw.

"You have had more sex in a year than I've had total. *Total*, Carol. Total in my entire life. And I've been having sex for a long time, every chance I get. You've had *more*."

I blushed guiltily and sipped my drink.

"Normally, people slow down after six months. It's like a thing. The six month slump. From then on, you have less and less sex. If you stay together long enough, supposedly you don't have any at all."

"We've been having more and more," I snickered. "I can only imagine how much we'll have once we graduate."

"I hate you, Carol! I want your sex life!"

"Would you be quiet?! People are staring!"

She didn't care. "Can I have it? Can you give it to me?"

"I'm not giving you Channing," I laughed.

"I don't want him! Just the sex. Can you sign it over somehow? Like in a contract? You're pre-law. Don't they have a contract for that?" She was laughing too.

"Maybe if you stuck with one person, you'd have more sex."

"What would be the fun in that?" she snorted.

One fun thing that happened?

Evan Urleigh came crawling back.

Turned out, Whitney dumped him for another guy. Poor Evan. I've heard just desserts are always served spoiled. Anyway, he missed the campus-wide announcement that Channing and I were a thing. It seemed like everybody knew except him. We bumped into each other passing between classes one day.

"Hey, Carol," Evan said. "Long time no see. You're looking good."

"Hey, Evan," I sighed, trying to be polite. I'd rather talk to an oyster than Evan Urleigh.

He projected loneliness like a lighthouse on a tiny rock island off the coast of Dumptown. I almost felt bad for him. I'd never be lonely again. We chatted for a few difficult minutes before he got down to business.

"Did you hear I'm not with Whitney anymore?" He dropped the hint like a bag of groceries, an emotional mess spilling out of him.

"Nope." I swung my head and my ponytail swung too, missing the hint by a mile.

"Yeah. I'm single now."

"Good for you, Evan," I nodded, still purposefully missing hints. His persistence required I jump over the rotten tomatoes rolling out of his pathetic attempt at reconciliation. Read: trying to get back in my pants, which were fully and permanently filled by Channing, thank you very much.

Evan slumped, "Whitney sort of dumped me."

"You don't say," I smirked. "That's terrible—"-ly fantastic! Haw! Haw! Haw! I didn't laugh at him. I stood there stoically.

"Maybe we could get lunch some time?" he ventured with his customary timid precision. "Patch things up?"

I was about to explain that patches couldn't mend broken hearts when Channing walked up and put his arm around me.

"Hey, babe. Who's this?"

"This is Evan. You remember I told you about Evan?" Eventually, I had given Channing the full story in bits and pieces over the past year. Pumpa, pumpa, pumpa. Glorg! He also knew all about Whitney-It's-not-what-you-think!-Vinson, and vowed that if he ever met her, he'd shamelessly flaunt his abs at her, per my request.

"Yeah, yeah. I remember all about Evan." Channing grinned and extended his hand. "Channing Peyton."

"I know." Evan sniffed and shook hands. His looked very small inside Channing's.

"Her boyfriend," Channing added.

"I didn't know that."

"Who else would I be?" Channing grinned.

Evan's face dehydrated like an old apple.

I wanted to laugh.

Through thin lips, Evan said, "Great season so far this year."

"*Perfect* season," Channing added. "Won every game two years running, and we'll do it again this year, I'm thinking. Go to the Rose Bowl, a-*gain*. How about that?" Channing was gloating. "Not bad, huh?"

"Too bad you lost the Rose Bowl last year. A second time." Evan said it with the slightest snideness.

"You win some, you lose some."

They were dueling.

It was amusing. There was no way Evan would win, even if he was right about the Rose Bowl, which was a sore point with Channing, the entire Cheetahs team, the rest of KCU, half of King City, and a third of the state. Most everyone was a fan. I had tried telling Channing many times it didn't matter, that simply *getting* to the Rose Bowl was victory enough. He wouldn't hear it.

"We'll win this one," Channing growled.

"There are no guarantees," Evan chuckled, biting on his annoyed irritation. "You have to get there first."

"We will. You know what, Ev?"

"What?"

"We should get you on the field to help out. We need every *man* we can get. You look wiry, Ev, like you might be fast on your feet. Ever think about special teams?"

"Oh, I couldn't," Evan laughed, believing Channing meant it. Channing had that effect on people. He inspired them.

"You couldn't, could you?" Channing grinned, ripping the rug out from under poor Evan.

Evan's smile crumpled.

Channing's smiled blossomed, "Thanks for cheating on my girlfriend, Ev. Couldn't have happened to a nicer guy."

"Who, me?"

"No, me." Channing put his arm around my shoulders and led me away. "Catch you later, Ev!"

At that point, I think a waiter arrived with a silver plater full of crows for Evan to eat. Hours later, Evan was still standing their dumbly, chomping on dry feathers, trying to swallow them down without any luck.

Had Evan been in Pasadena, California that January to watch the Cheetahs lose their third Rose Bowl in a row, he would've been handing Channing the platter, but I would've been there to beat Evan over the head with it and chase him off.

Nobody made my boyfriend feel bad about himself.

After losing that third Rose Bowl and returning to King City, it was a dark few weeks of me cheering up Channing. It was also the week I discovered how effective lingerie could be for cheering up a sad man.

Thank Sienna for taking me shopping at Victoria's Secret and making me buy practically one of everything.

Other than that minor blip, the rest of junior year and the summer after was a season of continued bliss. Channing and I were inseparable. Our sex life hadn't slowed. In fact, the lingerie and other bedroom games had sped it up. But it wasn't just about sex for us. Not anymore.

Channing and I started talking about life after college, about me picking a law school based on which NFL team picked him. He insisted I would handle all his contracts so nobody took advantage of his money, that he would never trust anyone as much as he trusted me. I can't tell you how honored and flattered I was that he put so much faith in me, in us. We talked about marriage, of me being an NFL wife, of having a family. It seemed a foregone conclusion at that point. Channing eventually wanted kids as much as I did. Now both our lives were on the same glide path to success and satisfaction.

Not only did it pay to be Channing Peyton, it paid to be his wife, he was fond of saying. Not that I wanted his money. I just wanted his love, and he gave me a treasure trove of that.

We would have sailed off into the sunset of a happy ending if senior year didn't happen.

But it did.

That year, the merry-go-round of our lives decided to spin wildly out of control and throw us in different directions forever.

If only I could go back in time and change things.

Sadly, wishing never fixed anything.

Chapter 21

CAROL

The muggy summer weather forced its way through screen doors and open windows, pestering the populace of King City to the bitter end of September. Summer never left quietly. Every fall, King City kicked it out on the butt end of a thunderstorm. The crackle of lightning this year should've given me a clue that things were about to break.

Good luck can't last.

The truth always comes out.

People closest to it are often the last to know.

I was no exception.

I ignored the warning sounds, the rollercoaster clanking during our ascent to the peak of relationship perfection. I was too busy enjoying the view to notice the swift descent into disaster just over the horizon and the catastrophic end awaiting me at the bottom of a deep, dark pit.

\#

&

&*&

&*&*&

&*&*&*&

M

"SPORT THE WAR! WAR SUPPORT!
THE SPORT IS WAR, TOTAL WAR!"

Loud heavy metal music blasted through Channing's penthouse louder than a rock concert when I came home. Slayer, I think. He always listened to them and a bunch of other metal bands during the season. I didn't like it, but he loved it. Our compromise was that he used headphones when I was home. Since I was supposed to be in class, he had cranked it. Since class had been cancelled at the last minute, here I was.

"Channing! Can you turn it down!" I shouted as I closed the front door. The music boomed so loud I literally couldn't hear myself. "Channing?!"

When I got to the bathroom and saw Channing standing there in his boxers injecting something into his ass with a needle, I gasped. On the bathroom counter was a leather case with lots of vials and spare syringes.

I was horrified. "What are you doing?! Is that drugs?"

Channing looked up and his eyes head-lighted. He ripped out the needle and tossed it on the counter. He said something I couldn't hear over the Slayer.

I shook my head in disbelief, backing up slowly. "Are you a drug addict, Channing?"

He said something else, but again, the music was too loud.

I couldn't take anymore.

I turned and ran.

Channing caught up with me in the hallway halfway to the elevator, grabbing my arm. "Carol, stop! It's not what you think!"

Whitney Vinson had used those exact words and it *was* what I thought then, so it had to be what I thought now. "Yes it is!" I looked at his hand on my arm like it was poisonous. "Let go of me!" I yanked.

He released me. "Can we talk? In the apartment? Please? I can explain everything, Carol. It'll all make sense. I swear."

"Putting it into words doesn't make it better, Channing? What else have you been hiding? Victoria the cheerleader? Have you been hiding her too?!"

"What? No! There's only you, Carol. I love you."

"And your drugs!" I was freaking out. At that age, I'd never known a single person who put a needle into themselves on purpose. Not even a diabetic. I knew Channing wasn't diabetic and didn't have any other medical conditions. He was healthy as a horse. You didn't live with someone for almost two years without knowing that. For me, seeing him injecting himself in the ass meant heroin or something worse. If there was something worse. I didn't even know. Illegal drugs were so foreign to me.

"Please let me explain, Carol. Please."

I loved him too much to run away without letting him explain. I nodded solemnly. "Okay."

"I'll turn the music down." He rushed into the apartment and I followed.

"Can you turn it off?"

He did, then closed the door behind me. Led me over to the couch. Sat me down.

Said quietly, "It's steroids. Anabolic steroids. Where do you think I get my muscles from?"

"Working out. You lift weights *all* the time."

"Weights won't make me this big," he chuckled. "It's no big deal, Care. Half the guys in college football juice."

"No they don't! They have drug testing."

"Drug testing," Channing chuckled. "There's a hundred ways to beat those tests."

"You mean cheat them."

"How is it cheating if everyone does it?"

"So it's not murder if everyone is murdering?"

"That's called war."

"I'm serious, Channing!"

"About murder?" he snorted. "Who said anything about murder? It's just steroids."

"No, I'm making a point. Whether it's illegal steroids or murder, everyone doing a bad thing doesn't automatically make it a good thing. That's a basic tenet of any society. Everyone agrees some things are okay and other things aren't. In this country, everyone agrees drugs in sports are wrong. I can't believe I'm telling you this."

"The only thing anyone cares about in sports is winning."

"They care about cheating."

"It's not cheating," he sighed, exasperated. "We all do it!"

"Oh? Have you asked every single player in college sports if they do drugs?"

"It's not drugs, Care. It's steroids. You make it sound like it's heroin."

"You make it sound like it's a banana."

"What?" he chuckled. "That doesn't make any sense, Care."

"You can't just rename it and treat it like something else. Bananas are legal. Heroin is *illegal*. Steroids are *illegal*."

"No they aren't. My grandma takes steroids for her arthritis."

"Does she take them for her college football career?"

"Huh?"

"Heroin is an opiate. Opiate is used as a painkiller. It's only illegal when you use it how you're not supposed to. That's what you're doing, Channing. You're not supposed to use steroids for football! Don't try to convince me otherwise! Anything you say will just be rationalizations and convenient excuses to avoid an inconvenient truth."

My minor in Ethics suddenly had a real world application that I was not enjoying one bit.

Channing opened his mouth to argue, closed it with a sigh. Looked at his bare feet.

I said, "Is this why you've had so much acne since summer? You didn't used to."

"Yeah," he nodded shamefully.

"Why, Channing?"

He shook his head, "Last season wasn't easy. We almost lost the last two games because of me. Three years of this has taken its toll. I've got eight more games to get through this season. I feel like I need an edge. I'm feeling my age, Care."

"Your *age?*" I snorted. "You're twenty-two years old! Same as I am."

"You try playing four years of D-I ball," he glowered.

"I'm sorry. I know how hard it is on your body." I'd seen him get sacked on the field and the huge bruises afterward enough to know.

"Steroids help."

"But it's wrong," I squeaked.

"You think so." His brewing anger said he obviously didn't.

"I also know they're bad for you. How does that help your body?"

"That's propaganda. There's guy's who've used steroids for decades without any bad effects. The trick is not overdoing it. I'm just doing one cycle to get me through this season. That's it."

"That's it? You won't use them in the NFL?"

He glared at me. "What do you want me to do? Be a fucking lawyer?!" He shot to his feet. "I'm not you, Carol. I'm fucking dumb when it comes to school! But I'm a fucking genius at football!" There was no arguing that. "You try being a lawyer with a bunch of 300 pound gorillas trying to break your fucking neck!"

I sighed. "Is this what 'roid rage looks like?"

"What?"

"I've never seen you this angry."

"Yeah, because you're asking me to throw away my whole fucking life for some dumb fucking idea nobody agrees with except you!" There was terror in his eyes, not rage.

"Channing, I..." I didn't know what to say.

He stormed out of the room, went to the bedroom. Emerged wearing jeans and a Sepultura T-shirt, no shoes. He held jingling car keys.

"Where are you going?" I asked.

"Anywhere but here."

"You need shoes!" I called out the open apartment door.

"Fuck shoes," he grumbled without closing the door.

I almost chased after him.

Thought better of it because I had a lot of thinking to do.

\#

&

&*&

&*&*&

&*&*&*&

M

"So what if he is?" Sienna said. "As long as he doesn't get baby balls and grow man boobs, who cares?"

"Does that really happen?" I asked.

"I've seen pictures. But that takes a while. If he's just doing it once, so what? Seriously, Care. It doesn't matter." We were having lunch again at the Student Center, in a quiet corner away from the other tables and students where we could talk without anyone hearing.

"Don't you care that it's illegal?" I asked.

"Blow jobs are illegal in Georgia."

"What?"

"Look it up."

"You mean they *used* to be."

"Nope, still are."

"Still?"

She nodded. "If I lived there, I'd be locked up for life."

"Me too," I giggled guiltily.

She reached over our sandwiches and slapped me a high-five. "Did you know, in Wisconsin, it's illegal for a man to fire a gun while his woman is climaxing."

"You made that up," I laughed, trying to imagine it while nibbling on a potato chip.

"Yee-haw! She's a comin! Blam, blam, blam! My woman is a comin!" Sienna giggled, miming the shooting of two six-guns.

Also giggling, I said, "Sex is different than what Channing's doing. Sex is between two people in private."

"Not always," she grinned, gnoshing on a French fry. "Sometimes it's just begging for public spectacle."

I snickered. "You know what I mean. They ban them to keep things fair." I was talking about steroids but I was trying to not say it out loud in public overmuch. So was Sienna.

"Fair? How is it fair that you're prettier than me?"

"Am not," I snorted.

"Look in a mirror."

"You're pretty too."

"Okay, bad example. How is it fair that some guys are born stronger than others? Or faster? Or better at throwing a football? Is that fair?"

"People don't have any control over how they're born."

"Is it so bad that some people want a leg up to even the playing field?"

"But Channing's already at the top. Why does he need it? It's the other people on the bottom who need help."

"Too bad it's illegal for them to get help."

I winced. "I see your point."

"Tell Channing that."

"Maybe I should."

\#

&

&*&

&*&*&

&*&*&*&

M

That night, I was trying to sleep in bed alone and having no luck. Ever since I'd moved in with him, I'd discovered during Channing's away games that I couldn't sleep without him beside me. Not well, anyway.

Those times, I always knew he was coming home.

This time, I wasn't sure.

He'd been gone all day and hadn't answered his phone.

I was too worried to sleep.

Around 3:00am, the apartment door opened and I heard keys jingling on the kitchen counter.

"Channing?" I whispered, sliding out of bed in my KCU yoga pants and T-shirt.

He stood in the dark living room, a brooding shadow of silence, his chocolate eyes burning dimly brown.

"Channing? What's wrong?" I approached carefully.

"Where's my juice?" He sounded like an angry junky seething for a fix.

"In the refrigerator."

He shouldered past me into the kitchen, opened the fridge, and leaned down to look. "Where?"

"Right there. Next to the milk."

"Not my OJ. My steroids." He slammed the fridge door closed.

"Oh. They're right where you left them. Have you been drinking?"

"I was at TT's." He'd almost kissed Victoria Bissette at TT's back when. Sure, Channing and I had gone there many times since, as boyfriend-girlfriend, but for me, TT's would always be a place he went with Victoria first, the place he'd *almost* kissed her, and *might* kiss her again.

I tried not to let that frighten me and asked calmly, "What were you doing at TT's?"

"Drinking." He opened a cupboard, grabbed a plastic trash bag. He was making me nervous.

"Did you drive yourself home?"

"Yes."

"While drunk?"

"I'm not that drunk." He went into the bathroom and started pulling vials out of the leather case on the counter, jamming them in the trash bag.

"What are you doing?"

"What you asked," he grunted.

"You don't have to do that. I was talking to Sienna about it today and —"

"Did you tell her?" He stopped stuffing and hit me with a hard glare, his anger a dark hammer.

"I had to tell somebody. I needed to talk about it."

"She *goes* here." He meant KCU. "Why'd you tell her?"

"Who was I going to tell? My parents? Do you want them knowing you're on steroids?"

He clenched a grunt and continued shoving vials with feral fury.

"Stop, Channing. I decided it's okay for you to use steroids."

"*You* decided?"

"I, no, that came out wrong. I mean—"

"I know what you mean." The leather case now empty, he knotted the trash bag. "I need to go dump this somewhere." He grabbed his car keys from the counter where he'd left them.

"Channing, you don't have to do this."

"It's already done."

"I don't want you driving around this late when you've been drinking."

"I don't want you leaving me because I'm on fucking gym candy *one* time."

It took a moment to process what he'd said. "I'd never do that."

"You didn't sound like it earlier. You sounded like you wanted to turn me in to the cops yourself."

"Why would you ever think that?"

"Because my mom almost left my dad over football. Football wives leave all the time. Same with football girlfriends. Football fucks up relationships. It's a given. I see it with guys on the team. None of them can keep a girlfriend for long. I'm trying to hold back disaster as long as I can."

"So you're getting rid of your steroids for... me?"

He smirked, "Who the fuck else, Care? I love you. I don't want to lose you any sooner than I have to. Is that ethical enough for you?"

"I'm not leaving you, Channing."

"You might. So this shit goes in the trash." He held up the bag of vials.

I suddenly felt incredibly grateful and like a complete ass. "I'm so sorry, Channing. I was being ridiculous. If you want to use the steroids, just for this season, it's okay. I did some research on the internet. It sounds like it won't hurt you if you do it just once. I just don't want you getting hurt permanently. Or in trouble with the school or the police."

He shook his head. "Losing you isn't worth the risk."

"Oh, Channing." I opened my arms to him and we hugged. "I love you so much. You have no idea how much."

That night, I drove him in his Mustang to a distant neighborhood that had unlit alleys between houses. Beneath power poles and hickory trees, we found a random trash can and threw the steroid bag inside.

Back home, we lay in bed together, for once not having sex. I cuddled against Channing and told him a thousand times I'd never leave him, not for any reason.

After the 1,000 and 1st time I'd said it, he whispered, "You're the only thing that really matters to me, Care. I'll be too old for football someday, but I'll never be too old for you."

"You might," I teased.

"Never," he grinned. "When you're old and wrinkled, I'll still fuck you until we both come."

"Care to give me a demonstration?" I giggled, reaching down to grab his growing length.

"With pleasure."

We made sweet love that night and fell asleep in each other's arms after the second time coming for both of us.

Channing was insatiable.

Good thing I was too.

He would blindside me with a break up three months later.

Chapter 22

CAROL

"And now," the announcer said in a rolling voice, "I am proud to announce, this year's winner of the Heisman Trophy is... Channing Peyton of King City University!"

Applause from the audience as Channing jumped up from where he sat in his suit in the front row of the luxurious PlayStation Theater with several other Heisman candidates. The theater was in Manhattan, in Times Square no less. We had flown in together two nights ago and stayed in a skyscraper hotel nearby. Lots of sex ensued. Yesterday, even though it had been another cold day in December, we went to Rockefeller Center to see the gigantic Christmas tree, and to Central Park with Channing's parents, where we warmed ourselves up touring the museums. His parents had flown in with us but had a separate room. On a separate floor, per Channing's orders. Not blushing! I didn't want them hearing us either.

His parents sat next to me in the front row across the aisle from where Channing had been sitting. Channing's mom Karen and I wore fancy evening dresses, and his dad Lee wore a tux, same as everyone else here.

When Channing had seen me walk out of the hotel bathroom in my dress earlier this evening, he'd said, "Your black dress looks like an explosion at a diamond mine. It's all black widow silk and defiance." I had thanked him with an impressed laugh and asked what book he'd stolen that line from. He said Broken Lion, the romance novel I'd brought to read on the plane. He admitted to reading it over my shoulder during the flight, and reminded me he sucked at math, not English. He was right about that, and I was impressed he remembered the line. I'd forgotten it already.

While the Heisman crowd cheered, I waited while Channing hugged his parents.

"I'm so proud of you, Channing," Karen cried, hugging her son fiercely.

"I knew you'd do it," Lee grunted approval, shaking Channing's hand hard, pumping it with enough force to bring up a geyser of well water if Channing had been attached to the ground. Don't let Lee's gruff exterior fool you. He was holding back enough tears for that geyser. I could see them shimmering in his eyes.

Channing turned to me. Hugged me with an exaggerated clap that was nothing like him, and whispered in my ear, "You're the real prize, Care. I'd give all this up for you in the blink of an eye."

I sniffed back my tears while he jogged onto the stage. Channing had told me the Heisman was the Nobel Prize of college football, given to the most valuable player in the entire country that year. The two other candidates here at the theater vying for the trophy were both incredible too, a running back from Texas A&M, and another quarterback from Florida State. Both had very impressive records, but Channing was always a little bit more incredibly impressive than anyone else.

On stage, he shook hands with a lineup of previous trophy winners, some quite old, then he stepped to the podium and thanked the suited members of the Heisman Trophy Trust, the two other candidates, who he'd played against during the regular season, two of his coaches from KCU sitting behind his parents, and three teammates sitting in the back and hooting "Chandy Man!" whenever Channing paused in his emotional speech.

"Most of all," Channing sniffed. "I want to thank Mom and Dad for never giving up on me, for making so many sacrifices in their lives so I could be here."

When I looked over, tears were streaming down Karen's face. Lee was fighting them back so hard his face was red.

"I put you both through hell to get here," Channing said, his tears starting to fall. "You guys taught me the meaning of loyalty. It means never giving up on someone you love even when you can't stand them." He said it with a tearful laughing grin.

Karen laughed through her tears and nodded, squeezing Lee's hand.

That broke him. Lee hitched and heaved, unable to control himself, sobbing in sniffing gasps, hiding his eyes and tears with his free hand.

"I love you Mom, Dad," Channing said, sniffing back his own. Then he looked right at me. "I love you too, Carol. I'll never give up on you. I'll never stop fighting for you."

While a man on stage led Channing over to the Heisman trophy, which he picked up from the stand and held over his head to a round of cheering applause, Karen reached over Lee and squeezed my knee. Smiling affectionately, she said, "Don't give up on my son, Carol. He can't say it so I will. Don't give up on him. He loves you with all his heart."

I balled.

It was the happiest day of our lives.

#

&

&*&
&*&*&
&*&*&*&
M

"I'll take another slice of your mother's amazing fruit cake," Lee Peyton said from across the table, winking at me, then Mom. His wife Karen sat next to him, Channing sat next to me, and my parents were at either end of their dining room table, which had been covered in a linen table cloth and Mom's finest china.

"Sure," I said, sawing off another slice of Mom's moist and juicy fruitcake with the bread knife on the platter. "Here you go."

We had just finished Christmas dinner, and the table was now covered with Mom's infamous cakes and cookies. Channing and Lee had eaten half of them already.

Inviting his parents to my parents' house had been Channing's idea. Since mine hadn't been there for the Heisman ceremony (they couldn't afford the trip to New York or the time off work), we had agreed to have Christmas dinner here. Fortunately, it had fallen on the one day Channing didn't have practice. The Rose Bowl was just around the corner, and it would be Channing's last before he graduated next year.

The team was nervous about Channing's three-bowl losing streak. This would be his last chance to finally win a Rose Bowl. If he could. No matter how well he played during the regular season, he could never quite get it together for the Rose Bowl. It's like he was cursed. There was even talk amongst the coaches of him not starting as quarterback, of letting Matt Budd, the second string QB, take over for him.

Lee said confidently, "You'll win the Rose Bowl next week, son, and after that, National Championships. Right?"

"Oh, Lee," Karen said. "Don't put so much pressure on him. He just won the Heisman trophy."

"I know, Karen, but he's taken the Cheetahs to the Rose Bowl three times already and lost. Last year, you said third time would be the charm. It wasn't." Sensing the tension, Lee joked to the table, "Can someone charm the Rose Bowl for me? We really need a win."

"I'll get my magic wand," I giggled.

"Please do," Lee laughed.

Karen rolled her eyes.

I found myself remembering what Channing had said about loyalty during his acceptance speech. It was obvious Karen worked hard to tolerate Lee's intensity regarding his son.

"You should be proud of Channing," Dad said. "Your son has done something no player has ever done. Taken his team through a perfect season *and* to the post season Rose Bowl four years in a row. He has the Heisman. What more do you need?"

"I know, I know," Lee nodded vigorously. "But if he could just *win* once, what a finish that would be! You don't even have to win the National Championship, Channing." Lee pleaded across the table. "Just get there. That's all I ask!" He couldn't let it go.

"More fruitcake, Lee?" Mom asked. "I see you already finished your second slice."

"How can I say no?" Lee laughed.

"Carol, cut him another slice."

I did.

With the help of Karen, Mom made coffee and tea for everyone in the kitchen while Lee and I talked football. I had learned a surprising amount since dating Channing, had watched all his games, and I could hold my own talking to Lee. My dad briefly excused himself from the table to adjust ornaments on the Christmas tree. He was always fiddling with them, but I think he was really avoiding Lee, whose energy was too much for him. Channing shot up from the table and went to help Dad. I would've joined them, but Lee was too busy pontificating about the relative merits of running back sweeps and slants. I actually knew what he was talking about, thanks to Channing, and counter-argued him for fun. I think he actually liked that I wouldn't give in.

Eventually, everyone returned to the table for coffee and tea and more cookies, cake, and conversation.

Ting, ting, ting!

Channing was clinking his coffee mug with his spoon. "Pardon the interruption, everyone. I'd like to say something."

"This should be good," Karen smiled, folding her linen napkin on the table.

"It always is," Lee laughed and winked at Dad.

"Great boy you've got there," Dad said. He wasn't exactly Mr. Sociable, but he seemed to like Lee and Karen well enough, all things considered. I knew he liked Channing just fine. They'd spent enough time together in the past two years. I just wanted our parents to like each other.

"Where to begin," Channing said. "It all started at a frat party. Mom, I'm not talking about you and Dad."

Karen blushed, "Your father and I did *not* meet at a frat party."

"Yes we did," Lee said.

"No, it was at *my* sorority fund raiser hosted at *your* fraternity house. It wasn't a party. It was during the day."

"That's right," Lee nodded. "But it was still a party."

"No it wasn't!" Karen clucked.

"We had beer. How is that not a party?" Obviously, they were enjoying the long-standing debate. It had a flirtatious quality that showed they still loved each other.

Channing said, "Okay, you two didn't meet at an actual party, but me and Carol did."

Karen looked at me.

I nodded and said, "We did."

"The thing that impressed me most," Channing said, "was the way Carol stood up to a drunken guy at the party like he wasn't three times her size. Your daughter has guts of steel, Mr. Duffey."

"She does," Dad smiled. "Ever since she was little."

Mom whispered to Karen, "Carol was always skinning her knees and falling out of trees like it was business as usual."

"Sounds like my Channing," Karen agreed.

Channing nodded, "She's also smarter than I'll ever be."

"No I'm not," I chortled.

"Book smart," Channing added.

"Okay, maybe," I giggled. That Channing managed to pass all his classes every quarter amazed even me. I knew how busy he was with football.

Channing grinned, "We can all see how gorgeous she is, so I don't have to mention that."

I blushed.

"The one thing we can't see is her heart. You can't see anyone's heart from the outside. You see it by what they do. Actions define a person's heart. Not a bunch of bullshit talk. Dad, you're always saying that."

"I am," Lee grinned.

Karen tittered at that.

Mom sniffed. She wasn't a fan of swearing at the dinner table.

"Carol is all heart. You know how I know?" Channing asked.

"How?" Karen asked.

"She's never given up on me. No matter what I put her through, no matter how much football I jammed down her throat, she never gave up." He reached into his pocket. "And that is why," he pulled out a velvet box, "I'll never give up," he got down on one knee beside the dinner table, "on you, Carol Duffey."

"Ohmygod," I gasped, covering my mouth with both hands.

"Will you marry me?" Channing smiled, opening the ring box with shaky hands, revealing an antique ring.

Karen gasped. "Channing! Where'd you get Mamaw's ring?"

"It's okay," Lee said, squeezing Karen's hand. "Your son and I discussed this."

"You discussed it?! Without telling me?"

"I didn't want to spoil the surprise. I brought the ring on the plane without telling you."

Channing chuckled, "Mom. Dad. I'm trying to ask Carol to marry me."

"Yes, of course," Karen laughed guiltily. "I'm ruining their moment," she muttered to Mom.

Mom rubbed Karen's arm and smiled.

"Ahem! As I was saying," Channing cleared his throat, shaking and nervous, beads of sweat sparkling on his forehead. "Carol Duffey, will you make me the happiest man on the planet and do me the honor of marrying me?"

I was biting my lower lip because it wouldn't stop quivering. "Yes," I choked out and threw my arms around Channing's neck. "Yes, forever yes."

We didn't set an exact date, but we talked about this coming summer, after we both graduated, which would be at least six months after Channing dumped me.

The holidays that year were a very happy time.

Ignorance truly is bliss.

Chapter 23

CHANNING

"Can we go to Disneyland after you win the Rose Bowl? I've never been." Carol asked, sitting in the seat beside me on the flight to Los Angeles.

"*If* we win the Rose Bowl," I forced a smile.

"Don't say that! Think positive. You'll totally win."

"Hope so," I said absently.

Lashawn popped his head over the seat in front of us. "I don't wanna hear any of that noise, dog! This is our time to shine! We're gonna win the Rose Bowl! From there, we're gonna win the championship! Tell him, Iesha."

Iesha peered over her seat back and said, "If anybody can do it, the Chandy Man can."

I was happy to see them sitting together. In the three years past, Lashawn always sat with the fellas on our flight to California. I liked to think he and Iesha were making progress.

"He's got that Heisman magic in his arm," Lashawn cheered. "Nobody can stop us now!"

"Yeah," I sighed, looking out the window at the blue skies. They weren't blue back home. In King City, it was a snowy blizzard.

"Why are you like this every year, dog?" Lashawn asked. "Every time we go to the Rose Bowl, you get downer than a dirty shoe."

"Got a lot on my shoulders."

"We'll help you carry it, dog. You aren't on your own out there. Remember that."

"Yeah," I said.

If they only knew.

#
&
&*&
&*&*&
&*&*&*&
M

New Year's Day.
Game day.

The Granddaddy of Them All.

The Pasadena Rose Bowl.

It had been going strong since 1902. Also going strong was the historic Rose Parade that started at 8:00am sharp game day (game was in the afternoon).

Rose-covered floats (almost 50 of them), 20 marching bands (including King City's), and horses galore, over 400 of them clacking horseshoes down Colorado Boulevard to bleachers full of cheering crowds not far from Rose Stadium.

I sent Carol, her parents, and my parents to watch the show. After four years, I had yet to see it myself, but I'd seen video of the parade on the news. The floats were epic, as big as boats.

Me, I was busy having the team breakfast, going over last minute details for today's game, armoring up in the locker room with the fellas, and listening to last minute pep talks from the various coaches, with Head Coach Slaughter wrapping things up with a rousing speech worthy of General Dwight D. Eisenhower revving up the troops the day before hitting the beaches of Normandy on D-Day. Anyway, team management filled our schedule from wake up call to running on the field to the sounds of the roaring crowd and fireworks before we faced off against the USC Trojans. There wasn't time to watch a bunch of rose floats motoring down a city street, no matter how much I wanted to be there, not here.

Same shit every time.

Somewhere in the middle of preparations, Coach Rucker pulled me aside, same as he'd done the last three years here.

"You ready to put on a show?" Rucker asked, over-smiling while over-thrashing his chewing gum. Chew, chew, chew.

"Yeah," I grumbled grimly as Rucker led me through the maze inside the locker room at the stadium. It was bigger than Cheetahs Stadium. You could easily get lost in here and never find your way out.

Rucker took me to a small side room, an impromptu storeroom with stacked furniture collecting dust. I'd been here three times before and knew it well.

Rucker closed the door behind us.

Two men stood inside. Both wore KCU team jackets, and caps, the kind you could buy outside from dozens of different vendors. These two could be anybody. Your neighbor's dad, your best friend's uncle, the guy at the grocery store, a hazy memory of nobody you'd ever met. Completely forgettable. The only memorable detail: they looked like brothers because they were.

Rucker said, "Channing, you remember Tony and Jake Martinelli."

I didn't answer. I glared.

"Channing Fucking Peyton," Tony chortled. He was the shorter and older of the two, his hair silver, his finger rings gold. He grabbed my neck like we were best friends and pulled my head down to his level. It was a show of dominance not friendship. "Good to fucking see you again, kid."

"Yeah," I grunted.

"Great fucking season, kid! Fourteen and oh! Again!" He glanced at his silent brother Jake. "Four perfect fucking years undefeated in the regular season! I don't know how you do it, kid."

"Good coaching," I said.

"We try," Rucker smiled. Chew, chew, chew.

"He tries," Tony said to Jake, who made up for his lack of speech with his imposing presence. "He fucking *tries*." Tony laughed.

No one else laughed.

Rucker wore his stage grin and continued killing his gum. Chew, chew, chew.

"Remember, kid," Tony said, "I want a good fucking game. I want them on the edges of their fucking seats, right up to the bitter fucking end."

I nodded.

"You know what to do then. Right, kid?"

I scowled and barely nodded.

"Is that a yes?" Tony demanded, a razor's edge of anger glimmering in his voice.

"Yes." I ground out the word like broken glass.

Tony laughed, "Yes that's a fucking yes!" He turned to his brother. "Of course it's a fucking yes. What else would it be? It's a fucking yes!"

Jake was drilling me with his eyes.

Rucker was chew, chew, chewing.

And I was fucking stew, stew, stewing.

When you were barely a 19 year old kid like I'd been four years ago, and the devil himself whipped out a contract written on human skin and handed you the quill pen dripping your own blood, signing on the dotted line seemed like a good idea because you couldn't see past the empty promises to the lies behind. Back then, my first time at the Rose Bowl, I'd been too young to realize what I was getting myself into. Too bad Dad hadn't been in this room then to talk some sense into me. I might have done things differently. But I hadn't.

If I told him the truth now, would it make him feel better about me losing the last three Rose Bowls?

Or worse?

I'd never know because there was no way I'd ever tell him. Especially not now, when I *was* old enough to know better. He'd never forgive me for throwing away everything he'd worked for, and at the last possible minute, at the last game of my college career, for the fourth and final time.

If I told him that, it *would* kill him.

That left me with only one choice.

\#

&

&*&

&*&*&

&*&*&*&

&*&*&*&

M

Two things in my life were beyond compare.

One was loving Carol Duffey with a heavy emphasis on the fucking. You know you're jealous.

The other was being on the football field in the zone.

Not the end zone.

The mental zone.

It was a physical zone too. When your body was a Ferrari supercar or a Formula 1 racer like mine, and every cylinder was firing in perfect time and the suspension tuned to perfection, the physical world was a different place for you than it was for mere mortals.

You didn't fight it.

You flowed through it.

When you were in the zone, every handoff was flawless, every pass a smooth spiral on a wire, you saw every blitz seconds before it hit, you were one with the green, green grass of the gridiron and the blue sky high overhead.

Nothing could stop you.

Play after play, we racked up yardage like points in pinball. The points on the Rose Bowl scoreboard racked up seven by seven. No matter what the Trojan defense did, we were ten steps ahead. Even at my worst, I was better than anything they had.

During one play, their outside linebacker on my blind side slipped past my left tackle *and* the guard, aiming for a blitz. I felt the blitzer diving for my knees without even seeing him, hopped over his head and fired a 14-yard pass while still in the air, both feet off the ground. Lashawn caught it with hands of glue and ran 42 yards to the end zone for a touchdown. That shit impressed even me.

It was like that the entire first half.

I was on fire.

The roar of the crowd a constant explosion.

Whenever the Cheetahs' D was on the field and I was on the sideline with the coaches, I tossed Dad glances where he sat with Mom and Carol on the 50-yard line at field level.

He'd grab my glances out of the air in his fist and shout, "HELL YEAH, SON! HELL! YEAH! WOOOO!" He was on his feet constantly, punching the air on every completion like he'd done it himself and was aiming for a heart attack.

I wasn't worried.

If he died today, he'd die a happy man. Who was I kidding? Dad was tougher than that.

Mom never stopped clapping and cheering.

And Carol?

Fuck.

Every time I saw her whooping and jumping up and down, I knew *my* life was fucking complete.

After four years, I was finally going to win the fucking Rose Bowl for the Cheetahs, my family, and me. From there, we'd go on to win the NCAA National Championships.

Those Martinelli brothers could go fuck themselves.

I didn't give a fuck *how* much money they had riding on me losing.

I was a winner and I was going to fucking win.

#
&
&*&
&*&*&
&*&*&*&
M

"What the fuck are you doing out there, kid?!" Tony Martinelli was raging semi-quietly in the same side-room Coach Rucker had taken me to earlier. Now it was half time. "You're throwing the fucking game!" Tony barked.

"Not this time, I'm not," I smirked.

"The fuck you ain't!" Tony snapped, inches away. He was too short to get up in my face, but we stood toe to toe.

I simply smirked down at him.

We had ended the first half up 31 to 14. I didn't have any control over the Cheetahs' defense, and by any measure, the Trojans' offense was killing it out there. The only thing I *could* control was *our* offense. If I'd been putting on a show for Tony and Jake, the score would've been more like 10 to 14 with us losing, a close but entertaining game.

Fuck.

That.

We were going to win, no matter how hard the Trojans played.

Here in the maze of the locker room facilities inside, there was less than twenty minutes of the halftime break remaining while The Bod Squad and the Cheetahs' Marching Band did a rousing halftime show outside.

I would've much rather been out there enjoying that than this shit.

"You're making a big fucking mistake, kid." Tony looked ready to chew my face off. "Tell him, Jake. Use that fancy fucking mouth of yours to make sense for this dumb fucking kid."

Jake locked eyes with me and said calmly, "What do you think happens when the good people of King City find out their darling quarterback threw the last three Rose Bowls?"

"You can't prove that," I smirked.

"You know what we can prove? We can prove you cheated your way past the academic admissions board at KCU because you didn't have the grades in high school. We can prove you cheated through four years of classes so you could play for the Cheetahs every year."

It felt like someone had tied a hundred pound weight around my balls and hung me up to let them stretch. I tossed a glance at Rucker. His face was a bland, plastic mask, his eyes lifeless. Chew, chew, chew. He wasn't going to save my ass now.

Jake added, "We can prove you're juiced up on dope."

"I didn't even finish the cycle," I smirked, my body starting to burn with anger and adrenalin. "That was months ago."

Jake nodded, "That's not what your piss says."

"I tested clean last week."

"Did you?" Jake asked ominously.

"Yeah." Random drug testing was a regular thing. How random it actually was was another story.

Jake smiled, "You think the Heisman Trophy Trust will be happy to hear about your four years of nonstop juicing? Body like yours, it's a given."

"I only juiced once! For less than a month!"

"Tell that to the Trust. Personally, I think they'll strip you of your trophy when they find out. How would your dear old dad like that, Channing?"

Dad would be crushed.

Jake continued, "You think your pops wants to see his boy humiliated in front of the whole football world? After all those years he spent making a winner outta you? Man like him has pride. You take that away from him, what's he got left?"

I was starting to broil under my pads.

"You think they let cheaters into the NFL Hall of Fame?" Jake asked. "Shit, you think they'll let you *play* in the NFL once this shit hits? Fuck no. You don't throw this game, Channing, and you're fucking ruined. You won't be first on next year's NFL draft. You won't even be on the fucking list. Say goodbye to your NFL life. Say goodbye to your big dreams."

As big as Jake was, I was a bit bigger, and I sure as fuck was stronger and faster. I could rip his face off and feed it to him if I wanted to. But I knew Jake and his brother Tony had friends. Lots and lots of friends. The kind you did not fuck with.

"Personally," Jake smiled, "I don't give a fuck what you do. It's you I'm worried about. *Your* future."

"What he said," Tony spat bullets. "I'm worried about ya, kid. Really fucking worried!"

Coach Rucker said quietly, "Think about the team, son." Chew, chew, chew.

"I am thinking about the team!" I insisted.

"Keep your voice down," Rucker warned. Chew, chew, chew.

I growled, "We deserve a win. The Cheetahs haven't had one in fifteen years. Now's our chance. We've worked for it. We paid for it with our blood, sweat, and tears."

Tony said, "Who the fuck you think paid for that brand new Ford fucking Mustang of yours, kid? Did yoouuu pay for it? No, you didn't. Iiiii fucking paid for it with the money I made because you did what you were told. Have you lost your fucking mind, kid? You wanna keep that fucking car, throw the fucking game. I'll buy you two more fucking cars with the money I'll make today. Use your head, kid. You think some fucking bowl trophy and a title mean shit? They don't."

Maybe not to him.

This man only understood one thing.

Money.

My dad only understood one thing.

Winning.

I only understood one thing.

I wasn't throwing the game for this greedy fucking schmuck. I was winning it for my dad, my mom, my girlfriend, myself, my team, and tens of thousands of people from King City, no, hundreds of thousands.

I'd disappointed them enough times already.

They were counting on me to win.

For once.

Fuck the consequences.

Chapter 24

CHANNING

The second half was disaster.

The tide of battle had turned.

I was miserable.

The Trojans offense chewed through our 31-14 lead, marching through what had been our impenetrable first-half defense with ease. We could've put newborn babies in pads and helmets and left them to drool on the field, and the Trojans would've had a harder time of it.

Their defense was also on fire, shutting me down with no remorse. Believe me, I was trying but things weren't gelling. Two critical turnovers by our team had propelled the Trojans further ahead on the scoreboard.

With a minute to go in the fourth quarter, the score was 35-31 with the Trojans now leading. With our D currently on the field, there was nothing I could do but watch from the sidelines. I could imagine Tony & Jake smiling somewhere in the stands.

They had gotten their show.

This would soon be one of the greatest comeback games in the history of the Rose Bowl. The USC fans in the stands were loving it and our fans were sitting silent.

For the fourth year in a row.

My last year with the KCU Cheetahs.

Maybe it was for the best. Crossing Tony and Jake was a bad idea. I knew that. But I'd been high on hope the first half of the game. Now that we'd lost our momentum, sanity had set in.

It didn't make the thought of losing any easier.

My dad was dying a slow death in the stands, practically pulling his hair out every time the Trojans scored. He was sitting now, bound up in a knot of frustration. Mom sat hunched next to him, her arms folded over her stomach. Carol leaned against the railing looking tired, her chin resting on her forearms, her face dragging with disappointment.

And then, hope.

The Trojans fumbled the ball.

A mad scramble ensued, men piling on top of the ball. When the refs peeled everyone away, Rance Pridemore cradled the ball. That meathead motherfucker just saved our asses.

Our O-team rushed onto the field.

Coach Rucker grabbed me by the arm, stopping me on the sidelines. "Don't fuck this up, son." Chew, chew, chew. He wore the evilest smile I'd ever seen.

We both knew what he meant.

Behind him, my dad was back on his feet and fighting like his life depended on it. "YOU GOT THIS, SON! YOU FUCKING GOT THIS!"

Mom, cheered, "You can do it, Channing! I know you can!"

Carol was energized. "Goooo Channing! This is all you, babe! Wooo-hooo!"

The adrenalin hit me and I trotted onto the field to join the huddle.

"We're gonna win this joint," Lashawn said, shifting from foot to foot, agitated and adrenalated. "I can taste it, dog. Taste it!"

The rest of the men were equally eager for victory.

Around us, the stands were relatively quiet. The Rose Bowl wasn't the Trojans' home field, but it may as well have been. The USC campus was twenty minutes away. Only a small contingent of ultra-loyal KCU fans had flown out to be here, leaving 90% of the stands rooting for a Trojan victory.

We were the underdogs today.

In the huddle, all eyes were on me.

I looked at each man, men I'd fought with year after year, my brothers in arms. I'd let them down the three previous years. Not anymore.

I grunted, "This is it, fellas. We're gonna fight our way to that end zone or die trying. No mercy. No fucking mercy!"

Their eyes fired and I called the next play.

For the next sixty seconds of game time, we clawed our way down the field. Thirty yards from their end zone, the Trojans launched a sneak attack, breaking our O-line and letting a sack slip past.

I went down hard under two Trojan backs.

Landed wrong on my knee.

Pain shot up my leg.

After the tackle, I lay there wincing and wondering if the bottom of my leg was still attached at the knee. Fucking perfect. We were close enough for a field goal, but a field goal would not win this game. We needed a TD.

Bigger question was, did I need an NFL career?

Without two good knees, I wouldn't have one.

There was no telling how serious the injury was.

If I played on it, I could make it worse.

If I got hit again, that could destroy it.

I grit my teeth, looking over at Dad, Mom, and Carol. They were small at this distance, but I could see the fear on their faces.

The sensible thing to do would be to bring in Matt Budd to replace me. It was second and short, we had twenty seconds on the clock and two timeouts remaining. More than enough. Budd was competent, but could he get it done? No, would he *choose* to? Or was he on Tony and Jake's payroll too?

I didn't know.

I rolled over and pushed to my feet wincing.

Doc Gillard, our resident sports medicine guru, and the medics were already rushing onto the field with med kits and a stretcher.

I put weight on my foot. Faint sensation started to return.

"What happened?" Gillard asked.

"Got hit," I smirked.

"No shit. You okay to play?" Gillard was a good guy.

"Yeah," I nodded, not entirely sure. "I'm solid."

"Flex it for me."

I did, shaking it out, shifting weight on and off it.

"You want me to look at it?"

"I think I'm good."

"You sure?"

"Yeah, yeah. I got this."

A slow smile stretched across Gillard's face. "We're rooting for ya." He meant it. "Take it in for the win."

I did.

We fought like hell pushing up another twenty yards to the ten. There, the Trojans stopped us cold. They blocked two running plays. On third down, they almost intercepted my throw to Lashawn in the end zone. On the fourth, their cornerbacks were all over our receives, even Lashawn. My only choice was to sprint the ball in myself.

Two Trojan backs saw me coming and charged.

I angled around them and dove over the goal line and under their flying tackles for a fucking touchdown.

A wave of disappointment quaked over the stadium, save for the tiny contingent of KCU loyalists screaming on their feet.

I lay there trying to decide whether or not I was hallucinating. Next thing I knew, I was being lifted in the air by the fellas.

"You did it, dog! You fucking did it!" Lashawn was under me near my ear. "I knew you had it in you! Fucking knew it! National Championships here we come!"

They carried me bouncing across the field on my back. Every Cheetahs player on the sideline rushed out to join us. I was mobbed by a sea of gold and black uniforms.

Finally, after four years of trying, I'd won.
At last, I knew the ecstasy of gold.

Chapter 25

CHANNING

The victory partying in Pasadena went strong until the restaurants and bars kicked us out. We started at some upscale steakhouse with fancy furniture and migrated to the streets after. Eventually, my parents wandered back to the hotel with a crowd of other tired team parents.

The Cheetahs ballers and The Bod Squad were too amped to sleep. Lashawn had the bright idea to hijack some shuttle buses from the fleet the team had rented to move us and our gear between the airport and here. With the bars closed, we used them to make our own party buses. Found a 24-hour grocery store called Vons. Loaded up with liquor. Thousands of dollars worth. Everybody pitched in.

Then we drove to Disneyland an hour away and drank until the park opened at 8:00am. Half the team were too drunk to go in.

Not me.

I dragged Carol, Lashawn, and Iesha in with me.

"Ohmygod!" Carol grinned. "I can't believe we're here!" She tiptoed up and kissed me as we walked down Main Street, U.S.A. past the Disneyland railroad.

"We're doing that drop tower," Lashawn said. "I hear that shit is dope!"

"What is it?" Carol asked.

"They take you straight up, chug, chug, chug," Lashawn sputtered, raising his hands high. "Then drop your ass straight down! Zoom!" He jumped high in the air and landed in a squat.

"Is that it?" Carol asked.

"I hear it's scary as hell."

"That sounds like nothing," Carol grinned. "Let's do that! What's the ride called?"

"Twilight something."

"The Twilight Zone Tower of Terror," Iesha said, studying a map, "That's over in California Adventures. We're at the wrong park."

I said, "We'll do that later. We got alllll day."

"Yeah we do," Carol giggled, leaning against me as we strolled deeper into the park. "Where should we go first?"

"How about Tomorrowland?"

"Get ready for Space Mountain, y'all!" Lashawn cheered then laughed, "Huh, huh, huh, huh."

"You are such a dork," Iesha grinned.

Carol whispered in my ear, "I think they like each other."

"Took 'em long enough," I smiled.

It was a great day.

The best ever, really.

Riding high on my Rose Bowl victory with Carol on my arm? What could be better? It would've been perfect until we ran into Tony and Jake on the Pirates of the Caribbean ride.

Lashawn and Iesha hopped into the front of the boat. That row now full, I jumped into the second row and offered my hand to Carol for her to climb in. She jumped past it without help and we scooted over to the far side, encouraged by the ride staff to "Please move all the way over!"

I sat down by the rail with Carol closer to the middle. Two men wearing sunglasses and matching Mickey Mouse Club T-shirts and Goofy hats with eyes on the front, teeth on the brims, and dangling ears, sat next to Carol.

"This your pretty lady?" the guy sitting next to Carol said, staring right at me while people pushed into the row next to him and the rows behind.

Tony Martinelli.

Next to him, his brother Jake.

How long had they been following us? All yesterday after the game? All last night at the restaurants? All morning on our drive here? All over the park?

Carol's eyes volleyed between me and Tony.

"Aren't you Channing Peyton?" Tony played dumb. "You won the Rose Bowl yesterday for KCU, didn't you?"

I smirked.

"He did," Carol said bashfully.

"What a win that was," Tony said with imitation enthusiasm. "I was so *sure* the Trojans would win." Cats toying with rats before the kill had never been so sweet. "But you didn't let that happen, did you, Mr. *Peyton.*"

Carol was starting to pick up on Tony's odd behavior. She didn't know what to say and wasn't sure what to do.

With the boat now floating into the darkness, there was nothing either of us could do.

I squeezed her hand in mine.

"This you girlfriend?" Tony asked innocently.

I grunted.

"Fiancée," Carol said, holding up her ring.

"Nice ring," Tony gushed. He elbowed Jake. "I love young love, don't you?"

Jake stared straight ahead, inscrutable behind his Mickey Mouse sunglasses and floppy Goofy hat.

"They're getting married." Tony's sarcasm was a razor he savored with every slicing word. "I was married once." He shoved the comment in Carol's face, demanding a reply.

"Oh? What happened to her?" she asked.

"She died," Tony growled, his warning as subtle as a knife in the stomach shot from the barrel of a cannon.

I pulled Carol close and was about to warn Tony off with a threat of my own when our boat suddenly plunged down the first watery fall. I nearly bit my tongue in half and left my stomach floating up above. For the rest of the ride, I sat in silence while Tony ignored us and Carol commented happily on the amusing pirate antics in the torchlit animatronic dioramas.

It was the worst experience of my life.

When the ride ended, Jake and Tony filed onto the dock with the other passengers and never looked back.

I now had a very serious problem, a very serious decision to make, and a very serious regret.

I should've thrown the fucking game.

For Carol's sake.

Chapter 26

CAROL

"I need my ring back," Channing said robotically.

"Oh," I said. "Does your mom want it back? I totally understand if she does. It's your grandma's ring. At Christmas it sounded like you took it without telling her."

"I'm giving it to Victoria Bissette."

"What?" I snorted and my blood iced.

"Please give me the ring, Carol. I'm breaking up with you." His robotic delivery was creeping me out.

My body flushed with acidic heat. "What are you talking about, Channing? I thought we were engaged."

"You need to move out. Please give me the ring."

I sank onto the couch in Channing's penthouse apartment in Faulkner Hall. We'd been back from California for one day. One.

Channing walked into the bedroom.

My head was spinning, my heart had fallen out of my mouth, and I was ready to vomit up my stomach.

Channing walked out holding a bunch of clothes on hangers. He carried them out the open apartment door and set them on the ground in the hallway.

"What are you doing, Channing?! Those are my clothes!"

"I need them out of my apartment. Victoria is moving in."

"What?!" I shrieked and jumped to my feet. "You did kiss her, didn't you?!"

"Yes." He walked into the bedroom and robotically grabbed another armload of clothes from the closet. He stopped and held out a big palm. "Give me my grandmother's ring. Please."

I ripped the ring off my finger. I would've thrown it out a window if it wasn't his grandmother's. I couldn't do that to Karen. Rather than set it in his hand, I turned my back on him and set it on the kitchen counter.

"Start packing," he said.

I whirled on him. "Fuck you, Channing! Fuck you! I hope your dick rots off!" I tore my clothes from his arm and walked them out to the pile in the hallway. Then I marched back into the bedroom to get more of my stuff.

Channing watched me make several trips. Didn't even help. Eventually, he said, "I'll be back in an hour. Be gone by then."

"Why?" I sneered defiantly. "So you can move Victoria in?"

He stared at me, eyes robot cold.

I snarled, "You are such a fucking liar! You never were a virgin when we had sex, were you?!"

"No."

With that, my betrayal was complete.

Holding back the tears he didn't deserve, I quietly gathered up my stuff over the next hour, then went looking for a place to live.

Chapter 27

CHANNING

"I heard you broke up with your girlfriend," Victoria Bissette smiled, sliding into the empty seat beside mine on the plane ride to Tampa, Florida where the Cheetahs would play the Alabama Crimson Tide in the NCAA National Championship game at Raymond James Stadium.

Victoria looked as good as ever, worthy of a movie screen or a fashion model catwalk.

I gave her a zombie stare.

"Are you okay?" she asked, soft concern in her comforting voice.

"No."

"Want me to brighten your day?" Victoria gave a wicked grin and let her hand fall from the armrest to my thigh.

I stared at her feminine hand like it was a barnacled sand crab teeming with disease.

"After you win the championship," she purred, leaning into me with substantial side breast, "we should rent a car and drive to Disney World. Orlando is only an hour away from Tampa. Then we can finally do Disney together. And I do mean do," she giggled. "I wanted to do you at Disneyland, but you and that frumpy midget were attached at the hip the whole time. I don't know why. She's so little. Let me show you what a real woman can do, Channing. I'll do things to you that'll make your head spin."

With one luxurious nail, she traced a line up my thigh toward my dick.

"Shut the fuck up, Victoria." I grabbed her wrist hard and threw it away like lit dynamite. "Do me a favor. Stick your head in the nearest airplane toilet and start flushing."

#

&

&*&

&*&*&

&*&*&*&

M

There was a knock at my hotel room door.

I was lying on the bed in my boxers, staring at the ceiling. Been doing it for two hours. Couldn't sleep. Empty mini liquor bottles surrounded me. I was buzzed, but it wasn't helping me sleep any. I needed to ask Doc Gillard if he had pills for that.

Another knock.

I guess it was real.

I rolled off the bed and stumbled to the door. Opened it without looking through the peephole.

"Channiiiiiiiing," Tony Martinelli said. Jake stood behind him. They wore matching Hawaiian shirts.

Behind them was Coach Rucker. Chew, chew, chew.

"Look at this miserable fuck," Tony Martinelli smiled. "You been drinking, kid?"

I slammed the door in his face. It bounced off Jake's hand.

"Manners, kid," Tony frowned, shrugging it off. "I was gonna say, strange piece of ass you got, kid."

I frowned.

"Cute little thing on the Pirates of the Caribbean ride? I always pictured you with someone hotter. Some supermodel or some shit. Like one of your cheerleaders."

"Fuck you."

"She here?" He peered around me into the room, obviously looking for Carol.

"She dumped me," I lied.

"Your fiancée *dumped* you?" he chortled. "She got a screw loose? You're a golden meal ticket, kid."

"I fucked a cheerleader," I lied. "She caught me."

Tony chortled, "You gotta hard time keeping your agreements, kid."

"What the fuck are you smiling about?"

"I'm here to make you an offer."

"Fuck off."

"Hear me out, kid," Tony chuckled, his patience straining string tight. "I got a little ahead of myself the other day. I have now had time to think things through. If you would be so kind as to invite us in, we can discuss like men."

Chew, chew, chew. Rucker said, "You should listen to what Tony has to say, son."

I sighed and walked into the room. Sat down on the bed. Waited.

Tony said, "Here's what I'll do." He pointed at me with both hands, "You take care of your upcoming game," he pointed at himself, "and I'll call us even."

"Even?"

"You owe me for your little fuckup in Pasadena."

"I don't owe you shit."

"Kid," Tony laughed, "keep your shit together. I'm offering you a way out of a very bad situation. Work with me here. You take care of me, I will take care of you. *And* your family. Your mom and dad are coming to town for the big game, right?"

I scowled.

Now he was threatening my parents?

I couldn't break up with them.

This was fucked.

"Don't worry, kid," Tony grinned, patting my shoulder firmly. "You take care of me, I take care of you. I'll make sure nothing bad ever happens to your parents *or* your girl."

"She's not my girl."

"Sure, kid. Sure. Either way, I'll make sure she's safe. We have an understanding?" Tony smiled graciously.

#

&

&*&

&*&*&

&*&*&*&

M

I threw the game.

We lost 24 to 21.

If I didn't have to make it look good, we would've lost 24 to 0 because I didn't feel like fucking trying.

I'd also lost the only woman I would ever love because I'd thrown her away too, stupidly thinking I was protecting her. She'd never want me back now. She'd never believe the truth about Tony and Jake. Nobody would. It wasn't like those two were going to explain things to Carol for my sake. Or hers. Thinking about it, she was better off without a dumbshit like me making her life more dangerous.

Oh, and remember that shot I took to my knee when I foolishly won the Rose Bowl? I took another shot because I didn't give a enough fucks to pay attention to my blindside when a linebacker railroaded over me.

Wasn't playing in the mental zone now.

Throwing a game didn't exactly take skill or focus.

The second hit aggravated the damage done by the first. I limped my way through the end of the game. Had to make sure Matt Budd or somebody else didn't win by accident. When Doc Gillard had me X-rayed later, my knee was hamburger from a meat grinder. There went my NFL career.

Lesson learned.

Winning wasn't worth shit.

I should've thrown the Rose Bowl. I would've had both knees, a career in the NFL *and* Carol.

Anybody have a gun?

Or a noose?

No?

Okay, I'll try beer.

Maybe I can drown in a pitcher of gold.

Some old fuck once said in a book I never read, you'd find ecstasy waiting at the bottom of a glass if you drank deep enough.

May the suds of gold cleanse my soul.

Nothing else would.

Chapter 28

CAROL

"Carol, hun? Would you like some lunch?" Mom asked from the doorway to my dark bedroom. "It's almost one o'clock."

I lay dead in bed, answering her with a sad sigh.

"You should really eat something, Carol."

"Later," I whispered.

"Okay. I'll come back in an hour."

I wouldn't be hungry then either.

I'd moved back in with Mom & Dad because Sienna and my other friends at KCU all had roommates, and winter quarter had already started. The way I was feeling, I wasn't making it to class any time soon.

My life was over.

```
      #
      &
    &*&
   &*&*&
  &*&*&*&
      M
```

For three months, I couldn't function.

I lost weight, hoping to wither away.

The only fight I had left was the fight to keep my parents from feeding me.

By default, I dropped out of all my classes. That should have been a very serious, carefully considered step. It meant I was screwing up the upper div class series I needed to take to finish my Legal Studies major. I'd crammed most of them in fourth year because I'd busted my butt finishing my minors third year. If I wanted to graduate, which was a big if because I really wanted to die, I'd have to wait until next fall.

Nine months of waiting.

Would I make it nine months?

Or would the seed of defeat growing inside my belly germinate into a carnivorous cancer that ate me alive long before?

It had already eaten my heart, so why not?

#

&
&*&
&*&*&
&*&*&*&
M

My hateful self-indulgence broke its hold the day I almost broke Mom's neck. She was trying to help me into the shower, the standard tub-shower combo I'd used growing up.

"I can't stand up, Mom," I gasped. I was so thin, I had no strength. Recently, breathing had become difficult.

"Yes you can," Mom said. "You need to shower, Carol. You smell like a trash can! You're filthy!" Lately, she had been using any tactic she could to spur me into action. Insults were her latest. She just wanted me to live.

I didn't. "No, Mom."

"Please just get in the shower." She grabbed the shower curtain with one hand and my bony waist with the other. "Please, Carol! Get in the tub! Please!" She strained against my weight, trying to lift me with her hip.

The shower curtain tore off the rings in quick succession.

Pop, pop, pop!

Mom slipped.

I fell.

On top of her.

She cushioned my fall, smashing her wrist against the side of the tub with a bang as she crashed down, then bonked her forehead against the edge. Her skull made a hollow, sickening thud.

"Mom?" I whispered hoarsely, struggling to roll off her.

She didn't answer.

"Mom!" The way she'd hit her head, I thought she was dead. "Wake up, Mom! Wake up! Please!" I cried dry tears, my dehydrated body too sad to have any.

"Carol," she moaned. "What happened?"

I hugged her hard and sobbed silently.

She had to roll out and help *me* to my feet.

That's when I started eating again, literally minutes after crawling into the kitchen and opening the refrigerator on my knees to open a can of Coke. I wanted to drive Mom to the ER, but I didn't have the strength. I had to call Dad. I crawled into clean clothes, then the car. Dad put Mom in by himself and drove us.

Later, the ER doctor told Mom she'd suffered a mild concussion.

Thank goodness.

My hunger strike was officially over.

I wasn't going to kill myself or anyone I loved over some asshole who had never loved me.

\#

&

&*&

&*&*&

&*&*&*&

M

With no classes to attend, I started working part time at the Target near Mom and Dad's a few weeks later. It was close enough to walk. When I got my full strength back, I worked full time. It felt good to live like a normal person again.

For some reason, I kept The Football Games journal Channing gave me. I just couldn't bear to part with it.

I'd considered burning it or throwing it away, but I wanted to hold onto it for some strange reason. In a way, it was a totem of something *I* had done, not him. It was *my* story. He'd just copied it. Sure, I had the original journal, the scribbled version, but his had significance.

Maybe I kept it because it was a piece of Channing's heart. According to Jordyn Hoyle, Channing still had at least a piece of mine, if not more, so it was only fair I had one of his. Maybe some day we could exchange them so I could forget him forever.

When I was older.

I'd need at least a decade before I could talk to him without trying to stab him while crying over his bloody body. I was sane enough to know no amount of stabbing would get back the pieces of my heart he'd stolen. He needed to return them willingly.

What I didn't know was how Channing would shortly shatter my heart a second time, and Mom and Dad's with it. This time, his actions would ruin all our lives.

The evil of that man knew no bounds.

Chapter 29

CAROL

"Hey, Dad," I said in early May as I walked in the door wearing my red Target polo shirt and khakis, my keys jingling in the lock.

"How was work?" Dad asked from his easy chair near the TV.

"Good. Watching the news?"

He nodded. "You can join me if you want."

"Can I get you anything from the kitchen?"

Dad leaned over in his chair toward me and whispered, "I hid a bag of Circus Animals in the cupboard over the refrigerator." He didn't mean actual circus animals. He meant the pink and white cookies with the rainbow sprinkles, his favorite. "Don't tell your mother."

"I'll get it," I grinned and returned a moment later with his cookies and a bowl of Breyers vanilla bean for me.

"You didn't say anything about ice cream," Dad grinned, eyeing my bowl.

"Should I get you one?"

"No." He dipped a pink elephant in my creamy vanilla mountain, prying off a good sized glop. "This'll do."

"I'm telling Mom," I joked while local news played.

Sharon Bancroft, the newscaster who'd been anchoring King City 7 News since I was a kid, said, "Local heartthrob and King City Cheetahs' quarterback Channing Peyton was arrested last night on misdemeanor counts of public drunkenness, public indecency, public urination, and defacing private property. Video recorded by a local teenager out skateboarding with his friends captured the moment."

The video was dark, showing Channing standing on top of the four-times life-size bronze cheetah statue outside Cheetahs Stadium. His dick was pixelated and he was obviously peeing on the head of the cheetah.

Off camera, you could hear the laughter of teenage boys.

"What're you doing?" one of them called out in a squeaky teenage voice.

"Taking a BLEEEEP! leak," Channing chuckled, his words slurring and blurry. He was loaded. "What the BLEEP! does it look like?"

"Are you Channing Peyton?"

"Who the BLEEP! else?"

More teenage laughter.

"Why are you peeing on the cheetah?"

"Because I hate this BLEEEEP! thing."

"Why?"

"This BLEEEEP! cheetah stole my BLEEEEP! girlfriend."

Dad said, "You're dripping."

This entire time, I'd been holding a spoonful of vanilla ice cream halfway to my mouth. It was dripping in my lap. "Shit!" I dropped my spoon clinking in the bowl and dashed into the kitchen to blot my khakis with a wet sponge. I walked back into the living room still blotting.

Dad said, "Channing said your name."

"He did?"

Dad nodded, "He said the cheetah stole you."

"Huh?"

"Shh, listen."

Channing said, "If it wasn't for her, I woulda beat Alabama in Tampa." He was talking about the national championship game back in January.

A teenager in the video snickered, "No, you lost because Alabama kicked your ass."

"BLEEP," Channing snorted. "I lost because I wanted to. For Carol. I did it for you, Carol Duffey! For you!"

Horrified and disgusted, I gasped, "What is he talking about?"

"I don't know," Dad said.

Channing looked skyward as he made his proclamation, his pixelated dick still dangling in the wind. He took a shaky step, lost his balance, and slipped off the statue, arms flailing as he rolled over the side.

The video shook as the teenagers ran, shoes slapping concrete around the cheetah statue to where Channing lay on the concrete steps surrounding the base.

"Dude! That was epic! Do that again!"

"Are you okay?" another teenager asked.

Channing moaned, covering his eyes from the camera light. "Point that BLEEP! somewhere else."

The camera turned to reveal two King City PD officers strolling toward the camera. The video ended there.

"What was that all about?" Dad asked.

I would've answered, but the sensation of several live squid writhing in my intestines told me I had a very bad feeling about this.

#
&
&*&
&*&*&

&*&*&*&

M

The harassment didn't start right away.

It took the help of KC 7 News to get the ball rolling. Not just any ball. The giant rolling boulder that chases Indiana Jones out of that jungle temple at the start of Raiders of the Lost Ark.

Sharon Bancroft sealed my fate the next night.

"Since Channing Peyton was arrested last night, everyone has been wondering, who is the mysterious Carol Duffey? Several people have alleged she is the same Carol who appeared at last December's Heisman Trophy awards ceremony in New York City with Channing and his parents."

The TV showed Channing at the podium inside the PlayStation Theater giving his acceptance speech. He looked down into the audience and said, "I love you too, Carol. I'll never give up on you. I'll never stop fighting for you." The video showed a closeup of me weeping in response to Channing's lying declaration of love.

In the living room, Dad was sitting next to me, sneaking more pink and white Circus Animal cookies. He wiped his hands on a paper towel and reached over to grab my hand, giving it a squeeze. For Dad, that was a bold move that meant he understood the gravity of this situation fully.

Reliving that Heisman moment was a piano falling on my heart and dropping the rest of me crashing into oblivion. Seeing it on camera oddly felt like an out-of-body experience. I had completely believed Channing that night, taken his public declaration of his undying love as somehow binding. It had been tangible proof.

Now I knew better.

It was tangible proof he was a lying hypocrite, a man with no morals, no ethical code.

What I had forgotten was the cameraman kneeling in front of me and Channing's parents that night, recording our reactions during the speech.

Sharon Bancroft said, "We showed this video to an acquaintance of Channing Peyton and this is what she said."

"Yeah, that's her. That's Carol Duffey," said a blotchy college girl wearing a KCU T-shirt standing on campus near the Ernest D. Caldwell School of Engineering building. The iconic Wurtzell clock tower was visible across the long grass field receding into the distance. "I remember him winning that trophy and her being there."

A reporter holding a KC-7 microphone asked, "How do you know Carol?"

College girl said, "I know Carol from dating Channing. I mean, *she* dated Channing. Not me," she giggled. "I knew him. I met her from him and we became friends."

"What was it you said Carol told you?"

College girl looked sidelong for a moment, bit her lip, dropped her chin, then said, "Carol told me she told Channing he had to prove he loved her more than football."

"How was he supposed to do that?"

"She said he had to lose to Alabama on purpose. So she'd know he loved her more than anything."

I barked at the TV, "I never said that! I don't even know her!"

"You don't?" Dad asked innocently.

"No! I've never met her before in my life! She's lying!"

It didn't matter.

Over the following week, seven more women I had never met came forward publicly, each alleging they knew me personally, and that I had manipulated Channing into "throwing" the championship game, each of their claims increasingly salacious. In one, I was his dominatrix lover, complete with whips, chains, ball gags, and an overly-controlling bitchy personality. In another, I made Channing pay me every time we had sex, as if our relationship was entirely transactional, the implication being that I was literally a craven prostitute high on greed. The accusations only got worse from there.

My assumption?

Someone was masterminding this spectacle from behind the scenes. My list of suspects? I'll give you a hint. It was very short.

Channing Peyton.

Did I confront him?

Considered it.

But I knew there was an even chance someone who worked for the King City Cheetahs football program was pulling the strings. Many tens of millions of donor dollars went into KCU's coffers every year. The school was *that* prestigious. For all I knew, the media lies had been born out of a wealthy cabal of vengeful mega-donors sipping brandy in a wood-paneled country club somewhere, the group of them guffawing and scheming about how to best drag my reputation through the mud and leave it lying in the road. Then they'd turn their team of horses around and have them stomp their hooves over my reputation seven more times before they left it and me to die.

In the end, I didn't confront Channing because I didn't want to end up arrested for *murder one with malice aforethought*. Believe me, I considered it many, many times, and very maliciously, but his actions had already imprisoned the hole in my heart that would likely never again be filled because there was now a corrosive cage around it. I didn't want the rest of me locked up for life too.

He deserved that fate, not me.

Another reason?

He had literally disappeared.

No one knew where he had gone, not even Lee and Karen Peyton, who called me frightened out of their minds one night, begging me if I knew where Channing was.

"Please, Carol!" Karen sobbed. "Where is my boy?! I can't find my little boy!"

I didn't know what to tell her.

Thank goodness, Dad took the phone and tried to soothe her with penny platitudes as best he could.

I went to my bedroom and cried for Karen and Lee, and probably a tiny bit for myself, if I was being honest.

Anyway, whoever it was instructing the liars on TV, within two weeks, half of King City believed I was to blame for the Cheetahs losing to Alabama. This was the early days of social media. Facebook and Twitter were just getting started. I didn't even have accounts. Had this happened today, the death threats would've hit my smart phone minutes later. As it was, it took almost a week before they hit me in the face.

\#

&

&*&

&*&*&

&*&*&*&

M

"You're that Duffey bitch," some woman snarled at me while I was stocking shelves at Target. She pushed past me with her loaded cart, almost running over my toes.

"Hey! Watch it!" I snapped, hopping back. "That's my foot!"

"Big deal," she snarled. "After what you did to him, it's the least I can do!"

"Me?! He dumped me!"

She got right in my face and hissed, "Not soon enough, you stuck up bitch!" A piece of spittle from her mouth hit my lip, warm and moist.

I spat it off and wiped my wrist across my mouth, wanting desperately to run up behind her and soccer kick her ass sailing over every aisle in the store. Wanting to keep my job, I did not.

"Is there a problem?" asked Ray Baca, my shift manager, who appeared from around the shelves at the end of the aisle nearest the spitter.

She glared at me and said, "Fire her. That'll solve your problem." Then she walked away, nose in the air.

"What happened?" Ray asked quietly.

While I explained, he nodded and attempted to comfort me with his incredulous frown. It didn't help.

At least Ray didn't fire me.

That was the first time the public harassment happened. It would not be the last. Within a week, I had at least a dozen people come up to me and say similarly mean things. As far as King City was concerned, I was the Delilah to Channing's Samson. Somehow, I had ruined him. What a joke! He was the ruiner!

Things got scary the night I came home from work and found a dead Cheetah hanging by a noose someone had pinned up under the porch roof at Mom and Dad's house. It was a full-size plushie Cheetahs mascot wearing a KCU jersey. You could buy them at the KCU bookstore. I'd sold quite a few when I'd worked there.

I pulled it down and went around the side of the house to stuff it in the trash. I didn't want Mom and Dad having to see it.

Then I went inside to eat a snack with Dad in front of the news. It was becoming our thing. Dad and daughter time every night I came home from work. We both enjoyed it.

Until a brick crashed through the living room window, scaring the shit out of both of us.

We both gasped, me jumping off the couch and him from his easy chair while an engine revved and tires screeched outside.

"Jack?" Mom called from the bedroom. "What was that?"

"Everything's okay, Bev!" Dad called out while I cowered behind the couch.

We called the police.

They said there was nothing they could do.

I helped Dad take a piece of plywood out of the garage and cover the window while Mom stood there in her bathrobe fretting about who would do such a thing.

We had no idea.

I know who I blamed.

#

&

&*&

&*&*&
&*&*&*&
M

Stocking shelves at Target one evening while wearing my red polo and khakis, I overheard this conversation between two college age women in Housewares while they stood in the blender aisle.

"The Cheetahs footballers are so dumb."

"You know who's the dumbest?"

"Who?"

"Channing Peyton. Like, a bag of rocks dumb."

Hearing them attack him didn't make me feel any better. I had a strange urge to defend his reputation, but it was washed away by a wave of nausea.

"I don't see how any of them graduate."

"You know they cheat, right?"

"At football?"

"No. They'd never do that. I mean school. They cheat on their tests and term papers."

"Who says?"

"My girlfriend is dating one of them. She wrote an English Lit paper for him last quarter."

"People do that stuff all the time. I've done that."

"Did you get paid?"

"No."

"She did. Her boyfriend got an A, so his buddies on the team in the same class came to her asking for her to write their papers too. I think Channing was one of them."

That was news. Except, it wasn't. Once we started living together, Channing had always been bugging me to help him with his papers. He had to write a lot for his Communications major. Honestly, he wasn't that bad at writing when he bothered to do it. But he didn't. He just wanted me to do the work for him. I'd never do that. It wasn't ethical. This had sparked several arguments until one day he stopped asking.

"Anyway," the girl in the aisle said, "she made like two thousand bucks by the end of the quarter. Five hundred a paper."

"What?! No way! Why am I not getting paid to write other people's papers?"

"Maybe you could."

"I totally should."

"All you have to do is hang out with footballers."

"How do you do that?"

"Show them your tits."

They both giggled and wandered off.

I stood there scowling, considering a revenge fantasy wherein I put my skills learned from my Investigative Journalism classes to use, went digging for a treasure chest worth of evidence, and took it to the media as proof that the entire Cheetahs football program was a corrupt sewer of liars and drug abusers cheating the system. It would spark a new nickname for the team.

The King City Cheaters.

Sadly, that wouldn't make the pleasant citizens of King City hate me less. They would roll out the guillotine and behead me in the center of Cheetahs Stadium with everyone watching and cheering.

"KILL CAROL DUFFEY!" they'd shout in unison.

"KILL THAT BITCH AND STUFF HER HEAD IN A DITCH!"

On that day, the beer, popcorn, hot peanuts, and admission for children under 12, would be free, as would the souvenir severed Carol heads. "Look how it rolls, kids!"

At least I had a morbid sense of humor about being shunned.

It was the only thing keeping me sane.

To be completely honest, lately my morbid laughter was the only thing keeping me from crying all the time.

#
&
&*&
&*&*&
&*&*&*&
&*&*&*&*&
M

Once word got out I worked at Target, I had to quit. Too many people coming in specifically to harass me in the aisles.

Nobody on staff made me quit. Target corporate was very supportive and concerned about my safety, but they did suggest I transfer to another store not in King City.

I wasn't doing that.

The closet one was fifty miles away. I could find a closer job.

Probably the worst thing that happened was getting booed out of Denny's one Sunday morning. We were having breakfast at the one between the KCU campus and our church.

It wasn't everyone booing.

Just half the restaurant.

They were literally booing and jeering and hissing like the pit of vipers they were. I think the only reason they weren't throwing food (other than snakes not having arms, ha, ha, ha) at us was out of respect for the Denny's staff.

Mom refused to leave.

Dad wanted to hide under the table.

I suggested we go for everyone's sake.

On our way out, someone threw a Smucker's Concord grape jelly package that hit Dad in the back of his head, one of those white plastic ones with the sharp edges.

"What was that?" Dad asked sheepishly. He wasn't very confrontational.

I was. I picked the package off the ground.

"You're bleeding, Jack," Mom said, inspecting the back of Dad's head, eyes narrowed in concern.

"I am?" Dad asked, momentarily cupping his head with his palm before pulling it away smeared with a stroke of red. The blood was minimal.

I didn't care. I held up the package like an accusation and shouted, "WHO THE HELL THREW THIS?!" I could be loud when I wanted.

The entire restaurant silenced.

"WHO THREW IT?!"

"You did!" someone heckled. "We woulda won nationals if it wasn't for you!"

I ignored the comment. "WHO THREW THIS AT MY DAD?! NOBODY?!" Waited a moment. Snarled, "COWARDS!" I threw the package skidding down the tiles between the row of seats at the kitchen counter and the booths behind, then dragged Mom and Dad outside. "Let's go," I grumbled.

That was the last time we went to Denny's.

Or out to eat.

King City hated us.

The feeling was mutual.

\#

&

&*&

&*&*&

&*&*&*&

M

A few days later, I gave a press conference in front of City Hall with Mom, Dad, and my new attorney, Helen Powell standing behind me. She was working for free, I think for the publicity. Whatever worked. Free was a price I could afford.

KC-7 and a few other local affiliates (ABC, CBS, Fox, NBC) had their microphones attached to the podium the King City police in attendance had set up for me. I had called the TV stations myself to tell them about today, and KCPD.

I was dressed in one of my nicer Sunday numbers.

I gave my prepared statement at 11:00am.

"A persistent rumor has been spreading like a cancer here in King City. Several people I do not know and never met claimed I made Channing Peyton throw the NCAA championship game in Tampa last January. This is not true. What is true is that Channing and I dated before the Tampa game. He broke off our relationship before that game."

Someone shouted, "Because you wanted him to lose on purpose!"

I improvised a measured response. "During our two year relationship, at no time did I *ever* ask Channing to lose the Tampa game or any other game on purpose. What Channing did on the field was entirely up to him. I was there to support him. That's it."

I returned to reading my prepared statement.

"Instead of blaming me, people should ask themselves why any football team wins or loses a game?

"Is it skill?

"Coaching?

"Preparedness?

"Luck?

"The other team?

"Whatever you decide is the answer, don't blame the girlfriend.

"Don't scapegoat me.

"I had nothing to do with it. I cheered from the stands at every game like the rest of you. Probably louder than the rest of you. If you don't believe me, watch the replay of the Rose Bowl. You can see me screaming in the stands with my and Channing's parents near the end of the game."

I allowed a small smile and continued reading from my printed pages.

"I ask that everyone in King City stop harassing me and my family. People have called us names, thrown bricks through our windows, thrown things at us in public, and harassed me at my Target job, which I quit because of people who couldn't deal with their anger issues coming into the store and giving me a hard time.

"My parents certainly didn't do anything and I didn't either. If you're angry about losing to Alabama, ask yourselves what is more important? Obsessing over a football game your team lost six months ago, or ganging up on an innocent family and hurting them every single day because you can't accept defeat in a college football game?

"There will be another game next year, and the year after, and probably long after my parents and I have passed away.

"Remember, you can't hurt a football team. It's an idea, an identity. It's not a person. It can't bleed. But you can hurt me and my parents. We *are* people and we *can* bleed, and have.

"I ask that you please stop attacking us.

"This whole thing started because someone I never met lied about me to the media. Lies are poison. Every kid knows that. What is happening to me and my family is proof. Lies can spread like wildfire, and kill like one too.

"For the last time, the Alabama loss was not my fault, King City.

"I respectfully ask you to stop blaming me for bad luck, and leave my family alone so we can get on with our lives, like the rest of you have the luxury of doing each and every day.

"Thank you for your time."

Reporters and a handful of ambitious bloggers hurled questions at me like rocks at an archaic stoning ceremony.

I didn't answer any of them.

I had spoken my piece.

Chapter 30

CAROL

The ceaseless ringing of Mom and Dad's telephone, and the thu-u-u-u-umping of circling helicopters over my parents' house heralded the arrival of the national news crews and their many vans with their tall microwave antennas and their cigarette-smoking fast-food-eating reporters with their phones glued to their ears like my story was more important than the President's.

Maybe it was on that particular day. I don't know.

I gained a new appreciation for the term "media circus." It was as if Ringling Bros. And Barnum & Bailey had parked on my neighborhood street. It wasn't what I'd call The Greatest Show on Earth, unless you liked being under a media microscope.

They came because my press conference was picked up by the national news shows and rebroadcast. USA Today called asking permission to reprint my speech in its entirety.

Being briefly famous because the city where you lived your entire life hates you is not an honor. The media calls were so continuous, we unplugged all the phones in the house after a while.

When I was interviewed on camera in front of a wall of bright and blinding lights in my parents' living room, I clenched fists in my lap to hide my nerves. Celebrity news reporters from every major network interviewed me that day, including Lesley Stahl from 60 Minutes. They were going to air a lengthy Sunday segment about me, complete with the ticking stopwatch. I didn't watch it because I lived it.

The only reason I agreed to the interviews was to again send a message to King City that every single citizen would hopefully hear:

Stop attacking me.

The outcome?

Slowly, the overt attacks stopped.

The shunning did not.

My parents generally went about their business as usual, but everyone recognized me, and many people still gave me dirty looks or ignored me like I wasn't there.

It wasn't quite a Pyrrhic victory (read: the fight cost you more than the win was worth), but it was close. This was a battle I had to fight, win or lose. I wasn't running away. Mom and Dad certainly weren't. They couldn't afford to up stakes and relocate their lives, and they shouldn't have to. Unlike the media, the Duffeys weren't a traveling road show. Both sets of my grandparents had been born in King City. It was our town too.

You know how I knew?

To everyone's surprise, a vocal contingent of feminists at KCU marched in my honor, led by none other than my favorite instigator and former roommate, Sienna Winters.

She'd never been a feminist that I knew (she liked dick waaaaay too much), but she was clever enough to find willing supporters for her cause. Before the march, she asked if I wanted to march with her and her Gyrl Gang (her name for it, their spelling). I declined because I needed to show less of my face in public, not more, especially when there was media coverage.

I saw everything on the news.

Sienna's Gyrl Gang carried handmade signs that said things like:

CAROL DUFFEY IS INNOCENT (with an enlarged photo of me taken from my King City High School senior-year yearbook photo, which Sienna said they scanned out of one of the other girl's yearbooks, who had been a freshman at KCHS when I'd been a senior)

JAIL CHANNING PEYTON (his Cheetahs team photo enlarged behind prison bars)

FOOTBALL OPPRESSES WOMYN (Sienna later told me her Gyrl Gang demanded that one on general principles)

CHANNING THE CHEATER (unclear if that meant he'd cheated on me or the football field or both)

HOW CAN YOU LIVE WITH YOURSELF, KING CITY?

One block-lettered sign read "QUEEN king CITY" with the word "king" crossed out with a red X.

And so many others that pled my case *in absentia.*

It was basically Gyrl Power day, in support of my plight.

Throughout their tireless and vocal march, they made their way boldly through the shopping district near KCU, bullhorns blaring slogans and handheld cowbells clanging in support of me. Then they wove their way through campus, ending up at Cheetahs Stadium near the oversized cheetah statue where they circled symbolically, predators penning their prey before the slay. They threw water balloons filled with milk at the cheetah. I guess it was supposed to symbolize breast milk?

Seeing them fight so hard for me, when so many had fought so viciously against me, made me want to cry. Knowing you were not alone meant everything.

Sienna in particular was a relentless force of support.

"I got your back, bitch," she'd said nonchalantly when she'd told me about the idea in the first place. "We'll show the assholes in this town who the real asshole is."

I want to say their protest engendered nothing but good.

It didn't.

That day, as they gained the attention of King City, many were not happy and did not take the attack sitting down.

The Gyrl Gang was verbally harassed by a growing number of young men wearing KCU Cheetahs T-shirts who gathered at the stadium to watch and lob taunts.

The scariest part, after it was dark and the Gyrl Gang ended their march, a group of men wearing shadowy hoodies skulked after Sienna, following her home.

Sienna later told me they taunted her incessantly, calling her a lesbian, dyke, carpet muncher, pussy lover.

"And you aren't?" she'd spat back proudly.

When they started joking about raping her, she got scared. There were at least ten of them and Sienna was alone.

She did reply, "If you want a protest sign up your ass, go ahead and try." By then, she was freaking out, gearing up for a desperate run.

There was a minute there where she was sure they were going to drag her into some dark bushes beside a building and attack, but by then, she was nearing her dorm in Hemingway Hall on campus, and a bicycle cop rode up just in time to scare off the beasts in the hoodies.

Violence averted.

Until the next morning.

When she told me she found red paint splattered all over her car, and a butcher knife jammed deep into the crack between the driver window and the doorframe, I made her promise to never march for me again.

I would feel terribly guilty if Sienna of all people, were to be hurt or even killed for trying to protect my reputation, of all things. *My* reputation would never be worth *anyone* dying over.

To my immense relief, when Sienna graduated that spring, she moved to New York to look for work. King City was too small for Sienna's big personality anyway. As long as she remained my friend and vocal supporter — "Carol Duffey is innocent, bitches!" — she'd be safer there than here.

One nagging worry festered blackly in the back of my brain: how long would it be until an angry young mob of men joking of rape followed *me* home, where there was no campus bicycle police waiting to stop them?

I knew my remaining time in King City was short lived, courtesy of Channing Peyton.

I *never* should've opened my dorm room door for him.

#
&
&*&
&*&*&
&*&*&*&
M

My departure was hastened by the biggest surprise of all.

I never had to uncover the truth about the Cheetahs cheating on their exams or drug tests because somebody else did it for me.

The scandal broke harder than a bursting dam, hitting like a hurricane in late August, a few months after my initial press conference.

A number of corrupt KCU administrators, professors, and members of the Cheetahs football coaching staff, including Head Coach Bill Slaughter, were arraigned on charges of felony conspiracy to commit mail and wire fraud (which included email and texting), and honest services fraud (because KCU football players who didn't have the grades to get into KCU took academic slots from kids who did have the grades).

Their elaborate criminal scheme involved copious bribery of KCU administrators and professors (tenured and adjunct, even several graduate student teacher aides) by the coaching staff. The shifty administrators were paid to let academically unqualified football players into KCU, and the unethical professors were paid to pass failing football players enough to meet the NCAA academic eligibility requirements.

No mention was ever made of where the bribery money came from. Consequently, many of the guilty KCU staffers went to jail in jumpsuits.

Worse, every football player who received fraudulent admission to KCU was stripped of their NCAA eligibility until such time as they could meet all academic requirements.

That meant them sweating nervously through the retaking of admissions tests under close and merciless scrutiny. Many pencils were chewed, multiple choice answers written and erased and rewritten so many times, holes were torn through answer sheets, and much metaphorical hair was pulled out by grossly under-qualified football players who, in many cases, had never even seen the tests they were forced to "retake."

It also meant them slogging their way through entire college classes they had previously "taken" to similarly frustrating results. This time, they had to pass on their own merits.

No surprise, most players did not pass.

To make matters worse, based on tips given to prosecutors during the admissions fraud investigation, the DEA and Justice Department swiftly launched a biting investigation that dug its fangs into illegal drug use of anabolic steroids (a felony crime) by the Cheetahs players, the coaching staff who supplied them, and the conspiracy to coverup fraudulent drug testing, which Channing must have surely known about. The results were sparse, but a few guilty pleas by players and coaching staff sealed the fate of the King City Cheetahs.

Channing, the lucky boy that he was, never was implicated. His image remained untarnished. People even appreciated the balls it took to piss on the bronze cheetah statue outside the stadium. They said it showed Channing marking his territory, laying claim to the team and their Rose Bowl win, as if Channing Peyton not only bled gold (the school colors were gold and black), he also pissed literal gold. Good for him.

Can you see my sour smirk?

Spurred by public pressure, and pressure from the NCAA, the dean of KCU gutted the Cheetahs football program, firing much of the remaining coaching staff.

With the scant remaining players on the team who *did* pass all academic requirements, and the football season already into its fourth week, the Cheetahs bowed out for the rest of the season.

For the first time in its storied history, King City University had no football team, and Cheetahs Stadium went dark. Only a skeleton crew of loyal maintenance personnel tended to the lonely indoor bleachers and field. They had to keep the heat going during winter for the sake of the structure, lest it freeze to death and suffer the same fate as this year's team.

You can imagine this crushed the football spirit in King City, sending the entire town into a deep depression. You could feel it in the streets. People were more somber, less friendly, more mopey, less patient, more confrontational. Until you've lived in a football town like King City, it seems insane. If you grew up here, you'd know the Cheetahs were as important as church, amen.

The Cheetahs gave so many King Citians a sense of purpose, of significance, of community.

If the Cheetahs won, then by gosh, *you* were a winner too.

If your neighbor was a Cheetahs fan, then by jove, they were your brother or sister in gold and black, and you would fight alongside them in any battle.

Fearing I would somehow get the blame for stealing the team from everyone, I decided it was time to move on. Wherever I went in public, I was still getting dirty looks and verbal threats, some almost impossible to believe.

"I know you! I wish you'd die!" an old lady said to me one day at the grocery store in the frigid meat department, spitting out the words like a foul taste in her mouth. "You're that Carol girl who ruined everything!"

An old freaking lady! She looked like she was at least 90, maybe 95. Total great-grandma type who looked like she kissed stray kittens wherever she went.

"I know you!" echoed her hate.

She didn't know me. But she was wearing a gold and black Cheetahs sweatshirt. That explained it.

"I wish you'd die!" Her face had been incredibly vicious. Like I had killed every one of those kittens she should've been kissing instead of cursing me with her vexing hex.

Do you know how it feels to have a complete stranger wish you were dead to your face?

Awful.

A sign of the tortured times: some T-shirt shop downtown near KCU started selling silkscreened shirts featuring my smiling toothy high school yearbook photo and the catchphrase CAROL DUFFEY, CHEETAH KILLER.

When I found out, my attorney Helen Powell and I quickly shut that down based on a claim of copyright infringement and threat of a whopper of a civil lawsuit ($2 million in damages), only to have a new version of the shirt pop up with a cartoon drawing of someone who was obviously me, but a much uglier version, the mutant monster villainess version, with the name CAROL DUNCEY. The new shirts sold like heroin-laced hotcakes, and I'd see them all over town. There was nothing Helen or I could do legally except accept it.

I want to tell you those shirts were funny, that I bought them to give to friends as ironic gag gifts, but I didn't. They weren't funny. I hated them. It felt like King City was a gigantic nightmare grade-school playground I'd never be able to escape.

The best remedy was for me to simply leave.

The only question was where to go?

I needed to pick a college to finish my Legal Studies degree, one that was far, far away, in a galaxy where people didn't care so much about football or me.

Good fortune finally shone on me.

I was contacted by, of all places, San Diego University in California. They had seen my story on national news and they wanted to offer me a full ride scholarship to finish my senior year there. They even had a prestigious Legal Studies undergraduate program, and their own Law School that would be happy to have me.

As sad as Mom and Dad were about the idea of me moving halfway across the country, we all agreed it was an incredible opportunity.

That fall, I packed up everything I needed, which wasn't much, and put it in a rented U-Haul van. Dad took time off work to make the three-day journey west with me. I said a tearful goodbye to Mom and joked, "At least we're not taking a covered wagon."

"Be safe, Carol," Mom had practically whimpered.

It would be the first time I was away from home more than a week without seeing them, save for the one sleepaway camp I went to for three weeks when I was twelve.

Growing up, I thought I'd spend my entire life in King City with Mom, Dad, and my extended family. When I set foot in sunny San Diego and smelled the Pacific Ocean, I had no idea I would never go back home. Having nobody hating you was good enough reason to stay. They also had an amazing art program, and on a whim, I took a life drawing class for an elective. Little did I know that meant drawing from nude models. It turned out one of their naked male models was a hot hunk of man candy named Christos Manos. Next to Channing Peyton, this guy Christos was to die for, but that's not my story. I chose to make my story man-free for the next ten lonely years. I wouldn't let myself fall for any hot hunk ever again.

You can probably guess the hollow hole where my heart used to be, the sad cavern in my chest abandoned by Channing Peyton, had never gone away.

Over time, one thing became clear:

Channing had taken *every* piece of my heart.

As the years passed, and I avoided romantic relationships like the plague, I learned one thing that Jordyn Hoyle had *not* taught me. I had always assumed she meant that men took pieces of your heart and kept them for themselves, holding onto them forever like prizes, pocket lint, or bottle caps for their broken-hearts baseball card collection.

What I learned?

Some men, men like Channing Peyton, took pieces of your heart and flushed them down the toilet.

I know because I never heard from him again.

That is, not until ten years later when he came skulking drunkenly up my parents frosty driveway to torment me one last time, and gloat over the pieces he'd flushed.

Floosh!

There goes my heart.

I hope the dolphins enjoy the pieces.

I hear broken human hearts are a favorite delicacy of theirs (they don't like us as much as you think).

Ha.

Ha.

Ha.

Thanks a lot, Channing.

No, seriously, thank you *ever* so much.

Asshole.

In ten years, I'd feel very differently when Channing dropped into my life like a falling star.

I'd heard you were supposed to wish on those.

Christmas Present

"Jake Martinelli is always making a list.

"He's always checking it twice.

"He damn well knows who's naughty, but he sure as fuck ain't nice.

"Know why?

"Jake Martinelli isn't fucking Santa Claus.

"Don't piss him off unless you want a bomb in your Christmas stocking."

—*Channing Peyton*

Chapter 31

CAROL

A loud sound woke me.

It took me a moment to realize I was in my high school bed at my parents house, and another moment to realize I wasn't 14 or 18 or 22. I'd left those lonely girls behind a decade ago.

Another thud startled me.

"Dad?" I whispered. "Mom?"

Had he or she fallen?

They were getting dangerously close to that age.

I threw back my covers and jumped out of bed, ripped open my bedroom door and padded down the carpeted hallway in my bare feet and pajamas.

The living room was lit by the soft reddish glow of the Christmas tree lights. Dad insisted on keeping it on all night whenever I was here. Arguing it wasted electricity was impossible because that was his argument every other time of year *except* Christmas.

A boom!

Followed by a poof!

Black clouds puffed from the fireplace.

Had the chimney fallen in?

How much would that cost to fix?

I hated to think.

Out rolled a soot-stained Santa.

I gasped and grabbed the fireplace poker, holding it like a baseball bat. Realized it had a point. Switched to a spear grip. I had taken self-defense classes. They taught you how to use everyday household items to defend yourself.

"Don't move," I hissed, pushing the point of the poker into the ribs of Santa Claus. My behavior definitely fell into the naughty category, not nice. So much for any presents under the tree for me this year.

"It's me, Carol." Sooty Santa tried to stand up.

"I have no idea who you are!" I gave a shove with the poker, pushing him rolling onto his back.

"Ow! It's me! Channing!" He pulled down his sooty beard, revealing his face.

"Are you insane?!" I hissed. "You just broke into my parents' house!"

"The chimney was open," he smirked.

"Ha! What were you thinking?"

"That I love you, Carol. I always have. I never stopped."

"You have a funny way of showing it." I was too amused to be angry or take any of this seriously. "You've made a huge mess. Let me grab some of Dad's tarps from the garage and lay them down so you can walk outside. Then I'll clean this up." When I thought about the amount of work Channing's little show of chivalry had just created, I got angry.

"I'll help," he said.

"No, you'll go," I whispered. "If you wake my parents, I'm going to kill you. Stay there while I get tarps. I don't want you spreading your mess around." I walked through the kitchen into the garage. Dad kept it well organized and I knew where to find the tarps.

Grumbling, I carried several back into the house.

"Let me help," Channing said.

"No. You'll get soot everywhere. Just stand there." I unfolded three tarps in a path between Channing and the front door. "Get out." When I looked up, I tightened.

He'd stripped down to his sooty red Santa pants (held up by suspenders), and boots. The hat, beard, and jacket were folded neatly on the tarp. That was so Channing, always folding his own clothes. I'd have to send Karen a thank you note in the morning for good parenting.

I forgot to mention, Channing wore nothing underneath the Santa jacket.

That body.

It brought back memories.

Vivid sexual memories.

It was better than I remembered, and I remembered perfection.

I had not been alone in a room with a half-naked man since... Channing. Although I had been strictly celibate since he dumped me, I had kissed several men along the way. I wasn't a nun. Some part of me did *not* want to die a spinster. So I had dated now and then, kissed a few men, nothing more.

Kissing told me all I needed to know about how attentive and responsive a man would be in bed if I ever let any of them go there. So far, none had measured up to Channing's kisses. Why bother with more? Empty, emotionless sex had zero appeal for me. I had a vibrator. The unfortunate truth: Channing's passionate and skilled bedroom prowess had ruined me by spoiling all other men.

None had ever measured up.

The unfortunate truth of it stood in front of me, looking unfortunately gorgeous.

"Channing," I sighed, "put a shirt on."

"Didn't bring one. I didn't want my jacket dusting soot everywhere, so I carefully folded it."

"Gee, thanks," I snarled, remembering the blast zone of soot underneath the tarp, which I would have to clean up before Mom and Dad woke up in the morning, if that was even possible without a wet vac? Dad didn't have one of those. "Can you go now?" I stood with my hand on the front doorknob, the opposite side of the living room and dining room area from Channing and the fireplace. "I have a lot of work to do, thanks to you."

"I told you I'd help."

"No, Channing!" I hissed. "I want you gone. What part of that don't you understand?"

He lifted one booted foot, slid the boot off. Then the other.

"That's not leaving," I warned.

"My boots are loud."

"Gee, maybe if you hadn't snuck down the chimney in your *loud* boots, you wouldn't have to worry about it, would you?"

He put the boots on his folded clothes and carried them under his arm across the crackling tarps toward me and stopped.

"Bye." I opened the door for him. "Don't come back. Ever. Please. For my parents' sake."

He cocked a smile, which was relatively clean compared to the rest of his soot-black face, which oddly intensified his chocolate caramel eyes as they searched mine.

Those eyes once loved me.

I now hated them.

My body disagreed.

My head knew better and I threw up a shield of humor, saying, "You look like a chimney sweep."

"You look like an angel."

"Go, Channing," I grumbled, twisting the doorknob.

"Do I at least get an A for effort?"

"Would you please stop stalling?"

"Give me a grade and I'll go," he grinned.

"No."

"How about an A-minus?"

"No, Channing."

"B-plus?"

I rolled my eyes, "More like a D-plus."

"D-plus?" He laughed.

"You made a huge mess."

"Granted, but the effort alone is at least a C. The costume, the chimney, and the *sleigh*. The sleigh, Carol."

"You mean your car and driver?" I smirked. "The black Mercedes or whatever it was."

"No, I mean my sleigh. Look out the window."

I leaned over to look through the front picture window and gasped. "You did not."

"I did too," he grinned proudly.

Eight actual reindeers and a fancy Santa sleigh strewn with a rainbow of Christmas lights stood in the snowy street, puffs of breath pluming from their snouts.

I said, "Where'd you get eight reindeer?"

"Nine. Don't forget Rudolph."

I looked again. Sure enough, a ninth reindeer led the team, red nose glowing. "How did you...?"

"A red LED light and very small battery pack."

"Wow. That's amazing. Did you rent them or something?"

"The North Pole," he winked.

"No, really. You rented them, right? That and the sleigh must've cost a bundle."

"It was nothing. We have all the money in the world."

"We? You and Mrs. Claus?"

"No, Carol. You and I. I have more than I'll ever need. You can have the rest."

"I don't want your money," I sneered. "I've never wanted your money."

"How about a sleigh ride? I can take you someplace warm. How about Barbados? We can be there in five minutes."

"Cannot," I grinned.

"Can too, but we'll have to make a few more stops in Europe before the sun rises there. That'll take an hour, I hope you don't mind. I have to finish up Spain first."

"What about Africa?"

"Did that already," he chuckled. "Started with Asia, worked my way west, then went to Africa, then Europe."

Trying not to laugh, I folded my arms across my pajamas and smiled. There had been a time when I had loved *this* man hard, and with good reason. He sparkled with positive energy, the indomitable Channing Peyton, the man who never stopped fighting for his dreams. But I would never forget the one who had dumped me harder, or his absolute lack of reasons why.

"I missed you, Carol. My life has been empty without you in it. I haven't loved anyone since you. I'm lost without you."

My ice was starting to melt. No, I couldn't let him in. "Go, Channing," I sighed, twisting the doorknob and opening it.

He banged into me, closing the door and turning me around with my back to it. His naked heat and hard abs pressed me against it.

I was trapped. "Channing..." I squirmed.

"I need you, Care," he muttered and thrust his hips into mine, which required he spread his long legs to bring his crotch level with mine.

"No, Channing." I pressed my palms against his rock hard chest. It was hot to the touch. It was also naked. Touching him bridged an electric connection that transcended time and brought me swooping back to before he'd left me.

My body suddenly remembered what love felt like.

It felt like Channing Peyton.

My ice dripped away in a flood of passion that sent the rest of me dripping into my panties and pajamas.

"Please forgive me, Care," he whispered. "I left you because I loved you."

"If you loved me, why didn't you stay?" I whined, softly hitting his chest with the bottoms of my little fists. "I was so lonely without you. Everyone hated me. It was just me, Mom, and Dad against the world. I needed you then, Channing. Why did you leave?" I could feel my 22 year old self, the one I'd been *before* Channing left me, expanding and filling my body with a hot hunger for his love as the sensible rest of me melted completely away.

"I'm here now," he muttered. "Forever, Care. Forever."

His lips found mine and we kissed.

Soft, hot, slow.

We had always fucked with our tongues.

Always.

It was no different now.

After ten years, this man was my puzzle piece. We locked together perfectly in a passionate embrace.

Channing picked me and carried me across the crackling tarps to my high school bedroom, closing the door behind us. "Remember when we made love all over this house?"

"How could I forget?" I sighed as he set me on the bed.

My pajamas disappeared with his Santa pants.

Naked, he smothered me in lust.

He filled me with his need.

Started a slow thrust.

The ecstasy was instant.

Channing fucked away all the pain, the hurt, the betrayal, removing it from my body and filling me with the love I'd craved for ten empty years.

We came together like always, snuggling into a warm and loving orgasm that was over too soon and not nearly as intense as it should've been.

He weighed into me and whispered in my ear...

"Carol? Are you awake? It's already nine. Aren't you getting up? I have breakfast ready."

Why did Channing sound like Mom?

Oh, shit.

My eyes fluttered open in my empty bedroom. Morning light leaked around the edges of the curtains.

Channing wasn't here.

The door was closed.

My hand was tucked between the heat of my legs under my pajamas, my fingers nestled in my wet folds under my panties, and my clit was sizzled in the after glow of my orgasm.

Fuck, fuck, fuck.

Had I been masturbating in my sleep, or...

"Mom?" I asked.

"Yes, hun?" she said through the door.

"Were there tarps all over the living room floor when you and Dad got up?"

"What? No." She laughed. "Of course not. What ever gave you such a strange idea?"

"Any soot stains in front of the fireplace?"

"No. Carol? Are you okay? You're starting to worry me."

I sighed, "I'm fine. I'm up. I'll be out in a minute."

"Don't take too long. You don't want your breakfast getting cold."

What a disappointment.

Had I dreamed all of it?

Not just the Santa thing, but also Channing being here last night before I went to bed? I had been drinking at TT's with Sienna and Jordyn. No, I'd had nonalcoholic cider. Channing had absolutely been here at the house and drunk when I'd come home. He'd offered his grandma's ring before falling in the snow. Then he'd gone home. All that happened. But he had *not* snuck in through the chimney and we had *not* had sex.

My body obviously wished we had.

I pulled my hand out of my pajamas and examined my fingers in the dim morning light.

They glistened.

I debated taking the time to give myself a satisfying orgasm while my breakfast got cold. If I didn't do it now, I wouldn't any sooner than bed tonight, and I certainly wasn't getting cold. I was literally hot and bothered and wet from the dream. And I often masturbated to memories of sex with Channing anyway. Nothing else came close.

This wouldn't be any different.

I imagined him entering me in this very bed.

It didn't take long to come hard. I was already turned on from either the dream, or seeing him last night, or I don't know what, but I came hard enough I had to cover my face with my pillow and bite it to keep from screaming.

Then I did my best to forget Channing existed while eating breakfast with my parents.

Chapter 32

CHANNING

I woke to someone smashing in my skull with a pillowcase full of padlocks. No, that was my whiskey hangover. When I opened my eyes, morning light stabbed my retinas. I clamped them closed and groaned.

Waited to see if my bed was spinning on a gimbal.

Not spinning, only swaying.

I'd had worse.

The whiskey buzz was gone.

What had I done last night?

Not Carol.

That would've been nice.

She hadn't been in the mood.

I'd gone to her house to win her back.

Didn't work.

Based on her reaction, it was a safe bet the Pope would sooner open a drive-thru abortion clinic in the Vatican than Carol would ever forgive me for how I'd dumped her in college without an explanation.

We'd have to see if I could rectify the situation. I would attempt making amends, whether or not she forgave me.

Where to begin?

For starters, I would ignore her request to leave her alone. Blame Dick. I felt compelled to burrow my way back into her heart so Dick could burrow his way back into his favorite destination.

Breaking down Carol's barriers would require a diligent campaign of charm and ingratiation, thoughtful gifts, romantic gestures, the works. I could do that. It was no different than courting money from suckers flush with cash. Seducing people out of what I wanted from them was half of what I did with my time. How hard would it be to seduce Carol into reopening her heart? She'd done it once before.

With no money involved, it might be a challenge.

But if I involved vast sums of cash, how hard could it be? Everyone loved money. Not as much as me, perhaps, but everyone was on a first name basis with it.

I slowly swung my legs to the floor and stood up.

"Are you up, sir?" Terrance suddenly materialized in the corner. Scotty from Star Trek had nothing on Terrance.

"Fucking Terrance! Do you always have to do that? It's like you're my baby sitter, not my butler."

"Sometimes I'm both, sir. Mr. Martinelli is waiting for you downstairs."

"Jake's here?"

"Yes, sir."

"Fucking great."

"Did you tell him I'm here, or can I sneak out?"

"Mr. Washington mentioned it, sir." Terrance generally called Lashawn Mr. Washington. "They're having a rather rousing chat at the moment."

"Fuck. Fine. Tell Lashawn to keep rousing. I'll be down in a minute."

"Very good, sir."

There went my day.

I took my time in the shower. Jake could fucking wait.

Leaning one hand against the marble wall while the hot water rained down, I clamped my eyes shut and fucked the best lover I'd had in the last year: my hand. Mentally, I focused on all the times Carol had made me come so hard it turned Dick inside out. I throttled him until I shot hot ropes dribbling down the marble wall.

I had never thought that an orgasm could be lackluster, but that one was.

Call it a boregasm.

A memory of Carol was not Carol. I needed the real thing. I needed her. Not once, not twice. Ten thousand times. A hundred thousand. No, a million.

A vague memory floated up from the past.

I had once told Sienna Winters I would fuck Carol a million times before we died, or something like that.

I distinctly remember Sienna liking my answer.

I also distinctly remembered Carol loving the ferocious wolf fucking we did afterward in my penthouse dorm room.

Fuck, that had been good fucking sex.

It always was with Carol.

As the sex memories of her came filtering back in, so did the feels. I had loved Carol harder than Dick had ever been for her, and that was harder than he'd been for any other woman. Carol was special. For me, as an innocent kid who'd never known the love of a woman before Carol, I'd given her everything I had when we'd had sex our first time, and every time after. I had never questioned it. She'd made it so easy to open up and give her my all every day of our relationship.

It hadn't been like that with anyone else.

With every other woman, I'd always mailed it in.

I didn't fully realize in college how special a treasure Carol had been. She was very different from the sort of women I met after her, the sort who ran over your heart the second you gave them the wheel to your feelings. I'd known quite a few of those since Carol. Opportunists, gold diggers, the usual bunch of lampreys and leeches. Women like that led with their pussies, making it difficult to see them for who they really were. Because of them, I'd learned to lock my feelings inside the bomb shelter I'd built around my heart.

I had not loved *any* woman since Carol.

Thinking about her reminded me how much I *still* loved her, that my feelings weren't dead and buried. Seeing her again had resurrected them. My heart pumped with lust for the woman I *loved*. That was enough to make Dick instantly raging hard again, pulsing his way to straining attention.

I grabbed another squirt of conditioner from the bottle and this time, it wasn't a boregasm.

It was a moregasm.

Because I desperately needed more of Carol.

One fuck would never be enough.

Every fuck until forever was the only option.

When I came hard, I nearly shot a hole in the marble, and nearly clawed gouges with the fingernails of my free hand.

I'm coming for you, Carol.

In every way that counts.

#
&
&*&
&*&*&
&*&*&*&
M

While strapping on my $90,000 Vacheron-Constantin chronograph (I paid a mere $48,000 for it because, let's face it, I never paid full price for anything), I walked down the grand staircase and across the pattern-inlay marble floor past the statuary dancers on their pedestals, heading toward the sitting room or whatever Terrance called it.

The soles of my Testoni's echoed pleasantly off the floor and walls. Nothing like the sound of leather on marble in the morning to start your day.

As for my watch, you didn't call a Vacheron-Constantin a fucking watch. It was a goddamn chronograph. One-syllable words were for the poor. Two-syllable watch company names were also for the poor.

Timex.

Rolex.

Do you notice a similarity?

Enough said.

The decor of my mansion evoked a historic ambiance by design. As a restoration project, it had been my goal to recreate the house's original interior, as envisioned by the builder and original owner, Pascal Fournier, the wealthy financier.

With the help of Lily Yang, one of my full-time interior decorators who handled the details for many of my builds, we had painstakingly researched historic sepia-toned photos of Fournier's home from when he'd finished building this place in the Roaring '20s. Lily could find anything your heart desired (when it came to decor, not love), and she spent several years tracking down or in some cases, having custom furniture built while the interior was restored to its current state by expert craftsmen. It had been a labor of love for me, her, and them.

When you didn't have a person to love (Lily was gay, otherwise who knows, we might have married over our quest to recreate Fournier's home as accurately as possible), you tended to end up loving things more than people.

I loved old things. Old things were good things. To me, the dazzle of new often smelled like desperation, the hypnotic song of some factory somewhere begging for a few dollars so you could be like everyone else who owned the exact same thing. "Buy me and I'll make you happy!"

You know what made me happy?

Making money. Anybody could fucking spend it. Making it was an art form and I was the Da Vinci of that shit.

When I walked into the sitting room, Jake and Lashawn were sitting and bullshitting in the fancy antique chairs near the wood-framed wall of windows.

"Huh, huh, huh, huh," Lashawn chuckled at something Jake had just said.

"Jaaaaaake, you piece of shit," I smiled. "How are you?"

"There you are," he smirked at me. "We were starting to worry you had slit your wrists in the tub."

"Why would I do that?"

"Haven't you heard?"

"No." I adjusted my cufflinks, already dressed in a shirt, tie, and slacks. It was a workday and this was my uniform.

"Morris Pilkington backed out."

"What?" I chuckled in disbelief, still adjusting a cufflink.

Jake nodded ominously.

I protested, "I had Pilky locked in last night." Had it not been for fucking Pilky, I would've found Carol at TT's with her two 10 friends, Sienna and the raven-haired beauty, made it a party, and probably made more progress with Carol than I had.

"Pilky changed his mind," Jake said.

"Fuck me."

"Fix it."

"Today?" I chaffed. Babysitting Pilky was the last thing on my agenda today. I had been about to clear my schedule so I could devote it to winning back Carol.

"Yesterday," Jake pinched.

"Oh, good," I smirked. "Because I have plans today."

"Get it done, Channing." It was a warning.

"Is this why you drove all the way out here? To ruin my morning? They have these things called phones. Wonderful invention. Nowadays, you can even carry them in your pocket."

"Funny," Jake said seriously. "I have some non-phone business to discuss."

"Can we discuss it while I eat breakfast?"

"What're we having?" Jake asked.

"You're having generic corn flakes, no milk. No, cold gruel, no salt. Lashawn and I are having whatever gourmet thing Frenchy is cooking up."

We migrated to the kitchen, which was fit for a king, namely me. Frenchy wore traditional kitchen whites and hovered over the gas burners fixing my feast. He was my personal chef. His real name was Frankie Delgado and he grew up in New Jersey. Never once been to France, but he trained at the Culinary Institute of America in New York and could cook the fuck out of any kitchen in the world.

"What's cooking, Frenchy?" I asked, popping a strawberry into my mouth from the platter that was already prepared, a fruit rainbow waiting on the long island, which like most things in the kitchen, was made of marble. I often made jokes to Frenchy about having him to work on "Long Island" (implying the one in New York), which he notoriously hated and considered too snooty and uppity for a Jersey Boy like him.

"Hey, boss! Good morning to ya!" Frenchy grinned quickly over his shoulder, focused on the sizzling stove. "I'm making Greek omelets."

"My mouth is already watering."

He chuckled. "You sleep okay?"

"Like a man who died from too good a blowjob," I lied.

"Only way to go," Frenchy chuckled, taking note of Lashawn and

Jake, who were already plucking fruit from the platter. Frenchy automatically adjusted for Jake, cracking more eggs onto the stove's big griddle.

"Oh," I said, "Jake will be having cold gruel."

"Sure, boss," Frenchy said, ignoring me.

Jake said to Lashawn, "You see the Cheetahs last Saturday?"

"Awwwww, dog," Lashawn enthused. "Absolute massacre. We wiped the field clean with Rutgers." Lashawn still talked about the KCU Cheetahs like they were his team.

I didn't talk about football at all. I'd left that life behind. Lashawn still followed it and loved to jaw about it with anybody who'd listen. Jake liked to bring it up in front of me to remind me who was top dog. His way of saying he still held the keys to my misery.

Lashawn continued, "They should rename them the Yellow Knights, because they're so scared." The official team name of Rutgers was the Scarlet Knights. "No, the *Scared* Knights. Huh, huh, huh, huh." He chuckled.

"Aaaaaay," Frenchy chortled. "That's my boys youse talking about." Rutgers University was in New Jersey. "Show some mercy."

They argued team stats like quarterback passing yards and completions while I ignored them.

I hated talking about football. It reminded me of everything I had ever lost that mattered to me. That included Carol. I shoved fruit in my face while the three of them talked. Frenchy finished cooking and plated our breakfasts, including a plate for himself and one for Terrance. He set them out on the bar.

"T-Dog!" I called out. "Come get your food!"

"Thank you, sir," Terrance breathed in my ear, startling a grimace out of me as always.

"Can you call ahead before you try to give me a heart attack?" I think Terrance got off on scaring me.

He dodged the question and said, "If you don't mind, sir, I'll take it in my room."

"Go for it."

Terrance refused to eat with us because "Such things just aren't done." Truth was, meals were his private time and I didn't begrudge him that. I also suspected that Jake gave him indigestion. Jake had that affect on most people.

Frenchy always ate with us and was already cutting into his food.

Jake said, "Do us a favor, Frenchy, I have some business to discuss with Channing and Lashawn." That was a hint for him to vacate.

Frenchy flicked eyes at me.

I nodded.

"Enjoy your breakfast, everybody," Frenchy said, putting his silverware on his plate with a clink and taking it out of the kitchen and heading in the general direction of the big-screen theater. "I'll go see what's on SportsCenter."

Frenchy gone, I glared at Jake, "Could you at least wait until he finishes eating?"

"No." Jake straddled a bar stool and calmly cut into his omelet. "Unless you want to drag Frenchy into family business. If that's what you want, be my guest." Jake chewed his food in my face. The family he was talking about wasn't one you'd ever want to join.

I hadn't.

But here I was.

Hip deep in Jake's shit.

Same as every year for the last ten.

Even though he and Tony had made back the money they had lost on my last Rose Bowl a decade ago (they nearly tripled what they started with after I threw the championship a week later), they still held my fuckup over my head like a guillotine. Tony's favorite threat when I got bitchy about dirtying my hands on their more questionable schemes? "We'd hate for something bad to happen to that old girlfriend of yours from college, kid. What was her name again?" Like Tony ever forgot. Tony could barely read, but he never forgot a name or a face. "Carol something. Duffey! That's it. Carol fucking Duffey. Cute girl. You ever check up on her, kid?" Only to make sure she wasn't dead because of me or these assholes. Tony knew how to keep me on a leash.

I sat down next to Jake and sighed over my breakfast, "What is it this time?"

Jake chuckled and chomped, "You'll love this."

I was confident I would not.

"I need you to throw someone out a window." Jake smirked his devil's smile.

What did I tell you?

I smirked back, "If it's Pilky, I'll be glad to. Point me to the nearest window." I was exaggerating for effect. I hadn't murdered anyone and didn't plan on it any time soon.

"You can throw him too. I meant someone else."

Lashawn had been sitting through this discussion chewing his food silently, looking very much like someone who wished he was somewhere else. Lashawn always had my back, but I didn't like dragging him into the worst of it.

"Who?" I asked.

"You know Tipple Town?" Jake queried.

Lashawn perked up. "We were there last night. I love that place."

"Yeah." I said to Jake, "Tim said to give you his best."

"I already gave him mine," Jake said cryptically.

"Gave him your what?"

"Best offer. That crip refused it. I need you to make him one he can't."

I frowned, "Are you trying to buy TT's?"

"Plow it under," Jake said, stabbing a piece of omelet into his mouth. "We're putting up another tower. Tim the crip doesn't want to sell his Daddy's fucking business. I don't give a fuck about whose business it is or was. Make him sell. I don't care how. Convince him."

Chapter 33

CAROL

"What should we do today?" Dad asked over breakfast, cutting into his buttered french toast and mopping up maple syrup.

Try not to think about Channing Peyton, I thought.

Mom said, "We could go to the museums downtown." King City had several world-class museums, most notably the Pascal Fournier Museum of Art. Fournier had been a rich financier who'd built up one of the country's largest art collections in the early-to-mid-20th century. He'd also built an impressive museum to house it and donated it to the city upon his death.

"I was hoping to try flying my drone at the park," Dad said. "We're supposed to have sun all week. A nice change from the snow flurries."

I was hoping to not think about Channing. He wouldn't leave my thoughts alone today.

When I had set the breakfast table for Mom, I had literally went to put down a fourth plate and silverware until Mom laughingly asked who it was for. Santa Claus had been my guilty answer. Mom's concerned reply, "Are you sure you aren't running a fever?"

If being hot and bothered counted, yes. Otherwise, fit as an un-effed fiddle. Was I obsessing about sex? No more than usual when the one man I'd ever had the best sex with (the best imaginable), came waltzing back into my life and my dreams with an engagement ring.

"Which do you prefer, Carol?" Mom asked, sipping her coffee mug with both hands.

I preferred not to think about Channing, but my heart wondered what Channing wanted to do.

Traitor.

\#

&

&*&

&*&*&

&*&*&*&

M

CHANNING

"Are you really gonna tear down TT's?" Lashawn asked from behind the wheel of the black Mercedes, driving us through the recently snowy roads that had been freshly plowed and salted before sunrise. Jake had already left my mansion to go murder more babies, or whatever he did when I wasn't looking.

Lashawn was driving because my hangover was still pounding nails into the backs of my eyeballs whenever I looked at the blinding white snowscape of King City surrounding us. With the sun full up, my sunglasses weren't enough to cut the glare. Lashawn didn't mind. It meant we could discuss the day's business in private.

"You listening?" Lashawn asked.

"Sorry, what?" I sat in the passenger seat and had my nose buried in my phone going through emails. I swear to fuck I got a thousand a day.

"TT's. Are you really gonna pressure Tim until he sells?"

"I'll get to it when I get to it," I grunted.

There was a cookie-cutter office park on the northwest side of King City where I had my main business offices nestled with the rest of the bland buildings. Three floors, 215,000 square feet. Place was immense. R&D for Peyton Solar was on the ground floor. Operations, sales, and management were on floor 2 with Peyton Construction and Peyton Auto Parts (we now had 74 stores in the midwest). Accounting, HR, and admin for all three businesses were on floor 3. My gratuitously large executive office was in the corner of 3. The only thing not here was everything related to Peyton Auto Circle. There wasn't room here. Fortunately there was there.

Lashawn accompanied me into the atrium to the glass elevators. Christmas decorations festooned each floor and were visible on the ride up. Trees, tinsel, garland, ornaments, candy canes, the usual. Hundreds of people in cubicles were busy making me money. Okay, the bulk of the profits went to Jake and his family, but you get the idea. Just because my name was on everything and I was the one calling the shots day-to-day didn't mean I owned it all. But I owned enough to make me filthy rich.

The elevator doors opened and out we stepped.

Behind the reception desk was the PEYTON INDUSTRIES signage mounted on the wood wall, the letters cut from etched titanium, also gratuitously and unnecessarily expensive.

"Good moooorning, Mr. Peyton," purred Ashley the hot receptionist, her lips wet and red where she sat behind the wide desk smiling invitingly.

"Good morning, Ashley," I said politely, scrolling through emails without making eye contact. Only five hundred to go.

"Morning, Ashley." Lashawn tipped her a nod.

He and I kept walking.

Did you expect me to stop for Ashley? I had yet to fuck her, not for *her* lack of flirting. Like all of my employees, Ashley was too good at her job to lose, and I never fucked the women who worked for me. Besides, I couldn't fuck everybody. I'd tried in years past, but like I'd told Carol last night, I hadn't had sex in over a year. Chasing unforgettable ass that I quickly forgot had become pointless. Carol had really done a number on Dick a decade ago, hadn't she?

"Oh, Mr. Peyton?!" Ashley called out.

"Yes, Ashley?"

"Rosa told me to tell you she has the checks ready."

"Which checks?"

"The Christmas bonus checks."

"Fuck. I almost forgot." I turned on the toe of my loafer and strode toward accounting while Lashawn continued to his office.

Did I mention I was better than an equal opportunity employer? 60% women (who wanted to look at men?), equal pay, and it was the United Colors of fucking Benetton around here, the over 18 version. I didn't care what nationality a woman's pussy was, I wanted it. Okay, used to want it. Fucking Dick and his Carol obsession.

Without stopping, I walked past Rolando, Rosa's man-candy assistant. If I wasn't mistaken, he was Rosa's great-nephew, but he was a good looking kid either way.

"Mr. Peyton!" Rolando gasped. "Ms. Ramirez is on the phone! You can't—"

Nobody told me what to do in my office.

Rosa Ramirez, my head of accounting, was indeed on the phone and held up a finger while chattering away in her Puerto Rican accent. If Ivonne Coll, the *abuela* from Jane the Virgin had a sister with bigger hair and a business suit, she would be Rosa.

I stood patiently.

When Rosa finished and hung up her phone, she folded her hands on her executive desk and smiled, "Channeen, *mijo*. Are you ready to play Santa?"

"I'm ready to hand out checks," I smirked defiantly.

"You have to wear the beard. You always wear the beard. I have it ready for you." She walked over to a low filing cabinet and picked up a white Santa beard and red Santa hat. "Put it on." Her eyes twinkled.

"Must I?"

"Everyone loves the beard."

"*You* love the beard."

"You do too," she laughed the lie. Rosa had the persistence of a river.

She could wear down anyone, even me. If you're having trouble picturing it, picture the Grand Canyon. It was worn down over a period of 2 billion years by that bitch the Colorado River. I was pretty sure "Colorado" was Spanish for Rosa Ramirez. It was easier to give in to her than resist.

I put on the hat and beard. "There. Happy?"

"Look how cute you are, *mijo*." She reached up and pinched my cheek quite hard. "Now the other one." She reached up.

I cringed and waved her away. "Are you trying to pop a zit?"

"You don't have any." Her pinching hand wavered like a determined cobra. "To give you that Santa glow. Don't be such a baby, Channeen. Come here." She pinched again and grinned. "There. Perfect."

We spent the next two hours walking from cube to cube and floor to floor handing out bonus checks. Rosa didn't have to tell me which checks went to who because I already knew. Everyone had been working here long enough it was easy to remember. If I hired you it was because you excelled at your job. If you did that, you could work for me forever. If you didn't, run for the nearest exit door and cover your ass because my foot was aiming for it.

I skidded to a stop when we got to the 2nd floor wing where the solar panel sales team sat. Most of the cubes were empty. I muttered to Rosa, "Does everyone have the Christmas flu or something?"

Rosa winced, "Didn't Jake tell you?"

"Tell me what?" I grumbled.

"I'll tell you after," she whispered. When we finished and were back upstairs in her office, she said, "Jake decided to cut costs and farm out sales to independent sales agents. He said we were paying too much in salaries and benefits, so he let them go."

"When did this happen?" I scowled.

"Six weeks ago."

"Why didn't you tell me?"

"I thought you knew."

"Fucking Jake." This wasn't the first time he'd done something like this. For a guy who rarely showed up here at the office, he sure liked to drop in on a whim and fuck things up for the fun of it. "Can you have Lekisha in HR try and get back anyone who hasn't found another job yet?"

"You better tell her. I don't want to come between you and Jake." Jake was the one person Rosa could not wear down, not even with a jackhammer. Man was made of stone-cold steel.

"Right." I grit my teeth, took off my Santa hat and beard, and went looking for Lekisha. When I found her in her cube, she wore an intentionally ugly knit Christmas sweater. The ladies had a competition going, same as every year, and I famously picked the winner who got a night out for two, including tickets to The Nutcracker Ballet at the opera house downtown. Lekisha was more than happy to make the effort to get back our sales team on my behalf.

I said, "If Jake gives you any pushback, tell him to talk to me." I'd fight it out with Jake later.

"You got it, Mr. Claus," Lekisha giggled and winked.

I reached for my face, expecting to find the beard still there. Nope, back in Rosa's office were I'd left it. "Next year, Lekisha, you wear the beard. No, better yet, you're wearing a frumpy Mrs. Claus dress and wig, and *you're* handing out the checks while I watch and laugh."

"Long as you wear the beard, I'm down."

"How did I know you'd say that?"

She laughed and I left.

Collected another box of checks from Rosa and drove myself out to a build site on the south side of King City, on the leading edge of King City's suburban sprawl, where we had a new housing development in progress. Cypress Gardens. 320 new homes just waiting to be filled (some already were) once construction was done (it was mostly interior work at this point) and the solar panels were in place (we got ample winter sun in King City).

I would not wear the Santa hat and beard for the fellas. I would wear my old Cheetahs jersey, this time at the insistence of Reggie Brown, the lead job site foreman.

The collection of office trailers were set in the dirt lot near the last of the houses waiting for siding installation, windows, doors, etc. Standing inside the office, Reggie held up a brand new PEYTON number 12 jersey (you could still buy them new from KCU where I was considered a legend, or so people told me) like they were going to tar-and-feather me with my own team jersey if I didn't put it on myself.

"Don't make us put this on you," Reggie chuckled. He was a huge dude.

I smirked and wagged fingers. "Gimme the damn jersey already."

I didn't mind, really. Most of the fellas working for Peyton Construction, whether full time or jobbers, remembered my football career at KCU better than I did, and treated me not just like their boss's *boss's* boss, but also a celebrity.

Whatever boosted morale.

My jersey on, the three of us set off to hand out the big box of bonus checks, fresh Krispy Creme doughnuts, and coffee, courtesy of Reggie. Courtesy of me, an extra bonus gift. With so much stuff to move, we drove from house to house in a company pickup truck loaded with everything.

My personal gift for the men?

Because money was nice, but a token of gratitude was even more effective at locking in their loyalty (you didn't get rich being stingy with your people), every man working today got a bottle of Jack Daniel's Holiday Select (if they were over 21). Me being a connoisseur of whiskey, this gift was a given. I passed out gift certificates for the bottles (Reggie's idea), collectible from Reggie's office *after* finishing your shift. Reggie knew better.

If a fella was unfortunate enough to be under 21 (we had quite a few kids between 18 and 20 on hand), they got a $100 gift certificate for Racer's Gentleman's Club (best strip joint in King City, where I was practically a fixture, and a silent 10% partner, especially when it was time to audition new-hires). And yes, some of the younger men on the job site over 21 traded in their whiskey for the gift certificate.

Getting drunk was nice.

Getting drunk on looking at pussy was nicer.

The fellas were pleased and I shook a lot of hands and bumped a lot of fists.

With the fun stuff out of the way, it was now time to figure out what I was going to do about Tim Farkas and Tipple Town. Taking away a man's livelihood was not a pleasant thing. Maybe I'd push Pilky out a window and give his $30 million to Tim. I'd like to say that sort of a Jake move would fix things for Tim, but once Jake fixated on an idea, he held on like a barnacle. He was going to tear down TT's unless I killed him first. That was just how Jake was.

I'd have to give a think to a better solve than that. Killing Jake wouldn't sit well with his brother Tony or me.

Before I handled any of that, I had Carol business to attend.

For that, a little recon was in order.

Chapter 34

CAROL

"You're gonna crash!" Dad laughed.

"I can't steer!" I screeched a giggle before smashing into the cold asphalt, flipping over several times and sliding to a stop in the middle of the park's walkway.

"We're dead," Dad chuckled. "I'll go turn the drone over."

I pulled the goggles off to look. For the past hour, I'd been doing a sucky job of driving Dad's drone, or as he would say, piloting. It was hard enough doing it without the goggles, which meant watching the drone with your eyes from a distance, which was how we'd started until I sort of got the hang of things. Once you put the goggles on, which were like VR goggles, and the little goggle screens showed you the view through the cameras mounted on the drone, like you were flying *inside* the little drone yourself, it was even more confusing, but it sure was fun.

We were both bundled up from the cold. Ski jackets, mittens, beanies, boots. At least the sun was out and the heavy winter snows hadn't quite set in. What had fallen when I'd arrived a few days ago had started melting away the next day. This was our second day here in the park. The afternoon temperature was in the low 40s and the asphalt path was completely dry. A few inches of snow remained on the grassy areas, but that was it.

Dad squatted down with a grunting wince. His knees and back popcorned as he picked up the drone off the ground, looking more frail in his movements than I remembered last year. I hoped he wasn't getting arthritis.

"I could've done that," I sighed, standing up from the park bench and jogging over to help.

"Already got it," he sighed. "They say flying drones is a young man's sport," he joked.

"I'm too old for it, obviously," I quipped. "And the wrong gender."

"We shoulda had you play more video games as a child," he winked.

"No thank you." I loved spending daddy-daughter time with Dad. We did so little of it nowadays. "Why don't you take over? It's more fun to watch the pro fly. Too bad none of your friends are here to race."

"They'll show up," Dad said, putting on the goggles.

Sure enough, after he flew around the trail loop by himself, he reported another drone joining in the race.

I looked around. Quite a few people in snow clothes were strolling through the park enjoying the ice blue skies and sun (Dad assiduously steered around them so as not to annoy), but none of them had goggles on, meaning they weren't flying drones. "I don't see anyone."

Now focused on flying, Dad noted absently, "They don't have to be within your line of sight. They could be sitting anywhere in the park and piloting."

"Oh."

"This guy's good!" Dad laughed cotton puffs, sounding sixteen instead of in his late 60s, which put a smile on my face. He looked it too, sticking his tongue out unconsciously while holding his controller in the air and turning it side to side like a steering wheel, even though you only used the thumb controls.

Dad may not live forever, but this moment would shimmer in rose-colored clarity as my treasured memory long after he passed away. I sniffed back a tear thinking about it, and tried to focus on the now.

A moment later, a new drone whizzed by our bench ahead of dad's. They both banked around a copse of trees and disappeared. "He's taking me around the big loop."

I couldn't see much from where I sat, but I was content enjoying Dad's action-packed narration.

"I passed him!" he laughed a minute later. "That sucker won't catch me now!" Dad cackled. "Damn!"

"What?"

"I just hit a tree branch. Came around that corner too hot and got tangled up. Damn, damn, damn." Dad's swearing was basically grade school approved. It never got any worse than this.

"What now?"

"We see if we can get the drone unstuck." Dad took his goggles off.

Together, we strolled down the asphalt path.

"There it is," Dad sighed, looking up at a high branch. "I'll never get that down. I'll have to get the extendable window washing pole from the car."

"I can get it down."

"How?"

"I'll climb."

He laughed. "It's too high. You'll break your neck. I'll get the pole."

"It's fine. I've been climbing at a climbing gym for five years, Dad. I think I can manage."

"Did I do that?" That voice, dripping with faux innocence that could coax lust from a nun.

I turned and saw Channing walking toward us holding goggles, a drone and a controller, looking fresh off the ski slopes in his puffy ski jacket, knit capped pulled low, snow pants, and snow boots.

"Was that you flying?" Dad chuckled turning to the voice. His face furrowed with hate when he recognized Channing. "What're you doing here?"

"I came to help you get your drone down." Channing was all smiles.

I smirked, "Are you wearing a disguise?"

"This? No. I always wear this."

"On a Wednesday afternoon?" I folded my arms across my jacket. Like me, Dad and Mom both used vacation time from work so we could spend it together over the holidays without spending any money on travel other than my plane tickets.

"This is my day job, Duff," Channing chuckled charmingly. "I always race drones on Wednesdays."

Dad was not amused and did his best to quietly wish Channing out of existence.

"How did you find us?" I asked Channing.

"The little birds told me. Listen."

All around us in the trees, the birds were chirping happily about the warm weather and sunshine.

Dad looked ready to leave until he remembered his drone caught in the leafless branches. He frowned at it.

"I'll climb up and get it," I said quietly. "Then we'll go."

"It's not safe, Carol," Dad warned. "I should get the pole."

"I've got a pole," Channing joked and tossed me a lascivious grin. "It should be plenty long enough."

I snorted and rolled my eyes.

Dad frowned, "Where? I don't see one."

I said, "He's joking, Dad. Don't worry about the washer pole. I'll climb up and get it." I started toward the tree trunk.

"It's up there very high," Dad warned. "Please don't climb the tree, Carol."

"Listen to your father," Channing said. "I'll get it. Can you hold this?" He offered me his drone, goggles, and controller.

"No." I smirked.

"How about you, Mr. Duffey?"

Dad eyed everything warily, "Is that a Mavic 2?" Now dad was drooling like it was a giant pink-and-rainbow sprinkled Circus Animal cookie.

"It is."

"Those go for around two thousand dollars."

"A grand," Channing smiled.

"Where'd you get it for a grand?"

"From Eric at E.T.'s Drone Home downtown."

"Eric sold it to you for a thousand dollars?"

Channing shrugged, "I never pay full price for anything. Take it for a spin while I get yours out of the tree." He set the drone on the ground and practically shoved the controller and goggles into Dad's hands.

"I couldn't," Dad said.

I smirked at Channing, "The first one's always free, isn't it?"

"It's not heroin, Duff," Channing chuckled. "I mean Carol." He was gauging Dad's reaction at having used my nickname. "Have at it, Mr. Duffey."

Dad was mesmerized by the controller.

"Let me help with these." Channing took the goggles and lowered them over Dad's head, adjusting the straps. "There! We! Go! Give her a spin while we get your drone out of the tree."

"Don't let Carol climb it," Dad warned half-heartedly, already focused on piloting the drone. Its little propellers spun up to speed and Dad started flying it.

"You heard the old man," Channing grinned.

"Don't call him that," I hissed.

"What, old?"

I gave him a "duh" look.

"Sorry," Channing said. He went to the tree and jumped up to the lowest branch, which he couldn't quite reach. He tried wrapping his arms around the trunk and shimmying up with his legs, but his snow boots kept slipping off the slick bark. He tried jumping several times before giving me a pained look. "My knee's never been the same. I lost four inches off my vertical after I injured it."

"Injured it? When did you injure it? I don't remember any injuries."

He scowled, "The NCAA championships."

"Was that one of the Rose Bowls?"

"No. It was the one after my last one." His face darkened.

Mine darkened too. "You mean the one after you dumped me."

"I'd take that back if I could."

"You can't."

"Let's focus on getting your dad's drone."

"Fine." I hated that we were again fighting like there was something significant between us, and once we finished we'd have the hot makeup sex I so desperately craved. That was a cruel fantasy that would never come true.

We both looked at the tall tree.

"What if I give you a boost to that branch?" Channing offered.

"Could you make it from there?"

"Easily."

"I'll give you a boost."

My heart didn't want him touching me because my body wanted him to. Badly.

He squatted down and laced his fingers together. "Use my hands for a step."

"Okay," I grumbled. When I stepped, it wasn't nearly high enough.

"What if I stand up, and *then* you step up my hands?"

"Okay."

This time, instead of squatting, he leaned with his hands clasped and said, "When you step, I'll straighten. You might need to brace your hands on my shoulders."

Not wanting to touch any part of him, I sighed. "Maybe I should get Dad's washing pole."

Dad was busy flying the drone, now sitting on a nearby bench, fascinated by whatever he saw whizzing by inside the VR goggles.

"Just try it," Channing said.

"Alright. Just don't try anything."

"How am I going to try anything with my hands laced under your shoe?"

"Just don't, okay?"

He rolled his eyes, "Your virtue is safe with me, Duff."

Was he referring to us losing our virginity together? It was crazy how much history I had with this man.

"You need a minute?"

"No, I'm fine. Get ready." I stepped onto his hands with one shoe and he lifted me.

Right.

Into.

His face.

By me, I meant my hips.

By my hips, I meant my crotch.

His nose was buried in it.

He inhaled deeply.

I let him.

For a languid, lingering moment, I felt a flutter of butterflies erupt in my tummy and I lost my mind as the pleasure zinged through me and I started to rain. No man's face had been in my lady business since Channing. It was rather sensational, I must admit.

Then sense returned.

"Oh no, uh-uh," Shaking my head, I collapsed my leg he was holding and landed on the other one safely and backed away several steps. "Not doing that."

"I could do that all day," Channing grinned. "Let's try that again."

"No. We're getting the pole." I angled toward Dad.

"No need," Channing chuckled. "Mine wasn't long enough before, but it is now."

I smirked, "*You* may be a 24-foot prick, but yours isn't. 24 millimeters on a good day." A blatant lie. I held up my thumb and index finger an inch apart.

"Not millimeters, Duff. Centimeters." He held up his palms at crotch level, spreading them slowly to the width of his waist. "You haven't seen it in a loooong time, Duff."

"Please, Channing, it's not that long."

"Would you like to measure?" His confidence was absolute, as was his exaggeration, which only bolstered his relentless appeal. "Having outgrown rulers, I brought a 30-foot measuring tape."

I laughed. "Can we keep this PG? Please? My Dad is *right* there."

"If PG stands for Prick Grabbing, be my guest."

"That's not even funny."

"But you're considering doing it, which is funny." He took a step toward me.

My cheeks burned with a blush, making me too distracted to back up.

"You always get red when you're turned on, Duff." He took another step, stalking.

"No I don't."

"When you take off your panties tonight and sneak them into the bathroom to hand-wash them, you'll remember the lie you're telling me now."

"No I won't."

"Liar. How many times did you have to hand wash your panties in college because you said you couldn't stop thinking about me in class?" He was now a foot away, his voice low, thrumming, and vibrating through me, old memories echoing between my legs.

"I was exaggerating." A blatant lie. "I just said that to turn you on." Why did I have to tell him that?

"Are they wet now?"

"No, Channing." Another lie.

"I'm so fucking hard for you right now it hurts."

"Not my problem," I muttered.

"Agreed. But your wet pussy is a problem I would be happy to explore in depth. I'm sure there's a sticky solution waiting for both of us at the bottom of a very long mutual orgasm."

"That's disgusting," I lied, trying not to squirm.

"There's nothing disgusting about true love."

Now I was disgusted. "You never loved me."

"I always loved you," he whispered so softly the chill breeze almost whisked his words away before they reached my ears.

But I heard.

Oh, did I hear.

I suddenly saw the 20 year old college boy who had promised to love me forever, the innocent boy inside the winning man who had bravely told me he loved me when we lost our virginity together. It had taken me some time to find the courage to say it back while he had patiently waited.

Back then, Channing had always been so patient with me, so tender, so caring. Those old feelings of love for him unfolded like spring flowers in my heart, a field of colorful roses holding me in their velvet-petaled embrace. I wanted to sink into those feelings and hug myself with gleeful abandon.

"I never stopped loving you, Care," he whispered.

That broke the spell, razing my field of flowers with a wildfire of hate.

"Ha!" I backed up. "You dumped, me Channing!" Not wanting to disturb Dad, I kept my voice down to a rattlesnake hiss. "You don't dump someone you love!"

"I had my reasons." His face paled. "I was protecting you. I owe you an explanation. Not here." He looked around cagily.

"I don't want to hear it, Channing. It's too late. We're done." I felt my heart reaching out to him, but my brain was battering it with both hands and saying, Bad idea, heart. Baaaaaad idea.

Dad suddenly interrupted, "Are you having any luck with the drone?"

Channing and I both looked at him holding his goggles up to show his eyes.

"Working on it," Channing said.

"Do you want me to get the washer pole?"

"We'll get it," Channing said. "How's the Mavic?"

"Better than my Emax Hawk 5, that's for sure," Dad laughed. "It's so much easier to pilot."

"Right?" Channing grinned. "Keep flying. We'll get yours down in a minute."

"Are you sure you don't need the pole? It's a short walk to the car."

"We're good."

"Are you sure?"

"Yes, Dad," my heart said out loud before flipping my brain the bird.

"Be careful," Dad said, then re-donned Channing's goggles and went back to flying.

I said to Channing, "Let's get Dad's drone and be done, okay?"

"Okay. I have an idea."

A minute later, Channing was leaning against the tree trunk. I climbed up his back, stood on his shoulders, and walked my hands up the trunk until I was standing tall. There was something symbolically satisfying about walking over him and standing on his shoulders. When I reached up for the branch and grabbed it, I couldn't resist stepping on his head with a giggling, "Oops."

"Ha, ha," he chuckled.

Once on the low branch, it was easy for me to climb up several more and shimmy out to the branch where Dad's drone was bound up. It was at least 30 feet off the ground, which was swimming and spinning beneath me, my branch swaying precariously under my weight, the thin patch of remaining snow on the grass offering a false blanket of security.

I could easily kill myself if I fell from up here.

I'd been this high on climbing walls many times at the gym, but then I'd always had a safety harness and a belay rope. Now my only choice was to set my screaming fear aside on a shelf where it could sit in silence while I focused, sliding slowly out on the branch toward Dad's drone.

"I can't go any farther," I called out, well short of my goal. "The branch gets too thin."

Channing asked, "Can you shake the one it's on and I'll catch it?"

"I'll try." I hooked my legs securely around the main branch, which was frighteningly slender, and grabbed the thinner one, reaching out all the way. It was just thin enough I could shake it. Doing so made my branch wave in the wind, but I ignored it. "I think it's coming loose!"

"That's what she said!" Channing laughed.

"Shut up," I giggled. "There it goes!" I watched the drone drop.

"Got it!" Channing caught it in competent hands. In a stage whisper, he said, "Now climb down before your dad sees you up there and has a heart attack!"

Dad was thoroughly enthralled inside Channing's goggles. I made my way down to the lowest branch where I hung above Channing.

"Drop and I'll catch you."

"No!" I laughed. "I'm too heavy."

"No you're not."

"What about your knee?"

"I lost vertical leap. I didn't say anything about strength."

"I would, but I might be tempted to kick you in the face on the way down."

"Do you want me to move?"

"No," I grinned, "I kind of want to kick you in the face."

"I'll move," he chuckled.

I let go and fell, landing in the snow in a half-hearted superhero pose. From this height, it was nothing. I was always dropping off the walls at the gym into the rubber pads. I stood up and dusted off my mittens.

"Nice work," he said. "Let me show my gratitude by making you dinner."

I tried to decide if that was innuendo or not.

Channing winked, "I'll feast on you after." He knew me too well.

"No, Channing."

"At least let me explain over dinner. You can go home unfucked after."

I almost teased, What if I want to get fucked? I kept my mouth shut. If I agreed to have dinner with him, I would have to leave my sex drive sitting in the garage at home, otherwise I'd get myself in trouble. There was an easy fix for that. "Can we have dinner at McDonald's?"

"I thought you hated McDonald's."

"I do. That's why I suggested it."

"Let me make you dinner. Come over to my place."

"No, Channing." I was picturing me and him in his penthouse apartment back in Faulkner Hall. That would surely lead to sex I shouldn't be having but desperately wanted to.

"Don't worry, we'll have a chaperone."

"Who?"

"Terrance."

"Who's Terrance?"

"My butler."

"You have a butler?" I snorted.

"Yes, and he's always popping up when you think you're alone. I can guarantee he'll cock block me without even trying. You have nothing to worry about."

"You seriously have a butler," I said rhetorically because I absolutely didn't believe him.

"Yes. His name's Terrance Wright. I brought him over from England myself."

"I don't believe you."

Channing smiled, pulled out his phone. Dialed. Put it on speaker. Two rings later, someone answered.

"Good morning, sir. To what do I owe the pleasure?" said an older-sounding man with a crusty British accent.

"Hey, Terrance. Can you put your phone on video?"

"Certainly, sir. One moment. Has that done it?"

"Yup." Channing turned the screen to me. "Terrance Wright, say hello to Carol Duffey."

"Pleasure to meet you, Ms. Duffey," said Terrance, who wore a dark gray suit jacket with shirt, vest and tie.

"Hi," I giggled.

"Ask him," Channing whispered.

"Um," I trailed off, not sure what to say.

"How can I assist you today?" Terrance offered a politely charming smile.

Channing whispered, "He's very helpful."

Annoyed that Channing was charming me into his clutches, I sighed. "Are you really Channing's butler?"

"Indeed I am."

"T-dog, can you chaperone Carol and me for dinner tonight at the house?"

"I would be delighted, sir."

Channing said to me, "Are you free tonight?"

I would've said no if Terrance wasn't staring at me hopefully. "Fine. I'll have dinner with you. But Terrance?"

"Yes, Ms. Duffey?" He was quick with names.

"Can I count on you to protect me from Channing?"

"Protect you, mum?"

I vaguely remembered from old movies that him calling me mum was a sign of deference. "If he tries to flirt."

"You mean if he gets cheeky?"

"Yes, that," I giggled.

"Rest assured, I'll set the hounds on him if he tries."

"We don't have any hounds," Channing said to himself. More loudly, "No hounds, Trey."

"I would never, sir," Terrance said with droll defiance.

"Yes or no, Carol. Dinner tonight? I don't want to leave Terrance hanging."

"Okaaaaaay," I laughed.

Channing's face practically unraveled in a giddy smile. "Terrance, tell Frenchy to cook up something special. Carol's coming over."

"I shall inform him, sir. Anything else."

"Nope, see you tonight." Channing ended the call.

I swatted his arm. "I thought you said *you* would cook me dinner."

"No, I said make. I'm *making* Frenchy cook it. Don't worry. He's well paid."

I laughed.

"That's a yes-I'll-have-dinner-with-you laugh, right?"

"You are such a manipulator, Channing."

"Let me get your phone number."

"Why, so you can cancel?"

"No," he chuckled. "I'm sure you want to spend the rest of the day with your Dad, and I have work to do before dinner tonight. That's not a crime, is it?"

"Fine," I smiled and told him.

"Did you get it?" Dad asked, lifting his goggles. Channing's drone rested at his feet on the park walkway, propellors no longer spinning.

"Yeah we did," Channing grinned, grabbing my hand with Dad's drone and holding it up like a victory salute, which it obviously was for him.

I prayed agreeing to dinner wasn't a horrible mistake.

Chapter 35

CAROL

"Are you sure this is a good idea, Carol?" Mom asked, sitting on the living room couch next to Dad. I'd told them about my dinner date with Channing when Mom had asked what we were doing about dinner tonight. I'd held off telling her as long as humanly possible and felt guilty when I'd admitted it.

"It's just dinner," I sighed.

"I don't know..." Mom fretted.

"He's here!" I said with unbridled excitement, feeling sixteen when Channing's black Mercedes pulled up in the street beyond Dad's inflatable snowman.

"What's he carrying?" Mom asked as Channing walked up our driveway.

"Gift bags?" I offered, barely noticing because my eyes were pinned on Channing. With his open wool coat and slick suit, he looked like a Wall Street tycoon. From the neck up, the familiar fashion model I'd once loved.

For the sake of safety, because I had stupidly shaved my legs this morning in the shower, long before I knew Channing would be spying on Dad and I racing drones, I now wore a bulky cable-knit turtleneck sweater, jeans, and snow boots. He'd need a pry bar to get me out of these clothes.

"Hey!" I opened the door before Channing knocked.

"Couldn't wait to let me in, could you?"

"Huh? No! I wanted to warn you off before the cops got here. I already called 911," I smirked.

"You mean Genevieve what's her name?"

My eyes lit up, "You remember Genny?"

"Of course I do, Duffin. She was our very first cock blocker."

"What did he say?" Mom chortled behind me.

"Clock blocker!" I blurted. "Genny in the dorms used to always stand in front of the clock."

"What clock? Your alarm clock?" Mom laughed. "She *blocked* it? So you couldn't see it?"

"Something like that," I tittered.

"Was she your roommate?"

"No," Channing said, "Genny was more of a clock thief. Always stealing other people's timepieces."

"Timepiece?" I smirked. "Where'd you learn to talk, the Walt Whitman school of poetry?"

"Robert Frost. He opened up a competing school across the street from dear old Walt. Put him out of business, sadly." Channing's eyes twinkled.

"You've changed."

"For the worse, I hope." He grinned. "Are you going to let me in?"

Dad complained, "You're letting out the heat, Carol. Let him in or close the door."

"Okay, okay," I grinned, pulling the door completely open.

When Channing stepped inside, there was a momentous quality to such a quiet moment.

"I come bearing gifts," Channing said, holding up the Christmas-themed gift bags, one with candles and angels, the other snow-covered gingerbread houses with glowing candle-lit windows and twinkling stars over a snowy valley.

"Have a seat," I said, pointing to the spot on the couch next to Mom. Dad was sitting in his easy chair. I sat in the chair opposite Mom.

Channing smiled at Mom, "Can we agree to keep our hands to ourselves, Mrs. Duffey?"

"I don't know why we wouldn't," Mom hemmed.

"Now that Carol is all grown up, I'm having trouble telling the two of you apart."

"Now Channing," Mom laughed, blushing.

Dad smirked to himself and rolled his eyes.

Channing sat down and reached into his gift bag. "You first, Mrs. Duffey." He handed her a bow-wrapped box of silver and gold. "Go ahead and open it."

"Okay," Mom laughed, untying the bow carefully. She opened the box, dug through tissues, and gasped. "Would you look at this?" She pulled out a figurine of a ballerina and a male ballet dancer. "This looks like Lladro."

"It is," Channing grinned. "I know how much you like them." He'd been here enough times to know.

Mom had several curio cabinets throughout the house bursting with porcelain figurines. She'd been collecting Hummel and Lladro since before I was born. When I was little, she'd take me hunting at thrift stores and flea markets, searching for underpriced figurines. Mom called them her lost children, and we saved them together, adopting each one with love and slowly adding them to the village living in her curio cabinets. I would often stare at them while Mom told stories about the checkered pasts of each figure, making up stories on the fly about the adventures of my miniature brothers and sisters.

"I haven't seen this one before," Mom marveled, holding it up. "Look how nice it is, Jack."

Dad grumbled a nod. He was worried. He'd told me as much after Channing had left the park the other day, warning me to be careful of him. He didn't want me getting hurt again.

"Isn't it beautiful, Carol?" Mom asked.

"It is," I nodded.

Channing said, "The ballerina reminded me of Carol. See the ponytail?"

"It does look like her when she was a girl." Mom smiled at me. "You haven't worn your ponytail in a long time. I miss it."

"Me too," I grinned, not meaning it. I had cut my hair in recent years, wearing it shorter and never in a ponytail. That broken-hearted version of me had been hiding since college for reasons standing in my parents' living room.

Mom inspected the figurine and said, "I guess we already know her story, don't we, Care?"

"We should make one up anyway," I grinned.

"I agree. We'll have to come up with one for both of them."

Channing asked, "Does it have a happy ending?"

I suddenly wanted to cry. I sniffed instead.

"Of course it does," Mom said, admiring the figurines.

"Dad's next," Channing said. "I mean, Mr. Duffey." He handed the other large bag to Dad.

"What is it?" Dad winced a smile and sat forward on his easy chair.

"Look inside," Channing prompted.

Dad dug through the red tissues and pulled out a red-bowed box that wasn't wrapped. He laughed, "A Mavic 2? No, Channing. This is too much. I can't accept this."

"I'll be honest with you, Mr. Duffey. A little bird told me you were a fan of drones."

"Who, Carol?"

"No, a little bird," Channing lied and winked at me.

I didn't say anything because I hadn't told him about Dad and his drones.

Channing said, "I bought my Mavic just the other day for you, Jack, but I couldn't resist giving it a test flight. Seeing how Eric doesn't accept returns on unboxed drones, I don't know what to do with it. I don't have time for it, honestly, so I thought, what better person to give it to than you?"

"No, I couldn't," Dad laughed.

Channing sighed, "Then I'll just have to give it to that annoying boy I passed down the street throwing snowballs at passing cars, most notably mine. That kid looks like the only use he'll have for a drone is peeping through people's windows, or he'll find a way to drop lit firecrackers from it. He seems very resourceful for a juvenile delinquent."

"Billy Varnick?" Dad frowned. "*That* junior hoodlum?"

"Gotta give it to somebody, Mr. Duffey," Channing warned, cocking an eyebrow. "Or you can keep it."

"Oh, alright," Dad chuckled, already drooling over the box.

Manipulator, I mouthed silently at Channing.

He grinned.

"What does Carol get?" Mom asked.

"Me," Channing winked.

Mom fluffed a blush.

"It's at my house," he said. "She can show you tonight when I bring her home."

"That would be wonderful," Mom smiled.

Channing's ability to know exactly what to say to my parents was new too. He used to be a bit clumsy around them, now he danced through conversations like Mikhail Baryshnikov. A decade had done him well.

"We should go," Channing said. "The reindeer are getting restless."

"The what?" I laughed, leaning to look at the window to make sure his Mercedes hadn't magically transformed into a sleigh and nine reindeer.

"Did I miss something?" Channing chuckled.

"No!" I blurted. "Let's go."

\#

&

&*&

&*&*&

&*&*&*&

M

"Lashawn!" I smiled when he stepped out of the Mercedes beaming a big grin. I threw my arms around him and hugged him hard.

"It's been a long time, girl," he chuckled. "Huh, huh, huh, huh." He opened the back door for me.

"Are you Channing's driver?"

"Only when he's drunk."

"Is he drunk now?"

"No."

"You should make him drive."

"Hell naw. The way he drives, we'd never make it back to the house. You should've seen him the other night at TT's," Lashawn smiled.

"Do you mind," Channing glared wild eyes at him.

I narrowed mine, "What night was this?"

"A few nights ago," Lashawn said.

"You're fired," Channing said.

Lashawn ignored him, "He was looking for you. Didn't he tell you?"

"No." I glared at Channing. "How *did* you know I was in town, *Channing?*"

"I told you, Duff. Lucky guess."

I smirked, "And you lucky-guessed I'd be at TT's?"

"Oops," Lashawn muttered without a hint of guilt. "My bad. Huh, huh, huh, huh."

Channing sneered at him, "Huh fucking huh. Thank you very much, Lashawn. Carol, kill him, not me. I kept my mouth shut."

"Forget it," I snorted. "But Channing is driving. Come on Lashawn."

"Are you sure? I'm not kidding about his driving, girl. He couldn't drive a driverless car without running into a tree."

"I'm not drunk," Channing said, exasperated. "You said so yourself. I haven't had a drop since the night Carol arrived."

"Is that true?" Carol asked.

"He hasn't," Lashawn nodded. "When the Chandy Man sets his mind to something, it's done."

Channing said, "Okay, you're re-hired, but no Christmas bonus this year."

Lashawn waved a hand and muttered at me, "You hear this baby?" He meant Channing. "Always with the empty threats."

I giggled, "You make it sound like you guys are an old married couple."

"Close enough." Lashawn chuckled. "We work together."

"And we're roommates," Channing added.

"What, like in an apartment?" I offered.

"Something like that," Channing said. "Do you want me to drive?"

"Yes," I grinned, happy to torment Channing. "You can be our chauffeur."

"Fine. Get in back with the blabbermouth." He smirked at Lashawn.

"Don't hit any trees. Huh, huh, huh, huh."

"You too, Duff." Channing motioned into the car.

Smiling, I climbed in after Lashawn.

Spank!

"Channing!" I blurted, rubbing my ass through my winter coat where he'd slapped it.

"Easy target," he smirked.

"Are you saying I have a big ass?" I barked.

"In the immortal words of Spinal Tap, '*The bigger the cushion, the sweeter the pushin.*' So, yes."

"Channing!" I tried to slap his hand but he closed the door in my face. I gaped at a grinning Lashawn. "Did you hear him?"

"I did," Lashawn chuckled. "He's right."

"About which part?" I glared.

"Take your pick."

"You too?!" I laughed.

"Huh, huh, huh, huh. Good to see you again, girl."

\#

&

&*&

&*&*&

&*&*&*&

M

"Your house is amazing, Channing," I sighed after getting a partial tour (it was literally too big to tour the entire house), guided by Terrance while Channing narrated details about each room and the antique furnishings. Lashawn wasn't here because he'd driven off in the Mercedes after dropping us off in the gravel roundabout earlier. He'd said he had something important to take care of tonight, but hadn't said what.

I said now, "This place reminds me of a Vanderbilt mansion, but not. I just can't think what. It seems so familiar."

"Thanks," Channing said. "Which Vanderbilt house were you thinking of?"

"They have more than one?"

"Too many to list, but I can think of a few off the top of my head. Hyde Park, Long Island, The Breakers and Marble House in Rhode Island, the Triple Palace on 5th Avenue Manhattan, the Vanderbilt House on West 57th Street. That one was the largest house ever built in New York City. Too bad it was demolished in 1926. If you look at the old black-and-white photos, that place was palatial. The king of France would've felt right at home."

"How do you know all this?" I wondered.

"I read a lot."

"Since when?"

"It's been ten years, Duff," he smiled. "Lots of time to read."

"Ohmygosh. I just realized something. Is this, this isn't the Fournier Mansion, is it? Your house, I mean."

"It was," Channing smiled proudly, "up until it became Peyton Place."

"Wait, isn't that a book? It is! I read it in high school English class. I loved that book! It was full of scandal and sexual intrigue. They made it into a 1960s TV soap opera."

"Don't tell anyone," Channing grinned. "We should go downstairs and see what's cooking."

"What scandals are you hiding, Channing?" I giggled girlishly.

"After dinner, I'll show you were Selena buried her stepfather in the basement," he chuckled as he strolled down the stairs beside Terrance.

I stood paralyzed where I was at the top of the sweeping staircase, my mind lighting up with a pinball of pinging memories as I remembered the novel. Through the medium of her book, author Grace Metalious had spoken to my teenage soul with her story, its poetic prose, and its angsty emotional turmoil. It had always been one of my most beloved books, a place I wanted to live that didn't exist.

I whispered a wish in the form of a question, "Channing, did you *read* Peyton Place?"

"It has my last name. How could I not?" Like the Pied Piper playing a tune for the children of Hamelin as he marched them out of town, Channing tossed the comment over his shoulder as a seductive song, a whimsical melody I couldn't resist.

Leaning forward on my toes, I gasped, "But that, that's a *woman's* novel, Channing. The first line of Peyton Place is literally, 'The Indian Summer is like a woman. Ripe, hotly passionate, but fickle, she comes and goes as she pleases so that one is never sure whether she will come at all, nor for how long she will stay.'"

"And to think, the critics called it porn," he chortled. "I just remember the overall story. I don't know how you can recite lines like that, Duff. I'm impressed."

"You *read* that?"

"You can report me to the Book Police after dinner." He smirked from the bottom of the stairs, standing on the patterned marble floor, surrounded by an elegant coterie of bronze ballerinas.

My mind zinged again as I remembered the Lladro statue he'd gifted my mom. Suddenly, Channing Peyton had become literally, and seemingly *literarily*, perfect.

"Let's eat." He turned and sauntered off, followed by Terrance.

It took everything I had not to chase after Channing on a flying carpet of floating hearts.

$$\#$$
$$\&$$
$$\&^*\&$$
$$\&^*\&^*\&$$
$$\&^*\&^*\&^*\&$$
$$M$$

"Nice to meet you, Carol," Frenchy said to me after Channing introduced us in the immense kitchen. "You don't look like Channing's usual type."

"Frenchyyyy," Channing snorted. "Don't say that."

"I mean it," he said earnestly. "Carol here looks real nice." It was an unassuming, friendly compliment.

"That better not be code for *not* hot." Channing amused.

"Don't get me wrong," Frenchy smiled, "She's pretty in her own way and she doesn't look like a bitch." He winked at me.

I had to smile, "Does Channing normally date bitchy women?"

"She said it boss, not me," Frenchy chuckled.

Channing sighed, "I may have earned a bit of a reputation since college."

"I hate to think," I grinned.

"Have some hors d'oeuvres," Frenchy said, sliding a tray across the long island marble countertop covered in crackers. "Lobster toasts with avocado and espelette pepper."

"Mmm! This is so good!" I grinned after taking a bite.

"Wait'll you eat the entrée," Channing grinned.

"What are we having?"

"I know what I'm having." Channing's chocolate-caramel eyes drizzled over with a flush of lust.

"I meant the food." I tried not to squirm as my body flared in response.

"I'll eat that too," he flirted.

"Get a room, you too," Frenchy chuckled over his stove.

I laughed like it was old times and Channing had never dumped me. Those memories suddenly threatened to spoil the buttery taste of the lobster toast melting in my mouth. I swallowed everything down before the past could ruin the present. Ten years of practice made it easy, and there was no reason to let Channing's ancient actions spoil Frenchy's cutting-edge culinary genius.

"First course is ready," Frenchy said a bit later. "Do you want me to serve it here? I can if you want."

At that point, the four of us (me, Channing, Terrance, and Frenchy) had been having a lively conversation while nibbling our way through two more platters of hors d'oeuvres. For being employees, Terrance and Frenchy seemed more like friends.

"I shall take my meal in my room, sir," Terrance said, "if the two of you don't mind." He smiled at me.

"Go for it," Channing said. "Frenchy, can you help me carry everything upstairs?" Over the last hour, Channing had discarded pieces of his suit, and was now down to shirt, slacks, and shoes, with his cuffs rolled up to his elbows.

"Don't worry about it. I'll use the dumbwaiter and a cart. You two go relax."

"Are you sure?" I asked. My bulky sweater and jeans were fine for carrying food around.

"Fuggedaboutit," Frenchy said. "Gimme a few minutes to get everything upstairs. The lighthouse, right?"

"Yup," Channing said.

"The lighthouse?" I wondered.

"I'll show you." Channing guided me through several corridors and up several different staircases.

"I don't know how you keep this place heated in winter," I said, clomping up more stairs. "It must cost a small fortune."

"I have several."

"Small fortunes?" I snorted.

"Large ones," he grinned.

"You know what else has changed about you?"

"Do tell."

"Your ego. It's bigger than your new house."

"But not other things," he chuckled suggestively.

"Why do you keep insinuating you have a huge dick? It's me, Channing. We have had sex. I know how big your dick is. It's just the right size. Unless you had a dick transplant in the last decade? Based on what you've said, I'm picturing a NASA rocket, in which case," I smirked, "can Lashawn drive me home now?"

"No transplant," he snorted.

"Then why?"

"Old habits."

"Old? You never used to talk about your dick like it was the Second Coming."

"Second?" He smirked, "You and I came together more times than there are numbers."

"Still suck at math, I see," I joked.

"Oh, I may suck at math, but I can *count* well into the millions. Check my bank account if you don't believe me."

I shook a smile, "And this money thing? I don't care how much money you have. I never did. You know that. It's like you can't stop trying to impress me."

"Here we are," he twinkled a grin when we reached the top of yet another curving staircase.

"Ohmygod," I gasped. "What is this? This is incredible."

"Welcome to the Lighthouse," he said impressively.

This time, he had every right.

We stood in a small circular room with windows all around and cushioned bench seats beneath. Dim white Christmas lights circled the ceiling. In the center of the smallish room was a table set for two. Two candles stood sentry, flickering over the elaborate place settings like little night-watchmen.

"Terrance must've come up to light the candles," Channing said. "Let me turn the lights down so you can see the view."

The lights dimmed.

King City sparkled around us in every direction, an ocean of twinkling stars with us floating above. It was breathtaking.

"Wow," I whispered.

"Would you like to see the gardens?"

"Which ones? Yours?"

"Yuh. Look over here." He guided me, a familiar arm around my shoulders, one that fit me like a favorite jacket, the heroic one that made you feel a little bit prettier, like the woman you'd always dreamed of being but never quite were until you put that jacket on.

I melted into that feeling and this man without even knowing I had. It was getting easier and easier to remember how much I had once loved Channing, but it was impossible to forget how he had betrayed me.

Then the gardens came to life.

In the distance, the grounds glowed, a midsummer night's dream in the middle of winter, a snowy wonderland lit by an ordered palette of colored lights hidden amongst the snow-capped greenery, a living picture postcard.

"This is all yours?" I whispered.

"Yes, but I'd rather share it." He gave me a knowing look, his eyes flickering the promise of insistent kisses.

The romance of the moment swept away my sanity. I didn't even bother to wave goodbye as it took flight. I was ready to surrender to this man, the one I had once known so well and loved so purely, as had he. If he kissed me now, I wouldn't resist. It was worth the risk.

"Foods coming up," Frenchy said from the bottom of the stairs. "What happened to the lights?"

"I'll get it," Channing said. The white Christmas lights glowed brighter, revealing Frenchy as he carried up two plates covered and kept warm under silver cloches. "I'll just set them down on the table and you can get to them whenever you're ready."

"Thanks, bud," Channing said.

"Thank you, Frenchy," I said.

He smiled, "I'll leave dessert at the bottom of the stairs. I hate being interrupted by waiters when I take my lady out."

"It's fine," I dismissed. "What's the entrée?"

"Seared scallops with brown butter and lemon pan sauce, creamed kale with grilled portobello mushrooms, and lemon asparagus risotto."

"Ohmygosh, my mouth is already watering."

"Wait'll you taste it," Frenchy winked. "Leave the cloches on until you're ready to eat, otherwise it'll get cold. G'night, you two. Don't do anything I wouldn't do," he singsonged as he disappeared down the spiral stairs.

Chapter 36

CAROL

"Have a seat." Channing pulled out my chair and I sat down. He removed the cloches and set them aside.

"It looks delicious," I grinned.

"Are you still hungry after those hors d'oeuvres?"

"Enough to try this." I cut into my scallop and took a buttery bite that literally melted in my mouth. "Ohmygod," I moaned around a mouthful. "Total foodgasm."

"You always did like it when I came in your mouth."

"Hush! You're ruining the scallops."

He chuckled and cut into his own food.

After sating myself on another bite, I said, "You speak very differently from what I remember in college. You're more refined."

"Like I said, it's been ten years."

"No, it's more than that. What changed?"

He smiled thoughtfully. "You want the truth?"

"That would be my preference," I smirked.

"The Football Games."

Those words arrowed my heart. Back in college, they'd been shot from Cupid's bow on Valentine's Day, piercing my heart in the best way possible when Channing had given me his handwritten version of my story, thereby making it our story, the one about Carol Everdeen and Channing Hawthorne fighting against death for the sake of true love. Now, hearing that title felt like a betrayal, like one of the three Greek Fates had pierced my heart with the killing stitch.

"Did I say something wrong?" Channing asked.

"No," I choked and took a sip of water from an elegant crystal wine glass. "What does my story have to do with anything?" I didn't even want to say the title out loud. That was an old ghost I'd rather forget.

"I used to hate reading before I read your Football Games story."

I wish he'd stop saying it.

He continued, "Something about reading it that first time always stuck with me."

"You mean when you came all over it and the pages stuck together?" I snorted a laugh.

He chuckled, "That, and something else."

"Tell me about it," I grumbled. Something about *writing* it had always stuck with me, something I'd rather forget, namely the pain and misery of the last ten years of disappointment.

"What?" he grinned inquisitively.

"Nothing. Please finish your story."

"Anyway, that first time I read The Football Games, it was better than any movie or TV show I'd ever seen, or video game I'd played. More vivid. More real. Best part, it literally got me laid many, many times." He chuckled luridly. "The best sex I've ever had, Care. Based on what you said the other night, the *only* sex you ever had. Good thing we had so much."

I couldn't disagree, so I smirked expectantly. "And?"

"Remember how you always had romance novels around our apartment?"

"Yes." I hated it when he said *our*, but *our* union was an undeniable fact of *our* history. My preference tonight had been to enjoy the moment here in this romantic Lighthouse with him, but *our* past was waiting in the wings to dart out every five seconds like shadowy assassins intent on ruining dinner for both of us. "What about my romances?"

He grinned guiltily, "Okay, *maybe* I paged through a few back then."

"I remember you reading over my shoulder every now and then."

"That wasn't the only time."

"That's news." I snorted, surprised. "Why?"

"I read for the sex scenes."

"That's it? Just the sex scenes? You didn't read a single other word?" I laughed.

"Okay, maybe a few other words."

"How many is a few?" I grinned.

"Enough to get ideas about what to do in bed. Or on romantic dates. To spice things up."

I laughed. "You never told me that."

"I was embarrassed. Studying game films before a football game? Absolutely manly. Reading your romance novels to be a more thoughtful lover? No way. It's my deepest, darkest secret," he chuckled rustily, the sounds suddenly fading to choked clanks. He frowned.

"What?" I could tell something was bothering him.

He reached for his glass of water and gulped down half of it.

"What, Channing? Just tell me."

Gritting his teeth, he nodded, "The Football Games. It all started with that. Now I read everything. Fiction, non-fiction, poetry, doesn't matter. Words are my jam, man."

"Uh huh," I said dryly. "You're not telling me something, Channing. What?"

"I was just telling you about my love of reading."

"Yes, but you're hiding something. What is it? Is it what you wanted to tell me in private?"

His face caved in. He fisted his fingers on the tabletop, popping the knuckles. He heaved a sigh. His head hung and a single lock of hair bounced over his brow. When he looked up, he shook his head with slow sadness.

"What, Channing?"

"Let me tell you a story." That voice of his was suddenly fragile, lost, uncertain. "My freshman year in college, that first year I led the Cheetahs to the Rose Bowl in fifteen years, that was before you and I met, it felt like I'd led every person in King City through the desert to the doorstep of the Promised Land."

"Meaning the Rose Bowl?"

"Yeah."

"The Promised Land is a very accurate metaphor," I smiled. "Winning around here is exactly like that. The Cheetahs are a religion to the people of King City."

"They are," he chuckled. "And that too is a great metaphor. Anyway, when the Cheetahs got to the Rose Bowl, you know what I did?"

"What?" I could already tell from his expression I wasn't going to like the answer.

"I threw the game because someone paid me to lose." Channing the man shrank before my eyes, shriveling into a dusty husk of his former self. One puff, and he'd blow away in wisps.

I closed my eyes as the disappointment hit me in a crushing black wave, knocking me completely off the high I'd been feeling this evening, now drowning me in dismal sorrow. Channing's words unearthed the dead bodies of *our* scandal, not Selena Cross's in Peyton Place. *Ours.*

This was *our* tragic story he was about to confess.

I could feel it.

He was about to show me the body of *our* dead relationship and finally explain all that trauma *he* caused, and the resultant shockwave that ripped through my life and my parents'.

Lowering his eyes to the table, he whispered his sins, "After, when I had to make empty excuses at the press conference, I felt like a complete liar, like I'd led all of King City across the Desert of Defeat to the Promised Land of Victory *knowing* I never had the keys to the city, like I'd led them to their deaths only so I could get paid to betray them. Total. Judas. Move."

I couldn't speak.

He mumbled, "Then I did the same damn thing three more times."

"Three?" I whispered dryly. "You *won* your fourth Rose Bowl. I'll never forget. It was the happiest day of your Dad's life. He was happier than when you won the Heisman."

"I know." His eyes were dark marbles. "And I fucking threw the championships a week later." He grit his teeth, the words a furnace of self-hatred. "Did you ever wonder where I got that Ford Mustang back in college?"

I grimaced. "Let me guess. Throwing games?"

"Yes. The stupidest thing I've ever done. If I could take it all back, I would. When you lead people, they put their trust in you. They expect you not to lie. I did." He heaved a sigh.

When he said no more, my heart wrenched with despair.

I wanted to tell him, when you loved someone, you weren't supposed to lie to them either, or lead them to the Promised Land of True Love, only to chain them to the door and leave them there while you ran off to let them die a slow horrible death because *you* were done with them. I wanted to tell him I had very nearly starved to death after he dumped me, but I'd already told him that the other night. He didn't need to hear it twice, didn't *deserve* to, and I was too angry, too overloaded with battling emotions to speak anyway.

"And I lied to *you*, Care. The only woman I *ever* loved. I lied to *you*. I regret that more than every game I threw, more than every mistake I've ever made combined. Abandoning you, Carol, is my biggest regret of all, and I will carry it to my grave."

My heart instantly bridged the gap between present and past, and my feelings were singing with the fragile sadness and confusion I'd felt when he'd first announced he wanted me out of his campus apartment and his life for no apparent reason.

In a frightened tearful voice I recognized as that of a much younger me, I squeaked, "Why, Channing? Why did you leave me?"

Channing sat there, his eyes dead.

#
&
&*&
&*&*&
&*&*&*&
M

CHANNING

How did you tell the woman you loved that people like Tony and

Jake Martinelli had privately threatened to kill her once upon a time?

What would be a bigger betrayal?

Telling Carol the truth or withholding it?

Was it better for her to know that her life was forfeit if I fucked up, or if I simply disobeyed Jake on something he considered important but I didn't?

Then there was Tony. He was getting older, sure, and was less involved than he'd been ten years ago, but Tony'd always had a short fuse. If he heard from Jake that I'd done something Tony didn't like, there was no telling what he might do. Or what Jake might do. Jake could be vicious in his own way.

Ten years working alongside Jake had established something of an easy rapport, but he wasn't always easy. He had his days. When he did, I was dancing on broken glass, always worrying one mistake on the wrong day might get Carol killed.

Was I supposed to tell her that? Burden her with that truth for a lifetime? Weigh her down with the heavy load of constant danger? Knowing an axe was hanging over your head year after year took a slow toll. I spoke from experience.

Was it better I hide the truth and lie?

So she could live lightly?

Then an awful truth I had missed snuck up and punched me in the heart.

My youthful stupidity had put Carol in this position.

My actions.

Her only mistake had been getting involved with me.

My biggest mistake had been pursuing her.

Had I been smarter, and stayed out of her life, Carol truly wouldn't have anything to worry about.

But there's no going back. I was in love with her as much now as ever. No, probably more. What was I going to do? Imagine me telling her: "Carol, I did something real dumb back in college. Now your life is in danger as long as I'm alive. Wanna get back together and have mad passionate sex?"

I could never tell her that.

My best option was to let Carol go.

Let her live a better life without me making it worse.

The truth always hurt, didn't it?

Sometimes, it hurt too much to endure.

#

&

&*&
&*&*&
&*&*&*&
M

CAROL

Channing's face lit up with a charming smile, his withered body suddenly inflating with good humor and charm. "So, yeah. That's what happened. I threw the games. Dumb move, right? What do you expect from a stupid kid?" He chuckled and shook his head like he'd just admitted to sneaking out his parents' car for a joyride after curfew, and got a speeding ticket in the process.

"That's why you broke up with me?" I moused in a thin voice. "Because you were ashamed of throwing some games?"

His winning smile cracked around the edges. "I, uh, yeah." He shriveled again.

"That's it?" I was starting to anger.

His eyes shifted thoughtfully. "You don't understand, Care. I grew up addicted to winning. You met my Dad. He's worse than I ever was. You know those four undefeated regular seasons we had? The games I didn't throw?"

"Yes," I pursed. "What about them?"

"Didn't mean a thing. Ask an addict: which hit is the best one? The next one. Always the next one. That's living for winning for you. I'm still doing it. Look around. You saw the house. Now I live for money."

"I hope it's worth it." I sat up stiffly and folded my arms across my chest.

"It has its perks," he said, running his fingernail around the base of his water glass like it was the most fascinating thing he'd ever seen.

"Does it?"

"Sure," he shrugged, not looking at me.

"Was it a perk when the entire town of King City wanted me dead? Because you *threw* some games for money? Was that a perk, *Channing?*" I was ready to fury, on the edge of vengeance. "Do you have *any* idea what that did to me?"

"You mentioned it the other night," he mumbled.

"Oh, I *mentioned* it," I said with savage sarcasm. "Did I mention a bunch of women came forward after *you* threw the game, and they *lied*, saying *I* made you do it? Did you know that?"

He growled.

"They said I was a prostitute."

"Who's they?"

"I don't know. Like, eight different women I've never met. They were all interviewed on King City 7 News and said they were my friends and I told them my secrets. Secrets about you. I had zero idea who they were. Complete strangers."

"That's odd."

"Not as odd as what they said. They said I was your dominatrix."

"Too bad you aren't," he snorted.

"Not funny. These women said on TV that I made you pay me to have sex with you, that I was some warped psycho who got off on controlling you, and I *made* you throw the championship game to satisfy some sick desire. King City hated me so much for that, people made T-shirts calling me a Cheetah killer with my face on it. They came up to me on the streets, wherever I went in public, and told me to die. Literally die. Did you know that, Channing? Huh? Did you?"

He stared blankly.

"No," I said, "probably not. Because you disappeared. You went missing or whatever you did. Did you know your parents called me looking for you? Your mom was sobbing. I could hear the tears. She thought you were dead, *Channing*."

"I know." His face aged thirty years before my eyes.

"Why'd you leave her in the dark? Your own mother. What kind of son does that? She was freaking out! I'll never forget that call." I shook my head in abject sadness.

His sad, old man's eyes darkened. "I was too damn drunk to call home. Took me months before I did."

"What were you doing?"

"Hiding."

"Obviously. What happened?"

"I drove my Mustang down to Galveston, Texas and slept on the beach for three months."

"You lived on the beach?"

He nodded, "For three drunken months."

"You should've called your parents."

"I was too drunk."

"To call them?"

He nodded, head heavy with shame.

I stared at him, puzzling over his bizarre choices ten years ago, trying to make sense of them. Without warning, another piece fell into place with a thick thunk. "You told me you were breaking up with me because of Victoria Bissette, the head cheerleader. You said she was moving into your apartment. Did that ever happen?"

His eyes flicked up quick. "No."

I thought for a moment. "Did you ever have a thing with her?"

"Never even kissed her."

My guard slipped a little. "Tell me the truth. Were you a virgin when we had sex?"

He clasped hands together and nodded solemnly. "You were my first."

Somehow, I knew he was telling the truth. "This isn't making any sense, Channing. It doesn't add up. You threw a game for money, which is incredibly unethical, by the way. But that's not the point. The point is, why didn't you tell me?"

He snorted, "It's not exactly something to be proud of."

"You're missing the point. Did you think I'd what, dump you if I found out? So you dumped me instead? Why?"

He shrugged.

"So you'd be the dumper and not the dumpee?"

He shrugged again.

"Is this an addiction to winning thing?"

"I guess," he mumbled.

"That is so incredibly immature, Channing. Relationships aren't a competition."

"I told you. I was a stupid kid." There was an easy cool to his claim I didn't quite believe, but I couldn't decide why.

I said, "How did this whole throwing games thing came about anyway?"

He chewed his lip and glared at me.

"What?"

He said suddenly, "Do you want dessert?"

"What? No! We're having a discussion. This is important."

"I'm going to get dessert. Frenchy said he left everything at the bottom of the stairs." Channing stood up and started for the stairs.

"I don't want any dessert, Channing! You need to explain yourself."

"Be right back." A minute later, a door closed, followed by steps ascending the stairs. Channing carried two plates of chocolate cake and set one down for me, one for him.

It wasn't just any old chocolate cake. It looked like it could win an award. Nine layers, an ombré fade of chocolate frosting (milk chocolate to dark), delicate white chocolate flowers and spidery decorative lines of white chocolate drawn on the sides with paisley precision. Had I been in a better mood, I would've devoured it with guilty glee. Instead, I ignored it.

Channing leaned over the table and whispered, "I'm going to tell you something that absolutely cannot leave this room."

"Is it criminal? Because if it is, and I don't report it, I could get disbarred."

"You're a lawyer, aren't you." It was more statement than question.

I smirked, "Finished law school, been a practicing attorney for almost seven years, so yes."

"I knew you'd be a great lawyer some day," he smiled.

"Who says I'm great?"

"Do you suck? At law, I mean. Not, you know, other things." He winked. "I know you excel at that."

"Now is not the time, Channing. Tell me what you were going to tell me. If it has to do with throwing games, that's fraud. Fraud is a felony."

"That was ten years ago. Isn't there a statute of limitations on that?"

"Depending on the kind of fraud, most likely seven years for federal. If any money changed hands over state lines, it would be federal. I'm assuming money changed hands? No, don't tell me. I don't want to know. I'm not your attorney."

"Fine. How long is the statute for state?"

"I'm not sure what it is here in King City, but state laws are usually similar. Assume seven years, if you're lucky, less."

"I don't need a calculator to do that math. Sounds like I'm in the clear either way?"

"Are you asking me if the crime you committed ten years ago will no longer get you thrown in jail?"

He smiled.

"I'm not your attorney, so I am not giving you legal advice when I say, probably not." It was finally starting to sink in. "You broke the law, Channing. Four times, one for each game."

He nodded an amused smirk. "I told you I was a dumb kid."

"Do you realize, if you had told me this then, I *never* would have dated you? Or slept with you? You'd already committed a felony *before* we met, when you threw that first game."

"Yup."

I scowled. "I never should've let you into my room that first day. Never, ever, *ever*. I was the dumb one, not you."

"Two peas in a pod," he smiled.

"No," I snorted. "Not even close. You're a criminal, Channing!" I was hissing my ire quietly, trying to keep my voice down. "Are you still a criminal? Is that how you paid for this place? Ten years isn't a long time to get mega-rich like you appear to be, unless you're a dot-com billionaire in Silicon Valley or something."

Channing smirked, said nothing.

"Oh no. No, no, no. You are, aren't you? You're a criminal. What is it? Organized crime? Don't answer that! I don't want to know! This was a bad idea. I never should've agreed to dinner. I should go." I pushed back my chair with a wrenching noise and stood up abruptly.

"Wait, Carol. Please."

"No, Channing. We can't work. You're a criminal. I'm an attorney specializing in defending people who commit white collar crime. Do you not see the problem?"

He grinned from his chair, "Actually, no. I see a golden opportunity dawning over the horizon for both of us."

"What do you mean? Wait. What kind of crime do you do? No! I don't want to know!" I shook frazzled hands.

He smiled.

I gaped.

He was literally wearing a white-collared shirt.

I didn't need any more clues than that.

He cocked a sloppy smirk, "I always said I wanted you as my lawyer, Duff. You watch my ass and I watch yours." He winked with lascivious charm. "We're a match made in heaven."

"Oh, no. No way. Uh uh. Too many conflicts of interest. It's a terrible idea that should never happen. The less we see of each other, the better. Do you understand me, Channing? This is bad for both of us. *Really* bad. We should not be involved in any capacity, personal or professional. Not ever. I mean that. We will now go our separate ways and part company forever. For. Ever. Understood?"

The light in his eyes died and he sat at the table, helpless.

We both were.

Shaking my head, I walked past him and went down the circular stairs. It was a short walk that got darker and darker. I could barely see, the only light coming from the dim glow upstairs. Working by feel, I twisted the antique doorknob, which barely turned, and tugged. The door didn't budge. I rattled it more firmly. No luck. I gripped the doorknob hard, and turned as hard as I could. Felt metal grinding as the knob bit into my palm. Worse than trying to open a stuck jar. "Channing? Did you lock me in?!" I was not liking this one bit. Was he trapping me now?

"No," he called out from upstairs. "It sticks."

"What?!"

"The door sticks! I'll be right down!" Shoes on the narrow stairs. It wasn't wide enough for two people. His huge shadow blotted out the glow from above. "Let me try."

I was so anxious to escape, I backed up a single step, sliding around him, trying to flatten myself against the wall, but the hand-railing stabbed into my back and I arched it. My breast brushed against his arm.

If he noticed, he showed no sign. He pulled on the door. "It's stuck pretty good."

"You locked it, didn't you?" I was right on top of him, agonizing to get out.

"No," he chuckled. "I thought I had this fixed. The house must've shifted when the cold set in. Let me try again."

"Try kicking it."

"It opens in."

"Oh."

"Back up."

I took a single step.

Gritting his teeth, he twisted, grinding the knob audibly, followed by a springy pop. "That's the plunger."

"The what? Aren't those for toilets?"

"It's the thingamajig that goes in the strike box."

"The what?

"Never mind. Just move. I have to yank it. I don't want to hit you."

I backed up another step.

"If this doesn't work," he said, "I'll call Lashawn and have him kick it in. Here goes nothing." He coiled his body and the muscles bunching under his dress shirt, stretching out the back of it in the dim light. Suddenly, he pulled with explosive force. The door flew open, sending Channing stumbling back into me.

I sat down under his weight on the steps with a thud.

The door banged off the wall and swung back to closed.

He spun over. "Care! Are you okay?"

"I think so." I took a moment to listen to the signals from my body. "I'm fine. Can you get off me?"

His face was inches from mine, his eyes dark desire.

I felt it too. Stood up before those feelings took root. Crowded up to the door and grabbed the knob. Channing was right behind me. "Move. I can't open the door with you here."

"Carol, I…" That voice. His body burned behind mine, trapping me in this dim prison.

I wanted to flee, but my body wouldn't let me. I pressed against the door, trying to escape my desire that this man take me here, now, in this sordid stairwell. I was no beauty, but he was a beast, a criminal, an unethical man with no principles. It didn't matter he had once been an innocent kid who handed me his heart the first time we made love.

He was a beast.

"Channing, I..."

His full weight pressed up against me, forcing me into the door.

"Channing," I gasped, biting my lower lip.

"Let me open the door, Carol," he grunted a hateful warning.

"No," I whispered.

"Move, Carol." His anger heated.

"No." My word was a silent plea for mercy, my heart begging my body not to do this. A sense memory of Channing deep inside me for the first time, after he had come and I had too, us cuddling after, a feeling of completeness I had never imagined possible enveloping me in a profound warmth, and his whisper so soft a mouse might miss it:

"I love you, Carol."

Only it wasn't a memory.

Channing had just said it, whispered it in my ear in that same boyish voice brimming with innocence. But the beastly weight pressing against me was the opposite.

"Take me, Channing," I hissed. "Take me."

Hard hands roamed over me from behind, diving between my thighs.

I moaned.

They pushed up against my folds soaking inside my jeans and panties.

I moaned.

Then smeared sexually up my stomach, lifting my sweater and shirt beneath, softly up my ribs, a chill thrill.

I moaned.

They squeezed my breasts with sweet need, twisting both nipples.

I moaned.

He nipped my neck and grunted.

I moaned.

He thrust into my ass.

I moaned, thrusting against his slacks.

He groaned.

I reached behind me and pulled his ass into mine.

He groaned and thrust me back into the door with a bang. He reached around and ripped my jeans open.

I pushed them down before he could, just pass my ass.

His thumbs dug into my skin and his fingers gripped my hips, jolting me into him again. He pushed my jeans down my thighs. Bunched his fingers in the back of my panties and pulled upward.

I moaned, sinking into their binding tightness, trembling with pleasure.

"I can smell how wet you are," he snarled in my ear.

I bit my lip and whimpered, my cheek pressed against the hard wood door.

"I love the smell of your sex, Care. It drives me fucking wild." He pushed my panties down and slapped my ass.

I jumped and whimpered again. My body was begging him to fuck me. My heart and head had left the building. I circled my ass for him in a slow dance.

He spanked a second time and I gasped a sensuous sigh.

"Fuck me, Channing."

A swift zip and the rustle of fabric.

A low, feral, leonine grunt.

I presented my ass.

Hard heat probed my folds.

I pushed against him, so wet he slipped right in.

Channing groaned deep, filling me whole.

Pulse.

Pulse.

Pulse.

He pulled my sweater over my head and I let him.

He ripped off my shirt and I let him.

He unhooked my bra with swift skill and I let him.

He grabbed my breasts and I let him.

He started a slow fuck and I let him.

Every in was sin.

Every out a pout for more.

I never wanted him to stop fucking me.

The relentless pressure of my first orgasm rose and exploded, mocking every feeble orgasm I'd given myself during ten years of lackluster masturbation.

The next orgasm hit minutes later, sweeter, harder, hotter, fuller.

"Come all over my cock, Carol." That voice. "Fucking come like you mean it."

Oh, I meant it, wailing away the pain of a decade of sexual emptiness as he filled me with his hot need that only fired mine.

Pulse, pulse, pulse.

Thrust.

Thrust.

Thrust.

I was dripping down my thighs at this point, a sopping mess of heady abandon and passionate sex.

For another ten minutes, he thrust steadily, steadfastly, and unrelentingly, grunting with every plunge, growling with the lust of fucking.

When my third orgasm started to build, his built with me. Every thrust we moaned, timing our cries in sexual synchronicity.

"Fuck, Carol," he rasped.

"Do it," I begged.

"Fuck! Carol! I'm going to!"

"Do it!" I pleaded.

"Fuck!" Channing roared. "Fuuuuuuuuck!'

Orgasms stole over both of us.

Pulse.

Pulse.

Pulse.

My sex milked every last drop until he had spent his last.

Chapter 37

CAROL

We had naked sex seven more times in the Lighthouse.

Lying on the cushions with me on the bottom.

With the cushions on the floor with me riding on top.

Doggy style with me standing on tiptoes, my hands on a bench, staring out at the twinkling stars over his gardens as he plowed my field, or at the shimmering lights of downtown King City where the two Tabor Towers stood proud.

We paused to refuel on chocolate cake and water. Thank Frenchy for leaving a full pitcher on the food cart at the bottom of the stairs.

Channing and I fucked, and fucked, and fucked until we couldn't come any more. The last time we came so hard it was almost painful for both of us. We collapsed onto the cushions by one of the windows, him leaning against the post, me cuddled between his legs, his arms wrapped around me as he kissed my hair and whispered.

"I never stopped loving you, Care. I've never loved anybody else."

"I loved you too," I said carefully.

"Loved? As in past tense?"

I sighed. "I don't know what to say, Channing. It's been ten years. You broke my heart."

"I understand." His sadness was a seduction, an invitation I wanted to ignore but couldn't resist.

"I need time to think, Channing. Can we just enjoy this moment for what it is?"

"Sure," he whispered and kissed my hair.

\#

\&

\&*\&

\&*\&*\&

\&*\&*\&*\&

M

I had Channing drive me home that night. Sleeping with him seemed like a bad idea, an old habit I had broken and didn't want to revive.

My parents were asleep when I walked in the house.

I slipped into bed without showering, not wanting to wake them, having done only a quick mop job over the toilet. For a long time, I lay under the covers in my high school room, wondering if Channing's seed was quickening inside me.

I hadn't been on the pill since Channing dumped me.

I had been ovulating this week, I was sure of it.

I wouldn't have foolishly had unprotected sex with him if I hadn't been.

The next morning over breakfast, Mom and Dad asked about my date with Channing. I said it was nice. They said that was great, asked if it might be serious. I laughed a no, I was only in town for the holidays. They knew that.

After breakfast, I drove Dad's car to CVS and bought a Plan B morning after pill. I sat in the car reading the instructions in detail. Two pills. No more than 72 hours after unprotected sex before you took the first pill, and the second 12 hours after that. The pills were identical, but you had to take both as scheduled for it to be fully effective.

I didn't have to take the first pill now, did I?

No, I had, what, 60 hours remaining to decide?

This was ridiculous.

What was I waiting for?

I couldn't have Channing's baby without telling him.

I needed to take the pill.

No, I needed some advice from my sister pirates.

I texted Sienna and Jordyn and met them both for lunch.

#
&
&*&
&*&*&
&*&*&*&
M

"What should I do, you guys?" I asked over my Panera sandwich. The three of us sat in a cozy booth that shielded us from the humming lunch crowd.

"Wait, wait, wait." Sienna waved her hands ominously, a pickle slice pinched between two fingers. "How many times did he come inside you?"

"Seven? Eight?"

"And how many times did you come?"

"Ten? Twelve? I don't remember. Does it matter? Do my orgasms mean I'm more likely to get pregnant? I heard that's a factor."

Sienna exchanged a serious look with Jordyn.

Sienna winced a whisper, "Twelve times?"

Wide-eyed, Jordyn said, "I thought eight was a lot."

Both broke into giggles.

"You guys," I sighed. "This is serious. I don't know what to do."

"He said he loved you," Jordyn said.

"But he dumped her before," Sienna said. "It wasn't pretty. I was there."

"I'm talking about the baby," I said. "What if I'm pregnant? I'm not thinking about Channing right now."

"You should be," Jordyn said. "If it's his, and he loves you, shouldn't you tell him?"

"But he's—" I stopped myself from telling them Channing was a criminal. "It's, we're, he's changed. We live very different lives. I don't see us working out."

"Do you love him, Rolo?" Jordyn asked.

Her calling that took me back to high school like a time machine. I had to stop and think.

"He still has a piece of your heart, doesn't he?" Jordyn smirked, suddenly looking seventeen, like the Pirate Queen I would always remember her as. "He does. I can tell."

"Carol's in luh-ove," Sienna fluffed.

"Maybe I am," I sighed. "But is he?"

"You said he said it," Jordyn said. "It's not like he's twenty. He's a grown man. Maybe he wants to settle down. These things do happen."

"Not to me," Sienna snorted.

"Me neither," Jordyn commiserated.

"And maybe not to me," I said. Again, I wanted to tell them he was a criminal. My ethics prevented me. I couldn't go around telling Channing's secrets. Technically, I was pushing the boundaries of propriety by *not* telling him I might be pregnant, whether or not I mentioned it, or took the Plan B pill. The honest and equitable thing to do would be to tell him I was considering it under the circumstances.

I texted Channing that I wanted to have dinner again.

At his place.

He agreed, responding immediately.

In the parking lot outside Panera, Sienna drove off in an Uber while Jordyn walked to her rattletrap car. We laughed about old times a few more minutes before I said Mom and Dad were waiting for me back home.

"Rolo?" Jordyn asked.

"Yeah?

"I feel lame asking you this."

"Asking me what, Jay?"

She lowered her eyes. "My, uh, my mom's health insurance payments are kinda crazy right now? Because of her chemo? Our electric bills are getting out of control because it's been so cold? We've got the heaters running 24/7, you know? And she isn't working full time since her diagnosis? And Medicare doesn't cover everything? I'm working and all, but I don't make much, you know? We've been trying to make ends meet, but they're not meeting." She laughed guiltily. "I don't really know anyone in town anymore, it's been so long, you know?" She offered a meager smile.

I'd never seen the Pirate Queen look so delicate and helpless. Not even her trusty leather jacket could protect from these enemies.

"How much do you need, Jay?" I asked.

"Anything you can spare. I'll pay it back right away."

I had to think. I made decent money for a junior attorney at a large firm, but I worked crazy hours, my San Francisco rent for a one bedroom apartment was insane, and much of what I saved was earmarked for my 401(k) or helping my parents out when they retired, which seemed like it was right around the corner these days, and they *still* hadn't paid off their 30 year mortgage. But I wasn't broke. I had some savings I'd saved for emergencies.

I said, "I can spare $1,500. Will that help?"

"Yeah," Jordyn smiled. "Definitely."

"How long will that last you?"

"I'll stretch it."

"How long?"

"It's plenty, Rolo. I already feel like a douche for asking."

"It's fine. If you were in my shoes, I know you'd do the same, sister."

"I would," Jordyn said solemnly. "I'll pay it back as soon as I can."

I shook my head. "No. You don't think about paying me back, sister. Not until your mom is cancer free. In the mean time, you think about taking care of her and taking care of you. That's what matters. Do you want me to drive you to your bank and deposit the money right now? I can if you want."

"Would you?" Her eyes glimmered hope.

"Let's go, girl."

Chapter 38

CAROL

This time, dinner at Channing's mansion included Frenchy and Terrance eating with the two of us in the kitchen. I didn't want a repeat of last night's romance.

Okay, I did want a repeat.

Not necessarily seven times.

At least three.

Okay, two would do.

At this point, it didn't matter if we had more unprotected sex tonight, did it? No. But we needed to talk first.

After another wonderful dessert from Frenchy, a vanilla cream and fruit torte to die for, Channing led me to the library. My jaw dropped when I saw it.

"Holy shit! How many books do you have?"

"Several thousand. I don't know the exact number. I told you, you got me into reading."

"That's an understatement," I snorted. "Have you read them all?"

"No," he chuckled. "Hope to some day. You know how it is when you start a hobby, it slowly takes over your life."

"I'll say," I mooned as I strolled past shelves, grazing a greedy finger across the spines of book after book. His library was a book lover's paradise, worthy of its own Pinterest page. What it had extra over any website was the wonderful smell of real. Not quite musty. More like lusty, the loving smell of real books.

"Take a gander at these." He opened a glass cabinet.

I grabbed a volume at random.

"Careful with that one," Channing said.

I turned the leather bound edition over in my hands. "A Tale of Two Cities, by Charles Dickens." I opened the cover with a creak. The pages were heavy paper, the edges intentionally ragged, the paper blotted with age spots. I read aloud the text on the bottom of the title page. "London: Chapman and Hall, 193, Piccadilly; MDCCCLIX. That's, what, 1859? That's really old."

"First edition. Would you like to know the price?"

"No. I told you I don't care about money." I giggled, "Okay, tell me."

"Asking price was $20,000."

I gasped. "Is that how much you paid?"

"Never," he said with faux-offense. "I bought it with a large lot of other collectible books. For this one I paid $15,000."

Cringing, I put it carefully back on the shelf.

We spent another hour touring the library while Channing told me stories about the books he'd bought. When he went to kiss me, I placed a finger on his lips.

"We need to talk," I said. Currently, I was cornered in the angle of two bookcases.

"We never had sex in a library, did we?"

"We didn't?" I squirmed, knowing we hadn't.

"This seems like a perfect place to end that trend." He pushed in for the kiss and I yielded.

How could I not?

Last night, we had kissed passionately many times.

This was no different, our tongues battling for control, his full lips tickling mine. It didn't take long until our clothes were off and he was inside me, still standing in the corner between the bookcases. He grabbed my thigh with a big hand and lifted it, opening me wider to his insistent thrusts. I planted a bare foot on a bookshelf. It was a bit too high and tilted my hips, so I used it to lift my extended leg higher, and felt myself tighten.

"Oh, that's fucking good," Channing hissed, thrusting with slow grunts. "Do the other one."

"My leg?"

"Put it on the shelf."

I did, sinking onto his cock, feeling him go deeper. I put both hands behind me on two higher shelves for balance.

"Fuck. So good. So fucking tight like that." His head rolled back on muscled shoulders and he groaned.

Now it was my turn to fuck him, working my pelvis in languid tilts, skimming my clit across his skin each time I sank down. The intensity was electric, at some point it became too much for my legs to support my weight. The overload of pleasure was blending my brain into a wet mess of zinging need. I sagged onto him, on the verge of coming but not quite there.

"I can't," I gasped. "My legs are too tired."

He pulled out.

"Where are you going?" I whined. "I'm about to come."

"You will now," he grunted and supported both my thighs with his big hands, his face diving between my legs. His tongue savaged my wet folds, whipping against my clit again and again.

"I want you inside me!" I gasped.

"Shut up and let me eat you. I want to taste your cum, Carol."

I felt one of his hands position one of my thighs with my knee over his shoulder, taking my weight. I had to shift my arms on the shelves to compensate.

Something plunged into me from below.

His fingers.

He fucked me with them while devouring my clit.

The orgasm was a firework burst.

I moaned throatily and drenched his face.

He lapped me for a long time before withdrawing his fingers, his muscles bunching, thick veins coiling and pumping, his shoulders and chest vibrating, engorged with enough blood to redden his skin from the exertion.

I braced myself and lowered my legs to the floor. When I went to kiss him, his cock jabbed my tummy just below my ribs.

Pulse.

Pulse.

Pulse.

A pearl of pre-cum appeared.

I wrapped my mouth around his swollen head and went to work, pumping with one hand and massaging his velvet sack with the other. It didn't take long before it pulled up tight against his pelvis, and he jolted into my mouth. I tasted his cum on my tongue and swallowed. I had always liked his taste. Strange, but pure. I'd given him so many blowjobs when we'd been together, it was like riding your favorite bicycle. And his was most definitely mine.

I swallowed him down, knowing how much he loved it when I did, drinking every last drop with enthusiastic moans of, "Mmm-hmmmmm. Mmmm."

"So good," he practically cried, his voice as tight as his balls as he hunched over me, leaning forward with both muscled arms propped against the bookcases.

I pulled away and kissed the tip before biting my lip coquettishly as I stood up and looked him in the eyes. Then mine bulged. "You've had a lot of sex. With a lot of people." I laughed nervously. There was no telling where his dick had been. I don't know why I hadn't thought about it until now, but there it was. "Should I be...?"

"Don't worry. It's been more than a year. I've been tested since. I was very careful and always wore condoms. I am absolutely clean."

"That's a huge relief." I sagged into the corner of the bookcases.

"Is that what you wanted to talk to me about tonight? Because of last night?"

"Yes. No." I shook my head. "We should sit."

He led me to the nearest leather button love seat.

"You're naked," I grinned.

"You are too," he smiled.

"It's hard to concentrate. I forgot how much I love your body."

"Me too." He caressed my cheek with the backs of his fingers. "As gorgeous as the day we met."

I slid my palm down his chest. Felt a thrill between my legs. "I should stop." I slapped my hands against my crossed thighs.

"I'm ready to go if you are."

To my amazement, his cock was slowly pulsing back to attention. "You are insatiable, Channing." I hid my guilty grin with my fingers because I was too. I wanted him again.

"Look who's talking, Feral Carol."

"What?!" I laughed.

"That's my new nickname for you. I don't know if you realize this, but you literally fuck like a beast."

"Do not!" I swatted his chest.

"Wolf sex? Who's idea was that?"

I blushed guiltily.

"I miss you so much," he grinned.

"Me too," I admitted. "You never should've broken up with me." I almost wanted to retract my statement, but he already knew how I felt from the day he'd dumped me.

"You're right," he sighed. "But that's in the past. Let's talk about the present where we both are."

"Ah, the present," I nodded. "Guess who isn't on birth control in the present?"

"You aren't on the pill?"

"Nope." I popped my p and wondered about popping that Plan B.

He blinked a few times. Frowned. "Do you think you're pregnant?"

"Yes. No. Probably."

"Did you take a pregnancy test?"

"It's too soon. I haven't taken my Plan B pill either."

"The morning after pill?"

"You're familiar with it," I said sarcastically.

"Not from me. I told you, I was always careful. I didn't want to get anyone pregnant," he hissed.

#

&

&*&

&*&*&
&*&*&*&
M

CHANNING

After dumping Carol to protect her from Tony and Jake, the last thing I wanted to do was get some other woman pregnant, or let another woman fall in love with me, or drag anyone into my shit with me.

Nobody deserved that.

It wouldn't be fair to anybody.

Definitely not a child.

And definitely not a child of mine.

#
&
&*&
&*&*&
&*&*&*&
M

CAROL

"Let me guess," I grimaced. "You don't want to get me pregnant either."

He frowned. "I didn't say that. I would love to have kids with you. I used to talk about that in college. Except..."

"Except what?" I folded my arms across my breasts and squeezed my thighs together on the couch.

"It's complicated, Carol."

"Criminal complicated?" I was more annoyed with myself for having sex with him again than I was with him.

"Yes." He hung his head and shook it, his hair hanging and waving in loose locks.

I wanted to grab it, pull it, caress it, pull his head to my breast and hug him hard, but I was in over my head. I rested my chin on my knees and sighed.

I was an attorney.

I had taken an oath to uphold the law. Sworn to obey, uphold, and defend the Constitution of the United States and the Commonwealth of California, where I had passed the State Bar and was licensed to practice law. My oath had not been empty words. Not for me, anyway. Some attorneys were corrupt, but I wasn't.

"Look at me," Channing said and lifted my chin gently.

Our eyes met.

That same, unrelenting, unyielding and powerful love Channing had given me daily for two unforgettable years washed over me in a hot wind of affection and devotion.

"If I wasn't a criminal, Carol, I would go get my grandmother's ring right now, get down on one knee beside this couch, and ask you to marry me and raise a family with me." He was absolutely serious.

I almost blurted yes. Had to clamp my mouth shut to stop myself from saying it.

"But I am a criminal, Care. I would say you deserve better, but I don't know that you'll ever find someone who loves you as much as I do, criminal or not. I can't take away who I am, but I'd never ask you to accept me. It's too much to ask of anyone."

My heart thumped in my chest. My body tingled with need. I tried to process what he'd just said. Not just the words, the emotional subtext. "You, Channing, it, it sounds like you're giving up." I didn't add, on me. To say it out loud might make it happen.

\#

&

&*&

&*&*&

&*&*&*&

M

CHANNING

The sad truth was that sooner or later, Jake would find out Carol had been here, even if she left this second and never came back. I could probably keep Lashawn and Frenchy quiet, and it seemed unlikely Jake would ever go asking Jack and Bev Duffey any questions, but that was only if I kicked Carol to the curb once again and avoided her completely from now on.

If I kept her in my life like I so badly wanted to?

Jake would know.

Tony would know.

They would have the ultimate leverage over me. They would suck me deeper into their criminal schemes knowing Carol was my Achilles' heel.

It had been incredibly selfish of me to invite Carol back into my life.

I never should've done this.

There was no way out without breaking her heart a second time. The only way to avoid that was to make her mine.

But I just couldn't.

No man was worth dying for, least of all me.

#

&

&*&

&*&*&

&*&*&*&

M

CAROL

"I guess I am giving up," Channing sighed. "I don't see how we could work."

I closed my eyes and tried not to cry. I cried anyway, a few tears slipping down my cheeks. I nodded vigorously, eyes still closed. "You're right!" I shook my head. "No, you're right. It *can't* work. You're a criminal. I'm an attorney. This was such a mistake." I slapped my thighs and stood up.

Channing stood too, grasping my hands. "Don't."

"You just said we can't be together, Channing." I trotted naked over to the bookcases where my clothes were piled with his. I tore mine out and bundled them up, hunched over as I rushed out of the room before I started sobbing.

I found a guest bathroom around the corner from the library and locked the door behind me while jumping into my clothes, hardly noticing the antique everything. Then I peed and cleaned up before flushing and closing the lid. I went to grab the doorknob, then stopped. I was going to cry again. I sat on the toilet lid, elbows on knees, head in my hands, and let myself weep quietly.

What a disaster.

I remembered I had the Plan B pill package in my purse. I considered taking it right now.

Didn't.

I wanted to take it with a clear head, not when I was an emotional wreck.

Footsteps outside the door distracted me.

I expected Channing to come knocking and mutter through the door about how much he loved me, how we would find a way to make it work, no matter what challenges life threw at us.

He did not.

When I was ready, I walked out, heading in the general direction of the front door. Channing's house was such a maze, it took a while to fumble my way there. Voices drifted to my ears in hissing whispers before I reached the marble entry hall. Angry whispers.

I stopped to listen.

"You can't be here, Reyna," Channing said.

"I have every right. This is *your* baby, Channing!" A woman's voice, soft but edged with aggression.

For a strange second, I was sure this woman meant mine. *My* baby. Yes, my baby *would* be Channing's.

Then I heard a baby's cry.

My eyes widened in alarm.

"How could it be mine?" Channing gasped.

"Not so loud! You're scaring him," the woman hissed.

"We haven't had sex in almost three years, Reyna!" Channing's voice was low, off balance, completely disbelieving.

"You're forgetting that one time you were drunk. Or was it two times? Could be three. Or more. There were quite a few toward the end of our marriage."

Channing had no answer for that.

I didn't know where to begin.

Reyna said, "He's your son, Channing. He turns one this month."

I wanted to vomit my balled-up emotions and send them skidding across the marble floor like so many rolling marbles.

Channing had lied to me.

Again.

He'd said he'd been careful about birth control.

Why had I believed his lies?

Again?

I turned on my shoe, intent on finding a back way out of the house. I'd trudge home in the snow if I had to. But my sneaker squeaked on the marble.

"Carol?" Channing called. "Is that you?"

"*Carol?*" Reyna spat my name like a poisoned curse. "Who's Carol?"

I readied myself to run. No. I would not run. This was not my shame. This was Channing's. I would march past him and *the other woman*, my head held high, and I would never look back.

I started marching.

Seconds later, Channing thudded up to me. "Carol I can explain."

I snarled, "Can you? Can you tell me how you were *sooo* careful with the women you slept with?"

"I was," he sighed.

"Except when it came to your *wife*," I scowled. "You are a liar, Channing Peyton. You always were and always will be. Let go of me. I'm done with you."

"It's not what you think," he begged.

"Oh, it is *exactly* what she thinks," said Reyna from around the corner. Pistol shots clacked off the marble walls as her high heels approached.

Channing's face glazed with hate.

A slender form appeared, the silhouette of a supermodel obvious from a distance. Tall, hour-glass, feminine and flaunting it. As she approached, cradling a baby in her arms, her face emerged into the light, a triumphant smile chilling her ice blue eyes. Her hair was obsidian black, as shimmery as her wet red lips.

Reyna.

"Who are you?" she asked me with royal flair. "The new cleaning lady?"

"I'm an attorney," I growled. "Who are you?"

"Reyna Peyton. Channing's wife." In her arms, the baby squirmed and started to cry. "And this is Channing's son."

Chapter 39

Seventy hours after first having sex with Channing in his Lighthouse, I stood in my high school bathroom with the door closed, looking at myself in the mirror.

The Plan B package sat open on the counter, tempting me to take it. Two little pills in the blister pack. I'd been in here for twenty minutes trying not to cry.

Time to get it over with.

After meeting Reyna the Royal Stain the other night (total bitch, if you hadn't noticed), and Channing's *son*, I had called an Uber. Channing had insisted Lashawn drive me home. I was okay with that because I wouldn't have to wait. But I was not okay with Channing being married *and* having a son.

Can you blame me?

Taking Plan B was a given.

I hadn't taken it the night I'd met Reyna. I was too angry. And sad. Again, I wanted to have a clear head and be relatively calm. I'd spent yesterday thinking it over. Again, I'd talked to Sienna and Jordyn. Both were very supportive, but neither were willing to tell me what to do. I respected that, and waited until now because I just needed more time.

And here I was.

My mind was clear.

Even though I had plenty more years before I was too old to have kids of my own, there was no sign of a meaningful relationship with any man waiting over my horizon, meaning there was a good chance this potential pregnancy might be my *only* chance to ever have my own child.

But.

Having Channing's baby without his knowledge would be the epitome of unethical. I couldn't do it. I pushed the first pill out of the blister pack and held the innocent little thing.

The gravity of the moment weighed down on my shoulders like a hundred elephants.

If I took this pill, I would never have the one baby I most wanted to have. Channing's. I certainly wasn't going to have sex with him ever again, so this was it.

Five tries later and I still couldn't get the pill all the way to my mouth without crying and hyperventilating and having to stop for a breath.

On the sixth try, I closed my eyes.

Opened wide.

I could feel my breath warm and moist on my fingers as the pill approached my tongue.

I couldn't do it.

I lifted the toilet lid.

Dropped the pill in the water.

Popped the second pill out of the blister pick and tossed it too. Flushed. Then I tucked the packaging under my pajamas so my parents wouldn't see and went back to my bedroom, stuffing the package in my luggage.

In bed, I sniffed myself to sleep under the covers, periodically wiping away tears. If I couldn't have Channing in my life, at least I could have his baby—no, *our* baby—and give her or him the love I wanted to give Channing, but never would now. Not with Reyna in the way.

I should tell Channing.

That was the ethical thing to do.

He should at least know.

No, it was too soon.

I might not even be pregnant.

\#

&

&*&

&*&*&

&*&*&*&

M

CHANNING

"What's the word on Tim?" Jake asked, tossing a pistachio nut into his mouth, shell and all. "You make him an offer on TT's yet?"

"No," I barked. "I've been busy."

"Better get on that," he smiled wolfishly.

"I'll get to it," I grumbled.

"If the crip won't sell, break his legs."

"They already are. He has Spina Bifida or whatever it is. He walks on crutches." I had yet to break anyone's legs and I wasn't about to start for Jake's sake.

"Fine. Break his arms."

I couldn't decide if he was joking or not. It was hard to tell with Jake, but he had never once asked me to rough someone up. If the Martinelli

Family did that kind of business, it wasn't on my watch. Then again, Jake was always full of smelly surprises.

Jake cracked the pistachio nut in his teeth and spit out the shell with an audible "Pfthoof!" It landed six feet away on the cold terrace stones behind my house where it overlooked the snowy garden. The only snow on the terrace currently were the tiny windblown pellets of ice piled in the corners and edges around the stone balustrade.

"Pick that the fuck up." I glared at the shell pieces glimmering with Jake's spit that would soon ice over. It was below freezing, but the windy air was dry as bone and had a bite to it.

"Have the gardener do it."

"No, you do it. Show some fucking class."

Jake was dressed impeccably in a suit and long tan coat, but he acted like he wore shit for a shirt and turds for trousers. He smirked, plucked another nut from the bag he held in his hand, popped it in his mouth, cracked the shell with his teeth, and spit it out. "Pfthoof!"

I glared at him.

He arched a smiling eyebrow, daring me to say something.

I didn't.

"How's Pilky?" he asked. "Haven't heard a word from that bird. You think he flew the coop with his cash?" He was implying I needed to collect said investment money before Morris Pilkington spent it somewhere else.

"I've been busy."

"I heard. Your lady is in town."

"Reyna?"

"Her too."

I frowned.

"Frenchy told me your other girl is in town. The college kid. What's her name. Carol something."

It was impossible not to scowl. Not because of Frenchy. I'd never once mentioned Carol to Frenchy before having her over for dinner. When Frenchy had asked about Carol after she'd left, I'd simply said she was an old friend and left it at that. Frenchy had chuckled, "Not that old. I could hear you two at the other end of the house. Going at it like dogs." I had simply smiled with pride, and Frenchy laughed, "I could take lessons from you two."

Jake asked, "What was the college kid doing here?" He spit out another shell. "Pfthoof!"

Raging inside, I stepped in front of Jake until we were a few inches apart. Jake was a big guy, but he was an inch shorter than my 6'4". He was also ten years older, less massive, had never worked out like I did to this day, and I knew for a fact he wasn't one-tenth the athlete I was.

Teeth clenched, I hissed death, "If you spit one more fucking shell on my terrace, I will beat the living shit out of you where you stand."

Jake's face reddened. His eyes vibrated. He carefully placed another nut in his mouth. Bit down on it between molars so I could see it. Cracked it.

"Go ahead and spit," I warned. "Spit it in my face if you want. If you aren't wearing your gun today, I will stomp your skull to a bloody mess here on the stones."

I would never kill Jake over spitting nuts. I'd put up with plenty of petty abuse from him over the years.

I *would* kill him over Carol.

If he so much as gave her a hangnail, I would chop off his fingers. If he gave her a black eye, I would pry out his with a screwdriver. If he killed her, I would kill Jake's entire family, burn down their houses, and salt the ground.

Jake kept the nut and shell fragments in his mouth, rolling them over to his cheek while he smirked, "Something bothering you, kid?"

I answered with a question, "What's on your mind, Jake?"

"Business."

"No shit," I smirked. "If you came here to remind me about TT's and Pilky, I'll take care of it. Anything else?"

"Make sure you do. We've got bills to pay and we can't do it without Pilky's money."

"I said I'd take care of it."

"You've got two women on your stick. That's two too many in my book. Don't let them take your eye off the ball, kid. You know what happens when that happens. You get blindsided by a linebacker." An obvious threat.

Again, I was ready to remove his skull from his spinal column and kick a field goal with it. I hissed, "You ever get blindsided by a quarterback?"

"No," Jake pursed. He cupped a hand in front of his mouth to spit his shells into it. He grimaced at the wet shells, shoved them in the pocket of his long tan coat. "Talk to Pilky. Get his money. And buy TT's." Jake strolled past me and walked away, his loafers grinding across the frozen stone.

I'd won that round.

Made my point without showing my hand about Carol.

I hoped.

Jake wasn't dumb.

```
        #
        &
       &*&
      &*&*&
     &*&*&*&
        M
```

CAROL

I found the texts on my phone several days after Channing sent them, and finally read them sitting alone on my high school bed.

Reyna and I have been separated over a year.

She disappeared before signing divorce papers.

She said she was on the pill.

She never told me she was pregnant.

I didn't know.

I swear.

Please call me, Care.

Please.

At least let me apologize one last time before you never talk to me again.

I sat there grimacing, reluctant to believe any of it.

One thing I knew for certain?

I could never be with Channing.

White collar crime wasn't exactly murder, but my parents didn't need to be worrying over me more than they already did. They'd worked hard to provide a home for me growing up, and they still hadn't paid it off. Once they did, they deserved to retire to a quiet life, not visit me weekly in my orange jumpsuit at the nearest minimum security women's prison for the remainder of their years.

I would talk to Channing one last time, but only to explain to him the sad reality of our situation. Whether or not I'd tell him about my maybe pregnancy was entirely up in the air. I'd be juggling that secret privately until I was ready to drop it in his lap like a baby boy hot potato, or maybe a baby girl bun from my oven, too soon to know which, if I even *was* pregnant.

What were the chances?

```
        #
        &
       &*&
      &*&*&
     &*&*&*&
```

M

CHANNING

"It's not your kid," Lashawn shook his head, leaning over the antique pool table in my private game room, lining up the shot. He snapped his cue stick and cracked the cue ball across the royal purple felt into the purple-striped twelve, pocketing it in the corner. He stood and walked around the table to line up another shot. Grabbed the blue cube and chalked his stick, shaking his head, "It's not yours, dog. I'm telling you."

"But that's what she said," I sighed, leaning against my pool cue on the corner.

"Bullshit," Lashawn barked angrily. "You never fucked Reyna drunk."

"She said I did," I sighed.

"Uh uh, dog. Every time you were drunk, I was there, keeping your ass out of trouble. Before Reyna, during, and after. She's high."

"Every time? Are you sure?"

"Sure as I'm gonna sink the thirteen." He cracked it into the side pocket with authority and smirked, "What did I tell you? Kid. Isn't. Yours. She's lying."

"Do I ask Reyna for a DNA test?"

"You're making a mammoth mistake if you don't. How long are you gonna let her live here in the house?" He aimed for the 14 ball and sank it.

"At least until she gets a DNA test. She has my baby. I can't kick them out on the street."

"A baby," Lashawn insisted before pocketing the 15. "Either way, make it quick. The last time you got rid of her was the happiest day of my life. Due respect, I can't stand the woman."

"Most people can't," I sighed. "Can you at least try and cut her some slack for now?"

"Me?" he chuckled. "Every time I see her, she gives me the same old look she always did."

"Which look is that?"

He smirked seriously, "The one she gets like I'm supposed to call her massuh."

I knew that Reyna could be snootier than the average bitch bear during a food shortage, but this was a big house. Immense, for lack of a better word. I sighed, "Try to avoid her. Stay in your wing if you have to. At least until the DNA test. If it's negative, we'll both boot her to the curb. If it's positive and the baby is mine…"

"It isn't." Lashawn lined up the winning shot. "Big black ball in the corner pocket. Huh, huh, huh."

Crack!

He sank the 8-ball with ease.

In my experience, Lashawn rarely missed.

But he wasn't psychic.

Chapter 40

CAROL

I texted Channing to meet me someplace public.

Although I was still somewhat gun-shy about being seen too publicly in King City for various reasons like:

CAROL DUFFEY, CHEETAH KILLER T-shirts,

and

Random Old Lady: "I know you! I wish you'd die!"

I felt more comfortable meeting Channing somewhere public where we would *not* fall into bed and have sex again. I had been hornier than usual in the past few days, which seemed impossible after all the sex we'd had, but I was. I had no idea if that meant I was already pregnant or not, and my biological clock was starting to speed up and demanding action.

I briefly considered my parents house as a location to meet Channing, so they could chaperone us, but I couldn't have an open conversation with him in front of them, and they didn't deserve to be inconvenienced by my bad decisions anyway.

So I decided on a Starbucks not far from their house, which was more than far enough from King City University, meaning minimal risk I'd be triggered by random people walking around in gold and black Cheetah's jerseys who may or may not recognize me as the woman who singlehandedly murdered KCU's football program for a time.

I was already inside the crowded Starbucks at a table cupping a warm glass of blonde cappuccino when I heard thunder outside. A black race car drove up and parked. I had no idea what kind but I had a pretty good idea who was driving it.

Out stepped Channing, breath clouding the crisp winter air. As always, he was dressed sharp enough to poke out the eyes of all the women craning their necks to gawk out the windows at him. To my dismay, none of their eyes did get poked out on his designer coat or designer suit underneath. But, when Channing opened the front door, their eyes popped out and their tongues followed.

I waited expectantly for a flurry of panties to pelt Channing in the face, and for him to catch at least one pair in his teeth.

Neither happened.

But the whispery gossip was instant.

Every woman in this Starbucks knew Channing Peyton by name.

Since the day I'd met him, he'd been a rock star, and he still was. In this town, anyway. I doubted anyone in San Francisco would know him on sight. But they would drool.

Channing was effortlessly dashing.

"Carol!" He brightened when he saw me. "You saved a table. Should I order or...?" There was a long line up to the counter.

"Go ahead," I said. "I'll wait."

He glanced at the line. "Forget it. We'll share." He dropped into the seat across the tiny table and motioned at my cappuccino. "May I?"

"Sure," I sighed.

He took a swallow and licked foam from his lips. "Not bad, but you taste better."

"Please don't, Channing."

"Don't what?" he asked innocently.

"Make this any harder than necessary."

"Sorry. So, yeah. Where to begin?"

"Your wedding day," I smirked.

"Ah, that. I was married to Reyna."

"You said you were only separated."

"Technical detail. Reyna is, how can I say this politely, she, Reyna would frighten the mane off a lion. She has claws like you wouldn't believe."

"Yet you got her—" I noticed people around us were listening closely while pretending not to. I leaned over the table and lowered my voice to a thin whisper, "— you got her pregnant."

"The jury's still out on that one," he said equally quietly. "I have good reason to believe she might be, mmm, misleading me."

"What reason?"

"It's complicated."

"Did you get a—" I silently mouthed the rest, "—paternity test?"

"As soon as she'll agree to one."

"Have you asked?"

"It's a delicate subject."

"I can imagine," I smirked and reached for my cappuccino. Stopped myself before I grabbed it. I could see Channing's lip prints on the opposite side. I wasn't worried about a germ thing. I was worried about giving him any ideas.

I sighed, "What else?"

He reached over the table to grab my hands.

I withdrew them and folded them in my lap.

He sighed and hung his head, keeping his hands where he'd left them. Glanced around at the crowd. This was the opposite of a private conversation. Quietly, he said, "Carol, I never meant to hurt you. That's the last thing I wanted. I know I've probably fucked things up beyond repair, but I wanted you to know I have always loved you, past tense. I still love you, present tense. I will always love you, future tense. Whether you lay your head to sleep in my bed every night, or one on the other side of the world, you will always be in my heart, Carol. I couldn't get you out if I tried."

I almost asked him if he had the pieces of my heart trapped in his. Almost asked if I could have them back. Almost blurted I was pregnant with his baby. Almost blurted I *might* be pregnant with *our* baby, and if I was, I would raise our child with or without him.

Ultimately, I sighed and said, "I don't know what to tell you. It's sweet, Channing, but your, um, *line of work* isn't exactly going to work with mine. We talked about this."

He closed his eyes and nodded, "I know. Believe me, I know. If I could trade in my past for a normal job, someplace like here," he motioned around the Starbucks, "I would."

"Why don't you?"

"Dump my life to be a barista?" He grinned. "It does have a certain vagabond appeal, doesn't it? But I'd have to grow out my hair into dreadlocks."

I laughed, picturing it. He'd still be sexy as hell.

"You can grow dreads with me," he smiled.

"No," I snickered. "I'd never do that to my hair."

"If we sold everything we own, moved into a van, and lived like nomads, driving from one trailer park to the next, you wouldn't have a choice. There aren't enough trailer park barbers between National Parks."

I grinned, "Where do you come up with these fantasies of yours?"

"From my muse." His eyes pinned mine.

I couldn't move. My heart thumped a happy tune. I collected my thoughts into a picnic basket of idyllic hope and said, "Could you do that? Walk away from your life and give up everything for me?"

"Define everything."

"That's a no," I snorted.

"No, I'm asking for specific terms. You don't sign a million dollar contract you haven't read, or at the very least, have your lawyer read. Know any good lawyers?" He said suggestively.

"No, but I know a good attorney."

"Is her name Carol?"

"No, his name is Mitch and he's my boss and mentor."

"Oh. I get it. Funny. Back on topic, let me think. Could I give up everything for you?"

"If you need to think about it, the answer is no."

\#

&

&*&

&*&*&

&*&*&*&

M

CHANNING

I would give up everything for Carol in an instant.

One problem.

Jake Martinelli would never give up anything for anybody, not Carol, and sure as shit not me.

Worse, if I gave up everything, I wouldn't have any resources to protect Carol from the likes of Jake and Tony and the Martinelli family.

I needed to do something about those fucks.

But what?

\#

&

&*&

&*&*&

&*&*&*&

M

CAROL

I shook my head, "I appreciate the sentiment, Channing, but I understand. You've built a life for yourself. There isn't room in it for me."

"Yes there is. You saw my house."

"I also saw Reyna and your—" I mouthed silently, "—baby."

"Like I said, jury is still out."

I wanted to believe we could be together, but there was just too much drama in Channing's life.

"Do you like being the other woman?" Reyna blurted from where she'd popped out of hiding in the crowded line not far from our table. She was gorgeous, but something about her makeup and her jilted energy reminded me of a Jack-in-the-Box toy, or in her case, Brunette-

Barbie-in-the-Box.

"What're you doing here?" Channing grimaced.

"Checking up on you," Reyna sneered.

"Is that what they call spying these days?" he smirked.

Reyna rolled her eyes at him and pointed a French-manicured nail at me, "Sweetie, you don't want to get between me and my man, okay?" Her tone bled bitch. "It won't end pretty, and I'm not talking about me."

Channing had been right about her claws.

I had been right about his drama.

I pushed back my chair and stood to go.

Smirked at her, "He's alllll yours, honey."

Smirked at him, "Have a nice life. When this doll wears out," I whipped a switchblade glare at Reyna, "call Mattel and exchange her for a new one."

Chapter 41

CAROL

"Oh my gosh!" I sang and clapped my hands over my mouth after opening the front door at Mom and Dad's. It was Christmas Eve. Outside stood Jordyn and her mom in winter coats and knit hats. Both held glass dishes covered in plastic-wrap steamed over from the cold. I smiled, "You look exactly like Jordyn." Her mom really did. They were twin raven-haired vixens, both pictures of a Pirate Queen.

"Invite them in Carol," Mom clucked behind me. "It's too cold outside."

They clomped through the door.

"Where's you leather jacket?" I asked.

Jordyn smiled, "Mom loaned me one of her coats."

Her mom said, "You can't wear leather for Christmas Eve. Even I know that. Duh." She laughed nervously.

Jordyn said, "Rolo, this is my mom Jennifer."

"Nice to meet you, Rolo," Jennifer said, extending a hand for me to shake.

"Rolo?" Mom snorted.

"It's Carol," I said.

"Rolo is sweeter," Jennifer said.

Mom frowned.

Jordyn looked slightly embarrassed by her mom's comment. She said apologetically, "I'm sorry, Rol— I mean Carol, I don't know your mom's name."

"Beverly Duffey," Mom said. "This is my husband Jack."

"Hello," Dad smiled and tipped nods at everyone, never taking his hands out of his slacks.

When I again noticed the dishes in Jordyn and Jennifer's hands, I smiled, "I told you not to bring anything."

"I'm not showing up to a party empty-handed," Jennifer laughed defensively. "What side of the tracks do you think I came from?"

"She made fudge," Jordyn explained.

"I love fudge," Dad chuckled.

"One's chocolate, the other butterscotch," Jordyn said.

"Best fudge ever," Jennifer said.

Jordyn said quietly, "It is."

Mom said politely, "Sounds delicious. Let me put these in the kitchen.

Jack? Can you help?" Mom left me with Jordyn and Jennifer because she knew better than to leave Dad alone with two strange and incredibly beautiful women. He wouldn't know what to do with them other than ask them about drones. I also suspected Mom wasn't sure what to do with Jennifer either. She had a brittle brusqueness my parents weren't used to.

"Your parents seem really nice," Jordyn said.

"Wait'll they start drinking," Jennifer said.

"They don't drink," I said.

"Don't mind Mom," Jordyn apologized. "She thinks everyone grew up in a bar like she did."

"Did not," Jennifer chuckled. "I was eighteen the first time I waited tables." She was a lot like Jordyn, rougher around the edges, but no less beautiful. I could see she was older, but not by much. Compared to my parents, Jennifer looked youthful and vibrant. If I didn't know she had breast cancer, I'd think she was still going to live forever like her daughter and I.

The doorbell rang.

"Is that the male strippers?" Jennifer chuckled.

"It must be Sie." I crossed my fingers it wasn't Channing come to surprise me. My chest tightened when I opened the door.

"Caaaaare!" Sienna sang, jumping into my arms. When she broke away and saw Jordyn and Jennifer, her eyes lit up. "Nobody told me I'd be having a three way!"

Jennifer frowned, "What's she talking about?"

"She's kidding, Mom," Jordyn said.

"I'm not," Sienna said.

"Calm down," I laughed, not wanting Sienna and Jennifer to start punching, because neither seemed like the clawing type. Fists would fly if they went at it.

"Who're you?" Jennifer asked.

"Sienna Winters," Sienna said, opening her arms. "Bring it in, sister. You must be Jordyn's mom."

"Last time I checked," Jennifer chuckled while Sienna crushed her in a hug. "Easy on the boobs, babe."

"Oh, right, sorry," Sienna winced and said seriously, "How are you doing?"

"Never better." Jennifer looked like the last thing she wanted to talk about was her breast cancer.

Jordyn wore a hopeful smile.

"Let's sit down, you guys," I said cheerily and led everyone to the couches for a change of scenery and topic. Sienna quickly shifted from flirting with Jennifer to entertaining all of us with her New York stories. She had an endless supply of those after living there ten years. I half-expected Jennifer to find Sienna's stories annoying, but it turned out Jennifer had some crazy stories from her own youth that put Sienna's to shame. By the time dinner was ready, you'd think they were best girlfriends.

Mom called us to the table that I had set an hour before everyone arrived and we worked our way through traditional Christmas Eve dishes. Turkey, honey ham, sourdough stuffing, candied yams, gravy, cranberry sauce, mixed vegetables, salad, and roasted chestnuts (a holdover from Mom's mom). Dessert followed, including Mom's fruitcake, cookies, and Jennifer Hoyle's infamous fudge. It really was delish.

I am happy to report, the dinner conversation was effortless. Sienna and Jennifer had established a rapport and they entertained everyone. Sienna figured out quickly how to tailor her stories for Mom and Dad's PG tastes. Jennifer wasn't quite as adept at keeping it clean, but Sienna constantly distracted or interjected with jokes in such a way as to bolster Jennifer's story without stealing her thunder.

I found myself frequently thinking of Channing and wishing he was here, even though he never could be. But he was on my mind.

\#

&

&*&

&*&*&

&*&*&*&

M

CHANNING

"Why are you torturing yourself like this, dog?" Lashawn asked from the front seat of the dark Mercedes.

I watched Carol and her family, Sienna, and the two raven-haired babes through the open front window, savoring their Christmas dinner, passing food and conversation back and forth like the rare delicacies they were, their laughter flowing like wine as they got drunk on one fun story after another.

I'd never seen a family look happier.

"You're right," I sighed. "Let's go. We can have our Christmas Eve dinner with Reyna."

"You can," Lashawn chuckled. "I'm eating with Terrance in the kennel with those hounds you're always talking about. They're way nicer than that... *woman*."

It wasn't the word I would've used, but he had a point.

```
                    #
                    &
                  &*&
                &*&*&
              &*&*&*&
                    M
```

CAROL

Over coffee, Mom continued her annual tradition by asking laughingly in the middle of some boisterous story Sienna was telling me, "When do I get grandkids, Carol? I'm not going to live forever, you know."

I had been laughing so much at what Sienna had just said, I almost blurted, "I'm growing one right now, Mom! Nine more months!" Before I could actually say anything, Jennifer spoke for me.

"Yeah, Carol. Listen to your mom. You get any older, you won't be able to have any."

There went the record needle.

The conversation bus stopped on a dime.

Jordyn looked ready to die of embarrassment.

Jennifer stood proudly over the grave with a shovel.

Dad looked like Billy Varnick down the street had broken Dad's new Mavic drone from Channing.

Sienna finally, for once in her life, had nothing to say.

Mom's eyes shimmered with hidden sadness.

Then I almost did tell everyone I was pregnant, for Mom's sake. But I didn't know if I was, otherwise I would have announced the good news.

Then, a stray thought.

The night Channing had me over at his mansion for dinner, he had arrived at this house bearing gifts. Mom's Lladro figure that he said reminded me of him, and Dad's slightly-used Mavic 2. Channing had said he had a gift for me at his house, but he'd never given me one.

He'd given me sex.

Lots and lots of sex.

Was that his gift?

Or would it be the baby growing inside me?

Assuming there was one?

#
&
&*&
&*&*&
&*&*&*&
M

CHANNING

"He's *your* baby, Channing," Reyna insisted, folding her arms across her embroidered Versace jacket, bought yesterday at Neiman Marcus. Reyna never wasted any time spending my money. Fortunately, I had a large fortune. "Channing junior is *your* son," she said. "Why do you think I named him after you? I'm not taking a DNA test. It's disgusting for you to even ask," she snarled. "I already know. He's yours." You'd think we were arguing over whose pile of shit was soiling the oriental rug between our feet, hers or mine.

I heaved a sigh.

It was late Christmas Eve, I really didn't want to have this discussion now or ever, but there would never be a good time.

Reyna and I stood in the East Sitting Room. Channing Jr. was sleeping elsewhere in his brand new crib in his brand new nursery. He didn't need to hear us hashing things out. And, if you saw his new nursery, you too would rather be there than here.

Two days ago, I'd had my decorator Lily Yang drop everything she was doing for a day (she was currently managing interior design on an upcoming 60-unit luxury condo project), so she could transform one of my many guest bedrooms into Channing Jr.'s baby paradise.

In a mere 24 hours, Lily had worked her magic and it was like Disneyland's A Small World in there. I'd pulled a couple workers off the Cypress Gardens housing build to help her move furniture and paint. They'd done wonders.

Reyna had, of course, stuck her nose into things halfway through, trying to gum up the works while I'd been at the office tending to business. It had started when Lily had called begging me to let her get back to managing her condo project.

Lily had sounding very frustrated. "I don't know what to do, Mr. Peyton. She won't—"

"Channing," I said. "Don't start mistering me now. What's wrong, Lily?"

"It's Reyna. She's," Lily ughed. "I'm *trying* to work with her. She doesn't like any of my ideas. I've given her five different design options, each distinct, but she tears down every one. It's like trying to please the queen when she's hormonal."

That sounded like Reyna, but it didn't sound like the Lily I knew. I tried not to laugh because I'd never heard Lily so flustered. She was impeccably professional and level headed. Lily never lost her cool and never talked shit about a client. She prided herself on being able to take care of business herself. Normally, I only saw her at the beginning of a project and at the very end when she showed me her incredible results. Now she sounded like her dress was on fire and I was the only one with a firehose.

I said, "Is there any way you can—"

An incoming call beeped my phone.

Reyna.

"Hold on, Lily," I grunted. "It's the queen calling." I switched over. "Hey, Reyna."

"Your decorator is ruining junior's room!" Reyna shrilled. "Ruining, Channing!"

Did you notice how Reyna didn't say hello?

Just dove into the harangue like it was her favorite thing?

"What do you mean ruining?" I asked calmly. "Did Lily paint the room black? Install wall-to-wall asbestos carpeting? Put rats in the walls?" I knew how Reyna thought.

"*Noooo*," Reyna sneered. "Her color choices and furniture selection are all wrong. She's trying to make it too kidsy."

"Kidsy? Isn't my son a baby?"

"You need to set the right aspirational tone, Channing."

"He's a year old. The only thing he should aspire to is regular bowel movements, getting enough sleep, and enough breastmilk. How is that going, by the way? I know my doctor cleared you for breastfeeding, even with your breast implants. Have you tried it yet?"

"I told you, *Channing*, I don't want my nipples getting stretched out." You'd think I'd asked her to allow every man on the planet with a breast fetish to join in the fun.

"Fine," I grumbled. "I've already started the paperwork at the milk bank to get you donor milk like you asked. You should get the first shipment in a day or two."

"Now tell your Asian decorator to do what I say."

Did you hear a thank you?

And how she mentioned Lily's ethnicity?

Seemingly the day after our wedding, Reyna suddenly developed the bad habit of pointing out everyone's race, unless you were white, which she never mentioned. I'd pointed out her habit many times. Her response would always be something like, "What? She *is* Asian? How is it a problem that I mention it?"

If you want to argue with Reyna, be my guest.

She had developed a number of other bad habits after our wedding, spending my money being number one. I should probably tell you, Reyna wasn't like this when I met her. She was very reserved and she wasn't greedy, unless we were in bed. There, she was a ravenous wildcat starving for my cock.

Believe it or not, I had been sober when I had proposed to her. After our wedding day, that trend turned downward until I slid over a whiskey waterfall and drowned myself in the pool at the bottom. The most sober moment of our marriage was probably the day I'd crawled out of said whiskey pool and gone to my lawyer to draw up separation papers.

Anyway, it had taken another thirty minutes of placating Reyna on the phone about Channing Jr.'s nursery decor and promising to buy her a Porsche Cayenne SUV so she could drive him around King City in style before she had relented and let Lily do her thing. That was an easy enough fix: I had slapped a dealer plate on a fully-loaded Cayenne that had been sitting on the lot for six months at Peyton Auto Circle and let her drive it. Didn't cost me a dime.

Now we were arguing about the DNA test.

I said, "All it takes is a cheek swab. He won't even notice."

Demonic fury sliced up Reyna's face. "Are you accusing me of fucking someone else, Channing?"

"No, I'm asking your permission to swab our son's cheek for a DNA test."

"This is Lashawn's idea, isn't it?"

"No."

"I know how you two are. He put you up to this, didn't he?" Her voice was venom.

I sighed.

She sneered, "Don't you think it's time we turned our house into a home, instead of a frat house?"

"It's not a frat house," I chuckled.

"As long as Lashawn lives here, it is."

"What? Half the time he's here, you can't even tell, the house is so big."

"I see how he looks at me. Whenever I'm in the kitchen, his eyes are all over me, Channing. All. Over. I've been taking my meals upstairs because Lashawn won't stop ogling me. If I'd let him, he'd fuck me on the dining room table. Is that what you want? Let your football friend live here in this frat house with us so he can fuck me, Channing? Would that make you happy? Do you want Lashawn to fuck me in your own house?"

I frowned, "It sounds like you do. Why do you keep saying it so much?"

Reyna's eyes circled for a second. "I'm just letting you know what your horny African friend is up to when you aren't around."

I closed my eyes and wished desperately that Reyna would disappear before I opened them. "Look, Lashawn gets plenty of ass. Believe me. He doesn't want yours." I wanted to add, because hers wasn't worth it. Lashawn already knew that. The day I'd told him about my separation papers, he'd danced a dab and I'd danced with him, both of us shuffling back and forth in the kitchen, throwing dabs left and right like I'd thrown and he'd caught the winning touchdown pass at the Super Bowl.

I said to Reyna, "Can we stay on point? I'd like my son to have a DNA test. If he's mine, what's the problem?"

"The problem is you won't trust your own wife. We're still married, in case you forgot. Or do you want a divorce? Is that what you really want? If it is, I'll expect half, *and* child support. I won't have *your* son growing up any other way."

We had not signed a pre-nup.

In my book, you didn't marry someone you didn't trust. I had trusted pre-marriage Reyna. As a test, I had given her a credit card in her own name. Before we were married, she used it *one* time when her car battery died unexpectedly and she had to have a new one installed at the nearby Pep Boys where her car had been towed. She had called and asked me permission to pay for it, apologizing profusely for the money she promised to pay back. Post-marriage Reyna was a different person. She spent on her credit card like it drew funds from the Federal Reserve. I swear, someone had switched her brain with Genghis Khan's on our wedding day, or an alligator's, I could never decide which.

I sighed, "So, no DNA test?"

"You won't let this go, will you?" Her voice softened.

I shrugged.

"I know what will get your mind off it," she purred.

"No, Reyna."

"Don't no me," she grinned, her lips spreading into a wet smile as she slid toward me and snaked a hand around my neck. "Why won't you fuck me, Channing? I'm your wife. Don't you want your son to have a little sister?"

Make no mistake.

Reyna was a supermodel. Literally. She had once walked the fashion runways in New York and modeled for Victoria's Secret. When I met her, she was one of their Angels. If they only knew how miscast she was for that part. If you're wondering how a woman who once modeled for Victoria's Secret couldn't afford a car battery, so was I. Reyna was very evasive about her own money.

She dragged her palms down the front of my dress shirt. Grabbed my silk tie and tugged it suggestively. "You know how much I miss your cock." She bit her lower lip. "How about I show you?" She squatted down enough to stick out her hourglass ass and lower her lips to the level of my crotch. Slowly unbuckled my Stefano Ricci belt with sensual delight and sultry snickers. She let the leather tip hang like a half-erect dick. She cupped my balls through my slacks. Pushed her palm against my crotch. Frowned. "Why aren't you hard?"

"Why won't you do the DNA test?"

Her sensual expression deadened into a snarl.

Then she punched me in the balls.

Not hard enough to sterilize me, but hard enough to startle me and send a toxic cloud of pain wafting up my guts.

"Fine," she barked, stalking away on high heels, throwing up her arms. "Don't fuck me. Let your African friend suck your dick. I know you want him too."

"He was born in Arkansas," I grumbled.

She stopped in the doorway to the Sitting Room and whirled. "His ancestors are from Africa, aren't they? Or have you made him take a DNA test too?"

Had they outlawed murdering your own wife?

I'd have to ask my lawyer.

Before I did that, I needed a fucking drink.

Or ten.

My plan was to be blackout drunk starting now until the day after Christmas. The idea of spending it with Reyna was only slightly more appealing than having Hannibal Lecter feed me my brains for breakfast. No, it wasn't even that. Someone open the fava beans.

Chapter 42

CHANNING

"Did she agree?" Lashawn asked from behind the wheel of my black Mercedes twenty minutes after talking to Reyna about giving Channing Jr. a DNA test.

"Fuck no," I snorted, sitting beside him. Yes, I was feeling guilty about *Reyna's* insensitivity. I was also pre-loading on a swig of Old Crow whiskey. I'd made Lashawn stop at a liquor store so I could buy a bottle. Shit wasn't half bad for gasoline. Barely burned going down. "Reyna wouldn't agree to a coronation unless it was her idea."

"Get a court order. Then she has to do it."

"If I do that, she'll want a divorce."

"Don't you think it's strange she disappeared before signing divorce papers, then she comes back with a kid? *Then* she asks you to fuck another one into her? Uh uh. She's lying."

"If she isn't, and I piss her off, she'll take half. Do you have any idea how much she could fuck up my businesses if she owns half of my half? She'll make it her mission to ruin anything with my name on it, just to spite me."

"Jake won't let her do that."

"If she fucks him, he will."

"That dude is literally dickless," Lashawn chuckled.

"You sure?"

"I've never seen him fuck anybody. Have you?"

I shook my head, "The only thing I've ever seen him fuck is his competition."

"True that."

"Let me ask you a question, LD."

"Lay it on me."

"No disrespect, you ever make a play for Reyna? She says you're ogling her since she came back."

"Ah hell naw. You think I want that ice pussy freezing my dick off? Hell naw! I'd fuck a meat grinder before I'd ever fuck Reyna. Huh, huh, huh. Honestly, dog, I don't know how you did that shit."

"Did Reyna?"

"Yeah."

"Enough whiskey for a whale." I pounded another glug of Old Crow.

Lashawn gave me a side eye. "You better not get me a DUI with your open container. I told you to sit in the back."

"Don't worry. If you get pulled over, I'll deal with the cops. You're not even drinking."

"Doesn't matter."

"Does to me. The day I can't get KCPD to see things my way is the day I change my last name to Goodbitch." Reyna's last name was Goodrich, and she'd never changed it after our marriage. Obviously, I was making fun of it and Lashawn caught the joke.

"You said it. Huh, huh, huh, huh."

My man.

\#

&

&*&

&*&*&

&*&*&*&

M

On the red neon Tipple Town sign over TT's, the name Tim's was flickering on and off as Lashawn drove up. If I was going to drink, no reason not to do it here, and I needed to have a discussion with Tim Jr. about selling this place.

They said you couldn't mix business with pleasure, and this was proof. I didn't think Tim would enjoy the conversation we would soon have.

I popped out of the Mercedes and opened the front door of TT's for Lashawn, following him inside.

TT's was packed for a Christmas Eve. Why weren't these people home with their families? I'd pay any amount of money to be back at Carol's house with her family laughing around their turkey dinner and enjoying some of their genuine Christmas cheer.

Speaking of Carol, the mere thought of her sent Dick fishing around in my slacks looking for my smart phone so he could dial her himself. That woman made me harder than a carbide drill bit. Reyna couldn't even make jello, yet she seemed to have me locked in a steel cage.

"Mr. Peyton!" Tim called out, crutching toward the front doors. "Mr. Washington! Great to see you guys!"

"What's up, Tim," Lashawn grinned, extending a fist. "Hit me with it."

Tim leaned an armpit on a crutch and bumped back. "Haven't seen you two in forever."

"Looking good, dog," Lashawn grinned. "Looking good. Can you still do a handstand like the old days?"

Tim rolled his eyes, "Gave that up when my doc said my blood pressure was getting too high."

"I feel you," Lashawn nodded. "You did some gold medal shit back in the day, player."

"I'm afraid those days are over," he sighed. "What brought you two dirty dogs off the bench tonight?"

I smirked, "The she-dog that chased us off."

"Bitch *is* the dictionary definition," Tim winked. "I won't ask her name."

"You're a cool cat, Tim," I said.

"Said one to another. Now you two cool cats go heat up some seats and I'll send Wanda over to take your orders."

"Tell her to bring whiskey," I said. "And whatever LD is having."

"Coke straight up," Lashawn said.

"You got it," Tim nodded.

"Before you go," I said, "I have a business question for you, Tim."

"Shoot."

"If I made you a very generous, top-of-market offer on this very fine establishment you run, what would you ask for it?"

"Jake sent you." Tim's big eyes dimmed behind his thick glasses.

"Let's say *I* sent me. Throw a dollar figure at me, Tim. Think big. Lots of zeroes and commas. How much? Before you say anything, think about how nice it would be to retire, to kick your feet up like the old days when you did the handstands, without any of the stress of paying bills or paying for renovations." I looked around. "The building is showing its age. Sooner or later, you'll have to bring in a team to spruce this place up. Good craftsman don't work cheap. Reno and repairs for a building this big, inside and out, could run you $200,000 easy."

Tim shook his head slowly, "It's very kind of you to ask, Mr. Peyton, but—"

"Channing. You can call Jake Mr. Fuckface for all I care, and don't say it to his face if you want to keep your teeth, but you call me Channing. You hear me? I'm still the quarterback kid who came in here with a fake ID and a beer-hollowed leg, and you looked the other way. I'm not Mr. Anybody to you, Tim. I'm Channing. Now give me a number. High as you can count."

Tim sighed, "TT's is my dad's dream. It's how I keep his memory alive. I can't sell it for any price." He perked up, "But if you know anybody good who can give this place a facelift, let's talk dollars and cents. I hear that Peyton Construction is pretty good." He winked.

For a semi-second, I considered playing a Jake card and asking Tim if he had any kids. I didn't think he did. He'd never been married that I knew. If he said he didn't have kids, I would tell Tim he wasn't getting any younger, that he'd be too old to keep this place open much longer and he'd have to retire or turn the business over to someone then. Who would run it for him? Who could possibly do justice to his dad's dream? Then I'd sell him on how much better retirement would be with the mountain of money he made selling this place to me and Jake, that his dad would want that for him.

But I wouldn't play Tim like that.

He didn't deserve that bullshit.

I felt like a prick for even considering it.

I squeezed Tim's trapezius. "You're a good man, Tim. Call my office and we'll figure something out. I'll charge you wholesale on everything. No markup on labor, and I won't take my cut. It's on me, my man."

"I appreciate the offer," Tim smiled. "Soon as I scrape the money together, I'll give you a ring."

My shark brain again wanted to start thrashing away at Tim. Don't have the money now? You short on cash, Tim? What do you think about selling? Again, I would never do that to Tim.

I said, "Sounds like a plan."

Tim smiled, "I'll go get your drinks. Whiskey and a Coke for Lashawn."

"You got it," Lashawn nodded.

Tim crutched off.

Lashawn said, "You want to shoot some stick?"

"Sure. Why not."

We ambled back to the pool room and found an open table. The usual percentage of hotties (all of them) were eyeing me, as were the former Cheetahs fans. Quite a few came over to chat while Lashawn schooled me at pool, which gave me plenty of time to shake hands and take selfies with the fellas and the women who wanted to flirt. Didn't take too long for me to be too drunk to care.

"Channing Peyton!" gasped a sexy female voice behind me.

I turned around and chuckled. "Well, fuck."

Iesha Taylor stood there looking hot as all hell.

She jumped into my arms for a hug.

"Shay-shay Taylor," Lashawn chuckled. "Huh, huh, huh. You're all grown up. Bring it in, woman." They hugged too.

"What're you guys doing here?" she gasped. "It's been years. So good to see you again!"

"Where have you been?" Lashawn said. "I haven't seen you since college."

"I'm cheering for the Dallas Cowboys now," Iesha said with a hint of pride.

"You go, girl!" Lashawn grinned.

I smiled, "I knew you'd go all the way one day, Iesha. What're you doing back in King City?"

"My parents are still here," she smiled. "Came home for Christmas. I gotta fly out in two days for the next Cowboys game."

"Your boys are killing it this year," Lashawn said. "You think you'll make it to the Super Bowl?"

"We'll see," Iesha grinned.

"Now I know why they're playing so well this season."

"Why?"

Lashawn grinned, "They see your ass bouncing on the field, they go hog wild. Tell me I'm wrong."

Iesha rolled her eyes, pretending she wasn't flattered, and shook her head, smiling at me, "He's always like this, isn't he?"

"Only around you," I said. "LD here has plenty of game everywhere else."

Lashawn smirked, "Why are you throwing me under the bus like that, dog? I act the same around Iesha as I do around every woman I know."

I knew better. "Bullshit, Lashawn. You've always been gameless when it comes to Iesha." I sipped my whiskey. "I see Iesha doesn't have a ring on her finger. You got a boyfriend, girl?"

"You asking me out, Chandy?" She smiled coyly.

"I'm spoken for. But Lashawn here is taking you out for Christmas dinner tomorrow night."

"I am?" he blurted. "Says who?"

"Says me. Part of your job requirement. Take Iesha out for dinner tomorrow or your fired."

Iesha frowned, "I'm having dinner with my family tomorrow night."

"Even better," I nodded. "Can I invite him over?"

"Now wait, wait, wait," Lashawn said.

"Shush. Iesha, is it cool for LD to meet your family on a first date?"

Iesha was smiling, "Uh, I don't see why not."

"There you go, Lashawn. Dinner tomorrow at Iesha's. Make it happen."

"What are you doing, player?" Lashawn asked, shocked.

"You mean, why am I setting you up with the hottest hottie ever to cheer for the Dallas Cowboys?"

Lashawn hemmed, then hawed, then he danced around the topic for two minutes straight. Iesha rolled tired eyes. She'd heard this story before.

"Spit it out, Lashawn," I said. "None of us are getting any younger."

"Okay, fine. Fine!" He threw up his arms in defeat. "I have no game around Shay-shay Taylor. There, I said it. I have no game when it comes to the *hottest* cheerleader in the NFL. Can you blame me?"

I winked at him, "Maybe you don't need any."

He smirked, "What kind of girl wants a man with no game?"

Iesha pursed her lips and shook her head.

Desperate, Lashawn hissed in my ear, "Look at her, dog! She makes Halle Berry look butt-ass ugly! She doesn't want me!"

"Have you ever asked?"

Iesha ticked the air with her index finger, "Chandy, can you change his diaper? This girl needs a drink." She turned to go.

"Last chance," I warned Lashawn.

"Okay, okay. Iesha, may I have dinner with you tomorrow night?" He said it with the amount of embarrassment you would expect if he had publicly asked to sniff her dirty panties.

"Are you asking me out? Or just as friends?"

"Will your dad kill me if he knows it's a date?"

"Yes." She folded her arms across her sweater. "That a problem?"

I said, "Man up already, LD."

"Fine! I'll go."

"Don't tell me, tell her," I chuckled.

Exasperated, he said, "Iesha, may I have dinner with your family tomorrow? I'll bring a bouquet of flowers for you, and gourmet chocolates for your mom. A bottle of something nice for your dad. What does he drink?"

"He doesn't. Bring extra chocolates."

"I can do that."

Iesha's pursed lips melted into a sly grin, "That took you what, ten years?"

"Sixteen," I said, "if you count all four years of college."

Lashawn laughed at me, "How many buses are you gonna throw me under tonight?"

I checked my watch. "The express bus'll be along in five minutes. Be ready."

He rolled his eyes. "Wait, hold up. Iesha, was that a yes?"

Iesha smirked, "You're right, Chandy. He really doesn't have any game. Yes it's a yes, Lashawn."

His eyes lit up. "She said yes! Iesha Taylor said yes! Woooo dog!"

They were inseparable the rest of the night, laughing, flirting, and shooting pool while I drank and watched. I'd never seen Lashawn be more real with any woman. Iesha liked it just fine. I wished them the best. Dallas wasn't exactly in King City's backyard, and I'd hate to see Lashawn move down there and take another job, but if he developed feelings for Iesha like I had for Carol, I'd ship him down there myself.

Ah, Carol.

I'd hate to see her leave town too when the holidays were over, but what can you do? Carol had her own life to live and I had Reyna and Channing Jr. taking up my time. They were more problems Carol didn't deserve. Nobody deserved Reyna in their life, that was for damn sure. I wouldn't wish that woman on an oil spill.

Time for me to suck it up and take one for the team.

I wasn't complaining.

If Lashawn and Iesha went the distance, I'd root for them every step of the way. It'd keep my mind off my own life.

\#

&

&*&

&*&*&

&*&*&*&

M

Hazy drunk, I started blacking out while still at TT's.

Vision came in flashes.

Lashawn and Iesha making out in a corner.

Laughter.

Tim doing walking handstands on his crutches.

Thought he wasn't supposed to anymore? Because of his blood pressure?

Tim on the ground in wrong angles.

EMTs thudding boots into the bar.

Tim wheeled out on a stretcher.

Lying in back of the Mercedes, Lashawn in front with Iesha fretting beside him.

Bright lights, a hospital.

Arguing, something about Tim not having insurance.

A waiting room, my first moment of clarity. Bright ceiling lights knifing my eyes.

"You awake?" Lashawn asked.

"Where the fuck am I?" My tongue a swollen slug.

"King City Presbyterian."

"The hospital?"

"Yup."

"The fuck happen?"

"Tim had a stroke. You passed out."

"TT's Tim?"

"Yeah, dog."

"Did he make it? Is he…?"

"Hanging in there. He doesn't have any insurance."

My mind was not my own, phantom hands moved my mouth and worked my vocal cords, "Make him an offer."

"What?"

"On his bar."

"What are you talking about, player?"

"Lowball him."

"What?" Lashawn asked, annoyed.

"While he's down for an eight count. Tell him I'll pay all his medical bills if he sells TT's to me."

"What the fuck is wrong with you?" Lashawn asked, angry. "He told you he doesn't want to sell."

"He did? When?"

"Tonight. You're drunk. Go to sleep and sleep it off."

Iesha said, "What's Chandy talking about?"

"Nothing. He's loaded. Just needs to sleep."

Christmas Future

"God rest you, merry gentlemen,
"Let nothing you dismay,
"Remember Christ our Saviour,
"Was born on Christmas-day,
"To save poor souls from Satan's power,
"Which long time gone astray.
"O tidings of comfort and joy,
"Comfort and joy,
"O-o ti-i-dings of co-om-fort and joy."
—*English traditional Christmas carol, as catalogued in "Christmas Carols, Ancient and Modern; Including the Most Popular in the West of England, and the Airs which They are Sung. Also Specimens of French Provincial Carols," William Sandys, published in London by Beckley (1833)*

Chapter 43

CHANNING

It was snowing when I woke.

I lay on the floor in a waiting room. Sitting up, I realized I was in a hospital. Outside the dark windows, I saw I was several floors up. Only the lights from the hospital and dots of distant streetlights revealed the snowfall quickly blanketing the buildings and streets. A thin layer already powdered everything.

Why was I here again?

Not sure.

What was sure: I was heavily buzzed from drinking. Been here, done that.

I got up and went looking for a restroom. Based on how quiet this floor was, and the dark hospital rooms, it was late. My phone said it was 3:46am, Christmas Day.

I wasn't feeling very merry.

Something was weighing on my mind like sated and lazy drug monkeys hanging from my back, but I couldn't remember what.

I passed several nurse's stations, all empty and dark. Found a restroom. Used it. After, decided to stretch my legs. Walking would help me remember why the fuck I was at a hospital in the middle of the night, but not injured from some drunken accident I had probably caused.

When I got to the elevators, the one working nurse looked up from the computer at her desk and smiled, "Merry Christmas."

"You too," was all I felt like saying.

"Excuse me, sir. Are, are *you* Channing Peyton?"

"No," I lied.

"You look so much like him," she grinned.

"I get that all the time," I smiled politely and pushed the button for the elevator. Took an empty one downstairs and walked across an expansive lobby, empty and dark, my shoes shushing. Walked out automatic doors to watch the snow fall from under an awning.

The access roads and parking lot were quickly whitening. Checked my phone again for weather. King City was supposed to get eight inches of snow tonight before sunrise. It would be a white Christmas like everyone hoped.

I could picture parents snoring while the kids still snuggled into beds everywhere were wide-awake and waiting for Christmas to start, presents to be torn open, milk and cookies to be consumed before hot maple-syrupy breakfasts were inhaled adjacent to chestnuts roasting on open fires crackling, some in actual fireplaces, others on big screen TVs playing HD Fireplace videos on Hulu or Netflix or YouTube.

Other TVs would flicker with Grinches stealing Christmases, or Will Farrell's Elves teaching human Grinches the meaning of it, or Bad Santas learning how unconditional love nurtured the birth of redemption, or countless Ralphies discovered the risk of wishes fulfilled as he shot his eye out over and over again with his one true love on TNT.

I wasn't sure what my Christmas would bring. Knowing Reyna, an extended argument that gave everyone an ulcer.

The distant tinkling of sleigh bells stole my focus.

Tracking the sound, I looked up into the dark and snowy sky.

A soft orange glow, too big to be a star, to orange to be an airplane, too sluggish to be a meteor, caught my eye. I tracked it as it grew in size, slowly at first, then faster and faster.

It was heading straight for the hospital.

Vague visions of disaster traipsed through my brain, but that was Hollywood movies talking. If it *was* a meteor heading for the hospital, shouldn't it have broken into a silent shower of sparks by now?

The loudening sound of sleigh bells said I was missing the mark.

"What is that?" I chuckled out loud to no one. I was out here alone. The unknown had a power all its own, and I started to wonder if it was wise for me to be standing here out in the open as this strange sleigh-bell thing approached closer and closer. Because, more than three decades on this planet had taught me there was no Santa Claus, it was wish-fulfillment to think otherwise, and yet it seemed to be him I was seeing.

Visible through the falling snow, the orange glow undulated through the air, a snaking train of glowing ember motion.

Then, newly visible movement.

Galloping legs.

Rhythmic, lunging heads.

Eight beasts of burden pulling a sleigh, a lone rider guiding them flying in the sky.

What.

The.

Fuck.

I clamped my eyes shut, shook my head, and opened.

Santa Claus and eight running reindeer.

I was drunker than I realized. Probably a good time to go inside and sit down before I passed out in the snow and froze to death. I turned to go. Jingling bells demanded I take one last look.

Not Santa Claus.

Not reindeer.

Four black horses with eyes of fire and flaming hooves. Four immense hounds with flaming paws and maws dripping liquid fire from their fangs. The hair on the head of the shirtless man in the sleigh was burning as brightly as his eyes.

I was transfixed.

The galloping horses and hounds snorted and slavered their fiery saliva as the oversized sleigh descended and touched down well short of where I stood. Snow steamed instantly at the stepping of hot hooves and cindering claws. The skids of the big sleigh were red hot metal, also sizzling the snow into clouds as the hellish coach plowed to a slushy stop in the middle of the snow-covered road.

"Channing," said the fiery driver, who wore red leather pants, a shiny black belt, and black boots, all adorned with dozens of elaborate golden buckles. He also had the razor-sharp antlers of a 16-point buck sprouting from his flaming hair.

"Jake?" I gawked.

"Hop in," he leered.

"What the fuck, Jake? Where did you get the horns? Or a flying sleigh? And these dogs? They're huge! Big as the horses!" They were also on fire, as were the horses. "Is this some kind of top secret DARPA thing? Is this military? What the fuck?" I couldn't make sense of what I was seeing, but it was impossible not to believe it. I could feel the heat from the beasts cutting the cold.

"I have something to show you."

"Is this thing nuclear powered?" I was trying hard to think of a single sensible explanation.

"Get in." His eyes flared with flames.

I suddenly felt compelled to climb on board. I reached carefully, expecting the hot sleigh to burn my hands if I touched it. It didn't, but it was hot to the touch. The sleigh was massive, the step was high, and I pulled myself up into it with a struggle.

Jake was huge and standing at the reins. Almost eight feet tall, if I had to guess. He was also ripped.

"You been working out?" I asked.

He simply offered a devilish smile and whipped the reins. The sleigh lurched and I fell back onto the leather-buttoned bench seat while we accelerated quickly down the snowy road. I was about to stand and grab the front railing of the sleigh when everything tilted and again threw me back into the leather bench. The sleigh banked to the side and I slid, my stomach sloshing in fear, warning me I would slide right out the opening on the low side if I didn't hold on for dear life.

I did.

We were already a hundred feet off the ground and climbing. I could see snow-covered King City spreading out around us in a grayish haze of snow fog, streetlights the firefly sparks dotting the ashen night.

"Where are we going?" I asked.

"You'll see."

I'd flown over King City in an executive helicopter many times before (best way to show off a skyscraper to a potential client), and this was like that, except the wind in my face and the lack of seatbelts. And I'd never seen snow fog this thick. Almost smoke-like.

A strange sound pulled my attention behind the bench where a huge velvet bag knotted with a gold rope squatted in the sleigh's bed. The bag appeared damp, and patches of it shimmered redly in the light of Jake's burning hair. It was also making... slithering noises, and the insides were shifting slightly, almost bubbling with internal movement. I decided I didn't want to know and kept my eyes forward.

"Here we are."

"Where?" I asked, sitting forward on the bench. "Hey, that's TT's."

"For the moment."

We circled Tim's Tipple Town, two hundred feet in the air. The sign was dark. This late, of course it was. Bars closed at 2:00am in King City.

"Watch."

The impossible happened. With rapid haste, heavy equipment rolled into TT's parking lot with the familiar jerking and jolting motion of time-lapse video. A wrecking ball demolished the retro building within seconds while dozers, loaders, and dump trucks hauled out the debris in fast-forward motion.

"No," I muttered. "What's going on?"

Continuing to circle in the sleigh, I watched the speedy scene play out. Asphalt was jackhammered away, the dirt lot excavated, pilings sunk, back fill replaced, foundation poured, steel rebar fingers clawed skyward then were clad in concrete. Floor by floor the building rose, workmen like ants on crack, working every level, carrying, hammering, welding, bolting.

Less than a minute later, the skyscraper was complete, a tall tower of faceless mirrored glass reflecting back the fractured image of Jake's burning sleigh and me in it as we spiraled around and around to the top.

"You fucking prick," I grumbled. "You tore down TT's for this empty monolith?"

"TT's wasn't worth the land it sat on. This building will generate ten thousand times the revenue of a worthless old bar."

"What?" I chuckled. "People *loved* TT's. It stood for decades, making countless people happy before you tore it down."

"Happiness is a losing business prospect."

"Fuck that. What about Tim? How much did you end up paying him to buy him out?"

"I didn't."

"You didn't *pay* him?"

"I didn't have to."

"Why? What happened?"

"I'll show you." He offered a heartless smile.

Everything around us smeared as we shot forward and I was thrown backward onto the bench. Seconds later, the smearing clarified and we circled briefly above low buildings in another part of town before landing in the snow-covered parking lot. The sign in front of the building said Goodfellow Assisted Care Home.

"Is Tim in a nursing home?"

Jake headed toward the automatic doors. A placard next to a button box said, "Please ring desk for entry." Jake waved a flaming hand and the doors opened.

I jumped out of the oversized sleigh and followed him inside.

The time-lapse thing started again. People rapidly came and went, came and went through the halls of the care home. Outside the windows, the sun rose and fell repeatedly as we walked to a random dimly-lit room. Tim lay shriveled in a bed near the room's one window, never moving, his big glasses strapped to his head, reflecting back the rapidly rising and setting sun. Another man lay in the bed near the door where I stood with Jake. Unlike Tim, this man was constantly shifting in his bed.

I noticed two groups of people flickering in and out of the room. Nursing home staff and family. The staff attended both beds. The family went only to the other man. Not a single family member visited Tim.

His magnified eyes stared blankly and blinkless out the window, drool dripped down the corner of his slack mouth, pooling on his pillow in ever-expanding time-lapse circles. His body withered quickly before my eyes.

The time-lapse slammed to a stop.

Two male orderlies walked in.

"Time to change the sheets," one said.

"You roll the oldy."

"Is he awake?"

"Wake up, Oldy." The orderly shook Tim's foot.

I muttered to Jake, "Don't they know his name?"

He said nothing.

The orderly sighed, "He's dead."

"Tim's dead?" I muttered to myself. "He can't be dead. He was just at the hospital."

"You sure?" the other orderly asked.

"Hey! Old guy! Wake the fuck up!" Chuckling.

"Don't talk to him like that," I said forcefully to Chuckles. "Show some fucking respect."

Chuckles appeared not to hear me.

I gave him a shove, but my hands passed through his body.

The other orderly said, "I'll check his pulse. Nothing. Get the gurney."

Chuckles walked out and returned rolling a squeaking gurney. The two men wrapped Tim up in bedsheets and rolled him thumping onto the gurney's mattress. One of Tim's arms dropped over the side and hung.

Chuckles saw it and shrugged.

They wheeled Tim out into the hallway.

I followed them through the building and out a set of back doors to some dumpsters. The two orderlies grabbed the sheets in knots, dragged Tim off the gurney, and started a swing.

"No," I groaned.

"One, two, three!"

They threw him unceremoniously banging into the dumpster, then pushed the squeaking gurney back inside without looking back.

"Aren't they going to bury him?" I protested. "Give him a funeral? Casket, flowers, the whole bit. I'll pay for it myself. There has to be a thousand people in King City who'll show up for Tim's funeral. I just have to get the word out. I'll call someone at KC-7 and have them run a retrospective story about Tim's life. People loved him. They'll show."

Jake stood beside me, quiet, eyes flickering flames.

"This isn't right," I sighed. "They can't do this."

"It's already done. We have another stop."

Jake started walking and I was pulled along against my will.

"What about Tim?" I struggled against the force pulling me, but it didn't matter. My stationary feet slid me along the snow like it was ice and I was being pulled by an invisible rope.

Seconds later, I was back in Jake's big sleigh and we were flying. Everything smeared until we circled my mansion and landed in the snow-covered grass of the back gardens. We walked through the snow, flaming antler-headed Jake melting footprints along the way.

Inside the mansion, we strolled from room to room. The walls were transparent and I could see everyone and everything ratcheting forward with relentless rapidity. People's speech was garbled insect ticks and clicks, but some moments stood out based on body language.

Reyna arguing with Terrance, pointing for him to go, Terrance packing his bags and leaving.

"Did she just fire Terrance?" I asked.

Jake didn't answer.

Reyna firing Lashawn.

Reyna firing Frenchy.

Reyna firing every other staff person who worked at the mansion, all who I knew by name, to be replaced by strangers in corporate uniforms from one service company or another.

Channing Jr. grew quickly.

With the transparent walls, I saw that Reyna was rarely in the same room as her son. She kept her distance and he was cared for by a parade of uniformed nannies. I saw myself come and go rapidly, frequenting Channing Jr.'s room at first, but less and less as he grew into boyhood. The reason: each and every jittery stop-motion tableaux featured Reyna standing guard between me and Channing Jr., and her haranguing me whenever I tried to get close to my son.

One particular moment that slew my heart more than any other was the one wherein I watched myself enter a boyish Channing Jr.'s room carrying tyke-sized football pads and a helmet which Reyna promptly threw in the trash before handing our son soccer cleats. I was relived to see myself later sitting in the stands at an outdoor game watching my growing son play soccer, cheering for him while Reyna's nose was glued to her smart phone or makeup mirror.

I watched my hair gray as I aged.

Reyna seemingly remained ageless and coldly beautiful, but the swiftly aging version of me didn't seem to notice because he was never in the same room as her that I could tell. It was a loveless marriage to a loveless wife in a loveless life.

Again, the time-lapse slammed to a halt.

Channing Jr. appeared to be late high school age, 17 or 18. With his jet black hair and cold blue eyes, he had definitely taken after his mother in the looks department.

She was screaming at him, "I don't care *what* you fucking want, Channing! You're going to Harvard if I have to buy your way in!" Reyna was shrill as ever.

"No I'm not!" Channing Jr. argued. "Dad said I could stay in King City and work for him! I don't give a fuck about Harvard! As soon as I graduate, I'm helping him build houses!"

"Over my dead body! You're going to college!" Reyna was furious.

Watching them, I was the opposite, happy to hear that Reyna's efforts to drive a wedge between me and my son hadn't made me or him so bitter or distant that I wouldn't extend a helping hand whenever he needed it, and that he would accept it when I did.

"No I'm not!" Channing Jr. shouted. "Dad said! I can work construction! I don't give a shit about school! I hate fucking school! I'm never going to Harvard or any college!"

What followed from Reyna was a lecture so acidic, so corrosive, so insulting, so hateful, I wanted to cut out her tongue for Channing Jr.'s sake.

When she finished, he glared at her, "Oh yeah? Maybe if you'd let me play football instead of soccer, I'd have a fucking scholarship to Harvard! But you wouldn't let me because you hate Dad!"

"Football is for losers like your father!" Reyna screeched.

"He's not a loser! He pays for everything you have!"

"Shut your fucking mouth, Channing! You will *not* talk to me that way!"

"Then don't talk about Dad that way!"

I bit back a hint of pride.

Reyna snarled, "I will talk about that man any way I want! He is a loser, and if you try to be like him, you'll be a loser too!"

Channing Jr. snapped, "You're the fucking loser, Mom! All you do is spend Dad's money and fuck other guys!"

Reyna recoiled in alarm, her eyes icy knives. She hissed, "What did you say?"

"Don't deny it," Channing Jr. grumbled. "I've seen you fucking Kurt a hundred times!"

"No you didn't." Reyna slithered calmly. "Kurt is my driver and nothing else. You're imagining things, silly boy."

"Yes I did! You're a liar, Mom! Always lying! What else do you lie about besides everything?! I bet you're not even my real mom! What do you think Dad would do if he found out?"

Reyna's voice dropped off a high cliff and she seethed in a low voice, "If you ever—"

"He'd divorce you! That's what he'd do! Then it'd be me and Dad living here while you live in Kurt's car! I hope you like sleeping in the back seat where he fucks you!"

Reyna rattled out an ear-piercing scream and charged her son, eyes wild and claws flashing.

I rushed forward, throwing my hands around her waist from behind to stop her, but my arms passed right through her and she wheeled forward.

Channing Jr. side-stepped his mother, and slapped a hand against the side of Reyna's head, throwing her down. She went head first into the sharp metal corner of a table. Her skull cracked and she rolled out flat.

Shock struck my son between the eyes.

His jaw sagged in horror.

He checked Reyna's lifeless body, lifting her limp hand and letting it drop.

Time accelerated into stop-motion haste.

Channing Jr. left the room, went to his bedroom. Sat on the edge of the bed for what had to be hours. Thinking, crying, thinking, crying, until he was hollow-eyed and frightened. Got up. Went to the men's sitting room with its old maps and oil paintings of frigates and ships-of-the-line on the walls, the big antique globe, the sextant and compass on the enormous antique desk, and the locked glass display cases with historic guns, from flint lock to a World War I era Colt M1911. Channing Jr. stood there zombie-eyed. Smashed through the glass with a hammer. Took out the automatic Colt. Loaded it with the copper-jacketed display rounds. Returned to his bedroom.

Sat on his bed.

Rocked back and forth at high speed.

Lifted the gun.

Rested it against his skull.

"No!" I shouted, reaching out with my ghostly hand that passed through air.

Channing Jr. pulled the trigger.

His body dropped and the blood pool expanded so quickly, it had no meaning. Seconds later, an accelerated version of me came home from a long day's work, walked into the room where Reyna lay dead, and frowned. Then sped-up me smirked in amusement, looking very much like he'd come home to merely find a toilet had overflown, or a bird had smashed through a window and broken its neck, nothing more. Then accelerated me grew concerned, walked through the house, found Channing Jr. dead in his bedroom, and rushed to his limp body, cradling him in his arms and sobbing at comical speeds.

I didn't find it funny at all.

"Stop!" I barked at Jake. "Just fucking stop! I don't want to see this anymore!"

The flaming antler man waved a hand and we were again in his evil sleigh, smearing through time and space. When the smearing cleared, we were outside a sunny home surrounded by palm trees with the blue ocean in the distance.

"What's this?" I asked.

"Watch."

At hyper speed, Carol walked out of the cozy little home cradling a baby, bouncing it on her hip. The baby grew quickly, crawling on the ground, learning to walk, learning to run, Carol playing with him and them both laughing every step of the way. Seconds later, they were tossing a football clumsily back and forth. As the boy grew, his sloppy passes turned into precise spirals, then he was passing them to other neighborhood boys running plays in the street while Carol aged gracefully and carried out drinks and snacks on trays for the boys. In no time, the boy was a young man, also high school age and looked like my own damn mirage.

I grunted, "Is that my kid?"

The evil flaming man said nothing beside me.

"Jake! I asked you a question!

"Is?!

"That?!

"My?!

"Son?!"

Finally, the Jake monster turned his head slowly from his eight foot height and glared a smile at me, revealing vampiric canines, eyes burning, his hair flaming and his antlers glinting in the unholy fire.

I threw a punch, aiming for his face, but he was so tall it hit him in the chest, right where his heart should be. No surprise, he didn't have one, and my fist was sucked into the black hole of his chest cavity. I went flying forward, vortexed inside his quickly growing body and into a black oblivion, falling faster and faster toward an ocean of fire far below.

High above, a gigantic Jake loomed over me, issuing a grinding villainous chuckle that literally powdered my bones. I rippled into a gelatinous airborne blob. His chuckles crackled into evil laughter as my blobby body plummeted. My beating heart raced in rabbit fear. The faster I fell, the closer I came to the ocean of fire, and the hotter my skin got.

Long before I reached the flames, my flesh melted away in a bubbling froth of impotent hate. The pain was extreme and stabbed me gasping awake.

The Final Piece

"We wish you a Merry Christmas,
"We wish you a Merry Christmas,
"We wish you a Merry Christmas,
"And a happy New Year!
"Good tidings we bring,
"To you and your kin,
"We wish you a Merry Christmas,
"And a happy New Year!"
—*English traditional Christmas carol, from the West Country of England, origin unknown*

Chapter 44

CHANNING

Hissing my last breath, I sat up in bed clutching my chest, completely convinced I was having a fatal heart attack.

"Sir?" Terrance inquired quietly. "Everything all right?"

"Where the fuck am I?" I rasped, twisting frantically under a knot of covers.

"At home, sir." Terrance's voice had a soothing grandfatherly tone I very much appreciated at the moment. It grounded me solidly on the bedrock of sanity.

A dream.

No, a nightmare.

Jake would never be eight feet tall with flaming hair and antlers.

I grabbed at my blankets, clutching them to make sure they were real. "When did I get here?"

"Mr. Washington brought you home shortly after sunrise."

"From where?"

"I believe the hospital, sir. And before that, some pub or another named Titties."

"TT's," I corrected.

"That, sir. Mr. Washington said something about a mister Tim having a stroke?"

That much *had* happened.

I jumped out of bed. "Where's Lashawn?"

"I believe he's sleeping in his chambers, sir."

"Thanks." I rushed through the house wearing pajama pants, my hangover head ballooned to triple normal size and pounding with every step. I again wished for a golf cart as I made my way to Lashawn's wing of the house and gently knocked on his elaborate bedroom double doors.

"I'm up," Lashawn said sleepily.

"Can I come in?"

"No!"

"It's important."

"I have a lady in here."

"Oh. Who?"

"Morning, Chandy," Iesha called.

That brought a smile to my face. Holding back a chuckle, I said, "I'm worried about Tim."

"Give us a minute," Lashawn said. "We're getting dressed." A few minutes later, he opened the door wearing pajama pants, his pecs and abs rippling.

Iesha sat in Lashawn's big bed wearing one of his button-down dress shirts.

"What's the word on Tim?" I asked.

"The doctors are keeping him at the hospital today, but they said he can go home tonight or tomorrow. The stroke wasn't as bad as we thought."

"Thank fuck," I groaned and sagged against the door.

Iesha added, "They're supposed to send him home with a nurse. He's supposed to take it easy for at least a week. Maybe two."

"Oh. So no work?"

Lashawn shook his head, "No."

"That's not good." I couldn't remember a night at TT's when Tim wasn't there. "I need a ride to the hospital. I can't drive."

"Now?" Lashawn said reluctantly.

"After breakfast?"

Lashawn looker over his shoulder at Iesha.

"Whatever works," she smiled and shrugged.

Lashawn whispered, "She looks hot as fuck in my bed, right?"

"Hotter than ten fucks," I grinned and raised a fist.

"You know it." He bumped the top. "Huh, huh, huh."

"What're you two laughing at?" Iesha asked.

"Nothing," he and I chuckled.

Louder, I said, "I'll get cleaned up. After we eat, we'll pay Tim a visit."

When I stepped into my shower under the hot waterfall, my nightmare grabbed me again.

Carol.

My son.

Reyna's son.

Was he mine?

Or was Lashawn right?

I needed to know.

I could swab baby Channing's cheek easily enough. Reyna didn't helicopter over him 24/7. Only when she knew I was around, otherwise she avoided him like he was an open sewer line. I'd sneak an opportunity. Not that it mattered. My nightmare and my gut told me I needed to protect that kid from Reyna. She could easily destroy the boy if she wasn't careful.

What about Carol?

Had that been just a dream?

Or had it been prophetic?

Was she pregnant?

With *my* son?

I had to know, whether or not I was part of their lives going forward, but I couldn't go barging over to the Duffey house on Christmas Day, asking if their daughter was possibly pregnant. Thinking about it, it had only been a few days since Carol and I had sex. It was still probably too soon for her to know either way.

I'd have to wait patiently and ignore the feelings of elation and disappointment ping-ponging in my chest every two seconds.

You're a dad!

You're not a dad.

You're a dad!

You're not.

Frustrating.

In the meantime, there was a mountain of good I could do for the other people in my life I cared about, starting with Tim Farkas.

\#

&

&*&

&*&*&

&*&*&*&

M

"How you doing, big guy?" I asked softly.

Tim looked tiny in his big hospital bed. Without his magnifiers over his eyes, his eyes looked tiny too, but they finally fit his face. He blinked sleepily. "Is that Channing? You sound like Channing," he smiled awake. "All I see is a big blur."

"It's me," I grinned, fighting back tears.

"We're here too," Lashawn said, standing with Iesha.

"How are you feeling?" she asked.

Tim said, "Like I got fucked up the ass by an elephant."

We laughed quietly, but it was the funniest joke ever told because Tim had said it without slurring his words. We sat with him for a while, making small talk. Tim's left side had been mildly affected, and he'd need help with getting around on his crutches for a few weeks, but it was fairly minor and the doctors didn't expect anything permanent. When the moment was right, I asked Lashawn and Iesha to give me and Tim some privacy. They went to get coffee.

I said, "Tim, we need to talk business."

"Not now," Tim grimaced. "We can talk about fixing up the bar when I'm better." That he remembered our conversation from last night was a good sign.

"That's a given," I nodded. "I'm talking about paying off whatever you owe on it."

"You can't do that."

"Why not?"

"I paid off Dad's construction loan ten years ago."

"What're you paying on now? Land lease and property taxes, right?"

He groaned, "Through the roof, Channing. Ever since downtown turned around, the city has been jacking up my property taxes every damn year."

"Sorry about that."

"What do you have to do with it?"

"Me and my business partner have been steadily revitalizing downtown. You know all those new buildings like Tabor Towers and the King City Spire going up?"

"Yeah?"

"Those are ours."

Tim smirked, "So you're the ones ruining my view."

"Yeah," I chuckled. "That's why I'm here. I want to set up a trust to cover your property taxes and land lease for the next thirty years. Who owns it, by the way? The land, I mean."

Tim smirked, "That tightwad Warner Olinger."

"No shit?"

He nodded, "The fifteen year lease I signed with him fourteen years ago is almost up. The one before that was thirty years. Dad signed that one for a reasonable price because downtown was for shit back in the 70s. Nobody wanted to go near it in those days."

"They do now."

"You're right, they do, and Warner Olinger knows it. That dusty old fart is getting stingier in his old age."

"Tell me about it," I chuckled.

"I think he's going to double my monthlies when I sign the next lease. If he does that, it'll break me, Channing. With all the new fancy bars going in downtown, nobody wants to go to old TT's anymore."

"They will if you renovate and market the shit out of it. TT's is retro as hell. Hipster heaven. You need a social media presence. You don't have shit online. I checked."

"I don't know how to do that stuff."

"I do."

"I can't afford to pay you. And I won't take your charity."

"No charity. Forget the trust idea. Here's a better idea. I'll buy 49% of your business for whatever 30 years of property taxes, land lease, insurance, and utilities costs you. You'll still be the controlling owner with 51%. Then I'll set up everything, have my people run your marketing, manage your books, everything. All you have to do is show up at TT's when you feel up to it. When you don't, you stay home and cash checks."

"What checks?"

"We'll pay you a hefty salary, profit sharing, and health insurance. You can help me work out the right numbers. TT's will still be *your* business, Tim. I'm just helping you keep the heart beating."

Tim's eyelids drooped sleepily.

"Sorry, I'm wearing you out," I said.

"It's okay. It's a lot to think about."

"I know, and now isn't the time. You need to rest. Listen, when you're ready, you find a lawyer you like, and I'll pay him or her to look over the contracts for you, so you aren't out any cash on lawyer fees, but I'll draw everything up now so you can sign them whenever you're ready."

"It's too much, Channing," he shook his head, his voice husky with emotion. "I can't ask you to do so much."

"Fuck that. I'm not asking. I'm doing it. Unless you say no."

Tim's lips quivered.

I nodded, "Hey, one thing I never asked. Do you have any family? Kids? Cousins? Nieces? Nephews? We should set up an estate for you, if you don't have one already."

"It's just me," Tim said softly, almost shamefully.

"Not anymore, brother." I grinned and extended a hand. "We'll keep your dad's dream alive together. You and me."

Tim gripped my hand hard with his still-strong right hand, which was surprisingly strong for a guy his size. His blinking eyes wet, he said, "What about Warner Olinger? He's going to jack up my lease in a year."

"Don't you worry about him, brother. I'll square Old Oli away. He owes me one. Big time." Or should I say Bible time, as in the Birdsong Fragment I gave him as a signing bonus for his $40 million on the King City Spire. "Olinger won't be a problem."

"I don't know how to thank you." Tim's voice was barely a whisper at this point. Tears dribbled down his cheeks.

"You don't have to thank your own brother." I still held his hand in mine and clapped my other one around it and shook. "We've got this, brother. We have *got* this."

I didn't bother discussing Tim's hospital bills with him (on the drive here, Lashawn had reminded me that Tim didn't have any insurance). I simply went down to billing and paid off Tim's bills on the spot, with any remaining balance to be billed directly to my office, care of Rosa Ramirez. I also arranged for Tim's in-home nursing bills to go to me as well.

No matter what happened, I would be there for Tim every step of the way.

Chapter 45

CAROL

When I woke up Christmas morning, I did *not* find Channing sitting in the living room next to the tree wearing Santa pants, a sexy smile, and a body that was better than I remembered from college. He sure had kept in shape all these years.

Instead, I found Dad sipping coffee and reading the newspaper, chuckling over the comic strips. He still subscribed to the King City Tribune. "You have to read today's Family Circus," he chuckled, handing me the paper.

I read it and forced a laugh. "Funny."

I told myself I wasn't disappointed about Channing.

I didn't need a man in my life to help raise my maybe baby. I had a good job, family, friends. If it turned out I was pregnant, I would figure things out on my own. I had already proved I could go without sex for years.

Who needed screaming animal sex in a lighthouse?

Or a library?

I didn't.

What woman really *needed* a man in her life?

It wasn't caveman days anymore.

"Feral Carol." Channing had called me that.

I blushed at the thought. It was frivolous. None of that was important anymore. I could take care of things. It was the 21st century. I and my maybe baby would be fine.

No, I was being narrow-minded and a little bit selfish.

Every child needed a mother *and* a father, or at least a father figure. I considered calling Channing—he would be the *actual* father, after all—to wish him a Merry Christmas.

Didn't.

This was torture.

If only I could know sooner if I was pregnant.

#
&
&*&
&*&*&
&*&*&*&

M

CHANNING

That night, Frenchy made a feast of a Christmas dinner for everyone in the house. Even though Christmas fell on a Wednesday this year, most of my house staff worked today. I paid anyone who worked on Christmas Day triple time (in addition to their annual Christmas bonus), and gave them the option of staying home with their families. Most chose to work because, who paid triple time except yours truly?

You're welcome.

Joining the bustling crowd eating and gabbing happily in the kitchen was a very pouty Reyna and a happy, laughing, and cooing Channing Jr. He was in love with his new nanny Maria (Reyna had insisted we hire her), and my daily maid staff couldn't get enough of cute little Channeen. He'd grow calluses on his cheeks if they kept pinching.

It came as no surprise that Reyna pushed off as much responsibility for her son onto other people as she possibly could, whining every time.

"Can you watch Channing for a minute?"

A minute always meant an hour or ten.

"I think his diaper needs changing. Can you do it?"

I'd gotten quite good at changing them. Who knew it was so easy?

"He won't stop crying! Can you, I don't know, make it stop?"

Could she, I don't know, try giving a shit?

"How am I supposed to know he's hungry?! Can't you just feed him?! I have to be somewhere!"

Where was more important than feeding your own son? And what was not to like about holding a baby in your arm and feeding him a bottle of breast milk? It was probably the most relaxing part of my day.

Unlike Reyna, I was grown up enough to know that what a baby *needed* was more important than what you *wanted* for yourself at any given minute. She would never wear the mantle of motherhood because it wouldn't fit over her enlarged sense of self-importance. Most airplane hangar doorways were too small for that.

Reyna was more focused on mission-critical activities like hair, nails, spa, massages, the gym, shopping for designer clothes, never for maintaining the house or the baby, not even diapers. Whenever I asked, she always said things like, "I forgot," or "They were out."

"Every store in town?" I'd ask.

"Every store."

The thing you had to love about Reyna was, whenever she lied, she didn't even try. You had to laugh, otherwise you'd strangle her.

Then there was her endless coffees and lunches with old friends, watching TV, obsessing over her phone, trying on the new clothes she bought daily, posing at home in front of the mirror with her bestest friend of all (her own reflection, followed a close second by her Instagram followers because, I swear, that woman took more pictures of herself than the Mona Lisa), navel gazing, asshole waxing (in Reyna's case, sadly, that did *not* mean covering her entire body with depilatory wax and removing herself entirely from existence, but it should), you name it, Reyna did it. That woman could squander time like life was her personal shopping spree.

Worse, none of my staff liked her. Before she had disappeared, her tyrannical tenure as my wife had left a rotten taste in everyone's mouth. Even the house cringed whenever she entered, creaking in offense when she walked its floors.

Was there any way I could, I don't know, kick her out of my life and keep Channing Jr.? I know, I know, we all had our crosses to bear. Mine was lugging around Reyna on my back with her arms out and legs stiff in a Reyna Christ pose, and her saying incessantly, "Channing, can you, I don't know, walk more carefully? You're bouncing too much."

My personal revenge fantasy lately: a classic British fox hunt, me, Terrance, Lashawn, Frenchy, and everyone else on my staff wearing the red jackets and black hats, on horseback, the bugle blowing, and Reyna running through the woods like a frightened fox. Me shouting, "Whoever catches her first gets a free Christmas turkey!" Only problem, nobody actually wanted to catch her, making me the turkey.

Anyway, Christmas dinner had a very familial vibe, as long as you ignored Reyna pouting over her phone in the corner of the big kitchen.

I wanted to taunt, "Not enough new views on your Instagram?" I did not. It would start an hours-long argument about how insensitive *I* was.

Raise your hand if you're surprised to know that Reyna sulked when she was not the center of attention.

Nobody?

I thought not.

It was her fault, really. None of my staff wanted anything to do with her. And with me around for the evening, I put the boot on Reyna's wicked stepmother routine well before she could sink her vindictive teeth in.

Lonely pouting was her only option.

While she huddled in the banish corner, the rest of us enjoyed a rousing White Elephant gift exchange using whatever people had on hand or could find lying around the house (except books from my library).

The laughter was continuous, the gifts ridiculous.

Through it all, I thought of Carol, of how much I wished she and her parents were here with us, of how much fun they'd have. But I couldn't ask Carol to occupy the same room, let alone the same building, as Reyna. My preference would've been to send Reyna to the moon and invite the Duffeys over, but NASA didn't launch any rockets on Christmas Day.

I did my best to focus on the festivities.

You probably already guessed that Reyna didn't play in the gift exchange. She drank herself to sleep, so I carried her to the guest bedroom were she was setting up shop for the long haul (outliving my dying day being her main end game), and put her to bed. Then I went and said goodnight to Channing Jr. where he was already sound asleep in his crib next to Maria's bed in the nursery.

Pardon me, I forgot to mention, Reyna said she couldn't sleep with Channing Jr. "Waking her every five minutes." That was the job of, as Reyna put it, "our Mexican nanny Maria. She gets paid. I don't." I never bothered to correct Reyna by informing her that Maria was in fact from Ecuador, or that Reyna lived here for free, and did not pay for food, electricity, heating, wifi, water, trash, gasoline, her clothes, her anything.

After standing in the very soothing nursery designed by Lily Yang (she'd done a terrific job), and staring lovingly at Channing Jr., I pulled $1,000 out of my wallet and handed it to Maria. "Merry Christmas, Maria. Your bonus." It was actually her second. Her next paycheck would have the first.

"For me?"

"Yes, for you. I couldn't take care of CJ without you." Of late, I'd taken to calling Channing Jr. CJ.

"Oh my goodness, Mr. Peyton. Thank you so much. I don't know what to say."

"You don't need to say anything," I smiled. "It's the least I can do." It really was. I couldn't be home 24/7 and I needed Maria to take care of the son who may or may not be mine.

After everyone went home or to bed (except for Lashawn, who was still out with Iesha at her parents' house, and having Christmas dinner with them), I went up to the Lighthouse with a bottle of whiskey and started sipping.

On every bench in the circular room, I saw after-images of Carol and I making mad passionate love under the soft white Christmas lights. It wasn't just sex with Carol. It never had been. Every time I slid into her heat, it felt like the first time. Every time I came inside her, my life felt complete. Only trouble was, I wanted her *more* each time we had sex, not less. After fucking her thousands of times over the years, it was an addiction that would never let go. Any addict will tell you: you never stopped wanting your next fix, you just learned to stop chasing it.

Was there a twelve step program for Carol Duffey?

Because I damn sure needed one.

I poured another shot and gulped.

It didn't take long before I had a good buzz warming my heart with whiskey lies. I stared out at the King City lights in the direction of the Duffey house, wondering what Carol was thinking, or if she knew how much I loved her.

\#

&

&*&

&*&*&

&*&*&*&

M

CAROL

In my dark bedroom, I lay in bed weeping silently, pretending my fingers were Channing.

When I came, I cried.

Ethics were very inconvenient.

I whispered softly, "I love you, Channing Peyton."

I hope he heard me.

Chapter 46

CHANNING

On December 26th, I visited a local DNA lab downtown and picked up a half dozen cheek swab kits. When Reyna inevitably went out to do who knows what (Teeth whitening? Plastic surgery consult? That Reyna-removing asshole waxing I mentioned?), I left Channing Jr. with Maria, waited until she took a bathroom break, and quickly swabbed Channing Jr.'s cheek myself.

Later that day I took his sample and mine back to the lab. Paid extra to get the results the next morning. Had Lashawn drive me because I was too nervous to concentrate. Sat in the front seat next to him.

When the technician showed us the results in the lab's reception room, my jaw clanked onto the countertop so hard, my teeth almost bounced out and went skittering across the laminated wood.

"I told you he isn't yours," Lashawn smirked.

Out in the Mercedes, I was a volcano ready to blow. My first thought was to tell Carol the not-so-good news so she'd know I hadn't lied. Maybe now was not the time. I whipped out my phone and scrolled through my contacts.

"Who're you calling?"

"Floyd Lunsford." I tapped his name on the list and my phone dialed.

"Your PI?"

I nodded. "I want him to start following Reyna and collect evidence."

Floyd had the nose of bloodhound, and the tenacity of a pit bull. He was worth every penny he charged. His phone went to voicemail and I left a message telling him to call me immediately.

Lashawn asked, "Is there anything I can do to help kick that liar out of your life?"

"Start polishing my kicking boots," I grumbled.

"You mean your cleats?"

"Those too," I smirked. "And any other suitable boots you can find in my closet."

"Huh, huh, huh, huh."

"I'm kidding. Don't ever polish my anything."

"Why would I?" he asked, confused because he never had.

"Never mind."

"You know what I *should* do?" he asked.

"What?"

"Keep tabs on Reyna whenever she's at home and you're out."

"Great idea."

"Floyd and I can rig up mics and hidden cameras all over the house for when I'm not there either."

"Love it. Whatever it takes to get the truth out of her."

"You got it, dog."

I pulled up Carol's number on my phone.

Hesitated.

Sigh and stuffed my phone in my pocket.

As much as I wanted to tell Carol everything, it was too soon. Nobody wanted to be embroiled in a cancerous battle over paternity. They wanted to be on the other end of winning it. I spoke from experience. I couldn't wait for this to be over with.

Reaching out to Carol would have to wait.

#
&
&*&
&*&*&
&*&*&*&
M

With my wheels of deceit now set in motion to shred through Reyna's web of lies, it would be a waiting game until the evidence started to accrue. I tried to create a list of the men who might have gotten Reyna pregnant, men Floyd could investigate, but she had literally disappeared on me for over a year. Hadn't even used her credit cards. She had her own private bank accounts, which I'd never bothered to track because I was glad to be rid of her.

There was no telling what she got up to on her own. For all I knew, CJ's father was a Russian oligarch or South American drug lord or a space alien from Mars.

Reyna had a crazy streak.

All I could do was wait and hope some other better man didn't swoop into Carol's life and steal her from me.

In the meantime, I had Pilky to deal with. He still hadn't signed the contracts for the $30 million he'd promised toward the King City Spire. Jake was ready to chew me a new one about that. So were the banks. We needed cash flow to keep making payments on construction fees, insurance, leases, etc.

Luck struck a few days after Christmas.

The chain of events that finally put a bow on that Pilky pain-in-my-ass problem started over dinner. It was me, Lashawn, Frenchy, and Terrance eating in the kitchen, all of us sitting on bar stools at the long island countertop, four friends after a long workday, silverware scraping and tinking as we shot the shit.

Lashawn unwittingly started the snowball rolling when he said, "Yo, T. When did you get laid last?"

Terrance practically choked on his food. Once the rest of us stopped laughing and he stopped choking, he said, "Pardon me, Mr. Washington, what was your question?"

"You know, sex. When was the last time you got any, T?"

Terrance blushed.

I said, "We know you've never been married. You aren't gay, are you?"

"No, sir!"

Lashawn said, "We're cool if you are."

"I'd rather not talk about it, sir. If you don't mind."

I said, "Come on, Trey. We're all men here. If you aren't getting any, your dick has to be as stiff as your British upper lip."

Frenchy and Lashawn both chuckled at that.

I continued, "If I went without sex for as long as you have, Trey, I'd be a walking hard-on. Be straight with us. Are you gay?"

"No, sir."

"But you haven't been laid since… when?"

"It's been years, sir."

"But you *have* been laid?"

"Yes, sir. It was a long time ago."

Lashawn said. "I'm picturing T with some World War Two hottie huddled together in some cramped bomb shelter when the Nazis bombed Britain, right?" Lashawn watched a lot of historical war documentaries and was always telling me about what he'd learned.

"That was before my time, sir."

"Oh, right," Lashawn said. "To be hooking up with babes back then, you'd have to be, what, eighty-five? Ninety?"

"At least."

"But you're like sixty, right?"

"Sixty-two, sir."

I said, "Does your dick still work?"

Chuckles from Lashawn and Frenchy.

Terrance sat up stiffly. "Last time I checked, it was in good working order, sir."

Laughter from all of us, including rumpled chuckles from Terrance.

Lashawn said, "You mean the last time you wanked? That's what you

British dudes do, right? Wank off?"

"It's wank, sir. We have a wank. Er, I meant to say, *one* has a wank. Not that I would know."

The fellas laughed again.

I said, "It's cool, Trey. We all wank, right fellas? No matter how much action we get, we still wank. A man's gotta do what a man's gotta do."

Frenchy and Lashawn both nodded solemnly over their food with arch smiles. It was true.

Terrance cleared his throat and forked up more dinner.

"We have to get Trey-dog laid," I said seriously. "I say we call Nicole and hook a brother up. Right, Trey?"

Terrance paused with his fork halfway to his mouth.

Lashawn said. "I don't think Terrance is interested, dog. Maybe we should drop it."

Terrance took his bite, set his fork down, patiently finished chewing, wiped his hands on his napkin, laced his fingers on the countertop. Staring straight ahead, he said, "Who is this Nicole, if I may ask?"

Me, Frenchy, and Lashawn nearly fell off our bar stools howling with laughter.

#

&

&*&

&*&*&

&*&*&*&

M

"This the place, boss?" Frenchy asked from the backseat of the Mercedes where he sat with a slightly tipsy Terrance. I sat up front with Lashawn, who insisted on driving because I was fully buzzed. I'd had to ply Terrance with enough whiskey to get him to say yes to our little outing.

Outside, the dark street was filled with Victorian row houses. This was an older part of downtown King City where the rich used to live. Not anymore. This neighborhood hadn't been revitalized. Most of the parked cars were older and shabbier, but the number of expensive cars parked *temporarily* on this street each and every night made you wonder what drugs were being sold.

Only the oldest drug of all.

Pussy.

"Yeah, this is it," I said. I turned to Terrance and grinned, "Sorry you get your Christmas present a couple days late, Trey."

"You already paid my bonus, sir."

"This is the real bonus," Lashawn chuckled. "Huh, huh, huh."

"He's right," I grinned.

"I should hope so," Terrance chuckled with uncharacteristic glee.

Frenchy jumped behind the wheel and sat with the car while Lashawn and I led Terrance up the steps of a tan Victorian with black trim. If that sounded like the description of a woman, it should.

Nicole McKinnon ran her high-class call-girl business out of this building. I'd never paid her or her women for their services because I never paid. I knew Nicole because Jake often came here to conduct business with her clients. I also knew Nicole's place of residence wasn't here. It was in Tabor Towers. I'd sold her the unit myself when she'd told me she was looking for a low-maintenance place to settle down. Said she had her eye on retirement.

Nicole was in her late fifties, a dark and sultry beauty who looked damn good for her age. In the dim lighting of her fine establishment, she easily passed for 30 or 35. That was a compliment, not an exaggeration. Good genes. Best part, I heard in the dark, she sucked dick like she was 18, which was tempting because most 18 year olds I'd known sucked dick like they were 81.

"Do I have to, Channing? Can't you just fuck me like last time?" Pout, pout, pout. Always with the pouting.

What can you do? That's post-millennials for you. Always wanting everything handed to them on the silver platter of their smart phones, even their own orgasms.

You know who had sucked my dick with abandon when she was 20 years old?

Carol Duffey.

Yes, walking into the best little whorehouse in King City made me think about the only woman I had ever loved. I told you I was addicted. It made being here slightly depressing, but I wasn't here for me. I was here for T.

"Channing Peyton," Nicole said when she greeted us in the dimly lit reception room with its Victorian decor. We'd gone through two layers of security to get here (meaning grumpy male bouncers). "It's been a spell since I've seen you."

"You haven't aged a day," I said.

"Still lying," she laughed and opened her arms for a quick hug. Her pile of just-fucked black hair looked smoking hot, and it also looked like it took her an hour to make it look that good. The rosy lighting in the room enhanced the lines of her black lace robe and lingerie underneath. She exuded heavenly devil.

Terrance stood there ramrod straight wearing his best tweed suit and driving cap. It was as close as he ever got to casual.

"What'd we tell you?" Lashawn prompted. "She's fine, right?"

"Yes, sir, she's very beautiful," Terrance nodded, his upper lip as stiff as the rest of him.

"Don't say it to me, player. Say it to her."

"Right." He offered Nicole a proper smile. "Madam, may I say, you are simply ravishing."

I muttered, "Listen to Trey Smoove over there making the moves."

Lashawn chuckled, "Our boy is all grown up now. Huh, huh, huh, huh."

"You know it," I chuckled.

Nicole flirted a wink in my direction. "I hope you came for me."

I grinned, "I wish. Terrance here needs some good company tonight. The best. Meaning you."

"You brought him to the right place," Nicole smiled and led a shaky-kneed Terrance upstairs. He was in good hands.

Lashawn and I went to the cramped billiard room in back to shoot stick on their one pool table while we waited. Ninety minutes into it, Lashawn chuckled, "What's taking T so long? You don't think he died, do you?"

"If he did, and Nicole fucked him to death? He isn't complaining." I leaned over the table for a fist bump, which he returned. "I forgot to ask, how was Christmas dinner at Iesha's? That go well?"

"It did," he nodded.

"Her parents like you?"

"Seemed like it."

"You hook up with her yet?"

He frowned and looked up from where he was aiming to sink the striped eleven ball, "Don't ask me that."

"I saw her in your bed."

"Then why are you asking?"

"LD, you tell me *every* damn time you fuck a chick. You go into extreme forensic detail. You take measurements. You list every position, every piece of furniture. Every orifice. You don't leave out a single detail."

"And you don't?" he challenged.

"Okay, fine," I chuckled guiltily, "but you do too."

"Not this time, I don't." He snapped his stick, hit the cue ball, and sent the eleven ball careening into a bunch of others. "Look what you made me do."

"Me?"

"Damn right you. Talking about Iesha makes me nervous."

"Why?"

He shot me a glare, "I don't want to wreck things with her."

"You won't if you be yourself." I leaned over the table and aimed at the four ball. Sank it. "You gonna see her again?"

"Hell yeah."

"When?"

"Super Bowl."

"She get you tickets?"

"Yeah she did. One for you too. We can both fly out and watch the game."

"Can't. Too much to do here."

"You need me to stay in town, keep an eye on Reyna?"

"Nah. Go enjoy yourself some of that Dallas Cowboys' Cheerleader ass for a few days."

"I've only got eyes for one ass now," he chuckled bashfully, eyes wistful.

"That's a yes."

"Yes what?"

"You hooked up."

"You didn't hear it from me, player. Huh, huh, huh."

"Whatever," I grinned. "Bring her back to King City when you guys are done at the Super Bowl. We'll go out for dinner or something."

"I can do that. As long as you don't bring Reyna."

I smirked because I agreed with his sentiment.

Thudding steps rumbled over our heads. A commotion and sounds of muted half-panicked female voices followed.

"You think T is all good up there?" Lashawn asked, concerned. "He isn't that young, and Nicole looks like she's got a motor that won't quit."

"I think you're right on both counts. Let's go check."

We rushed upstairs. At the end of the hallway, a brunette was pleading with Nicole in the wallpapered hallway, both of them wrapping robes around themselves in a panic.

The brunette said, "I don't know what happened! He just started having chest pains."

Lashawn muttered to me, "Are they talking about T?"

"I hope not."

Terrance leaned out an open door, hair mussed, looking concerned and wrapping a frilly pink robe around himself.

"You alright, T?" Lashawn asked.

"Never better," he grinned. "What's all the hubbub?"

I glanced over the shoulders of the brunette and Nicole into another bedroom. On the bed wearing a black leather bra and crotchless panties was white-haired Morris Pilkington with his limp dick hanging out. His wrists and ankles were roped to the bedposts, and his face was beet red with pain.

I rushed in to start untying ropes.

"My chest!" Pilky hissed.

"Heart attack?" I asked.

He grimaced a nod.

"I've got this," Lashawn said, whipping out a lockblade knife with his thumb to cut the ropes.

"Someone call 911," Nicole said.

"No!" Pilky whispered. "I don't want Lena knowing!" He meant his wife.

Nicole shrugged her hands. "I don't know what else to do."

I smirked, "Morris, do you want me to drive you to the hospital?"

"Please," he sputtered. "My nitroglycerin first!"

"Your what?" My first thought was dynamite.

"My pills!" he choked.

"Where?"

"In my jacket."

I fished out a bottle while Nicole got water from the bathroom inside the room and helped him swallow a pill.

I said, "Are you good, Morris? Or...?"

He shook his head with worry. "I think I better go to the hospital."

"Let's carry him out," I said to Lashawn. "I'll get his legs, you get his arms."

Lashawn nodded.

I didn't care that Morris's wrinkled dick was hanging out of women's panties and flopping in my face. The man was knocking on death's door and the grim reaper was about to open it and let him in for a very long visit.

"Not like this!" Pilky hissed. "I need my clothes!"

I groaned, "Would you rather live looking like this or die getting dressed?"

"Dressed!"

"Suit yourself," I said and used Lashawn's knife to cut off Pilky's black leather bra and panties. Then the brunette and I suited Morris in his clothes while I had Nicole call Frenchy on my phone to bring the car around. Lashawn and I left Terrance here with Nicole and carried Pilky downstairs.

We arrived at King City Presbyterian's emergency room twenty minutes later and they took Pilky straight to the OR. Lashawn went back to Nicole's to get Terrance. I stuck around to call Lena. She had someone drive her to the hospital in a bathrobe, slippers, and overcoat. We sat together in the surgical waiting room, her clutching my hand with frail fingers.

Lena said, "Thank my lucky stars you were there at Morris's poker game to help out, Channing."

I'd concocted the poker game story for her sake. "It was nothing. The least I can do."

"I do hope he makes it," she fretted. "I don't know what I'd do without my Morris."

"He'll pull through." I patted her hand. "Everything'll be just fine, Lena. I promise."

While we waited, the topic of the King City Spire eventually came up. Lena mentioned it because she knew all about it, that I was building it, and that Morris was interested in it.

"How is that going?" she asked.

"It's coming along fine," I smiled the lie. I wasn't going to sell her on it now. It wasn't the time.

Six hours later, the surgeons told us Pilky survived his double bypass and could expect a full recovery.

Six days later, without any prompting on my part, Pilky signed over his $30 million for the Spire. My daily visits to bullshit with him while he recovered from his surgery may have helped. We never once discussed his fondness for crotchless women's panties, but you could see the topic hiding just behind his eyes.

That was business for you.

Pilky was happy.

I was happy.

And Lena was happy.

It's the little lies that help so many get by.

Life was messy. I was used to it.

I still had two more major messes of my own to deal with.

#
&
&*&
&*&*&
&*&*&*&
M

"You sitting down?" asked Floyd Lunsford over my smart phone on the afternoon of December 31st.

"I'm in my office," I said, standing at the third floor window looking out at the view of downtown King City in the distance. It hadn't snowed all day, the air was bone dry, and the sky was crystal blue, the sun plating everything gold.

"Take a seat. What I'm gonna tell you is gonna knock your socks off."

"Spit it out, Floyd."

"It's her sister's kid," he said with grim glee.

"What?" I gasped.

"Your boy isn't even *her* kid. It's her sister's."

"My son—" I stopped to clear my throat because every muscle in my body suddenly locked up like they'd been torqued tight with an impact wrench. I could not move.

"I told you to sit down," Floyd chuckled bitterly. "He's not yours. Channing Jr. is the son of Shenka Goodrich, Reyna's younger sister."

"Reyna has a sister?"

"Half-sister."

"I had no idea."

"They ain't exactly close. Least they weren't until Reyna borrowed her baby."

What.

The.

Fuck.

I asked, "How'd you figure that out?"

"Those mics me and Lashawn put in your house work great. He sure knows his spy gear. Anyway, Shenka called Reyna every day asking a million questions about the kid. Is he eating, is he shitting, is he sleeping, that kind of thing. His name ain't even Channing. It's Jackson."

"No shit." I shook my head in disbelief. That woman had more screws loose than Home Depot. "How do we prove Channing, I mean *Jackson*, is Shenka's kid?"

"You need a court order to subpoena DNA tests from Shenka and him. This is fraud, Mr. Peyton. Outright fraud."

"Tell me about it," I groaned. "It's a felony, right?"

"That'll depend on how much money Reyna cheats you out of. She'll only go to jail if the DA wants to prosecute. At the very least, it's a civil case and you can sue the shit outta her. She already cheated you outta plenty so far, from what you told me. The clothes you bought her? That fancy SUV she's driving free? The pain and suffering? The—"

"I don't care about any of that." The more I thought about what Reyna had done, the more my mind reeled. How could she even conceive of such a vile plan?

"Any way you look at it, Mr. Peyton, it's time you talk to a divorce lawyer and cut ties with that vampire before she sucks any more life outta you. She'll be lucky if she don't end up paying *you* spousal support after the scam she ran."

"Yeah," I grumbled.

My challenge would be dealing with the sense of attachment I already felt growing for my son, I mean, Jackson Goodrich, or whatever his last name was. At this point, his father could be literally anybody.

What a fucking mess Reyna had made.

I could only imagine what new deceitful details would come out in court. I hated to think. I *really* hated to think what Carol would think. Hopefully, she'd never find out. I certainly wouldn't drag her into my drama voluntarily.

Worst part for me, things were going to get much worse before they got better. What a fucking mess I'd made for myself. Carol was lucky to escape when she had. If you took away my looks and my money, what did I have to offer her, really?

A dump truck full of nothing.

After my call with Floyd, I seriously considered blitzing my office window and taking a header through the glass. I probably would have if my office was higher than the third floor.

You know what had sixty floors?

The King City Spire.

Now *that* would make a fabulous splat.

I should go pay it a visit and enjoy the view a while before I—

Chapter 47

CAROL

New Years Eve was a quiet celebration at home with Mom and Dad. We did our usual thing.

The scent of cinnamon and vanilla filled the house while Mom and I baked snickerdoodles and shooed Dad away from dipping his finger in the mixing bowl.

We all drank too much egg nog, no rum. Played poker for Hershey's Kisses. After Mom inevitably cleaned out me and Dad (she was aces at poker), we all retired to the couch to nibble snickerdoodles and watch *It's A Wonderful Life* on the DVD Dad had bought fifteen years ago, a family tradition. As always, Mom fretted while a miserable George Bailey clung to the bridge over the river, desperately contemplating ending it all until his guardian angel showed up to save him.

When the movie ended and the people of Bedford Falls all sang *Auld Lang Syne* inside George's Building & Loan, I of course wished Channing could be my George Bailey, and our daughter would grow up to be as cute as little Zuzu, but wishes only worked in movies.

At midnight, I watched the ball drop in Times Square on TV, sitting between a very sleepy Mom and Dad, then it was off to bed shortly after.

The only thing out of the ordinary about the entire day?

I missed my period.

Chapter 48

CHANNING

My resolve broke on New Year's Day.

I had to go talk to Carol.

I had no idea what I'd say to her, or if I'd say anything. Maybe seeing her would be enough. I didn't know. Lashawn was in Dallas, so I sped through the snow-covered roads toward her parents' house in my Mercedes.

"She's gone?" I asked Mr. Duffey after he let me inside the house.

He nodded, "Carol flew home to San Francisco this morning."

"On New Year's Day?"

"She has a mountain of work waiting for her at the office. She wanted to get an early start tomorrow."

"Shit." I sagged.

Mr. Duffey slid his hands into his slacks and shrugged.

"How's that Mavic 2 working out?"

"Very well, thanks," he smiled.

"Wanna go fly it? I'll fly your old Hawk 5, you fly the Mavic?"

"Why not," Mr. Duffey grinned.

At the park, we flew for two hours without me saying another word about Carol. I promise you, she was the only thing on my mind. My race results reflected it. Mr. Duffey beat me every time.

When we packed up to go, he said, "Something troubling you, Channing?"

I winced a smile. "Did Carol…? Was she…?" Pregnant when she left? Because I foolishly fucked her without a condom a dozen times? There was no good way to pose these questions to the father of a daughter.

I drove Mr. Duffey home and headed back to the mansion. There, I tried calling Carol. I knew her flight had probably landed, but she didn't answer. I tried texting her. No reply.

For the next six weeks, I tried every single day, right up to the day after Valentine's Day. No matter what voicemail I left, or what text strategy I tried, she wouldn't communicate with me. I didn't blame her. I was the criminal, she was the lawyer.

With it being nearly two months since we'd had plentiful amounts of sex, I could only conclude that ethical Carol was not pregnant. If she had been, she would've let me know at the very least.

Since she obviously wasn't, I could only assume she'd said her goodbyes the day she'd walked out of Starbucks, after Raging Reyna had barged in.

It was for the best.

My life was still a shit mess.

Reyna and Channing-Jackson continued living with me. Both Floyd Lunsford and my divorce lawyer Penelope Chang encouraged me to maintain the status quo until Floyd had collected the last of his evidence. It would show good faith on my part.

When everything was ready, Lashawn personally served Reyna with a summons to appear in court and answer for the civil suit of fraud I had filed against her.

She moved out instantly after that, taking Channing-Jackson with her and finding her own divorce lawyer who served me papers for a countersuit soon after.

Lashawn suggested I call in a favor with King City PD to make Reyna's life even more miserable than she was making mine. Over dinner, Lashawn said, "You should have that woman arrested. Send the police over to cuff her and haul her ass downtown in the back of a squad car for what she did. Make her pay her own bail."

"Tempting," I grumbled, savoring the idea even more than the spoonful of lobster bisque Frenchy had cooked up.

"I'd like to see that woman behind bars for at least a year. She made you miserable for twice that long."

"I would, but I keep thinking about CJ."

"Yeah. I feel for that kid."

"Me too."

"He's got a shitty mom."

"That's too kind a word," I smirked.

"Which, mom or shitty?"

"Both," I grumbled.

When it came time to press criminal charges against Reyna, I didn't have the heart. She had enough problems already. A few weeks later, my civil suit against her went to court. She never showed. The judge decided the case entirely in my favor, entering a judgement against Reyna for the full $15 million in pain-and-suffering that Penelope had suggested but not expected we would get. We were also awarded court costs and attorney's fees.

I didn't expect Reyna to ever pay any of it.

I just needed a judgement in my favor to help with the divorce case. It took another month until those grueling proceedings got under way.

You already guessed correctly that Reyna refused to settle during mediation. She didn't care that I had won the civil suit. She fought for half of every penny I had like I owed her twice that and more.

She was vicious in court, taking the stand to rant accusations and a long litany of spousal abuse allegations. It was wasted breath. I had a parade of character witnesses *and* direct fact witnesses in the form of people like Lashawn, Frenchy, Terrance, Maria, and a dozen other employees of mine who were all present in the house so frequently that their testimonies peppered Reyna's heinous allegations full of holes.

When Floyd took the stand and presented his evidence collected for the civil suit, Reyna unraveled in her seat. Her attorney, a youngish good-looking kid in his late twenties who looked fresh out of law school, was shocked. I heard surprised whisperings from him suggesting Reyna had never told him about the civil suit. I also got the impression Reyna may have seduced his services out of him for free. That was how she operated.

In the end, the judge granted the divorce in my favor and gave nothing to Reyna. No child support. No spousal support on the grounds Reyna had never collected any from me for over a year after disappearing during our marriage, and she had been very evasive on the question of how she had supported herself during that time. When the judge had asked her on the stand why she had used her sister's son to defraud me, she blew a head gasket and screamed at the judge, "You're the dumbest fucking judge ever if you believe anything they're saying!" The judge was not pleased.

I walked out of the courthouse that day with a bittersweet smile on my face.

Reyna Goodrich was out of my life, thank fuck.

CJ was too. I was sad about that. I missed the kid.

Saddest of all, Carol Duffey was also out.

I missed her more than anything. I told myself I would give up everything to get her back.

And that's exactly what I did.

Chapter 49

CHANNING

"I'm here to turn myself in," I said to the cute clerk behind the front counter at the King City District Attorney's office downtown in City Hall.

"Um, let me call someone." The young clerk's eyes jumped when she saw the three lawyers behind me wearing suits so powerful they could light King City for a week. One man, two women. Neither were Carol. Conflict of interest and all that.

I'd already consulted these three, *and* an entire army of almost twenty other white-collar defense lawyers, about how to take this suicidal step. There was really no good way to do it. You just had to kiss the gun barrel, bite the bullet when it came out, and hope you caught it without getting your head torn off.

Eventually, my team and I were ushered into the back of the DA's office. There was no need for good cop/bad cop because I laid my guts on the table for the DA's suited team to examine under their legal microscopes. While the DA's video camera ran, I shared every bit of relevant information I could about the questionable business practices Jake and I had used for years, some more shady than others. Some of our most successful techniques had been legal but highly distasteful, others socially acceptable but flirting with illegality. The camera recorded every one of my carefully scripted words for this seemingly impromptu deposition. For them, anyway. My lawyers and I had prepared two months for this day.

It went flawlessly.

My team had even prepared for the FBI's inevitable involvement. Tony and Jake were still running football scams involving interstate wire transfers and the King City Cheetahs. I wasn't involved, but I knew about it (Tony could never keep his bragging mouth shut around me), and I didn't care what happened to those two fucks. They and their criminal family had effectively stolen the only woman I had ever loved.

Months later, after the King City DA did their due diligence, they made me an offer. In exchange for pleading guilty and helping them dissect the inner-workings of the Martinelli family and shining the light of day on their criminal enterprise, I got a mere eighteen months in the minimum security state prison in Springville because my business actions had danced at the edges of state laws as recently as last week.

The FBI didn't hit me with anything. I was well past the statute of limitations on any federal crimes. I'd been very careful about avoiding those.

Lashawn, whose only real crime was standing beside me to look imposing whenever a dubious situation called for it, was given immunity in exchange for telling the DA everything he knew, which was little, fortunately for him. From day one, I'd shielded Lashawn from anything that reeked of criminality.

Tony and Jake's asses were hanging in the wind when KCPD showed up to arrest them, and they both went quickly to trial.

The day the transcript of my video deposition went public, wherein I admitted that back in college, I had thrown three Rose Bowls and the NCAA National Championships in Tampa, Florida, King City News 7 led with the story, and the next morning, the King City Tribune ran the following headline:

CHEETAHS' QB ALLEGES CRIME FAMILY TO BLAME FOR PAST LOSSES.

The biggest surprise to me?

During Tony's trial, eight women came forward to testify they had been paid by Tony and Jake to lie and say publicly they knew Carol Duffey personally, and that Carol had told them she had convinced me to throw those games in exchange for sex.

Hearing that made me rage.

Tony and Jake had put Carol through a hurricane of pain back in college, simply to cover their asses after I pissed on the Cheetahs' statue and rambled on about losing to Alabama at the Tampa championship for Carol's sake. Thing was, when the news replayed that old clip of me piss-drunk and pissing on the statue, I had never said anything about throwing the game for money. I'd said I'd done it for Carol. It was a stretch to think my words would ever lead back to Tony and Jake's gambling fraud, but they hadn't taken any chances. Too much of their money was at stake.

So they ruthlessly murdered Carol's reputation.

As much as I wanted to murder Tony and Jake with my bare hands for what they did to Carol, I knew it was best to let the rusty wheels of justice grind the Martinelli family slowly into hamburger.

Exactly that happened when it came out their family had been paying off quarterbacks since long before my time (and after) to throw Cheetahs' games. When the good people of King City heard the news, they practically rioted in the streets. They wanted to string up anyone named Martinelli from the nearest lamppost. For whatever reason, they weren't mad at me. Someone even wrote an Op-Ed in the KC Tribune about how

I'd been used and manipulated by master criminals. That was truer than the article's author would ever know.

But it wasn't my reputation I cared about.

It was Carol's.

Turned out I wasn't the only one who cared about it. During Tony and Jake's trials, there were protestors outside the courthouse daily, waving signs that said things like:

EXONORATE CAROL DUFFEY

KING CITY LOVES CAROL

REPARATIONS FOR CAROL DUFFEY

CAROL DUFFEY CHEETAH LOVER

Guess who led the charge day after day? That crazy vixen Sin-Win, Sienna Winters herself, come out to support her old friend, same as she had back in college, I found out later when I saw the news footage. I also recognized the raven-haired vixen with her, the perfect 10 I'd seen in that Instagram photo of Carol and Sienna having drinks at TT's the night Carol flew into King City last Christmas.

While Sienna and the vixen were helping stoke pro-Carol public opinion on the streets, poor Tony had a heart attack in the courtroom when the jury read his guilty verdict. Died a week later. May he rest in shit.

Jake fared only slightly better. He stood there stone cold silent at his sentencing when they gave him a total of seventy-five years with no possibility of parole. Why so long a sentence for a white collar criminal? Over a series of separate criminal trials for Jake, it came out he hadn't been just a white collar criminal. Unbeknownst to me, he had been involved in quite a few blue-collar crimes (think physical violence). There was no statute of limitations on murder or rape in this state. That explained why I'd never seen Jake show any interest in women. His only interest in them was... you can figure it out.

If you're wondering *how* Jake was convicted on blue collar charges, which I knew nothing about, we can thank the Martinelli family as a whole. Because of my testimony against Tony and Jake, the King City DA tightened their noose around the necks of nearly every other Martinelli family member who'd had their fingers dirtied by the Martinelli money pot, rounding up more and more of them with the tireless help of the FBI and the detectives at the KCPD. Like blood hungry sharks, the once-loyal family suddenly turned on themselves, quickly tearing each other apart in the courts while trying to save their own skins and reduce their sentences.

End result, other lesser-known Martinelli family members went to prison for a variety of white collar charges. Blackmail, bribery, extortion, fraud, racketeering, tax evasion, you name it. If it was organized white-collar crime, they did it.

Really, the biggest surprise for me was that Jake was the only Martinelli with a prosecutable violent streak. I'd suspected he was brutal for a long time, but he'd always hidden it.

By the time the trials were over, half the Martinelli family was spread out in minimum security prisons across the country. The unconvicted other half fled for parts unknown. Nobody wanted them in King City and they knew it.

When the mayhem eventually faded, I had to report to the nearby Springville State Prison and trade in my silk suits for a khaki jumpsuit. Once I was locked up, I played a lot of cards, chess, backgammon, lifted a lot of weights, and mopped a lot of floors.

Time would have crawled if not for Lashawn visiting me five days a week. I had businesses to run and he was my proxy. Luckily, Lashawn knew the nuts and bolts of the entire portfolio of Peyton Industry businesses already, so he had no trouble juggling a thousand new responsibilities without dropping them.

Other notable visitors: Rosa Ramirez with accounting questions, Reggie Brown with construction questions, and countless other people from Peyton Solar or Peyton Auto Parts, or Peyton Construction, or Terrance who stayed on at the mansion to manage the upkeep, or Frenchy who I paid to stay and feed the house staff. Between all them, I had visitors daily.

Some days, it didn't even seem like prison.

Eighteen months started going by quicker and quicker.

Even better, my good behavior shortened it to fourteen months.

Although the state seized some of Peyton Industries' assets identified during the Martinelli trials as belonging to the family (and therefore forfeit), much of the assets remained intact, belonging to the company. You see, ten years ago, when Jake discovered how good I was at making legitimate money (I could sell shit to an asshole), he had invested less and less of his laundered money into growing the Peyton business empire. It made more than enough legal money to sustain itself. These days, it was fully legal and generated real revenue, thanks primarily to me. Meaning, the state couldn't touch the bulk of the company's existing assets.

What the state could do was fine the shit out of the Martinellis, Jake in particular. He had made the mistake of using his massive earnings from Peyton Industries to pump back into his illegal schemes: international commodity transfer fraud, cryptocurrency transaction fraud, online gambling fraud, and electronic payment fraud, to name a few, all of it hidden in a series of shell corporations I'd never heard of.

And you thought I was greedy.

Compared to Jake, I looked like a Boy Scout running a lemonade stand who had the clever idea of loading his lemonade with too much ice until the customers complained and demanded a free refill. Hence, my slap on the wrist. They did fine me $500,000. Yawn.

Jake's financial obligation to the state was much higher. But the state didn't want ownership of Peyton Industries. They wanted money, cold hard cash. Instead of dividing everything up in a low-ball auction, they sold Jake's stake in Peyton Industries to a high-dollar bidder who just happened to come knocking with a top-of-market offer at the exact right time.

Guess who that was?

Morris Pilkington.

Pilky was quite ecstatic his money in the King City Spire was earning out, and was happy to help me keep the company intact because he saw crotchless profit potential in the Peyton name, if you know what I mean. Remember I said some of my most successful tactics were distasteful?

Don't feel bad for Pilky. He was going to make mountains of money on profits from Peyton Industries.

Fortunately, my personal assets were safe from forfeiture to the state. They were locked up airtight, walled off behind the impenetrable fortress of my plea agreement with the DA's office. They had built that legal fortress for me, in exchange for me handing them the Martinelli family, which I did, filleted and fried on a platinum platter. I can picture Jake lying there in a bed of lettuce with an apple garnish clenched in his teeth. The total monies the state seized from the Martinellis made them very happy. I had no doubt some state officials went on to line their own pockets with some of that cash. Those officials could be as corrupt as the Martinellis.

I had no doubt Jake stewed in his dark cell every night, grinding his teeth and plotting revenge while cursing my name, but there wasn't much he could do to me from a different prison, or with the Martinelli family in turmoil. None of them wanted to make matters *worse* for themselves by helping Jake.

United they had stood until divided they had fallen.

I didn't care about Jake's revenge either way.

Not to toot my own horn, okay I'll toot, there wasn't anyone in Springville Prison who could take me in a fight anyway. It was a minimum security prison. The fellas here weren't big bruisers like in max. Still, I kept eyes in the back of my head just in case. But nobody tried anything, probably because I made so many friends during my stay.

My buddies always had my back. Some who got out before I did were so tight with me, they ended up working construction for me on the outside (Reggie hired them at my request). Any enemies lying in wait or around dark corners simply couldn't get close enough for a shank.

The biggest shocker of all?

Jake *did* get shanked. Ha! His assassin hit him a hundred times in the prison shower with a sharpened toothbrush handle, and Jake died on his way to the prison hospital, according to the juicy rumors that dropped off the grapevine and rolled into Springville one sunny afternoon.

Yeah, I smiled.

According to the rumors, Jake had some heavy-hitting enemies in Chicago he'd never mentioned. They had finally come to collect.

Good fucking riddance.

I'd always said I'd kill Jake one of these days. That I'd done it indirectly by ratting him out, and through someone else's hand, made victory taste that much sweeter. Jake had hammered it into my head: never *ever* do your own dirty work yourself. Lesson learned, you shit-eating Nutcracker. The student is now the master. You should've taken your own advice, dumbfuck.

Eleven months after I'd gone into the joint, I got an unexpected visitor. Floyd Lunsford. I'd asked him to keep tabs on baby CJ. Floyd brought news that the courts removed little Channing-Jackson Goodrich from the care of Shenka Goodrich, on the grounds she had used him to commit felony fraud. Consequently, the child welfare judge put CJ into the foster care system for his best interest.

I wouldn't let CJ disappear into oblivion. With my help, contacts, and money, CJ's former nanny Maria officially adopted him. She'd grown as attached to CJ as I had. It was easy to arrange because, after Reyna had moved out, I had kept Maria in my employ as house staff at my mansion, which gave her the stable home she needed to qualify for adoption. Once she officially adopted CJ, they both lived at the mansion full time. I had Lashawn pay for anything they needed.

They say it takes a village to raise a child. My extended "family" caring for the mansion wasn't technically a village or a family, but in spirit they were that and more.

For all the people who stood by me during my time in prison, one person was notoriously absent.

Carol Duffey.

I wrote her letters, sent her emails, called her phone number. She never responded.

I couldn't blame her. Who wanted to take a collect call from prison?

I'd officially become the criminal she knew me to be.

A convicted felon.

That couldn't possibly sit well with her ethical outlook.

Even so, once I finished paying my debt to society, I'd go looking for Carol. At the very least, I would say goodbye and wish her all the best one last time.

I knew I'd never have Carol in my life, but I wanted her to know she'd always have my love.

Chapter 50

CAROL

Late summer in King City.

At the park near my parents house.

The sky a blue ocean over a sea of green grass.

Dad sitting on a park bench with his VR goggles on, racing his drone with his friends. Mom sitting next to him reading a romance novel, something called Fearless with a tattooed blue-eyed hunk on the cover.

I sat with my son, laughing at a nearby picnic table.

Sitting with me and giggling, his three adopted aunts and favorite pirate queens: Sienna Winters, Jordyn Hoyle, and her mom Jennifer, all of them laughing over our summer lunch.

Eventually, Dad and Mom wandered over to rejoin us.

"Time to cut the cake!" Sienna cheered, pulling my son's colorful birthday cake out of the grocery store box. She put a "1" shaped candle on top and Jordyn lit it with her Bic.

"Make a wish, baby!" Jennifer chuckled. "You're only one once!" Jennifer had successfully completed her chemo and her breast cancer was in remission.

I held up my son and cooed, "Go ahead, baby! Make a wish and blow out your candle!"

He burped.

We laughed.

I made a wish for him before blowing out the candle with a quick puff.

"Yaaaaay!" we all cheered and he danced his bootied baby feet on my lap as I held him up by his arms.

"He is so cute," Mom laughed, happier than I'd seen her in years. She loved being a grandmother. It gave her new purpose.

Jordyn cut slices for everyone onto paper plates and served. When she handed my plate to me, she said, "Rolo, I'm so glad you moved back to King City. It wouldn't be the same without you."

"Yeah, me too, Jay," I grinned, my eyes suddenly misty.

Going back almost two years, when I had returned to San Francisco and confirmed I was for sure pregnant, I had made the abrupt decision to quit my job there and move back home to King City. I wanted Mom and Dad to see their only grandson grow up. Truth be told, I was getting a little bit sick of the fast-paced techie lifestyle of San Francisco, and I didn't want to spend more time with my co-workers than I did with my own baby. King City was a better fit and I had Mom, Dad, and his adopted aunties to help me care for him. The other good news, with my high-profile job experience, it didn't take long to find work at a law office here. King City had its fair share of white collar criminals.

I had once known one intimately.

Proof burbled and gurgled in my lap, making a mess of his slice of cake with his chubby fingers.

After everyone finished, we opened presents. Baby clothes and baby toys. Exactly what we needed. Then Dad wandered back to his bench to race his drone more, and Mom picked up her book to keep reading. Sienna, Jordyn, and Jennifer walked away from the table to play frisbee on the grass, passing it back and forth in wobbly tosses, dropping it a lot, and generally laughing constantly while I bounced my son in my lap and pointed at his aunties' antics.

It was a perfect day.

I couldn't be happier.

"Carol?" said a man behind me.

I froze.

That voice.

I knew it instantly.

The man who had once held every piece of my heart.

Channing Peyton.

Since having our son, I had slowly realized Channing now held only *half* of my heart. After getting pregnant with his son, my heart had divided like a fertile cell, splitting into two wholes that became twins. That feeling had intensified dramatically when I gave birth, teaching me that I had space for the pieces of *two* hearts in my chest, one for my son, one for Channing. The one for my son was complete and full to bursting, the one for Channing forever empty, the pieces gone completely. He still had every piece he'd taken from me twelve years ago. The frantic hammering of my heart now was proof.

"Carol?" he asked again.

I closed my eyes tight, afraid I was hallucinating.

I had dreaded this day as much as I had longed for it.

My lips were trembling when I twisted on the park bench.

What I saw shocked me.

It shouldn't have, but it did.

Channing stood there, tan and handsome as ever in a T-shirt, shorts, and flip-flops, with a backpack slung over his shoulders. He leaned to one side to hold the tiny arm of a little boy similarly dressed, with dark hair and cool blue eyes.

"Say hello, CJ," Channing smiled.

The boy hid behind Channing's leg.

"He's shy," Channing grinned.

"Your son," I gasped over my shoulder.

"Legally, yes. Biologically, no."

I frowned. Was this Reyna's son? My eyes went to Channing's left hand. No wedding band, not even a tan line. That didn't mean anything. He hadn't been wearing one when I'd bumped into him two Christmases ago either.

"Long story," he chuckled. "The short version is Reyna is no longer a part of his life or mine. In fact, legally and biologically, she never was."

"Oh." I had no idea where to begin with that puzzle.

Channing lifted his son laughing by his pudgy arms and seated him on his shoulders, holding his little ankles. "He loves heights. He'll either be a mountain climber or a skydiver when he grows up. What do you think, CJ?" Channing started bouncing.

CJ laughed, "Higher, Daddy! Higher!"

Now jumping in short hops, Channing laughed too.

My heart melted seeing their glee.

Channing finally walked around the picnic table from where he'd been behind me this entire time. He stopped short when he saw our son.

"Again, Daddy! Do it again!" CJ laughed.

"One second," Channing muttered, eyes wide. He lifted CJ off his shoulders and set him down. Knelt in front of me, his face swimming with emotions dark and light. "Is this...? Carol, please tell me, is this...?"

I started sniffing tears. How could I have ever hidden our son from him?

Channing's eyes reddened and pleaded with me for an answer.

I nodded silently, biting my quivering lip, tasting the sting of guilt riding my salty tears.

"Is this *our* son?" he muttered.

"Y-y-y-yes," I stuttered, smearing tears from my cheeks.

"Come here a minute, CJ. I want you to meet someone."

"Who, Daddy?" CJ asked innocently in his chipmunk voice.

"Your new brother," Channing smiled.

"I have a brother?" CJ wondered, magical curiosity shining in his eyes.

"Yes you do. Say hello to... what's his name?" Channing chuckled tearily.

"Gale," I said. "Gale Hawthorne. His middle name is Hawthorne," I giggled tearily.

Channing laughed a smirk and said, "You mean like Gale Hawthorne from The Hunger Games? Or should I say Channing Hawthorne from The Football Games?"

"You remembered," I sniffled.

"How could I forget. That story changed my life."

"Mine too," I cried.

He turned to his son. "Say hello to Gale, CJ. He's your brother."

"Hi." CJ waved with his whole arm. He looked at me, eyes unsure. "Who are you?"

"I'm Carol."

CJ was too shy to say anything more.

"Can I hold him?" Channing asked.

"Oh, uh, yeah, of course."

Kneeling closer, he scooped Gale out of my arms and cradled him tenderly with expert technique, like he'd done it a thousand times before. "He has my eyes, Care."

"I know," I sniffed.

"He's *our* son, Care."

"He is," I nodded, my tears now flowing unhindered.

"My own *son*," Channing marveled. "*Our* little boy."

"Yeah," I laughed, crying. "You're his father."

Channing's face broke and his tears flowed, dripping onto baby Gale's shirt. "Did you hear that, son? I'm your dad." His voice quavered with intense emotion.

"I'm so sorry, Channing," I blubbered, drowning in my own conflicting emotions. "I should have told you sooner. I never should have kept him a secret from you, but I was scared."

"Scared? Why? Why would you be scared of me? I'd never do anything to hurt either of you."

"Not you," I whimpered. "I followed your trial. I read the public transcripts for the Martinelli trials too. Jake, Tony, the entire family. They did some very bad things. Especially Jake." I had to shiver. "That man was a monster."

"Jake is dead. He'll never hurt anybody ever again." Channing frowned. Pain strained his face, "Now you finally know."

"Know what?"

Channing sighed, "I'm the one who should be sorry, Care. This is entirely my fault." He shook his head, miserable. "Now you know why I left you in college. I was protecting you from them. The only way to keep you safe was to convince them you meant nothing to me. That's what I thought, anyway." His face caved in under an avalanche of cold sorrow. "I never should have left you, Carol Everdeen."

I laughed a sob when he called me that.

"I never stopped loving you, Care," he whispered hoarsely. "Not for one second. I mean that with all my heart."

That was the moment I knew Channing Peyton had kept every piece of *my* heart safe all these years, same as I'd kept his. Jordyn had been right all along. You never got back the pieces of your heart you gave away. The trick was giving them to the right person.

Turned out I had.

Channing sniffed, "I've said it before and I will say it again, Care. If it wasn't for my criminal past, I would ask you to marry me. Especially now. But it's not fair to you or our son. You're safer without me in your lives. Both of you."

A series of complex thoughts flashed through my mind in a millisecond. It was true Channing was connected to some very unsavory characters. It was also true many of them were in prison. And it was frustratingly true that every attorney involved with the justice system ran the risk of making criminal enemies. It went with the territory. I had already made several enemies of my own. They were white-collar criminals, true, nothing like Jake Martinelli, but I knew some people were capable of first degree murder when enough money was at stake.

Most importantly, Channing had taught me love was never easy.

My aging parents and Jennifer Hoyle's breast cancer scare had taught me there were no guarantees in life. Sooner or later, your own body would inevitably turn against you.

If you made every choice in life hoping or waiting for the one that would give you a perfect ending, you would never, ever get it. There was no best choice. But there were better choices and worse choices.

I suddenly realized I had two options to choose from.

I could accept the risk of having Channing in my life in some capacity, or live with the illusion of *less* risk (there was always some), but with a half-empty heart because I was afraid of what might be. I knew I could carry the burden of the latter fate for myself, but was that fair to put on Gale? No. Then again, the painful truth was, the option of having his father close would add some amount of unnecessary risk to Gale's fledgling little life. I wouldn't do anything to put him in danger.

"Daddy," CJ said, tugging on Channing's arm, "I want to go play." He was eyeing the pirate queens and their frisbee.

"In a minute," Channing said, hugging the boy to his side and kissing the top of his head with incredible tenderness and love.

Such a simple thing, that kiss.

I suddenly realized CJ didn't have any choice who his father was. He had to live with the risk, whether he knew it or not. His ignorance didn't make the risk disappear. In exchange, he was given the love and adoration of a wonderful man.

Could I allow Gale the love Channing was offering *our* son?

Could I allow *myself* Channing's love?

I knew life was filled with risk.

I knew there were no do-overs in love or life.

There was only going forward.

This was the moment my heart said yes to forever after with Channing Peyton, no matter what happened.

Both halves of my heart were now full.

"Why are you sad, Daddy?" CJ asked.

"I'm not sad," Channing sniffed. "I'm happy."

"Why?"

"Because I love you so much." Channing again kissed CJ's hair and hugged him fiercely to his side.

Smiling at CJ, I felt my heart growing a third boy-shaped chamber next to the one that held Gale.

We would go forward into life and love together.

As a family.

The four of us.

Gale, CJ, Channing, and I.

Tears streaming down my face, I said, "Channing Peyton, will you marry me?"

"What?" He snorted a surprised laugh.

"Will you marry me?" I repeated and bit my lower lip.

"Yes." Also crying, he nodded and reached over to take my hand. Gave it a loving squeeze. "Forever yes."

In my lap, Gale giggled a bright smile and shook his little hands, bouncing his exuberant little body in a moment of pure joy.

At last, I knew true love.

\#

&

&*&

&*&*&

&*&*&*&

M

Thank you so much for reading The Nightmare Ex-Boyfriend Before Christmas. It means the world to me. While you're still here, may I ask you to leave a review online where you purchased this book? Every review matters, but yours means the most. :-)

If you want to chit chat with Devon, join his Facebook group here and tell him what's what on Devon Hartford's Heartbreakers here:
www.facebook.com/groups/devonhartford

Lastly, if you'd like an email telling you when Devon's next book drops (that's hip lingo for "is available for purchase"), sign up for Devon's newsletter here:
devonhartford.com

ABOUT THE AUTHOR

Devon Hartford spent most of his life in Southern California.
Devon also paints. His background in the arts was the inspiration
for his #1 bestselling romantic comedy series The Story of
Samantha Smith.

Devon Hartford's Heartbreakers

Join Devon's Facebook group to chat with Devon and stay
up to date on his new releases. Here's the link:

www.facebook.com/groups/devonhartford

A gift from Devon

Would you like a free copy of Devon's #1 bestselling romantic new adult comedy? To read it free, sign up for the Devon Hartford Newsletter here:

devonhartford.com

OTHER BOOKS BY DEVON HARTFORD:

COLLEGE ROMANTIC COMEDY
Fearless (The Story of Samantha Smith #1)
Reckless (The Story of Samantha Smith #2)
Painless (The Story of Samantha Smith #3)

NEW ADULT ROMANTIC COMEDY
Cover Model
Stealing Chastity

HIGH SCHOOL ROMANTIC COMEDY
Stepbrother Obsessed

ADULT ROMANTIC COMEDY
Taking Back Beautiful
Broken Lion
The Nightmare Ex-Boyfriend Before Christmas

THE CRUEL KINGS OF CASTLE HILL ACADEMY
Book 1: Rich Boys vs. Poor Boys

SLIGHTLY PARANORMAL ROMANCE
If I Were Beautiful (If I Were… #1)

BILLIONAIRE ROMANCE
ONE YEAR LOVE - Part One
ONE YEAR LOVE - Part Two
ONE YEAR LOVE - Part Three
ONE YEAR LOVE - Part Four
ONE YEAR LOVE - Collected Edition (Parts 1-4)

ROCKER ROMANCE
Victory RUN 1 (The Story of Victory Payne)
Victory RUN 2 (The Story of Victory Payne)
Victory RUN 3 (The Story of Victory Payne)
Victory RUN 1-2-3 (The Story of Victory Payne - Collecting Parts 1-2-3)

ACKNOWLEDGMENTS

A HUGE thanks to:

Jackie Barnett for her usual genius

Jessie Duchannes for all things Sailor Moon.

Bethanie "The Typo Hammer" Melander for killing those typos

Her Highness Samantha Sheeley, Queen of All Typos and Ouster of Oopsies!

Michele McKenzie for equally all-star eagle-eyed typo-snyping.

For last minute typo-snyping of the highest order and in the face of great personal danger, I award a Typo Heart to the recently promoted **Brigadier General Melanie Starr**, the one and only **Comma Bomber**, who saved this mission from certain disaster at the 11th hour, but not without significant personal sacrifice on her part. General, I salute you!

The HUGEST thanks to all my passionate and fantastic sneaky peeking readers: LisaC, Jessica Laws, julez, Erika Jackson, Megan Christmas, Lori JoRay, Tina Lewis, Lisa venn sims, Kim Byrd, Sade, Hayley picknell, Christy Klein, Katie Reeves, Carmela Dimattia, Lynn, Patricia Hill, Louise!, Anna Lamonica, Kat Tonseth, Paula DeBoer, Lynnese Chandler, Jessica Janis, Brandi, Iris Morante Rosanne Triegaardt, Cole, Cassie King, Kari H, Loren Hahn-Anthony, Clare-Louise Sandell, Nikki Mckellar, Mz Goody, Shawna Juarez Gonzalez, Sandy England, Stacey M, Kylee Waite, Donna Read, Esther Blair, Laurel, Susan Byers, Lisab37, Lorrie Vanmeter, Muriel Garcia, Dr. Oooh!, Laura. You guys rock the sneaky sauce!

Last but most of all, a thousand GINORMOUS thank-yous to everybody else who helped make this book a reality!

www.ingramcontent.com/pod-product-compliance
Lightning Source LLC
Chambersburg PA
CBHW050910250626
47155CB00001B/175